Rory reached out and jerked the blanket away from her leaving her wearing only the shirt he had loaned her.

"Don't push me too far, lady," Rory said. "If I have to leave you in this cabin stark naked to keep you from escaping, I'll do it."

Catherine grabbed furiously for the blanket but he held her at bay, his left arm going easily around her slim waist while with his right hand he tossed the blanket behind him, out of her reach.

There was a grim smile on his lips. "Shall I prove it to you?"

"You wouldn't dare!" she hissed.

"Don't tempt me."

He held her so close that his breath stirred the tendrils of hair curling against the long column of her neck. Catherine shivered slightly.

"Mr. O'Shay, I managed quite well before your arrival at my saloon, and will continue to do so without your interference. Now I'll thank you to release me!"

"A summary dismissal if I've ever heard one," he mocked, reaching up with his right hand to toy with the buttons of her shirt. He slipped open the first button. "Just say the words, Catherine, and I'll stop. Tell me you'll not leave without my say so."

"I won't be tricked into giving my word!"

He smiled, his chiseled lips parting as his gaze rested on the opening of the shirt. "Very well," he said. "I gave you fair warning."

FORTUNE'S DESIRE

ZEBRA'S GOT THE ROMANCE TO SET YOUR HEART AFIRE!

RAGING DESIRE (2242, $3.75)
by Colleen Faulkner

A wealthy gentleman and officer in General Washington's army, Devon Marsh wasn't meant for the likes of Cassie O'Flynn, an immigrant bond servant. But from the moment their lips first met, Cassie knew she could love no other . . . even if it meant marching into the flames of war to make him hers!

TEXAS TWILIGHT (2241, $3.75)
by Vivian Vaughan

When handsome Trace Garrett stepped onto the porch of the Santa Clara ranch, he wove a rapturous spell around Clara Ehler's heart. Though Clara planned to sell the spread and move back East, Trace was determined to keep her on the wild Western frontier where she belonged—to share with him the glory and the splendor of the passion-filled TEXAS TWILIGHT.

RENEGADE HEART (2244, $3.75)
by Marjorie Price

Strong-willed Hannah Hatch resented her imprisonment by Captain Jake Farnsworth, even after the daring Yankee had rescued her from bloodthirsty marauders. And though Jake's rock-hard physique made Hannah tremble with desire, the spirited beauty was nevertheless resolved to exploit her feminity to the fullest and gain her independence from the virile bluecoat.

LOVING CHALLENGE (2243, $3.75)
by Carol King

When the notorious Captain Dominic Warbrooke burst into Laurette Harker's eighteenth birthday ball, the accomplished beauty challenged the arrogant scoundrel to a duel. But when the captain named her innocence as his stakes, Laurette was terrified she'd not only lose the fight, but her heart as well!

Available wherever paperbacks are sold, or order direct from the Publisher. Send cover price plus 50¢ per copy for mailing and handling to Zebra Books, Dept. 2320, 475 Park Avenue South, New York, N.Y. 10016. Residents of New York, New Jersey and Pennsylvania must include sales tax. DO NOT SEND CASH.

ZEBRA BOOKS

are published by

Kensington Publishing Corp.
475 Park Avenue South
New York, NY 10016

Copyright © 1988 by Susan M. Anderson

All rights reserved. No part of this book may be reproduced in any form or by any means without the prior written consent of the Publisher, excepting brief quotes used in reviews.

First printing: March, 1988

Printed in the United States of America

Life brings many changes and challenges to each of us, and during the creation of this manuscript a great many of each entered my life. I am indebted to the following people for helping me through such a transitional period and filling my world with love. To these special people this book is dedicated:

To my mother, Betty Coleman, who is a heroine in the truest sense of the word. Her perseverance, bravery and unselfish caring have taught me much about living; to my father, William Coleman, whose quiet strength and indomitable spirit have proved to me that human determination is omnipotent; to my sister and brothers, Debbie, Bill, and Larry, who have proved time and again that I can always count on them; to my grandmother, Genevieve Augusta Kindblom, who has always been there for me; and to Randy and Jason, my husband and son, who together constitute the light of my life, the dreams of my future. . . .

I love you all.

Prologue

Schuylkill County, Pennsylvania, June, 1873

"I'll be a son of a bitch!" the man swore fiercely under his breath as he gave full rein to the Irish Thoroughbred mare beneath him. "The boyos have found me out, girl. Damned if I'm not a goner!"

The sharp pounding of his horse's hooves landing on hard-packed earth filled his ears along with a cool, rushing wind as he sped down from the hummock where the dingy coal town of Shenandoah rested. Before him, beyond the valley, lay the base of Bear Ridge, its dark mass sprinkled here and there with the creamy froth of blooming mountain laurel. The man only hoped he could reach the ridge in time. Faster. He had to go faster.

He gave a brush to his mare's sides and felt her power as she plunged forward, lengthening her canter into a full gallop. Gunshots, one after the other, rang in the air behind him and shattered the peaceful silence of yet another northern dusk as the man veered his horse to the right, leaving the valley behind him. He steered his beast toward the ridge and the wild, wooded land of Pennsylvania's hard-coal country.

Stinging branches, bowed with summer's blooming

greenery and appearing bluish-black in the waning light, slapped against his bare forearms and face. But Rory O'Shay paid them no mind. The sons of Molly Maguire were in hot pursuit, and if O'Shay wished to see the sun rise on the morrow, he had to outrun the lawless men and do it soon.

"That's it, girl," he crooned to the coal-black mare beneath him, wild now with the freedom she'd been given. "Easy now. Watch the dips in the land. I'd hate to lose you, Bess. We've paved a long road behind us and there's an even longer one ahead." Leaning low over the animal's long, graceful neck, almost at one with the beast, O'Shay spoke softly into her ear. His hands were loose on the reins and his body sure in the second-rate saddle. Pity, he thought, to waste a fine animal—one newly bred—on such rough terrain.

The animal's full name was Bess's Dream. She had been a gift, along with the foal growing inside her, bequeathed to O'Shay by a wealthy Baltimore widow. The mare was a pure Thoroughbred, as was the stud she'd been bred with only a few short months before. The untamed mountains of Pennsylvania were no place for such a fine piece of horseflesh, but O'Shay had no choice. Only a mile behind him, in the O'Reilly shebeen, lay a man with his neck snapped and the life drained out of him. This night, Rory O'Shay had killed a man.

Soon, the coal patches of Pennsylvania would echo with the news, and the name O'Shay would be blacklisted in every coal mine from Shenandoah to Nevada. The Molly Maguires had a long and powerful arm, and Rory O'Shay—shrewd enough to coolly think through his temporary advantage—did not believe for one minute that if he made it alive out of Pennsylvania he would necessarily live to tell of his adventure.

Somewhere, somehow, other members of the Molly Maguires would learn of his sin, and Rory O'Shay would pay with his life. The Irish blood upon his hands would never wash clean.

The Mollies were an organization that had originated many years before in Ireland, where farmers had long been victimized by their English landlords who collected excessive house and cattle rents. A woman named Mollie Maguire had led a revolt against these landowners, and her followers soon began to call themselves the Sons of Molly Maguire. Now, in America, the Mollies had sprung up once again — on behalf of the many poverty-stricken Irish immigrants who had come here to work in the anthracite coal regions. Instead of fighting English landowners on the "ould sod," the Mollies now fought against American mine owners who exploited the hopeful, unsuspecting Irish laborers with meager wages, no guaranteed amount of work, and generally disgraceful working and living conditions.

O'Shay didn't wonder that the laborers — most, but not all of them Irish — had banded together in an attempt to do something about such outrageous treatment. But the Mollies, more often than not, had turned to violence, brutally beating mine superintendents, dynamiting collieries, threatening mine owners' wives and children. Once, they had even set to fire to a house full of sleeping people. To O'Shay, such despicable acts would never solve the problems. But he was only one man — one man who had killed a son of Molly — and now there was nothing but trouble for him in Pennsylvania.

Rory O'Shay had lived with harsh treatment most of his life. His coal-mining father, always a heavy drinker, had not been happy with his lot in life and had invariably taken out his frustrations on his eldest son. Rory, more often than not, chose to try and forget the horrible nights when his father, reeking of whiskey, would come home and beat him for some imagined offense. But, at the age of seventeen, Rory finally decided he would take no more. The life of a miner was not for him. He did not want to follow in his father's footsteps. Saying good-bye to his mother, father, brother, and baby sister—and to his youth—Rory had walked away from Shenandoah.

Life had been hard for him, but Rory had forced himself to be strong. No longer willing to be a victim, he had put up his fists and dared all to defy him. In his travels, he'd faced clubs and knives and even guns, and still O'Shay had beaten the best.

But now, with fifteen or more men in hot pursuit, O'Shay wondered if his luck had finally run out. Ironic, he thought, that his life should end in the very spot where, ten years before, he'd vowed it would begin. He'd been a young man facing terrible odds then, and now he was a grown man in the same place, facing the same odds.

"No," he said aloud to his mare as he brushed her sides with his powerful legs. "I've got miles to go before I let any Molly put a bullet in me! I've got to find my brother, I do, and only then can the devil have me!"

With that vow, he sped his beast against the wind and never once looked behind him.

Chapter One

San Francisco, July, 1875

A wild colt, all legs and shimmering black, stood nervously before Catherine Diamond. Its proudly held head tapered into a long, gorgeous neck and sleek body. Fiery-eyed and filled with a sure sense of its own beauty, the animal emanated an aura of touch-me-not.

Catherine sighed longingly as she regarded the yearling situated smack dab in the middle of the Diamond Saloon. The blue felt gaming tables had been pushed against the walls, and a circle of patrons and employees alike had gathered round to admire the horse. Scores of mirrors lining the walls of the gaslit saloon reflected endless images of the fascinating young animal who was tied to the end of a stout rope. Ears pricked and alert, unblinking eyes holding a challenge, the colt brought up its well-shaped head, tightening the slack rope with a show of contempt for the coarse piece of hemp tied about its handsome neck.

Catherine was not concerned about a yearling being inside her father's saloon. Both she and her father had been labeled outrageous on more than one occasion. None of the patrons appeared surprised by the unusual spectacle, either. They knew there was always something exciting happening at the Diamond Saloon. What Catherine was concerned about was acquiring the beast for her own—as were many of the customers who stood nearby.

Male voices, roughened with liquor and heightened with excitement at the sight of such a gorgeous piece of horseflesh, buzzed around Catherine's consciousness.

"My, but he is a black beauty," one man said.

"Given the proper training, he'll be a sure winner at the Bay District Course."

"What's the pedigree, I wonder?" said another.

"Well, Miss Diamond?" came the gruff voice of the man holding the piece of hemp in calloused, blackened hands. "The stakes high enough for you now?"

Catherine unwillingly tore her gaze from the proud black beast and settled her gray eyes, cool and appraising beneath long black lashes, on the man who'd addressed her. His rough clothing contrasted sharply with her own exquisite appearance. In her amber silk gown and Jouvin elbow-length gloves, sleek ebony hair swept into a cascade of curls held in place with sparkling topaz pins, Catherine seemed to have stepped from the pages of *Godey's Lady's Book*. The merest dab of India ink had been applied beneath her lashes, and the evocative scent of California flowers rose gently from her creamy skin. Jack Reese, however, appeared to have just emerged from the murky depths of a mud-filled hole.

A huge man, well over six feet tall, with shaggy brown hair and bushy beard, Reese looked more animal than human. His hazel eyes, a queer greenish-brown, were small and sharp, and a perpetual squint deepened the wrinkles at their corners. Sporting a silver-tipped wolfskin vest over a coarse brown linsey-woolsey shirt, rust-colored, mud-caked trousers, and spurred boots of an indistinguishable color, Jack Reese was definitely not the type of man usually found inside the Diamond Saloon. Purporting to be a coal miner from the east looking to make his fortune in San Francisco,

Reese had entered the saloon and approached Catherine's table. No one had invited Reese to join the poker game; the man had simply dropped a fist full of gold on the table, yanked a vacant chair over, and gruffly ordered the players to deal him in.

That had been hours ago, and now Reese—minus his hoard of bits and the greenbacks recognized as legal tender in the east—stood before Catherine, offering this prize bit of horseflesh as his next wager.

Catherine slid another glance at the yearling. "I have to wonder, Mr. Reese, if the horse is truly yours to wager. How did you come by such a magnificient animal?"

Reese rubbed his tongue along the front of his teeth, shoving down a wad of tobacco. Grinning, he crossed his beefy arms over his chest, then tightened his hold on the rope. "He's mine," he assured her, offering no explanations. "Will you join this hand or not?"

"I told you once, Mr. Reese, I've played too long as it is."

Jack Reese scowled. "A man should be given a chance to recoup his losses. You are seven hundred fifty dollars richer, Miss Diamond; money that was mine when this night began."

Did she detect a threatening tone in the man's rough voice? Catherine felt certain she had. "Poker is as much a game of chance as it is skill. Besides, I've given you a fair amount of time to win back what you lost." Catherine moved to step away from the man and his horse, but Jack Reese unfolded his arms, giving a ruthless yank to the hemp. The yearling, skittish enough surrounded by so many people, danced nervously, jerking its head back and giving a loud whinny.

"Outta my way!" Reese yelled to the crowd, and immediately the circle broke, giving him a clear path to the double door of the saloon. Tugging on the rope, Reese headed for the exit, but the yearling held its ground, protesting such callous treatment.

Eyes wide and blazing, the black colt stood up on its hindquarters and pawed the air viciously, nostrils flaring and teeth bared. The sudden, powerful movement startled Reese, and in that instant the coarse rope was jerked from his meaty fist by the frightened beast. Cursing, Reese lunged for the colt, but the animal, wary and ready, came down on all fours and bolted to the left of the huge gambling room.

Screams filled the air as people scrambled out of the way. Bucking and kicking, snorting and raving, the colt was allowed his head within the gilded walls, and soon the place echoed with the sound of crashing mirrors, splintering wood, and shattering bottles. Patrons jumped atop the Russian briarwood bar and hooted the animal into an even wilder frenzy, while the piano player pounded out a lively tune. The scene was chaotic.

Shrieks of delight pierced Catherine's ears, but she paid them no mind, nor did she tally up the damage the colt was wreaking on her father's saloon. She thought only of the black yearling whose eyes showed simultaneously his fright and his courage. This animal's spirit would not be tamed by a length of tattered rope. No, the beast before her would never be led unless he wished to be. Plain and simple.

Catherine Diamond respected such valor. Her pulse quickened. She wanted the colt for her very own.

"Enough!" she yelled into the din.

Only a few of the patrons quieted and gave her their attention, but as Catherine strode purposefully to the corner of the room where the colt now stood, the loud shouts slowly died, as did the piano tunes. The poor animal's chest was heaving, and he sent out gusts of air through flared nostrils as he laid his ears straight back, watching Catherine's approach warily. Stopping only a few feet from the frightened beast, Catherine held out one gloved hand and cooed softly. "Easy now. Easy," Over and over, she repeated some unintelligible chant, and slowly, oh so slowly, the colt began to relax. "There, there," she whispered. "That's it, boy. I'm not going to harm you."

The horse shied away a bit, tail swishing, but Catherine repeated her gentle words, taking first one step and then another, until she stood beside the yearling. The colt rolled a watchful eye at her, and then, to Catherine's great delight, he dipped his nose toward her upheld palm and gently nuzzled her white glove.

"Feisty little thing, ain't he?" Jack Reese declared as he approached from behind Catherine. "He's got the devil in him, he does. One day he'll make a fine racer. A stern hand is all he needs."

Fire ignited the yearling's eyes at just the sight of the coal miner. Without turning toward the man, Catherine said in low, even tones, "Don't come any closer, Mr. Reese. I don't want you near this animal."

Jack Reese gave an amused snort. "You've got no say in the matter, Miss Diamond. That colt belongs to me. But if you're willing to make me an offer I can't refuse . . ." He let his words drift off, his implication clear.

Catherine felt her insides churning. It was obvious this man mistreated the animal. Jack Reese probably didn't even own the horse, and here he was trying to sell it at a high profit! Catherine was incensed. She wished she had enough money to purchase the colt outright, but she and her father were seriously short of ready cash. Turning to the man, she said levelly, "I'll join the poker hand, Mr. Reese, but if I win, I want to hear nothing from you about being able to recoup your losses."

Reese grinned. "Sounds like a reasonable request to me, Miss Diamond." He reached into his vest and pulled out a deck of cards, then motioned to a small table to his right. "After you, ma'am."

Catherine ignored his gesture. "You may put your cards away, Mr. Reese. Within these walls the only valid playing cards are Diamond cards." Looking past his shoulder, she motioned for Jake Randolph, her father's associate, to bring them a new deck.

Winking to one of the hired girls, Randolph made his way toward Catherine. Big and brawny with a bearlike chest and muscular arms, Jake Randolph's easygoing manner was in sharp contrast to his impressive physique. Good-looking beyond any doubt, Jake Randolph had thick, pale gold hair and sparkling blue eyes, a sunny smile and an easy way with women.

Those who worked at the Diamond Saloon called him Randy—which he was—and it was no secret that he had quite literally charmed the pantaloons off all the women who worked there. Surprisingly, the incorrigible flirt and rogue managed to keep the friendship of all the ladies he loved and left. In the eyes of most women, Jake Randolph could do no wrong. But Catherine knew better then to let herself be drawn to him. He was her father's business associate, and Randolph accorded her the respect he would have given royalty.

"Are these what you wanted, Miss Diamond?" he asked respectfully, handing her a stiff deck of cards, each of which was emblazoned with a huge silver D inside a glistening white diamond. Although Randolph openly courted nearly everything in skirts, he kept a purely business relationship with Catherine.

Helping to build the transcontinental railway, driving in spike after spike, mile after mile, Jake Randolph had made his way to California. He'd laid rail with the Union Pacific and was in Promontory, Utah, when the last spike was driven into the track that connected America's shores. He'd traveled on to California, and only when he'd seen San Francisco, the golden city by the bay, had he decided to stay. He'd become "Mad" Ned Diamond's righthand man. Not naturally quick with numbers, Randolph had nonetheless proved to be an astute pupil, and Ned Diamond trusted him enough to let him help Catherine run the saloon whenever he himself was called away on "private" business. Lately, it seemed, Mad Ned was away from the Diamond Saloon more often than not.

Catherine gave Randolph an affectionate smile as she took the cards. "Yes, Randolph, these are what I wanted."

Jake Randolph eyed the suspicious-looking Jack Reese. "Is there anything wrong, Miss Catherine?" he asked. "If there's a problem I —"

"Everything is fine," she assured him. "This gentleman and I are going to play a quick hand of poker and then he'll be on his way."

Randolph had been trained well. He took his cue and turned to leave.

"Oh, Randolph, one more thing," Catherine added.

"Yes, Miss Catherine?"

"Close the saloon for a few hours and get some men to clean up this mess."

As Jake Randolph went to do her bidding, Catherine stepped to a small round table covered with blue felt, and seated herself on one of the oval-cushioned chairs. A few men and women, all employees of the Diamond, gathered around, curious to see the outcome of the game while they waited for the saloon to reopen.

"Shall we begin, Mr. Reese?" she asked as she cut the deck. After a few deft shuffles, she dealt.

The playing cards flashed as, with skillful fingers, she flicked a card to her opponent and then one to herself. She repeated the process six times. Although she kept a strict poker face, she smiled inwardly as she glanced at the hand she'd dealt herself. Catherine knew for certain that had they used Jack Reese's cards, she would not be staring at an ace, deuce, and jack showing and a deuce in the hole.

Her knowledge of Reese's intent to cheat made Catherine's thirst for victory that much keener — also, she wanted the yearling Jack Reese claimed to own. Dealing the last card, she laid the deck on the deep blue table top and took a slow peek at her fifth draw. Her heart fluttered as a familiar sense of anticipation zipped through her. Another deuce!

"Well, Mr. Reese?" Catherine asked, her voice emotionless.

Reese squirmed a bit in his chair as he sucked a stream of tobacco juice through his teeth and down his throat. His coal-blackened fingers played nervously along the edge of the card in his hand. "I guess it's time you and me showed each other what we're made of, eh, Miss Diamond?"

Catherine bristled at his insulting tone of voice. She wanted nothing more than to be done with this game and to take the frightened colt to a comfortable stall. Slowly, she laid her hole cards on the table. Two deuces joined the ace, deuce, and jack there. Only when all five cards showed did she let herself smile. "Can you beat my hand, Mr. Reese?"

At the sight of the cards, a murmur swept through the small group of people around the table.

"Damn," Reese muttered to himself and threw his cards to the table. The king, ace, and ten he'd had showing were joined by another ace and another king.

Triumphantly, Catherine said, "Three of a kind beats two pair. I do hope you have a bill of sale for the yearling, Mr. Reese. I'd hate to learn the animal never truly belonged to you." Catherine pushed her chair away from the table, but before she could rise, Jack Reese was on his feet.

"Hold it right there," he growled. "I got a feeling those cards are marked, Miss Diamond. I don't take kindly to being swindled."

Again, there was murmuring among the onlookers, and one man took a step toward Reese. Catherine waved him away with one slim gloved hand.

"Indeed?" Her gray eyes flashed. "That makes two of us. You may inspect the cards if you wish, Mr. Reese. But I assure you, they are not marked. Now, if you'll excuse me, I'm going to take my yearling out of this saloon and into a warm stall where he belongs." She rose and turned away.

Eyes squinted nearly shut, Jack Reese reached out one meaty arm and latched his hand onto Catherine's elbow. Contemptuously he spit a stream of tobacco juice to the plush blue carpet beneath them, sneered at her, then said, "That colt is going nowhere until we play another hand—this time with *my* cards."

Catherine saw the group around them break apart and move back. Yanking her arm free, she opened her mouth to yell for Randolph to boot Reese out of the saloon.

But the words never passed her lips, for at that moment an army revolver was pressed against Jack Reese's neck and an ugly voice warned, "Spit one more time, Reese, and I'm gonna send a bullet winging down your throat." The voice that spoke was low and deadly calm.

Catherine had to tilt her head back to get a full view of the man who stood behind Jack Reese. His powerful legs were encased in snug, black breeches, and a red woolen shirt was tucked neatly into the waistband. The Remington revolver gleamed menacingly in his hand, hammer cocked as he held it against Reese's fat neck. His unruly black hair looked as though haphazard scissors had chopped it into three different lengths and then a loving hand had brushed it all back from his rugged features. Blue eyes, as cold as a Sierra snowstorm and as hard and impenetrable as a block of ice, glared down at Reese. His finely chiseled lips were set in a thin line as a muscle twitched in his left cheek. The stranger, tall and devastatingly good-looking, had the commanding presence of a rattlesnake.

With murderous intent, he ran the barrel of the revolver up Reese's neck to his bristly cheek. "Keep your paws off the lassie, boyo," he growled in a low voice. "And get ready to play a real game of poker."

Reese didn't move a muscle, although his eyes began to blink rapidly. "Get the goddamned pistol outta my face."

"Uh-uh. I should have blown your brains out long ago—

and we both know why."

"I don't know what the hell you're talking about, O'Shay."

"I think you do, Reese. Now, gather up those cards and deal me in. We play one hand and when I win, I take everything. *Everything*. Do you hear me, Reese?"

Jack Reese gave an affirmative grunt as he sat back down.

Catherine let her breath out, relieved. Finally, she could get away from this Reese character and take care of her yearling. Glancing at the man called O'Shay, she said, "Well, sir, I'm glad you're joining Mr. Reese in another hand. I've played long enough this evening and I—"

"Shush, lady, and sit yourself down," the stranger interrupted rudely. "Me and the boyo need a third, uninterested party in this hand and you're it."

Catherine blinked at his curt reply. The man spoke with just a hint of an Irish brogue. How long had it been since she'd heard such an accent? Over the years, her own father had worked very hard to speak without any brogue. Not only had Mad Ned changed their last name to Diamond, he'd also done away with his Irish past. Catherine was momentarily unsettled by the sound of the barely remembered accent.

Although she was tall, Catherine's dark head came only to the man's shoulders, and she had to tilt her head back slightly to meet his threatening stare. Such a menacing gaze for one with such a beautiful-sounding voice, she thought to herself. The stranger obviously knew the man called Reese—enough to know to pull a gun on the character—and Catherine was curious to see the outcome of this encounter.

"I'll join your game," she coolly informed O'Shay. "But there'll be no bloodshed in my father's saloon. Put your gun away, and after this hand is finished I want the both of you to take yourselves and your differences elsewhere."

The man did not acknowledge her agreement to join the

hand, nor did he holster his gun as she had ordered. He merely motioned for her to take a seat.

Catherine didn't budge. "I'll sit when I'm ready, sir. Now put your gun away. There's no need for you to brandish it about."

His blue eyes narrowed with impatience as he brought his gaze back to the young woman before him. To say she was incredibly beautiful with her rich, black hair and striking clear gray eyes would be a gross understatement. She was, perhaps, the most gorgeous woman he'd ever met. Fighting a familiar tightness in his loins, Rory reminded himself of his mission in San Francisco. He hadn't trailed Jack Reese across thousand of miles of rugged terrain only to be deterred now by a pretty face and a sharp tongue. Her intervention at this moment could destroy all of his well-laid plans. In an unnecessarily gruff voice he said, "I've traveled far this day, lady, and I'm in no mood for back talk. Just set yourself down and be quiet."

Angered by his rudeness, Catherine retorted, "No man tells me what to do, mister, and I've had more than enough from you and your friend. I want the two of you out of this saloon. Now!"

The man called O'Shay ignored her command; he simply raked his eyes from the top of her perfectly coiffed hair to the tips of her fashionable slippers with their French heels, letting his gaze linger for an uncomfortably long moment on the deep cleavage revealed by her tight, V-shaped bodice.

Catherine felt a momentary blush stain her cheeks, and then she yelled for Jake Randolph. "Randolph!" she bellowed in a very unladylike voice. "I want these two men out of here!" Her eyes never left the stranger's face; she seemed powerless to pull away from that electric gaze. *Where is Randolph?* her mind screamed as her whole body began to tingle beneath O'Shay's penetrating stare.

She was thinking about throwing both men out herself,

when Jack Reese, in a quick movement that startled both her and the stranger, jumped to his feet. Shoving the small table into Catherine and the gun-toting stranger, Reese drew his own pistol and began firing randomly into the air. Catherine and some of the other women screamed as Reese, still firing, bolted out the door and onto the street with one of the saloon employees after him. As bullets ricocheted off the walls, shattering mirrors and showering the floor with glass, people scattered in all directions seeking cover. The noise was deafening. Behind Catherine, the terrified yearling snorted and reared in panic.

"Get down!" someone shouted.

Catherine, worrying only about the horse and not the flying bullets, lunged toward the frightened animal, intent on leading it to safety. She had taken only two steps before strong arms were wrapped around her waist and she was yanked down roughly to the plush carpet. "Oof!" The breath was forced from her lungs as her body met the floor with a thud.

"I told you to get down, lady!" the stranger hissed into her ear as his lean body covered her own. He was a suffocating, dead weight atop her.

Trapped beneath him and barely able to breathe through the mass of her own thick curls which had came loose from their pins, Catherine began to struggle. "Get off of me!" she screeched, acutely aware of the intimate way in which the man's body was pressed to her own. She could feel his hip bones pressing against her buttocks. "I—my horse! I have to get my horse!"

"Do you now?" Arms on either side of her, his lips touching her right ear, the man stayed where he was, even when all sounds of ricocheting bullets ceased. Catherine could smell the manly scent of him—horseflesh and sweat and whiskey. Through her tumbled hair, Catherine could see only the top of the table Reese had pushed over. As she tried to blow a strand of hair away to clear her vision, the man atop her reached up and did it for her. Slowly, and much too tenderly for Catherine's taste, he brushed the strands from her face, his fingertips whisper-soft on her skin. Resting his hand at the base of her neck, the heat of his fingers nearly searing her skin, he shifted his body slightly, his hips pushing momentarily against her bottom.

"Better?" he inquired in a husky whisper.

Chagrined by the man's audacity and outraged at her own reaction to his nearness, Catherine could only sputter out her indignation as she placed her palms flat against the carpet and pushed.

No use. The man on top of her was rock solid.

"Miss Catherine! Are you all right?" Jake Randolph's voice cut into the air as did the sound of crunching glass beneath booted feet. Catherine lifted her head to reply.

Before she could speak, the stranger clamped a hand over her mouth. "Ssh." His cheek touched hers. "Wait a moment before you get up. Reese might still be in the saloon."

"Don't be absurd," Catherine said, her words muffled beneath his hand. "I saw him run out."

"Miss Catherine!" Randolph shouted again.

Catherine tried once more to push herself up from the carpet, but her attempt was unsuccessful. Even when she shook her head back and forth, her eyes wide and filled with anger, the stranger would not release her.

"Easy now, lass," he instructed, his hand still covering her mouth. "I suppose it's you that man is calling for. No sense getting all excited. I just don't want to see this pretty face of yours shot full of bullet holes." Turning her head slightly so that he could gaze into her eyes, the stranger said softly, "I can't recall a time when a woman beneath me thrashed as much as you. An old friend once told me women are a lot like horses—there's only one way to tame them." With that, the man closed the distance between their faces and, moving his hand from her mouth, he brought his lips directly over hers in a long, provocative kiss.

Catherine was taken completely by surprise. The room seemed to tilt crazily as his full lips crushed hers. Suddenly, there was nothing but his breath skimming across her skin, his lips moving atop her own, and the weight of his lean body pressing into hers. Back and forth, slowly, pressing harder without being rough, his whiskers rubbing against her own tender skin . . .

Abruptly, he released her, rolled to his side, then pushed himself to his feet. The look in his blue eyes chilled her.

As he stood, Catherine noticed the bright red stain of blood on his breeches. All thoughts of his audacity fled. "You've been shot!" she exclaimed.

He pulled a handkerchief from his pocket and tied it around his calf where the bloodstain was. "So I have," he replied calmly. "Why else do you think I didn't roll off you as soon as the firing stopped?" He lifted an eyebrow as he looked down at her. Rory O'Shay hadn't meant to kiss the woman, but the opportunity had presented itself. O'Shay was not a man to let such moments pass. Also, a kiss from such a gorgeous creature could do wonders to help a man forget he'd just been nicked by a stray bullet.

Catherine felt her face grow hot with embarrassment.

Rory's lips quirked as he noticed her chagrin. "I'd have followed Reese if one of his shots hadn't grazed me."

"I—I'll send for a doctor," she said, pushing herself to a sitting position.

"Don't bother," he said, straightening himself. "It's just a flesh wound. I've suffered worse."

The coldness in his eyes supported his statement. Catherine wondered who this man was and where he had come from.

"Miss Catherine!" Randolph gasped as he reached the upended table and saw her sprawled on the floor with a stranger standing over her.

Catherine's face grew hotter still. Although Randolph was every woman's fantasy in pants, he also had an irritating tendency to become as confused as a cocker spaniel. "Yes, Randolph," she replied flatly, pushing the hair back from her face and coming to her feet. "I'm here."

Randolph glanced from Catherine's anger-creased features to the stranger's harsh countenance. "What the hell is—?" He caught himself, noticing the bloodstained handkerchief around the stranger's calf. "What's happened Miss Catherine? Are you all right?" He righted the overturned table with one hand, then moved toward Catherine.

"I'm fine," she assured him, although she felt far from fine. Her mouth still tingled from the stranger's bruising kiss. "There was just a bit of a misunderstanding here. Nothing to alarm yourself about."

"But a gun—I heard shots . . ."

"It was that Reese character," she told him. "He started firing randomly into the air. Billy ran after him. Perhaps you should follow. Billy might have gotten himself into more trouble than he bargained for."

Just then, a medium-sized man dressed in blue twill ran into the saloon, barely able to breathe. "He got away!" he told Catherine and Randolph. "I tried to catch him but he jumped on a horse and rode like the devil!"

Though disappointed, Catherine gave the brown-haired Billy a nod. "You did your best, Billy. Let's just be certain Reese never returns to the Diamond." Turning to Randolph, she added, "Make sure the doors are bolted, then get to work cleaning this mess."

Jake Randolph gave her a quick nod, and after sizing up the stranger one last time, he turned away to see her orders carried out. Catherine and O'Shay watched him leave.

"I see you weren't just talking when you said your father owned this saloon," O'Shay said.

Catherine turned her face toward his and was once again jolted by those piercing blue eyes. "My father owns the Diamond but I am the one who oversees the operation. And I insist that you let me send for a physician."

The man shook his head and tugged the brim of his hat down low on his forehead. His eyes, now shaded from the bright glare of the gaslight chandeliers, were once again unreadable. "Sorry to disoblige you, madam. I can see you're a lady used to having her own way. Unfortunately, I'm a man who always gets his way."

"Yes, I've already had firsthand experience with that fact!" Catherine retorted.

Rory O'Shay laughed, a deep-throated sound that vibrated through Catherine's entire body. "You mean the kiss. You can't expect a man to look into a face like yours and not take advantage of it, Miss—Catherine."

"I am Miss Diamond to you," she informed him, uncomfortable with the smug grin planted on his face.

Catherine soon realized she need not have worried over the man's ungentlemanly behavior, for in the next second, his blue eyes rested on something behind her.

The yearling.

As his eyes beheld the animal, there was a sudden transformation in the man. No longer did he appear harsh and frightening. His features softened, and, for a split second—as lightning zips through an angry sky—Catherine saw naked tenderness in his cold eyes.

But in the next instant, the tender look vanished as the stranger walked right by Catherine and slowly held out his hand to the colt.

Catherine watched in fascinated silence as Rory O'Shay gently rubbed the colt's long neck and then its back, while his eyes took in the animal's every feature. With a disgusted grimace, he undid the coarse rope slung about the yearling's neck, then smoothed the black hairs, inspecting for any signs of injury. Throughout this inspection the yearling stood still; calm now beneath O'Shay's large, soothing hands.

Pulling out a leather halter from the back pocket of his breeches, O'Shay began fitting it into the colt's mouth.

"What are you doing?" Catherine demanded.

O'Shay, who'd had only soft words for the colt, spoke gruffly to her. "I'm taking my property out of this place." With the halter in place, he gave a soft click of his tongue to the yearling and then headed for the door with the docile colt in tow behind him.

Catherine stepped into his path. "There must be some mistake. You can't just walk out of here with my yearling. That animal belongs to me and he's not leaving these premises."

Rory O'Shay cocked a dark brow. "I'm afraid the mistake is yours. This boy is mine and it will take a lot more than you with your fancy clothes and husky friends to keep me from leaving with him. Now, please, step out of my way."

"I will not!"

"Lady, don't push me, I—"

Catherine didn't want to hear another word; she only knew that her horse—possibly the answer to her financial problems—was being led out of the saloon by a man who'd thrown her to the floor and treated her roughly. This yearling had seen enough harsh treatment at the hands of Jack Reese. She wasn't about to let it endure more. "Randolph!" she shouted at the top of her lungs. "Randolph, get out here!"

Jake Randolph appeared from behind a closed door near the bar and quickly made his way toward Catherine, his fist closed tightly around a Remington rifle. As he stepped up to the couple, he leveled the gun barrel at Rory O'Shay's chest. "I knew there was something wrong, Miss Catherine," Randolph declared triumphantly, finally having found his purpose this night. "Shall I shoot him, Miss Catherine, or should I run and get the authorities?"

Catherine debated the question briefly, while Rory O'Shay's blue eyes bore into hers. "No," she said finally. "Just make sure he leaves the premises and never returns."

O'Shay appeared nonplused. "I'm not leaving without my

animal."

"This yearling is mine, Mr. O'Shay. I won him."

"Did you now?" he asked with an Irish lilt to his voice. "I suppose Jack Reese told you he owns this yearling. If you believe a man like Reese, you're a fool."

Catherine hesitated a moment, then plunged on. "Have you anything to prove to me you are the owner of this animal? Have you a bill of sale perhaps?"

Annoyance flickered in his blue eyes. "I don't need a bill of sale, Miss Diamond. This boy is mine and I'm taking him with me." He took a step toward the exit with Jake Randolph's rifle still leveled at his chest.

"One more move," Randolph warned, "and I'll shoot you dead. Miss Catherine won the animal fair and square. We've got witnesses."

Rory O'Shay eyed his two opponents, his face cold and harsh in the gaslight. Randolph cocked the rifle, and Catherine felt a sudden shiver as O'Shay instinctively moved his free hand to his own holstered revolver. Several tension-filled seconds ticked by, punctuated only by the gentle snort of the yearling and the swish of its flicking tail. Rory O'Shay stood his ground, daring Randolph to make the first move.

Nervous and unsure, Catherine lifted a hand and touched Jake's arm — a mere brush, but enough to momentarily ease the tension.

O'Shay's hard gaze caught hers, narrow and appraising. Another second or two more ticked away. Then, quite suddenly, he dropped his hold on the halter. Catherine released a long-held breath.

"I'll be back," he told her. "You haven't seen the last of Rory O'Shay, I promise you that." With one last glance at the black beast beside him, he turned and strode from the room.

Catherine watched him leave, her eyes taking in his smooth, self-assured swagger, his lean and powerful build.

Watching him, she felt a shiver of fear wash through her. She knew he would return. She only wondered when.

Chapter Two

The light of a half-moon barely penetrated the gathering darkness and thick fog that covered the Embarcadero, San Francisco's main dock. Only the unending slap of the bay waters against the docks could be heard.

"Did anyone see you coming?" came a hoarse whisper from the far side of the abandoned warehouse.

"Of course not. Relax, boy, you're in good hands with me. Mad Ned'll take care of you. Here, I brought you something to eat. Did you get any sleep in the last eight hours?"

A tired-looking young man stepped out of the shadows, the dusty floorboards creaking loudly beneath him. "A little," he said as his china-blue eyes nervously scanned the area around him. He was dressed in creased, buff-colored breeches, a brown shirt, and dusty boots. His jet-black hair was uncombed and tangled. Small in stature, Connor O'Shay looked to be only fifteen or sixteen instead of nineteen years old. Of all the O'Shay children, Connor resembled his mother the most. His complexion was smooth and fair, and his eyes were a startling shade of blue. His dark hair and bushy black brows gave him a menacing air which was intensified by the slight crook of his once-broken nose. Bowlegged like his father, and full of the Irish charm that so many women, and their mothers, found irresistible, Connor O'Shay was accustomed to the many inquisitive stares he caused—so much so, he had developed a nonchalance that only heightened the appeal of his brooding good looks. He compensated for his lack of height by being quick on his feet and swinging his fists with a great deal of force. After his brother Rory had left home, Connor had taken to running with a wild group of boys, to the despair of his parents.

"A little sleep isn't enough," said Ned Diamond as he crossed the dimly lit room toward Connor. "If you're going to stay one step ahead of the Mollies, you've got to keep your guard up, and to do that, you've got to be rested."

"I can't sleep. Not in this place," Connor said moodily. He paced nervously, not even stopping when Ned pulled out a paper sack from beneath his stylish gray overcoat and handed it to him. "I can't stay here, Ned. I've got to keep moving. Reese is on my tail; I can feel it." Connor ran an impatient hand through his thick black hair. "Maybe I should leave the country."

"And go where?" Ned asked.

"I don't know," came the impatient answer. "The Orient, maybe."

"And then what, boy? If you run now, you'll always be running. Believe me, I know. There isn't a day I don't look over my shoulder and wonder if I'm being followed."

"So why the hell do you stay here, Ned?" Connor turned toward the older man and looked at him carefully for the first time. Ned Diamond stood tall and lean, looking for all the world like a gentleman banker just come from his office, dressed in a gray frock coat, white shirt with stiff collar, puffed ascot tie, and striped gray trousers. A ruby stickpin adorned the narrow lapel of his coat, and a tall, gray top hat sat on his graying black hair. He sported a thin mustache, curled at the ends, and his neatly clipped hair was groomed with just the right amount of Madagascar oil.

"Why don't you leave San Francisco, Ned?" Connor asked. "Surely you have enough money to take yourself out of the country!"

Ned Diamond narrowed his jade-green eyes and gave a short, bitter laugh. "I have a daughter to think of, Connor. Besides, it is the injustice of our situation that keeps me here. We have to fight the Mollies. We can't let them get away with murder!" he said emphatically. "The time is almost ripe to see the Molly Maguires brought low."

"I don't know," Connor said, shaking his head. "Who are we to stand up to such a powerful group? Their arm reaches longer than we could imagine. I don't know why I came here, Ned. I've been charged with blowing up the Trenton mine and putting them out of business. I was framed, but who's to say the law is going to believe me? I hear there's solid evidence against me."

Ned laid a comforting hand on the young man's shoulder. "You haven't done anything wrong, boy. And I promise not to let anything happen to you while you're here. Together, you and me, we'll dig our way out of this mess." His green eyes, so sharp and quick, were steady as he looked at Connor. Suddenly, he smiled. "Here now," he said. "Eat this chicken before it gets cold. Tomorrow, I'll move you into my saloon and you'll have comfortable quarters."

"And then what?" Connor asked as he sat down on an empty crate and took a huge bite of fried chicken.

"Then you'll become just another hired hand at the Diamond Saloon. We'll wait and see if any Mollies have followed you from Pennyslvania. If they haven't, then we'll lay low until the time is right to go."

"And if I've been followed?" Connor asked.

Ned Diamond pulled a cigar from the inside pocket of his overcoat. After lighting up, he replied grimly, "And if you've been followed, I'll take care of it."

Connor swallowed the piece of chicken in his mouth unchewed. He knew damned well he'd been followed, but he hadn't told Ned Diamond that Jack Reese, meanest of the Pennsylvania Molly Maguires, was hot on his trail. Jack Reese was the man who had tricked Connor into planting dynamite in Samuel Trenton's mine.

Memories of that fateful day nearly two years before now flooded Connor's mind. . . .

The clanking of metal links echoed in the dust-filled air as the rickety wooden cart carrying the six men was slowly lowered into the mouth of the tunnel. A few of the men, all dressed in unwashed nondescript clothing caked with sweat and grime, talked in low tones among themselves. Muted conversations floated around Connor's head: talk of home and family, the amount of work waiting below, the evening ritual of standing in line waiting to be paid. He wondered how they could all be so calm, so cool. His own nerves were taut and his muscles tight with tension.

Soon, the talk died away as did the clear light of the early dawn. The time for idle conversation was past. It was time to begin another back-breaking day of mining, time for Connor to do what he'd been instructed to do by Jack Reese.

He waited for the cart to come to a jolting halt before he climbed over the side, shovel and pick in hand, and landed on the damp, coal-covered ground. His nostrils were filled with the musty smell of the inner mine as it mingled with the odor of the lard oil in the lamp affixed to his miner's cap. The dim beam from the small lantern punched a small circle of light into the intense blackness before him.

Wooden rails positioned at intervals along the shaft supported the walls and ceiling filled with anthracite coal. Under the dripping moss that grew atop the beams, the surface of the ebony-colored coal glistened wetly in the shifting circle of light. The uninterrupted drip, drip of mine water was soon muffled by the shuffling footsteps of the other men as they piled out of the conveyance. Connor stood there, staring into the faraway darkness of the tunnel where his mine light could not penetrate. He was dying for a cigarette, but knew the danger of striking a light in this underworld. A naked flame could send the mine shaft sky high, along with every miner it. Although the fire boss had already been down to test the air quality, no miner was permitted an open light.

A large hand closed tightly over Connor's shoulder. He jumped nervously, then reined in his fright.

"Well, lad, are you ready?" came the low, gravely whisper. It was Jack Reese.

Connor did not turn toward the man. He said nothing, did nothing.

"The boys are getting into position. You know what you're to do?"

Again, he gave no response.

"Just give it some flame, lad, then run like hell. There'll be questions later. Just tell them what you're supposed to. The boys will want to see you tonight. You know where." With that, Reese stepped away and Connor was left alone.

His blue eyes narrowed as he gritted his teeth, his knuckles whitening around the pick of his right hand. There was no turning back for him now. He'd been assigned a job. Fighting down his conscience, he stepped forward, piercing the blackness before him with his lantern beam. Twenty yards ahead, buried beneath a small mound of recently dug coal, was a cluster of dynamite—small sticks, no more than two inches in diameter, but combining enough power to blow this mine operation out of business. The result would be lost jobs to himself and the other workers—possibly even Connor's own death. But the explosion would also mean no more profits for the mine owner, Samuel Trenton, and that's what Connor's "friends" were after.

Dropping to his hands and knees beside the black mound, Connor reached to undo the lamp affixed to his miner's cap. Damn! The light would not budge. It was stuck. Connor cursed his luck and the time spent fumbling with the light. The cluster of dynamite before him was to be the first to be set off in a timed sequence of explosions. The other two stacks of dynamite were situated near the opening of the mine shaft; one had been placed close to the spot where the miners' cart stopped, and the other just yards away from the tipple of the mine.

Throwing caution to the wind, he reached into his back pocket and pulled out three stick matches. His hands shook as he fumbled nervously with them. As one fell from his fingers, lost somewhere in the damp ground, Connor swore fiercely. His voice echoed so eerily around him that he glanced over his shoulder, half afraid that the mine boss would be standing there. But there was nothing except for the single beam of his light illuminating the narrow shaft.

"Easy now, Connor," he scolded himself aloud, and the quaver he heard in his voice disturbed him. He pressed his lips tightly together, focusing his attention on the second match. Frowning, he struck it against the sole of his boot, but thrust too hard and the thin stick broke in half, the sulphur end flicking away into the darkness. "Damn!" He had only one match remaining—and to his best calculation—only minutes before the second group of explosives was ignited.

If he didn't hurry, he would be trapped inside the shaft.

He struck the last match. It sputtered for a fraction of a second, then took flame. No explosion came from the naked flame, just a small light in a dreary world. Connor cupped his hand around the flame as he lowered it to a trail of gun powder that snaked toward the clump of dynamite. With a *fzzzzst,* the powder ignited and burned quickly toward its target. Connor dropped the match and scrambled quickly to his feet. He had exactly a minute and a half to climb out of the mine shaft before the whole thing blew.

One thousand one, one thousand two . . . He forced himself to silently count the seconds as he sprinted toward the opening. Even though the air in the mine shaft was no more than sixty degrees, he had broken out in a hot sweat. *One thousand twelve.* He passed the dilapidated cart which he'd ridden into the shaft. There'd be no time to ride out in it. Even if there had been time, Connor could not chance riding out of the shaft. There would be no reason for a miner who'd just come on duty to bring the cart back up.

Grabbing for the knotted rope he'd left dangling by the side of the cart on his descent, he began the short climb out. Straight up, hand over hand, he climbed. He could see the sunlight streaming in through the opening above. Bright and clear. Fresh air slapped his face and he sucked it hungrily into his lungs.

One thousand fifty-one . . . Almost there.

A deafening boom erupted behind him then, and the whole earth shook with frightening intensity. Connor felt his skin and muscles quiver with the explosion. Sheer terror gripped him as he realized too late that he'd miscalculated. A shower of rock, dirt, and coal tumbled down upon him, pelting his body with jarring force, knocking him onto his stomach. The iron rails of the cart track gave way and Connor's boots, wet with mine water, slipped. With sickening speed, he was dragged back down into the collapsing shaft.

Three knots of the rope slipped through his clutching hands. Rough hemp tore and burned his skin as he held fast to his only life line. His eyes were shut and his head was between his arms as he slid down. His face hit the hard rail and the crosspieces he'd been climbing up. Splinters burrowed into his cheeks, but Connor didn't release the rope. He clung to it, pushing himself back up the incline with his legs, then grabbing for a higher knot. Hand over hand, he inched his way toward the mouth of the shaft, wondering how long it would be before the second and third explosions occurred. Smoke and dust billowed around him, and an ear-numbing crash rolled up from behind as the mine roof—above the spot he'd been only moments ago—collapsed and crumbled. His hands groped for another knot.

Blinded by smoke and dust, eyes smarting, he pulled himself the last few feet through the mine shaft opening. But no moment could be spared to gulp in the clean air. He had to get away before the next explosion. Pushing himself to his feet, he swayed, dizzy and confused, then staggered away from the mine, coughing the smoke from his lungs . . .

Connor shook the memories from his mind. They were too painful. Not only had the Molly Maguires forced him to blow up the mine by threatening to hurt his father and baby sister, someone had told the authorities that Connor had done the deed. What Connor had thought to be carefully planned sabotage had, in fact, been only a plan to get rid of him. There had been no other dynamite set that day, no other explosions intended. The whole incident had been set up to eliminate Connor, and Connor knew the man who was responsible. Jack Reese.

It was Connor's belief that Reese had been acting under the orders of a key figure in the organization, someone who didn't want Connor repeating what he'd heard at the Molly meetings. Obviously, Reese and his cohorts had meant to silence Connor for good, and at the same time, sabotage a mining operation. But Connor had been lucky. He'd gotten out of the mine alive. As soon as Reese realized Connor wasn't dead, he submitted trumped up evidence to the authorities "proving" Connor had murdered the superintendent, and then Reese told them Connor was the one who had blasted the mine shaft.

"Damn!" Connor swore aloud, and ignored the raised eyebrow Ned gave him. How was he to prove his innocence? He would never have planted the dynamite if Reese hadn't threatened to harm his father and sister. Patrick O'Shay, also a coal miner and member of the Mollies, was a hard-drinking, hard-working man. After his eldest son, Rory, had left home, Patrick had undergone a metamorphosis. His moods were mercurial, switching dramatically from gentle, caring father to fierce and unforgiving tyrant. When his wife Kathleen died, Patrick O'Shay had gone over the edge. His days were filled with work and his nights with hard drink. It was then that Connor decided to join the Molly Maguires. Patrick had ordered him to stay away from the group, but Connor, never one to listen, had disobeyed his father. He'd joined the Brotherhood, and his own thirst for a good brawl had put him in direct contact with a violent group of Mollies. Because of Connor's stupidity, his father's life had been threatened, and Connor had had no choice but to do as Jack Reese instructed.

Connor tore off another piece of chicken, chewing quickly and following it with a healthy swig of Irish whiskey supplied by Ned Diamond. Connor knew of one more person who had followed him to San Francisco. His own brother, Rory O'Shay, had somehow picked up his trail.

Connor's bitterness toward his own brother almost exceeded the hatred he felt for Jack Reese. Rory was ten years older than Connor, and the two of them had never bridged the gap that time alone had created. Connor hadn't always felt animosity toward his brother. In fact, there had been a time when Connor thought the world of Rory. But that had been years ago—before Rory had walked out on their small family. Rory had written and had even sent money home, but he had still not returned when their mother, Kathleen, died. As Connor had watched his mother buried, he'd also buried any feeling that might have remained for his brother. There was only one thing Connor wanted from Rory now, and that was vengeance. Somehow, someway, Connor would make Rory pay for leaving their needy family.

"I think he's *hungry*, love. Or does he always have that wild look in his eyes? I, for one, wouldn't let the creature step one *hoof* in my room. No wonder you have no men in your life, Catherine. What healthy male would want to step into your bedchamber when it reeks of horseflesh!" Sallie Burt wrinkled her pert nose in disgust and stepped around the black yearling, who stood just inside the entrance to Catherine's private rooms above the Diamond Saloon. "Why not take the beastie to some stable in the city? Surely you can afford to board the thing somewhere other than your rooms," said Sallie in her deep-throated voice.

Catherine, seated on the edge of her lavender-covered bed, stared at her newest possession as she listened to her friend talk. She loved the sound of Sallie's voice; it had the husky quality of someone just awakening from a deep sleep. Catherine had seen the effect that voice had on the men who frequented the Diamond, and Catherine wished the words that spilled from her own lips would do so in the same wonderful tones.

"Really, Catherine, what *will* your father say?" Sallie continued.

Probably not a thing, Catherine thought to herself. *He'll probably be extremely pleased to learn I won the animal in a poker game and paid not a cent for it.* Ned Diamond, a dirt-poor Irish coal miner from Raven Run, Pennsylvania, had wiped his slate clean when he'd brought his young daughter to San Francisco. Sharp at all card games, Ned Diamond had won a sizable sum of money, all of which he recklessly invested in numerous stocks. More than a few of his card-playing friends had called him a fool, telling him the stocks he'd bought would soon be worthless. But Ned Diamond had stuck to his guns, and when the money started rolling in, people began coming to him for investment tips. "Mad Ned" soon became a common name among the stock enthusiasts. Wildly generous with his money and his booze, Mad Ned had the reputation of being the craziest but truest friend a man could have.

"I don't think Pa will mind," Catherine spoke up, thoughtfully gazing at the animal. "He's always been a horse lover and lately he's been talking about investing in horse racing. Actually, I think he'll be pleased that I've acquired this yearling." What Catherine didn't add was that her father was in desperate need of some capital. Catherine had learned from Randolph that her father was near bankruptcy and he hadn't enough money to pay the mortgage on the saloon. If Mad Ned Diamond didn't soon come up with a tidy sum of money, the Diamond Saloon would be lost to him. Catherine had no idea how her father had managed to go through his small fortune. Certainly, the man was noted for his heavy drinking and wild spending, but he had never spent so much that it would put his family and business into jeopardy. Catherine was determined to find some way to pay the bills and keep the Diamond going.

"I don't know, love," Sallie interjected as she sat down on a lavender-colored lounge between the two brocade-covered windows overlooking Montgomery Street. "You have no place to keep the beast and you said yourself that you're afraid one of those men will come looking for it. Although, from what you told me about this O'Shay character, I wouldn't mind if he came looking for *me*."

Catherine pulled her gaze away from the yearling to look at Sallie. She'd told her friend all about the episode in the saloon that evening, but she'd no idea she'd described Rory O'Shay in such detail that Sallie would be interested. Sallie was *never* overly interested in any man. Certainly, she'd had her share, but Sallie had always been the party to break off the relationship. No man yet had lived up to Sallie's expectations.

"Whatever did I say about Rory O'Shay that piqued your curiosity?" As Catherine asked the question, she wondered why she felt a pang of jealousy zip through her. But in the next instant, the green feeling was gone. Sallie was her best friend and had been ever since Ned had opened the Diamond Saloon five years before. She had always been there when Catherine needed the special guidance and support of another woman.

Sallie dealt cards in the gambling saloon six nights a week, and Catherine could not recall her having missed more than two days in five years of work. Even though Sallie was only five or six years older than Catherine, she carried herself like a worldly-wise woman. The two of them were very close. Ever since Catherine's twelfth birthday, five years before, she had vowed to be just like Sallie.

But Catherine had quite a way to go before she even remotely resembled Sallie with her rich auburn hair, delicate blue eyes and twenty-inch waist. Sallie was everything Catherine was not: sophisticated, enchanting, and definitely experienced in the art of seduction.

Catherine could count on one hand the times she herself had been kissed—and four of those five times had been by inexperienced boys, who were more nervous than she had been. Rory O'Shay had been the first *man* to kiss her—and so thoroughly had he done it Catherine still felt her head reeling with the memory of his mouth on hers.

"It wasn't what you *said* but what you *didn't* say about Rory O'Shay, love. The man obviously made an impression on you, Catherine. I should very much like to meet him. After all, it isn't every day you take an interest in a man. So many men have walked through the saloon doors and you've disdained them all. I was beginning to wonder if something was amiss!"

"Amiss?" Catherine echoed. "What do you mean?"

"My dear, when I was your age . . . well"—she lowered her lashes, smiling—"let's just say I knew enough to know better."

Catherine gave her friend a sidelong glance. Sallie, in her deep crimson gown of brocade overlaid with fine point lace on the tight, low cut bodice, her high cheekbones perfectly highlighted and her eyes artfully outlined, did indeed appear to know better. No doubt Sallie had been *born* knowing! The woman was absolutely gorgeous, and the best part was that Sallie knew exactly what to do with such loveliness. Catherine had been told numerous times she was beautiful, but she never *felt* beautiful.

"Rory O'Shay is an arrogant man and I want nothing to do with him," she announced.

"Ah, but, Catherine, those are the best kind!"

"Oh stop! You're teasing me now!" Catherine smiled and leaned back on her bed, then snatched up one of the round pillows and tossed it at her friend.

When their playful giggles finally ceased, Catherine asked, "Are they really?"

"Are they really what?"

"You know what I mean!"

"Oh. Yes, arrogant men are absolutely the best kind, but I've a feeling your Rory O'Shay will soon prove that fact to you." Standing and stretching her arms above her head, Sallie declared, "It's been a long night. I think I'll turn in now. You should do the same, love, although I don't know how you can sleep with this animal in the same room."

Catherine laughed. "You're too skittish around horses, Sallie. I do wish you'd overcome that fear."

Sallie stepped quickly around the yearling, her strides long and fast, and only when she pulled the door open and stepped safely into the hall, did she say, "I'll never trust them, love. You never know when they're going to turn on you. I was only ten years old when a horse nearly trampled me to death, and I haven't forgotten the episode yet. Good night, Catherine." With that, the auburn beauty disappeared down the hall and Catherine was left alone with the yearling.

Leaning back on her bed and gazing at the black beast, Catherine wasn't at all sure what she should do with the animal. She did know she didn't want it out of her sight. Both Reese and O'Shay were after the animal, and between the two men, Catherine didn't know who she trusted less.

"I guess I'll just have to keep you here," she told the colt, who pricked his ears at the sound of her voice. "It's no wonder both those men have laid claim to you. It's plain to see you're a born racer—so sleek and leggy. I wish you could talk, boy. Perhaps then, you could tell me who really owned you before tonight."

Standing, her amber skirts rustling, she walked slowly over to the animal and brushed one hand over his smooth neck. "There was something in Rory O'Shay's eyes when he looked at you . . . as though he were gazing at a long-lost friend." Catherine shook her head thoughtfully, smiling as the colt accepted her petting as his royal due. "Oh, so no one owns you, is that what you're telling me, boy?" She laughed, remembering the spunk and spirit the colt had shown earlier. "I suppose you will be your own master. You're full of fire. Irish fire."

The words appealed to her, and as she paused in her petting, the colt nuzzled her arm. "You like that name, do you?" she asked. Her smile deepened.

"So do I," she told her new friend. "Welcome to the Diamond, Irish Fire."

By sundown of the next day, Catherine Diamond had her newly acquired yearling comfortably situated in a small shed that stood only twenty feet behind the Diamond

Saloon. It was certainly less than a grand stable, but Catherine had visions of building the shed into something huge and beautiful and filling it with descendants of Irish Fire.

But that would be years away, and tonight, her only thoughts were of hiring a competent trainer for her colt. She needed someone experienced with fine horses, skilled and sensitive enough to groom Irish Fire into the fine racer she knew he could be. How she would pay this person's wages, she had no idea, but she did know she had to hire someone. She had been querying people all day about the matter, and so far she had gotten a different answer from everyone she asked. Not one person had given her the same name, and she began to wonder if the perfect trainer could be found in the city.

"Miss Catherine, the playing cards you ordered from the printers have not yet been delivered. Shall I stop by the shop tomorrow and find out what the delay is?" Jake Randolph asked as he stood behind the briarwood bar wiping glasses. The saloon was not scheduled to open for another hour and a half.

"No, Randolph, I'll take care of the matter. I have some errands to run before we open."

Jake nodded. "How's the yearling, Miss Catherine? Have you decided on a suitable trainer?"

"No, I haven't. I have Irish Fire out back in the shed, but he'll soon outgrow that small space. By the way, keep an eye out for both Reese and O'Shay. I don't want either of them stepping one foot inside this saloon."

"Will do, Miss Catherine. Ain't nobody gonna get near Fire without your say so."

Catherine gave him an affectionate smile. "I knew I could count on you, Randolph. I'll return before we open." With that, she made her way toward the closed double doors of the saloon, then stepped out onto the busy street.

She'd taken only two steps before she heard a familiar

voice that made her freeze.

"Hold it right there," Miss Diamond. I want to know where you've got my horse."

Catherine spun around, eying Rory O'Shay defiantly. "Irish Fire is *my* horse, and I certainly don't have to answer to you, Mr. O'Shay."

He ignored her declaration of ownership. Dressed in a peacock-blue twill suit, obviously new, and sporting a top hat of midnight-blue, O'Shay appeared only slightly less formidable than he had the night before. Not even the pressed clothes of a businessman could hide his ruggedness. He didn't look like a man with an injured leg. No bandage showed along his calf, nor did he sport a cane. He leaned arrogantly against the rough, boarded exterior of the Diamond Saloon and fixed his cold glare on Catherine. His topcoat was unbuttoned and Catherine could see his revolver tucked snugly into the holster on his shoulder. She tried not to think of how easily he'd pulled that revolver on Reese.

"That yearling is of pure blood, Miss Diamond. He needs a skilled hand to guide him, not a novice."

"Oh?" she responded dryly, bringing her gaze up to meet his. "And I suppose you deem yourself to be that skilled hand?"

"I do."

Catherine bristled at his presumptuous tone. Obviously, he didn't believe her capable of taking care of Fire. Attempting to brush by him, she said, "I know enough of horses, Mr. O'Shay, to decide what my yearling needs. I told you once I do not want you near the Diamond. I suggest you move on before I call one of my employees."

O'Shay stayed where he was, blocking her way with one arm. "I'm not going anywhere — not without my colt."

Catherine glanced down at the arm thrust out before her. Never before had anyone defied her. For as long as she could remember, she'd been given exactly what she wanted.

45

She decided it was time to teach Mr. O'Shay a lesson.

"Just exactly what are your qualifications, Mr. O'Shay?"

"Qualifications?" His chiseled lips turned up into a grin. "Concerning what, Miss Diamond?" His hand closed intimately around her silk-clad elbow, and Catherine felt the warmth of his grasp.

"Concerning the training of a racer, of course," she responded coolly, jerking her arm out of his grip.

"Of course." His grin deepened. "I've been around horses most of my life. I've kept birth watch over half a dozen dams, been midwife to their foals, and have nursed quite a few horses back to health. I've spent hours on Baltimore pastures readying horses for the track. When it comes to a racer, I've got the golden touch."

"I see," she said. "But that still doesn't tell me if you have the ability to train my horse. How many winners have you trained?"

Cryptically, he answered, "It takes money to race a horse. But every horse I've owned has been a winner."

"And you claim you own Irish Fire?"

"That's right."

"Have you any proof?"

He was silent for a moment, then shook his head. "Nothing." His voice was flat. "Jack Reese stole the animal from me. All I can give you is my word."

"And you expect me to accept just your word? Mr. O'Shay, I—"

"I know," he cut in fiercely. "You don't believe me. I've got nothing to prove my ownership—nothing but my hard work and sincerity." His blue eyes took on a hard glint. "I want to train that horse, Miss Diamond. And I aim to do so."

Something in his voice—some raw chord—tugged at her emotions. What if Rory O'Shay did indeed own Fire? What if Reese *had* stolen the yearling from O'Shay and then recklessly gambled the colt away in a card game?

46

But no, she decided in the next instant. She had no cause to believe either man. Irish Fire was a fine Thoroughbred, obviously bred to race the fast track, and any person with a smidgen of horse sense could see that. Any opportunist would jump at the chance of having Fire for his own. Catherine had been around opportunists all her life and she knew how to handle them.

"Irish Fire is my property now, Mr. O'Shay. If I intend to race him—which I've not yet decided—then I'll find the proper trainer on my own."

"If you don't race him, then you're a fool."

Catherine stiffened with his words. "Oh? And would I be a bigger fool if I hired you as his trainer?" Their gazes met. His blue eyes threw her an undeniable challenge, and Catherine felt the blood surge through her body. The urge to pick up the gauntlet was great but she pushed the notion aside.

"Never mind, Mr. O'Shay. I know the answer to that question." She took a step forward, as if to pass him by.

"You won't find a better man than me to train that horse," he said quietly. "You won the colt in a game of chance—let us draw cards to see if I'll be the one to train him."

The pale rays of the sun cast his face in shadow, but still the harsh lines of his countenance were clear to Catherine. It had cost his male pride much to suggest drawing cards. This man wanted Fire all to himself, and it was obvious he did not want to be in Catherine's employ. *He wants Fire so badly he is willing to be just the animal's trainer instead of his owner,* Catherine thought to herself. She grudgingly admired the man's persistence. She knew instinctively he would not let the matter rest if she didn't agree to his suggestion. Catherine's mind began churning. If *she* cut the highest card, then perhaps she could demand he work for her, for room and board only. . . .

"We'll each cut one deck, highest card wins," he continued.

"Your confidence is great, Mr. O'Shay. What if *I* am the one who draws the higher card?"

He motioned her toward the double doors of the saloon. "Then I guess I'll have to leave you in peace. But I'm not worried, Miss Diamond. I've the luck of the Irish." He flashed her a winning smile, then pulled open the doors of the saloon and followed her inside.

Chapter Three

Catherine crossed to the center of the dimly lit gambling hall and found herself relaxing by degrees with the familiar sounds around her. Low voices drifted in from the offices and kitchen at the back of the saloon where the many employees of the Diamond went about their duties before sundown. The doors just to the right of the bar swung open and a young woman bearing a tray of glasses moved to place them on the shelves beneath the briarwood bar and near the huge barrel of beer on draught. She smiled at Catherine and Rory, the tumblers clinking against each other as she set them down in pairs. Catherine waited for the woman to leave before she picked up a fresh deck of cards from one of the center tables. She turned toward Rory who had moved beside her, and handed him the cards.

He shook his head. "Ladies first."

"As you wish," she replied, setting the deck back upon the blue felt. She lifted half of the cards toward her, flipping the stack over so the bottom card could be seen. She breathed a sigh of relief. She'd cut a queen of hearts. She replaced the cards and waited for Rory to draw.

"Not bad," he told her. His blue eyes in the dimly lit room appeared dark as a deep ocean, and standing so close to him, Catherine could see the fine lines etched at the corners. Laugh lines? Distractedly, she wondered how it would feel to have Rory O'Shay bestow a genuine smile on her.

With nimble fingers, O'Shay cut the deck, flipping the cards. "King of spades," he drawled. "Looks like I'll be your new trainer."

Oddly enough, Catherine was not upset by the outcome of the draw. "By the sound of your voice I take it you have some reservations about your new employment."

He laid the deck back on the table, his face unreadable. "Let's just say I've never been employed by a woman before."

"But you'll suffer my supervision just so you can be near my horse, is that it, Mr. O'Shay?"

A moment of silence passed before he answered. "Something like that. Now where is the yearling? I'd like to get right to work."

Catherine blinked, surprised by his haste to be near the horse. "He's out back in a stall. Aren't you the least bit interested to know what wages I'll be paying you, Mr. O'Shay?"

"Call me Rory," he told her. "As for my pay, I trust you'll be fair." He was already headed for the main doors of the hall.

Catherine could do nothing but fall in step behind him. As soon as they were out of the main entrance, Catherine led the way through the narrow alley between the saloon and the adjacent tailoring shop. The smell of wet earth mingling with the stronger scents of baked goods coming from down the street wafted around her as her slippered feet sank nearly an inch into the spongy mud. The building occupied by the Diamond had once been a dry goods store, first erected during the Gold Rush, but the enterprising Ned Diamond had bought the structure and added rooms to the top and back, refurbishing the façade in a dazzling manner. Concerned only with outward appearances, however, he had not extended his golden touch to the back of the building. The property behind the saloon, what little there was of it, was badly in need of attention. Littered here and there were empty crates, cast-off furniture, and even some boards that had been used for shelving when the saloon had been a store. The small shanty, which stood a mere five hundred feet from the back exit of the saloon, was about the size of four outhouses. A dilapidated structure, once used as a kind of tack room by the previous owner, was a far cry from the stable. The door hung ajar on rusting hinges, tattered sackcloth fluttered in the single window, and there was a gaping hole in the roof where the wood had rotted.

"Here we are," Catherine announced.

Rory O'Shay glanced at the small shed. "This is it?"

Catherine straightened, keenly aware of the disrepair around her. "Yes," she answered as proudly as she could. "The—my yearling is in here." She gestured for him to follow as she lifted her skirts and stepped over a pile of dung she'd not yet had the time to clear away. There was barely room for the two of them to stand inside. The yearling, along with a half-filled pail of apples, and another pail filled earlier with water, but now tipped on its side, took up most of the space.

Rory's attention centered immediately on the horse who nickered softly in response to the man's low murmurings. He ran his large hands over the colt's silky neck, then brushed across the finely formed back, while his eyes took in every detail of Fire's form. Almost with contempt, he undid the coarse hemp that was tied around a piece of wood underneath the window, where Catherine had secured it that morning to keep the animal in place. He then removed the rope from the horse's neck.

"This won't do," he said gruffly, tossing the hemp in Catherine's direction. "And what in God's name are you doing feeding him a bucket of apples?" The half-filled pail followed the hemp into Catherine's arms. He bent at the waist and picked up the empty water pail, thrusting it, too, toward her. "He'll need water, and oats and some fresh hay. And while you're seeing to those things, find a shovel. This place smells."

Catherine's mouth dropped open as she stared at the pail swinging from its looped handle in his outstretched hand. Indignation welled within her. "Well! Surely you don't expect me to—" But the look on his face told her he did. "Mr. O'Shay! I hired *you* to see to the care of this horse—and—and what is so terribly wrong with feeding him apples?" She'd gone to great pains to find the freshest apples and see to it that Fire had a full pail of them!

"Miss Diamond, this animal is not a puppy brought home from a fair for the sole purpose of entertaining you. He is a fine Thoroughbred, a racer, with purer blood than any English sovereign. From this point on, nothing will be fed or done to him that does not meet my approval. As for my duties, you hired me to train him, and that I will do."

"But you expect *me* to shovel the stall and haul his water?"

"He's your horse, isn't he?" he replied, and somehow she felt he was mocking her. "As for this structure being called a stall, it is good for nothing more than kindling. You'll have to supply more comfortable quarters for the horse; preferably a stable with adequate pasture. The city is no place to train a racer."

A stable? *Pasture?* She felt the color drain from her face. What exactly had she gotten herself into? She could barely afford to pay the employees of the saloon, let alone house this beast in grand style. Turning her face from Rory O'Shay so he could not see her distressed expression, she grabbed the empty pail, and said, "I'll get some fresh water, and try to find a shovel. As—as for the other things you mentioned, I'll—it will take me a few days."

Rory shook his head. "He'll need oats and hay tonight. And there'll be other provisions we'll need before then."

Catherine nodded numbly, mentally figuring how much money it would cost to insure her new yearling's comfort. She had seven hundred and fifty dollars she had won from Jack Reese the other night, money she had hoped to put back into the running of the saloon.

She left silently to do Rory's bidding, and, once in the comfort of her own rooms, kicked off her dirtied slippers and gown and changed into apparel more appropriate for the task at hand. Then, she took several twenty-dollar gold pieces from her purse and headed back to the shed, pausing in the saloon to give Randolph instructions for the evening and to inform him she would not be in to oversee things until later on. Finding a shovel was not as easy as she had thought it would be. There simply was not one to be found anywhere within the Diamond. The best she could come up with was a worn broom and dustpan. These in hand, she greeted Rory who, in her absence, had cleaned out the interior of Fire's lodging with more than just a touch of the domestic.

A single, low-flamed lantern burned from atop a newly installed shelf just to the inside right of the door; crude pegs had been pounded into the back wall and were now slung with a leather halter and Rory's blue twill overcoat; two other pegs had been installed at a convenient spot to hold Fire's pails of food and water; and the ugly sackcloth that had covered the only window had been replaced with a perfectly cut piece of familiar blue material.

"I hope you don't mind," Rory said, seeing Catherine pause in the doorway, which had been stripped of its sagging door and rusty hinges. "I helped myself to a few things from the saloon's stores. I'll return the tools in the orning. I also intend to put up a new door then, too."

She was amazed the man had done so much in her absence. "Use whatever you see fit," she replied, stepping inside and noting he had removed all the refuse. "I—we didn't have a shovel. This broom is the best I could do." She propped the scarred wooden handle against one wall and let the dustpan clatter to the ground beside it. Irish Fire was leisurely lapping at a pail of fresh water; something she, in her haste and thoughts of other responsibilities, had neglected to bring along.

"He should be comfortable enough here tonight," Rory said, patting the animal's neck. "But we should see to more suitable lodgings as soon as possible."

"Yes, of course," Catherine instantly agreed, too proud to tell this man she didn't have the funds for anything more elaborate than what they were standing in. She reached into the pocket of her dress and withdrew the gold pieces she had brought from her rooms. "Here," she said, thrusting the money toward him, "this should take care of Fire's immediate needs."

Rory hesitated a moment before reaching for the coins. He now wore only a snow-white shirt, unbuttoned at the throat, along with his dark blue trousers and black boots. His ebony hair was mussed from his exertions, feathering back away from his forehead in soft waves, and his damp shirt clung to his muscled chest in the warm night air. Catherine tried to avoid focusing on his lean body, so evident beneath the tight material. Fingering the coins she gave him, counting them carefully but without any show of greed, he tucked them into the pocket of his trousers.

"Fire did you say?" he asked.

"What? Oh yes. I—I named him Irish Fire. It . . . seemed appropriate at the time."

He tested the name once, the words coming from his lips like a gentle caress. "Yes, I like it. I guess it is fitting to keep the Irish in him."

Catherine made no comment to this. To do so, would be to admit that he was Fire's true owner.

"I take it there's no feed on the premises?" he asked, breaking the awkward silence.

Catherine shook her head. "No. But I'll go and purchase some. How much—?"

"Don't bother," he replied, moving to stand beside her. "I'll take care of it. I have a list of things I'll need and I could probably bargain for a better price."

His words stung. "I'm quite capable of transacting a business deal, Mr. O'Shay. I do so numerous times a day with purchases involving the saloon."

He smiled. "I'm sure you do. Nevertheless, I'll take care of it." He took his coat from one of the pegs and slipped into it. Apparently, he intended to go in search of the provisions immediately.

"Is there anything I can do here tonight?" Catherine asked.

He leaned toward her, reaching past her body for the lantern. His arm brushed her shoulder. "No, nothing," he replied, his chiseled lips tilting in a faint smile as she quickly stepped away.

Catherine fought for composure. "Very well then. I—I've had a room readied for you, on the second floor. If you'll see me before you retire for the night, we can discuss details and I'll have a key for you then. If there is anything special you need, please let me know."

"I will," he assured her, then motioned for Catherine to precede him out of the stall.

It was inky dark outside except for the swinging lantern Rory carried and the soft yellow lights of the saloon streaming through the back windows of the building. Piano music, mingled with laughter and snatches of conversation, floated to them along with the sounds of wagons and carriages and the clip clop of horses' hooves moving along Montgomery Street. The air had turned cool, and Catherine shivered slightly. As she moved through the semi-darkness, Rory put his hand to her elbow and helped guide her through the alley. She did not protest his touch. Beneath the cover of darkness she was surprisingly comfortable with him.

"It sounds as if business is good tonight," he commented as they came around the front of the building. He paused for a moment, releasing her elbow and extinguishing the lantern.

"Yes, Thursday nights usually bring in a good crowd. I'll be in the main hall, Mr. O'Shay," she said, then moved away from him to the entrance of the saloon. He tipped his hat to her, then headed down the street. Catherine watched as he sauntered away into the nighttime bustle of the street, which blazed with gaslight from the many windows and storefronts of shops that were still open. San Francisco throbbed with life even in the hours of darkness. The city never slept, and round the clock gold and silver changed hands in never-ending stock transactions and other business deals.

To Catherine's left, an elegant caleche drawn by a pair of blanketed, perfectly groomed Friesian horses passed by, and Catherine looked with longing eyes at the stylish couple riding within. She felt a momentary stab of envy as she watched the carriage move down the street, for she had always dreamed of living the life of a wealthy, respectable lady, attending the circuit of gay parties, theater openings, and afternoon teas. But even though her father had acquired a substantial fortune since moving to California — and in San Francisco, wealth could certainly be a standard of social position — Catherine had never been to the theater or received a single invitation to any of the society galas. She was regarded as a social outcast by ladies of "gentle" breeding, and for Catherine this was a harsh reality.

In the early days of his newfound wealth, her father had gone to great lengths to see that she was included in the social activities of his business associates' daughters, but in the end, Catherine had been ignored and left to herself. There was no room among those young ladies for a motherless young girl who was raised inside a saloon where she was allowed to play cards, serve drinks and even gamble. Catherine had ceased even trying to gain entrance into the tight circle, and her father—perhaps embarrassed by his own lack of foresight—had not pushed. Instead, he allowed her even freer rein than before, becoming almost obssessed with the idea of Catherine's learning all there was to know about the operation of the Diamond.

Catherine had a head for business. Exceptionally quick with figures, and bold enough to argue her point of view with the many men she came in contact with each day, she took to running the Diamond like a fish to water. By the time she had turned seventeen, there was nothing she didn't oversee. From the ordering of liquor, to the preparation of food, right down to the scheduling of employees, Catherine supervised it all. The only thing she did not tend to was the books, and it was here, she realized in hindsight, that she'd made her biggest error. Her father had always approved the bills she handed him, and then saw to it they were paid. He approved her redecorating schemes, and even her innovative idea of a "free midday repast," a complimentary meal for patrons who bought drinks. Catherine made certain that the meals were of the finest quality—boiled salmon or roast beef served with potatoes, bread, and butter. The free lunch brought in quite a crowd in the daytime, and most of the patrons returned in the evening to let their money flow back into the saloon in gambling and drinking.

Not until Jake Randolph had let the secret slip that her father was in financial trouble, did Catherine think anything was amiss. By all her calculations, the Diamond Saloon was doing a booming business. But this just wasn't so. Somewhere, somehow, Ned Diamond was losing money by the barrel.

Watching until the caleche disappeared from sight, Catherine sighed heavily and turned. Three well-dressed men, each of whom tipped his hat to her, entered the saloon. She decided not to follow them inside since she wasn't dressed properly. Instead, she made her way back through the narrow alley and entered the saloon through the back door. The kitchen buzzed with activity. Oysters — free for the taking at the bar, along with toothpicks and matches — were steaming in a mammoth vat presided over by the efficient Chinese cook, Fong Ling. Deftly removing the oysters, one by one, he tapped them open and placed them in the half-shell on serving platters. The platters were then whisked away by the young lady whose sole job it was to see to replenishing all stocks at the bar. While empty beer barrels were noisily rolled to the side of the room where they would be carted away for refilling in the morning, one or two employees wandered in from the bustling gambling floor, seeking a moment's respite and perhaps a quick bite of food. Catherine smiled at Sallie, who had taken a break, seating herself heavily on a kitchen stool, her lavender skirts rustling. Sighing, she kicked off her slippers, one by one.

"I'll only be a minute, love," she said to Catherine. "I just *had* to get away. The place is bursting with rowdies tonight."

"That's fine," Catherine replied. "But you should rest in the lounge where it's more comfortable. You don't have to sit on that hard stool."

Sallie waved her hand. "I don't mind. Besides, I like the kitchen better than the ladies lounge, and Fong and I are able to exchange recipes. Aren't we, Fong?" She gave Catherine a quick wink, then turned her gaze to the elderly

Chinese.

Fong, who wore a black skull cap and a long queue that snaked down his slim back, frowned and shook his head. His forehead was shaved in the traditional style of his people, and he wore the loose tunic and pants, with soft black slippers that were a common sight in the Chinese Quarter.

"We no exchange recipes," he told Catherine. "Fong does all the talking; Miss Sallie only listen."

"But, Fong," Sallie replied, acting affronted, "didn't I share my secret with you for sumptuous chop suey?"

Fong muttered something unintelligible as he continued prying open steamed oysters. Both Catherine and Sallie laughed, remembering the practical joke Sallie had played on Fong.

The cook took great pride in his culinary skills, and his wonderful dishes were indeed a part of the Diamond's success. It was no secret to the employees that Fong continually strove to create something new and extraordinary that would win everyone's praise, and it was also no secret that he had more than friendly feelings toward the seductive Sallie. Sallie doted on the old man, spending her rare free moments with him, enjoying even his reprimands about her sorrowful lack of expertise in the kitchen. Sallie, in one of her playful moods, had informed Fong that she could indeed cook, and had then proceeded to describe to him a very detailed recipe for chop suey. Of course, there was no such recipe, but the gullible Fong with his thirst for supremacy in the kitchen, had secretly attempted the dish. The result was a total disaster that had left Sallie doubling over with laughter.

"Sallie, you are incorrigible," Catherine said, trying her best not to offend Fong by laughing. But she needn't have worried, she knew, for Fong was no doubt planning to repay Sallie with a practical joke of his own. Such was life within the Diamond Saloon. "I'll talk with you later," Catherine told her friend, then left the kitchen and headed up the back stairs to her apartment.

Once there, she changed into an evening gown of rust-colored silk, clipped on the one pair of diamond earrings she owned, and smoothed down her hair. She then went downstairs to face a long night of dealing cards and seeing to the comfort of the patrons.

The evening passed quickly for her. She spent most of it dealing cards, receiving many twenty-dollar gold pieces in tips. Catherine slipped them all into a scarlet drawstring purse which she carried for that express purpose. By midnight, the small purse was heavy and Catherine was tired. She rose and motioned for one of the other women to take her place at the table. Nodding to the circle of cigar-smoking gentlemen around her, she said her good evenings and sought the peace and quiet of her own rooms. An evening in the gambling hall left her drained, more often than not, and she was slowly coming to realize that she would rather not make a showing at all. But someone had to oversee the operation, and now that she knew they were in debt, the tips she collected each night would help to pay some of the bills.

She found Rory O'Shay sitting at the top of the steps that led to the private rooms. His back was propped against the wall and he had one leg stretched out before him, the other bent at the knee. He was cleaning his Remington .44 revolver, polishing the smooth, casehardened steel with a square of cloth. Catherine came up short as he raised the revolver and sighted it at the far wall.

"Evening, Miss Diamond," he said, eyes narrowed, hands steady, as he trained his gun on a speck on the wall. "Or should I say good morning?" Pleased with his aim, he lowered the gun and continued polishing it, now running the cloth over the rosewood grip. His movements were quick, meticulous, and he whistled softly as he worked.

Catherine was shaken for a moment as she recalled the sight of O'Shay pressing that same gun to the bulging neck of Jack Reese. Finding her voice, she said, "Guns are not permitted on the premises, Mr. O'Shay. I suggest you get rid of it. Now."

Cocking one brow at her, he spun the six-shot cylinder, let it whirl, then snapped it back in place. "I don't go anywhere without my gun, Miss Diamond—not even to bed."

"Well, I—I am sorry but you'll just have to—"

"No," came the calm reply. "I *don't* have to." Slipping the revolver back into his shoulder holster, he pushed himself up to stand above her on the top step. "I've been waiting on my room for the last three hours. You did tell me you have a place for me to sleep?"

Catherine let the subject of the gun pass. She'd deal with that issue at another time. "Yes, of course I have a room for you. I had thought you would come into the hall whenever you returned. I have the key right here." She reached into her drawstring purse and dug through the small pile of gold.

"I don't liken myself to the kind of men you cater to here at the Diamond. If it's all the same to you, Miss Diamond, I would just as soon transact our business outside of the gambling hall—and at a more reasonable hour, say, before the sun goes down and after it has risen."

Catherine brought her eyes up to meet his cold stare. Rory O'Shay obviously did not approve of her or of the saloon. Miffed, she thrust the key toward him, and said in imperious tones, "Your room is the second door on the right. Breakfast is served at seven, and if you have any questions, I can be found in the office between the hours of eleven and six."

He nodded, tipping his hat. "Those are more my hours."

He turned and headed for his room.

She waited a moment, allowing him time to enter his quarters and close the door before she wearily headed for her own apartments.

Their rooms were adjacent, the wall separating them thin enough so that Catherine could hear Rory's movements. Had it been possible, she would have given him quarters far removed from her own, but the only available room was the one next to her own. All the other upstairs chambers were occupied by employees of the Diamond. As she prepared for bed, Catherine tried to blot out the sounds Rory made; the creaking of the floor boards beneath his feet, the jingle of his spurs and the thump of his boots as he kicked them off. But even through the masculine voices that floated up from downstairs, along with a final tune from the piano — the ballad, "Aura Lee" — Catherine could not rid her conciousness of the man and his movements in the next room.

Of course this was only natural, she thought, considering the circumstances of their "partnership," her inability to pay the man a wage for his work with the colt, and the fact that she did wonder if Fire was truly his possession and not Jack Reese's to gamble away.

Discouraged and overtired, she finished slipping on her nightdress, then climbed into bed. The ropes beneath the mattress groaned with her slight weight — a comforting, familiar sound — and she bunched up her feather pillow, placed her head on it and rolled onto her stomach.

"Aura Lee," a ballad popular in the 1860's, was almost complete. There was only one refrain left. Catherine closed her eyes, concentrating on the music, her mind forming the words to the song. From the next room, she was surprised to hear Rory's voice as he began to sing in a low voice. His voice was mellow and caressing. Catherine listened closely to the words.

*When the mistletoe was green,
Midst the winter's snows,
Sunshine in thy face was seen,
Kissing lips of rose.
Aura Lee, Aura Lee,
Take my golden ring;
Love and light return with thee,
And swallows with the spring.*

Inexplicably, she was saddened when the music ended and all other sounds ceased from the adjoining room.

Chapter Four

The next day passed uneventfully for Catherine. There were numerous chores to be done and she was kept busy up until the time the Diamond opened for business. She hadn't seen her father all day and was now becoming anxious. She worried about Ned. Lately, he seemed very preoccupied and yet he would never share with her whatever was troubling him.

The night turned into a long one for Catherine. Her father had still not returned from whatever business kept him away for hours at a time, and Catherine was nearly exhausted with all the work she'd been doing over the past few days in her father's absence. Jake Randolph had been a great help to her, but he had asked to take this night off. Although Catherine could have used his assistance, she had let him go, knowing he wanted to escort one of his many lady friends about the city.

Now, as she hurried from the kitchen back to the gambling room, she wished she hadn't been so gracious. There was just too much work to be done. Every hired hand was busy, yet there were a dozen things left undone. Leaving a frazzled Fong in the kitchen, scurrying about and rattling on in rapid-fire Cantonese about how he needed another hand to properly prepare his dishes, Catherine stepped behind the bar and set down an armload of just-washed glasses. Billy, the bartender for the evening, scooped them up quickly, filling them with drinks. She gave him a reassuring smile, letting him know how well he was doing his job. He had just enough time to nod and tell her he would keep the drinks flowing. Business was unusually brisk tonight.

The customary, friendly hubbub in the saloon was suddenly broken by a disturbance at Sallie's table in the center of the room. One of the four patrons seated there—a red-faced, silver-haired man in an expensive pinstripe suit—had risen abruptly, knocking his chair over, and shouting at Sallie, who was visibly upset. As the man's voice rose, a small circle of onlookers quickly moved back.

Catherine hurried to her friend's aid.

"I say you cheated me!" the man fumed, wagging a long finger at Sally's astonished face. "You're dealing from the bottom of the deck, you are! There's nothing I hate worse than a card cheat, lady!"

A deadly hush fell over the room as Sally replied, "And I say you, sir, are a poor loser, and drunk to boot."

The man was indeed drunk, Catherine realized. She recognized him, although she didn't know his name. He was a regular at the saloon; in fact, he spent nearly all his time playing cards there. He had never been one to make a scene, but lately word had gotten around that the man's luck had run out. He'd been on a losing streak for some time now, and Catherine should have known better than to let her employees serve him too much to drink. A heavy drinker, down on his luck, was bound to stir up trouble eventually. She silently reprimanded herself for not paying more attention to the patrons. One lesson she'd learned well from her father was to always keep an eye on the customers, gauging their intake of liquor—and their winning or losing streaks.

"What is the problem?" she asked in a level voice as she

came to stand beside Sallie.

Sallie clenched her hands into fists, seething. "This *gentleman* claims I cheated him, Catherine. He says I've been dealing from the bottom of the deck."

The man's lip curled into a sneer. "Damned right you have," he replied menacingly. "And I aim to get my gold back, now!"

The air crackled with tension, and Catherine knew there could be bloodshed if she didn't calm the man. In soothing but authoritative tones, she said, "We deal only from the top of the deck in this establishment, sir. I can assure you Sallie did not, in any way, attempt to cheat you. She's been with the Diamond for years and is one of our best liked girls. I think, perhaps, if you take a moment to cool down, you'll realize you were mistaken. Please, why don't you find yourself a seat at another table and I'll have one of the girls bring you a hot cup of coffee."

"I don't want any gawdamned coffee!" the man shot back. "I want my gold, all of it, plus some compensation for the stress this *trusted* employee of yours has caused me!"

It was obvious the man was only seeking a way to reclaim all the money he'd lost, plus a tidy bonus. If Catherine relented now, she ran the risk of other patrons attempting the same ploy. She could not, at any cost, back down. There were too many customers listening, many of whom would not hesitate to use such underhanded tactics to recoup their losses.

From somewhere beyond the crowd that had gathered to watch, came a hard, male voice with a slight Irish lilt. "If Miss Diamond says you weren't cheated, boy, then you weren't. I suggest you forget the incident and move on. We don't need any troublemakers here."

Everyone turned to look at Rory O'Shay, his tall, lean frame dwarfing many of the dapper-looking men near him. He appeared as formidable as the first night Catherine had seen him in the Diamond—and with his left hand on his hip, which held back his coat, revealing the Remington in his shoulder holster, he looked all the more menacing. He made no move to reach for the gun, but the implication was clear.

"And who the hell are you?" the drunken card player demanded.

"I'm the man who's going to cart you out of here if you don't go willingly. Now, I suggest you give these fine ladies your apologies—and then I'm going to give you exactly ten seconds to clear out."

"I'm not going anywhere until I get my gold back!"

"Ten seconds," Rory repeated. "Starting now." He began to count slowly, his blue eyes diamond-hard as he stared at the belligerent card player.

Catherine feared the man was not going to leave without a fight, but soon the other patrons, who had kept out of the dispute until now, took a step closer to Rory, as though they agreed with his ultimatum. Outnumbered, and not wishing to be pumped full of bullets, the man mumbled a quick apology to both Sallie and Catherine, then turned and made a hasty exit.

Catherine, eager to have the whole incident forgotten, said loudly, "All right, gentlemen, the show is over. The next drink is on the house." She motioned to the bartender, who immediately began pouring more drinks. She didn't want to think about the cost of serving a free drink to every patron in a full house. But she had no choice, she realized; she needed to smooth over the moment. Turning to Sallie, she asked, "Would you like a few minutes to yourself?"

Sallie shook her head, then sent Rory a quick wink of thanks. "No, that won't be necessary. I'm fine, love. I've just never been called a cheat before. The man made me angry, but I'll be all right now." She resumed her seat at the table, and after flashing the returning card players a smile filled with soubrette sauciness, began to gather up the cards for the next deal. The usual, easy atmosphere of the Diamond prevailed once more.

Catherine moved toward Rory. "I owe you my thanks," she said earnestly. "I'm afraid without Randolph or my father here, things could have gotten terribly out of hand."

The hard gaze he'd given the card player softened as he looked at Catherine. "You should hire competent men whose sole purpose is to bounce out unwanted patrons," he replied.

"We usually have enough male employees to see to such matters. It's just that, well, lately we've been short-handed." She didn't want to admit they hadn't the funds to hire bouncers. "Usually my father, or Randolph, takes care of the sticky business."

"Even so," he argued, "a fine lady like you shouldn't be exposed to such riffraff."

Catherine felt herself blush. No one, ever, had called her a "fine lady." "Would you care for a drink?" she asked nervously, gesturing toward the bar. "Or perhaps something hot to eat?"

"A cup of coffee would be fine," he said. "But if it's all the same to you, I don't care to drink it in here. I'm not a gambling man."

His comment, easily made and with no demeaning overtones, nevertheless unsettled her. She knew there were those who viewed her involvement with the Diamond as disgraceful. Suddenly, the impression she made on Rory O'Shay mattered very much. "You can sit in my father's office," she said. "It's quiet and—and no one will bother you."

He nodded and then followed her toward the back of the Diamond where the office was located. It was furnished with a desk, two chairs, a settee, and stacks of ledgers. As Catherine lit a lamp and then went in search of some coffee, Rory settled onto the floral-patterned settee. He was glad he had walked into the gambling hall when he did. Rory had no doubts that Catherine Diamond could hold her own with any man, but it bothered him that such a gentle, beautiful woman should have to cater to such animals. Rory's own father had been a heavy drinker and he knew what ugly scenes could evolve from too much booze. Catherine deserved to associate with a more civilized clientele. Better yet, she shouldn't be forced to serve strange men at all. She was the type of woman who belonged at the head of a perfectly set table, one who would not be out of her element dining with heads of state or other illustrious guests. Her dark, sparkling beauty would enhance any formal dining room.

Rory smiled at his thoughts. His own background was far removed from the aura of wealth even though he had known such a life at one time. In Baltimore, at the age of eighteen, Rory had met a moneyed widow who was more than willing to take him under her wing. He had learned a great deal from Bess, who had been his senior by nearly twenty-five years. He'd lived in her home for nearly ten years, and if there was one thing he learned from her, besides how to manage a vast estate and breed horses, it was how to treat a lady. And since that time, Rory O'Shay had been searching for the right woman to shower all his skills and love upon. Catherine Diamond, in many respects, reminded him of the now-deceased widow.

Catherine was strong-willed, determined to succeed in a man's world, and yet, despite this hard outer shell evident when first meeting her, Rory detected a soft inner core. He also sensed a loneliness within her. Although surrounded by employees who were also her friends, Rory felt Catherine Diamond longed for something more in her life — just as he longed for someone to share his own deep thirst for living. Rory detected a certain vulnerability beneath Catherine's businesslike exterior. It was this vulnerability that drew him toward her. As he could picture her at the head of a glittering table, dazzling her guests with sparkling conversation, so, too, could he envision her in a homey kitchen surrounded by eager toddlers reaching for cookies she herself had baked.

He let out a long sigh, wondering why he had let his thoughts take such a course. Even though he was ready to take a wife and settle down, he knew such a future was not to be. He was a wanted man back east. He hadn't a proper home to offer a woman as lovely as the likes of Catherine Diamond—and he had yet to find his younger brother, Connor, who had gotten himself into trouble.

Just then, Catherine, bearing a small tray with two cups of steaming coffee, entered the room. "Here we are," she announced, setting the tray with its fragile china cups on one corner of the desk. "Do you take sugar or cream?" she asked, handing him one of the cups.

He shook his head, watching as Catherine placed one lump of sugar and a bit of thick cream in her coffee. As she daintily stirred the liquid, Rory let his gaze move down the curved length of her. She was absolutely the most gorgeous woman he'd seen, and, he admitted to himself, more than half of her allure had nothing to do with her looks. There was a certain aura about her that led one to believe she was a woman of great feeling and depth. Her whole being was suffused with a special luminosity and expressiveness. Her charm did not vanish with fatigue—and he could see she was very tired at this moment—nor was it erased by the harsh lighting of the office. Catherine Diamond was a rare breed, true to every word she spoke and every gesture she made.

"Are you certain you wouldn't like something to eat?" she asked.

"I'm sure," Rory replied, taking a healthy swallow of the hot brew.

Catherine, seated in the straight-backed chair directly opposite Rory, placed her cup and saucer upon her lap, sipped her coffee. She was glad for this time away from the noise and commotion of the gambling hall. Finally, after hours of mind-numbing activity, she could relax and enjoy a moment of peace. Only a moment, though, she reminded herself, for the Diamond was packed and her employees needed her assistance and guidance.

"I suppose you're anxious to get back to work, aren't you?" Rory asked.

Catherine looked up, startled to find his penetrating gaze resting on her. "I—ah, well, as I mentioned, we are a bit short-handed. We need all the help we can get."

"And it's not like you to leave your employees with too much of a burden."

She smiled in acknowledgment.

"I admire that quality in you, Miss Diamond. I've worked at many jobs, and I can tell you it has not been my experience to find a sympathetic employer. Most were just greedy for gold and nothing more."

Once again, Rory O'Shay had complimented her in a way no one else ever had. Despite their rocky beginnings, Catherine felt herself warming to him. "My father likes to think of the Diamond as a family business. Anyone employed here is like family to us."

"Then I guess I'm the newest member of the fold, aren't I? Here now, finish your coffee and then tell me what I can do to help. The—*your* horse is all taken care of for the night, so I'm free to help you here." His emphasis on Irish Fire's being her horse was not sarcastic. He seemed willing now to drop the argument over who truly owned Irish Fire. Catherine was grateful. She was too weary to continue to dispute, and, quite frankly, she realized, she didn't want to argue with Rory O'Shay.

"Have you ever tended bar before?" she asked.

Rory nodded, smiling wryly. "I have, many times. I guess you could say my father taught me the rudimentary skills."

Catherine, unaware of what lay behind his answer, was delighted to hear he'd had some experience behind a bar.

After lingering over their coffee for a moment or two longer, they headed back to the gambling hall where Rory took up a place behind the bar and proceeded to pour drinks for the thirsty crowd.

The rest of the evening progressed smoothly. Other than a minor mishap in which one of the barmaids spilled some drinks, there was nothing to dampen the spirits of the patrons. Throughout the night, as Catherine mingled with the crowd, she occasionally stopped to glance back at Rory. His good mood was infectious, she noted. Many of those he served remained at his station, allowing Rory to refill their glasses as he joined in numerous heated debates concerning horses and the racetrack. Once or twice he looked up and caught Catherine's eye on him. Each time, before she could turn away, he flashed her one of his endearing grins. Although the pace was hectic and she was tired, Catherine was surprised to find herself enjoying the work.

All in all, it was a profitable night for the Diamond. By two in the morning, all the customers had gone home, and the gambling hall had once again been restored to its usual orderly appearance. Exhausted, Catherine, Rory, and Sallie walked abreast up the wide staircase to the second floor.

"You did a wonderful job tonight," Catherine told Rory as they headed down the hall toward their rooms. "I don't know what we would have done without you."

"Oh, I'm sure you would have managed somehow," he answered easily, sending her that quick, appealing grin. "It was my pleasure though, I assure you."

Sallie, walking beside Catherine, yawned widely, covering her mouth with one slim hand. "I simply cannot *wait* to go to sleep," she announced. "But before I slip off to my room, let me add my thanks to Catherine's, Mr. O'Shay. There could indeed have been a nasty incident had you not intervened when you did." Acknowledging his gallant nod with a winning smile, Sallie bade them both good night and headed down the hall to her chamber, leaving Catherine and Rory alone.

"Good night, Mr. O'Shay," Catherine said quickly, feeling strangely uncomfortable to be alone with a man so late at night.

"Good night, Miss Diamond."

As Catherine entered her room, she heard Rory whistling softly to himself in the hallway.

Rory awoke early. He'd found, over the years, that he didn't need as much sleep as the average person. His favorite time of the day was dawn. He enjoyed the freshness of a new morning, the promise of a new day. Having been raised in a coal patch in Pennsylvania, he'd learned to rise early and he couldn't remember ever *not* being up with the sun.

Eager to be near his horse, he dressed quickly, then slipped quietly out of his room. He hadn't realized just how much he'd missed his yearling until he'd seen it the other night in the Diamond Saloon. He had been expecting to find the horse wherever he found Reese, but he hadn't expected to come across his Thoroughbred in quite the way he had. Tracking Reese from Pennsylvania clear across the country had been a long, hard journey.

His mare, Bess's Dream, bequeathed to him by the Baltimore widow, had given birth to the young horse in Utah. It was there that Jack Reese had paid Rory a surprise visit. Preoccupied with the new foal, Rory didn't notice Reese until it was too late. When he'd regained consciousness after a knock on the head, compliments of Reese, he'd found the foal gone, and Reese nowhere in sight. Climbing astride Bess, Rory had trailed Reese and the colt all the way to San Francisco, and then to the Diamond. Rory had moved himself into a mountain cabin which belonged to an old friend. Even now, Bess's Dream was at that cabin, awaiting Rory's return with the young horse.

Rory knew he and Reese were involved in a deadly game. It was a challenge for both of them to be the first to find Connor. Rory had no doubts that Reese would harm Connor if he found him first. Rory wanted only to help his younger brother whom he'd not seen in twelve years. He knew that Jack Reese had forced Connor to blow up the Trenton mine. But he also knew there was a fugitive warrant out on Reese, a man-for-hire who would do any lowdown, dirty deed if the price was right. All Rory had to do was let the authorities in San Francisco know that Jack Reese was in town and they could then lock him up. Unfortunately, Rory himself was now wanted for murder. True, he'd killed Big Pat Daugherty in self-defense. But he was still a wanted man.

Shrugging these worries away for the moment, Rory headed toward the shed that housed Irish Fire.

Irish Fire. He turned the name over in his mind. Yes, he liked it. Catherine seemed to understand the horse's special spirit. Someday, he told himself, he'd be rewarded with her smile when Fire sped across a finish line in first place.

"Need any help?"

Rory turned at the soft, feminine voice. Catherine, garbed in a simple skirt and blouse of deepest blue, stood framed in the doorway of the stall. The pale light of dawn spilled through her dark tresses.

"Good morning," he said, looking her over appreciatively. He turned back to Irish Fire. "You're up early," he commented as he groomed the horse with firm, even strokes of the brush.

Catherine felt something within her flutter at the sight of him. Though she generally slept quite late, she'd been awakened by the sounds of his getting ready for the day.

"Do you always rise so early?" she asked.

He nodded. "Every day. I want to get Fire out for a walk this morning."

"A walk? Where to?"

He continued to move the brush over the animal's gleaming black coat. Fire stood very still, obviously enjoying the attention. "I thought I'd take him up and down the streets before they become too congested with carriages and people. Would you care to join us?"

"Well," she said hesitantly, "I do have a few hours before I'll be needed inside."

Rory grinned as he reached to untether the horse. Together, they led the docile yearling out toward the main thoroughfare. The streets were nearly deserted. Except for a lone dray or two lumbering by—one filled with milk cans, another loaded down with dry goods headed for the wharves—there were very few people about.

Walking beside Rory, who led Fire, Catherine breathed deeply of the cool, damp air. The customary fog, which still lay in wisps over the steep streets, was beginning to lift. The world was quiet, hushed and peaceful.

They walked for some time in silence as Catherine drank in the morning sights of San Francisco. In the many, still-closed shops that lined the streets cunningly placed wares could be seen behind sparkling plate glass windows. The cobblestones beneath their feet were damp and slick, and the click of their heels upon the hard stones echoed pleasantly around them. The utter stillness reminded Catherine of the winter walks she had taken with her parents through the coal patch of Raven Run back in Pennsylvania. Huge flakes of falling snow had muffled all sounds, and everywhere that Catherine looked there had been a coating of pristine white. It had been as quiet then as it was now. As if the world was holding its breath.

A few feet ahead of them, in front of a bakery, two small boys played toss-penny with small, round wooden discs against the rough boards of the building. They were dressed in worn but clean-looking clothes, and from their similar mops of blond hair, Catherine surmised they were brothers. As she and Rory and the colt drew nearer, Rory called out a greeting to the boys.

They looked up, the smaller boy smiling shyly, while the older one only glanced at them.

Rory drew a gold bit out of his pocket and sent it skittering near the front of the bakery from which the delicious aroma of fresh-baked bread wafted. As the shiny coin rolled to a stop a mere inch from the boards, the younger boy screeched in delight. Rory only smiled, quickly flicking another twenty-dollar gold piece after the first as he and Catherine walked on. This time, the coin stopped directly beside the building, its curved side touching the boards. The boys scrambled after the coins, but Rory had moved on before they could thank him.

"You're very good at that game," Catherine noted. She'd also observed how pleased the children had been at being given a gold bit. "It was also very generous of you."

"I saw those boys playing there last night. I suspect one of their parents, if not both, works in the bakery. It must be dreary for them to have to entertain themselves all day long while their parents work their fingers to the bone trying to make a living."

Catherine glanced up at him. "You know," she said quietly. "You're not what I thought you were."

He grinned, his teeth white against his tanned skin.

"And dare I ask what that was?"

She felt herself blush, but refused to evade the subject. "You seemed cold, uncaring even. You pulled a gun so easily on that Reese fellow that I thought—"

"Jack Reese is a scoundrel," he cut in easily.

"Then it's not your usual style to pull a gun on a man?"

"Not at all."

"And what about taking advantage of a helpless woman?"

"If you are referring to when I kissed you in the saloon the other night, then the answer is no. I simply found it impossible to resist your beauty."

There was just enough mockery in his voice so that

Catherine didn't take him entirely seriously.

"I see," she said, somewhat primly.

After they returned from their walk, Catherine went to the saloon to meet with her father and discuss business.

Ned was seated at his desk in the office, an open ledger before him. He rose from his seat when Catherine entered the room.

Catherine's favorite room in the Diamond, besides the kitchen with its friendly banter, was her father's office. She enjoyed the quietness of the room, the smell of paper, and the faint aroma of cigars that clung to the furniture. This room was Ned's private sanctuary, the place he retreated to whenever he wanted to be alone. Recently, with Ned gone so much of the time, it had also become Catherine's private domain. She'd spent many long hours seated at the desk, pouring over the numerous ledgers.

"Katie, good morning," Ned said. "I thought you would still be asleep. It's so early, dear, why don't you go on back to bed and rest for a while longer? I can take care of things here. Although I haven't been tending to things lately, I'm here now."

Catherine noted how quickly her father had closed the ledger, and also how he now moved to the front of the desk, using his body to shield the papers scattered across its top.

"I'm fine, Pa. Actually, I think it's you who needs the rest and not I. You look as if you haven't slept a wink the whole night through. Have you been here all night?"

Ned Diamond gave his daughter a weak smile. Dressed casually in doeskin trousers, unbuttoned brown vest, and white cambric shirt with the sleeves rolled up to his elbows, he did appear to have spent the entire night hunched in his chair, awash in papers and ledgers. Ned, who was in his early fifties, stood just over six feet tall, with black, silver-tipped hair and fashionable mutton-chop whiskers that lent him a distinguished, man-of-affairs appearance. In just a few short years, he had managed to cast off all outward signs of his coal miner's past, and now he looked the very picture of a prosperous businessman. Hardships and the passage of time had added lines at the corners of his gray eyes and about his mouth, but nothing could take the shimmering light from the depths of his eyes. Those eyes, alive with an unquenchable zest for life, led people to think of him more as a man of thirty. Mad Ned Diamond was a man of visions and dreams, one who held tightly to his ideals. Though his skin now showed the ivory parchment hue of age, his spirit was still young and vibrant and utterly untamed. It was this quality that Catherine loved most about her father. And in this respect, she had been told by many, she was like him.

"I've spent more than one night immersed in business, and by the grace of God, I'll spend a good many more doing the same. Do not worry about me, Katie dear. I'm not as old as you might think."

"Of course you're not old," she replied. "I just worry about you. You don't have to take on all the tasks of running the Diamond. I'm here to help you. You know that, don't you?" She stepped up to him and gave him a quick, affectionate hug.

Ned returned the hug, and holding her tightly, he said, "Yes, I do. And it is indeed a deep comfort and a source of great pride to have such a lovely daughter. 'Tis a shame your mother didn't live to see what a beautiful young lady we created. She'd be so proud of you, Katie."

Catherine closed her eyes, reveling in the comforting embrace, unshed tears stinging her eyes at the mention of her mother. Her father didn't talk of her mother very often. He reserved such reminiscing for those times when he felt unusually pressured by the many stresses of his life. That he should mention her now bothered Catherine.

"What is it, Pa? What is troubling you?" she whispered.

Ned smoothed her hair with one hand. "Ah, nothing you should worry yourself about," he replied on a sigh. After a quick kiss to the top of her head, he released her, and continued, "Business, that's all. Speaking of which, I've hired a new employee. He'll be staying with us here, so I'll need you to remove the things you have stored in the room next to yours. Normally, I wouldn't ask you to give up the chamber, but we're short of space, and it will only be for a few weeks at the most."

Catherine smoothed and straightened the edges of his vest, then took a step back to look at him. "You need the room next to mine? I—well, I'm sorry, Pa, but I've already assigned the room. Actually, that was one of the things I wanted to talk with you about. You see, I was fortunate at the tables a few days ago and as part of my winnings I acquired a yearling—"

Ned lifted one brow, crossing his arms over his chest, an indulgent smile lifting the corners of his mouth. "So you've put the yearling in the room?"

"No," she replied, drinking in his loving, paternal gaze. She knew that if she were so inclined, her father would allow her to board a string of horses at the Diamond. "I've taken the liberty of hiring a trainer for the yearling which is, by the way, a perfect specimen of horseflesh. I've plans for the yearling, Pa. He's a true Thoroughbred and I'm certain that, with the proper training, he'll net us a fine sum at the track!"

"That's my Katie . . . so you've hired a man to train the beast?"

"Precisely, and since I haven't the cash to pay him wages right now, I thought we'd let him have room and board in exchange for his services."

Ned took a moment to absorb the information. Finally, with a nod, he said, "Very well, I'll leave the details of the matter in your capable hands. Although that still leaves us with the problem of where to house our new employee."

"Why did you hire another hand?" she asked, knowing the current state of their finances.

Ned moved away from his desk, bowing his head and muttering something about incompetent employees who couldn't be counted on to do a proper day's work—a comment that came as a surprise to Catherine. Ned Diamond and all the employees of the saloon were like family to one another, and Catherine knew firsthand how very hard every one of them worked. She could not imagine who had displeased her father and why Ned found it necessary to hire someone new, especially now when their funds were so low. Before she could question him on the matter, there was a knock at the door.

"Yes," Ned called out quickly, welcoming the interruption. "Come in."

It was Rory O'Shay who stepped inside the office.

He glanced from Catherine to Ned, nodding to the older man. "Excuse me for interrupting, but there are some details concerning the yearling I'd like to discuss with you."

"Yes, of course—"

"Katie, where are your manners?" Ned interrupted. "Introduce us, dear. Who is this man and what is his business here?"

Chagrined at her uncharacteristic lapse, Catherine felt a blush spread across her cheeks. Before she had a chance to rectify the situation, Rory spoke up.

"The name's Rory O'Shay. Your daughter has hired me to train her yearling." Rory took a step forward and extended his hand to Ned Diamond.

"O'Shay, did you say?" asked Ned skeptically. He accepted Rory's proffered hand but regarded him with narrowed eyes. "O'Shay? Where are you from, boy?"

Rory lifted one brow. It had been years since anyone had called him boy and even now the word rankled.

Rory had heard of Mad Ned. He had even visited the man's home, back in Pennsylvania, when Ned Diamond was still Ned McGuillicuddy. That Ned would remember him, or worse yet, have heard of his checkered past, was something Rory dreaded.

Answering Ned's question as vaguely as possible, he replied, "I hail from the east coast, but I hope to make my home in San Francisco."

"Is that so? Where on the east coast?"

Rory noted the shift in Ned's gaze, the growing mistrust in the man's green eyes. "Maryland," he answered. "Baltimore, Maryland."

"Baltimore, is it? Any family there?"

"Pa—" Catherine intervened, uncomfortable with Ned's interrogation.

"No," Rory replied in a flat tone. "I've no family in Baltimore."

"Where then, is your family, boy? Are they back east or did they follow you out west?"

Rory noted the dangerous glint in Ned's eyes and the set of his jaw as he posed the question. In that instant, Rory realized that Ned Diamond knew who he was—and knew also of Rory's past.

"I have no family to speak of," Rory lied. His words were quiet and hard as steel. He knew this was the only answer he could give to save his neck. "No family at all." He turned his gaze to Catherine. "Miss Diamond," he said, nodding his head, hating the numerous questions he saw in her eyes. "I'll be with the yearling when you're free." He turned and strode from the office.

"Pa!" Catherine exclaimed. "What got into you? Obviously, the man has painful memories of his past. What business is it of ours if the man has family back east?"

"I want him out of here, Mary Catherine. That man is dangerous."

Her father's use of her full given name caused her to straighten. "What do you mean, dangerous? What has he done? What do you know of Rory O'Shay?"

"I know enough to order you to stay clear of him. In fact, I aim to throw him out of this establishment, bag and baggage! Your mother would turn over in her grave if she knew he was near her daughter!"

"Pa, wait!" Catherine cried out, latching onto Ned's shirt sleeve before he could bound out the door after Rory. "What has he done? And how would Ma know him?"

Ned Diamond took a moment to control himself. Impatiently, he ran a hand through his silver-tipped hair before saying, "Your mother and I knew his family years ago."

"Where? In Pennsylvania?"

Ned nodded, saying nothing.

"Very well then, if you knew Rory's parents, you must realize Rory O'Shay cannot be such a terrible person. Perhaps he and his parents just had a misunderstanding. Perhaps—"

Ned silenced his daughter with a single glance. "He's wanted for murder, Mary Catherine. Rory O'Shay is a murderer."

At this thought, Catherine darted out of the office after her father. She was breathless by the time she reached the small shack behind the saloon. What would Ned do to Rory? she wondered. When she reached the shack, she realized that, for the moment at least, her worries had been in vain. Rory was nowhere to be seen.

Fire stood inside the stall, out of the morning sun, munching happily on a pail of oats, his water nearby, filled to the brim. His coat was gleaming as though he'd just been brushed, and all signs of refuse had been removed from the small interior. He looked up at the commotion that Catherine and Ned made as they bounded inside the small space.

"Where is he, Katie?" Ned demanded. Fire twitched his tail at the sound of Ned's loud voice.

Catherine smoothed the horse's back to calm him. "I—I don't know," she answered truthfully, thinking only that now she had no one to train her horse. Immediately, however, she put her selfish thoughts aside to consider Rory's situation. What would her father do with his knowledge? Would he go to the authorities, who would doubtless come and cart Rory away to prison?

Aloud, she said to her father, "Perhaps he realized you recognized him and he headed out of the city."

"I doubt it," said Ned dismally.

"But why? Why would he stay here when he knows someone has recognized him?"

"Because, Katie, the man I've hired as a new employee is his brother." Seeing Catherine's confused look, Ned added, "Never mind, do not let worries of Rory O'Shay bother you. I won't let the man near you ever again. He's a blackguard and is dangerous to even his own family. We'll take his brother in and protect him, and we'll see to it the authorities have Rory O'Shay behind bars before nightfall." Ned patted his daughter awkwardly on the arm, then strode away.

Catherine had heard her father's resolute tone and knew he would do exactly as he said. But she could not believe Rory O'Shay belonged behind bars, and he certainly did not deserve to be kept from his own brother. But how was she to explain her feelings to her father? There seemed to be no explanation to give Ned other than that Rory had kissed her and she had responded to that kiss. Perhaps her view of the man was indeed distorted because of the liberty he had taken.

She would do well to obey her father and tell Rory to leave the Diamond and never return. But then, what of her yearling? She couldn't afford another trainer and Rory had already proved himself a master with Fire.

How happy she had been only an hour earlier—and what a muddle it had all become!

With Ned away, the rest of the day passed uneventfully. After she'd seen the delivery of wine and barrels of beer, and the fresh produce needed for the evening meal, she retreated to her own rooms to freshen up before the night began.

The minute she stepped into her apartment, she sensed something was wrong. She hesitated a moment, listening. Her eyes scanned the darkness that was crisscrossed here and there by the shadowy light from the gas lamps in the street below. All looked as she had left it earlier. Even the contents of her jewelry box remained scattered atop her vanity, exactly as she'd left them the night before when she'd been rummaging through the box for her earrings. Surely if someone had been in her room, they'd have stolen her jewelry. Scolding herself for being silly, she shut the door and then moved across the room to close the curtains. As she crossed the thick carpet, she had the distinct feeling she was not alone. She paused midway, her senses alert. There was nothing but the brassy piano tunes coming from below, the jumbled voices of patrons, the heavy pounding of her own heart . . . and the whisper of wind coming through an open window. She felt her heart skip a beat. She had not opened a window earlier.

Just as she started to run from the room, a huge black shadow lunged at her. Thick, beefy arms, one about her waist, the other over her mouth, pulled her back roughly.

"Where is he?" the man hissed. "Tell me and I'll let you live."

Seized with terror, Catherine struggled to free herself. But the man's grip was like a vise, and she hadn't the strength to pry herself free. She tried to scream for help but all that came out was a strangled cry beneath the intruder's large hand.

"Don't scream, lady," he ordered, "or I'll be forced to snap this pretty neck of yours. Just tell me where you've got him hidden. I know Mad Ned's got him tucked away somewhere in this saloon. Unless you want the place ripped apart, you better start talking. Understand? Now, I'm gonna take my hand from your mouth. You scream and you're dead. Got it?"

Catherine nodded. Anything to get him to take his filthy paw from her face. Slowly, he released his hold and Catherine gulped precious, sweet air.

"All right, start talking."

"I—I don't know what you want," she gasped. "Who—who are you looking for?"

"Don't play games with me, lady. I can be real nasty when I have to be."

Her mind whirled. She recognized his voice, that deep guttural tone laced with menace. Jack Reese. Her heart thumped with fear and she was keenly aware of the arm he still had wrapped around her midsection. He squeezed her so hard she thought her ribs would crack.

"Is it O'Shay you want?" she asked.

He laughed. "None other. Now where is he? I saw your pa with him earlier. I know Mad Ned brought him here."

Her father? She hadn't seen her father for hours, and it was highly unlikely Ned would be seen with Rory. "You—you must be mistaken. My father didn't bring him here."

He shook her hard. "Don't lie to me, lady. I don't like it. Now quit stalling and start talking!"

"But I—I don't know what more I can tell you," she said, struggling again to free herself. "I—I swear to you I don't! I never even met O'Shay until the night of our poker game." As soon as the words were out, she regretted saying them. Sweet heaven, what would he do to her now that he knew she was aware of his identity?

"You're not as smart as I thought you were, Miss Diamond," came the cool voice in her ear. "So you knew it was me all along, did you? Well, for too long your pa's been sabotaging my plans. It's time I gave him a dose of his own medicine." He pushed her toward the vanity with its scattered jewelry and single gas lamp.

Catherine watched as he reached with one arm to pick up the lamp. Sudden dread washed over her. "What are you doing?" she demanded. "And what has my father done to you? I—I'm sure you've confused him with someone else. My father's only interest is this saloon. How could he possibly be involved in any dealings with you?" Still using one hand, he struck a match, which flared brightly. Catherine's mind raced. Perhaps her father was indeed involved in something illegal. Profits from the saloon were being filtered somewhere outside, and for the past eleven months, Ned had been letting Catherine see to the business on her own.

Lit match in hand, Jack Reese shoved Catherine down upon the carpet, then slammed his booted foot into the small of her back. She squealed with pain. "When you see your pa again—*if* you see him again—tell him Reese came calling." With that, he broke the lamp and its store of oil on Catherine's canopied bed, then tossed the match atop the oil. Catherine screamed, lunging for his legs, trying to stop him, but he kicked her away.

Within seconds, the lavender spread whooshed into spreading flames as Reese scrambled back out the window. Catherine had no choice but to let him go. Her bed was on fire! Orangish-yellow tongues of flame licked their way upward, roaring and crackling as they caught the overhead material in a fiery blaze. Catherine felt the heat sear her face and arms as she vainly attempted to douse the flames with one of the pillows from her lounge. Soon, billows of choking, black smoke were rolling about the room as the fire caught the back wall and raced along the flower-patterned wallpaper up to the ceiling.

Clutching her skirts close to her body so they wouldn't ignite, she raced to the window and smashed one pane open with a small stool. "Fire!" she screamed into the street. "Fire! Fire!"

From behind her, the door to the room was banged open and Rory O'Shay, wearing only his breeches and boots, burst in. "Miss Diamond!" he yelled, threading his way through the smoke-filled room. "Catherine!"

"Here!" she screamed. "Help me! Quick!" She was using one of her frocks to beat at the hungry flames that grew higher and higher, eating mercilessly away at one entire side of her room. "No, no!" she was screaming. "It can't burn! We can't let it burn!"

"Catherine!" Rory yelled, grabbing her from behind.

She tried to fight him off, screaming for him to help her douse the flames. But he wasn't listening. Why wasn't he listening? Rough hands pushed her down onto the floor, forcing her to roll over and over. Catherine fought him, wild with the heat and the fierce orange glare, knowing only that her home was burning to the ground.

"Stop fighting me!" Rory ordered. "Your skirts—they're aflame!" With one savage yank, he pulled the bottom half of her outer clothing from her.

The odor of melting silk filled her nostrils along with a noxious black smoke. She looked down to see Rory toss away the flaming material, some of it, still burning, clinging to his right hand. He paid it no mind as he lifted her into his arms and headed for the door.

"But the fire!" she screamed, reluctant still to leave. "We must stop the fire or the whole place will be lost!"

"It's already lost, Catherine. One minute longer and you'd burn right along with it!" They were in the hall now, heading for the front staircase, Rory yelling, "Fire! Everyone get out! Fire on the second floor and spreading fast!"

Catherine, trembling with fright, clung to him as he raced down the stairs, her arms laced about his neck, her cheek pressed tight to his bare chest. He smelled faintly of soap, his skin damp, as though he'd been washing when he'd heard the commotion. With her saloon going up in smoke and the terrified shouts and screams of people around her, she felt oddly safe within the shelter of his arms. His powerful strides took them to the first floor where utter chaos reigned as people pushed their way to safety, nearly trampling each other trying to reach the exit.

"Two at a time!" Rory yelled into the din, catching one man by the collar as he tripped and was almost trampled in the stampede. The double doors had been pushed wide and hung at odd angles on their hinges, the wood of the doors splintered where frenzied patrons had tried to exit four abreast. Rory had to shoulder his way out, clutching Catherine tightly and still yelling for some semblance of order in the melee. It was useless. Behind them, smoke billowed down the wide staircase. The sounds of licking flames roared like cannon shot, and soon the night came alive with the clanging bells of the fire brigade rushing to the scene.

Catherine peered over Rory's shoulder and tried to make out faces in the gray, smoke-filled air. Where were Randolph, Sallie, Fong, and the other employees? Had they made it out alive? And her father? Had he made it back to the Diamond, and was he even now in his bed asleep and unaware of the danger?

"I have to go back," she cried. "Let me down, Rory! I have to find my father—I—I have to help the others!" She fought to get free then, pushing at his chest.

Rory held her fast. "No, there's nothing more you can do. Do you hear me, Catherine? Stop fighting me, will you, lass? Look, here comes the fire brigade. They'll do what they can."

Catherine heard the sharp pounding of horses' hooves on the uneven pavement, heard also the shouts for water. Even as Rory set her on her feet in the middle of the road, men were lining up to form a fire line. Buckets were being heaved in capable hands and tossed up at flames that now spewed forth from the second-story windows. She couldn't bear to watch, yet she couldn't turn her face away from the towering blaze. Explosions like rapid gun fire cracked in sharp staccato, and a woman screamed as the second story collapsed from within and the whole front of the saloon tipped backward. Flooring gave way then, showering down into the main gambling hall with flaming timber that crumbled like toothpicks.

Catherine, shivering in her torn gown, with soot smudging her face and arms, watched in shocked silence as all her father's dreams and years of hard work fell apart right before her eyes. "Oh, Lord," she moaned. Firelight flickered eerily over her grief-stricken features. Someone—perhaps a member of the fire brigade—draped a coarse blanket across her shoulders. She turned to thank whoever it was, but the man was gone. Not even Rory stood beside her any longer. She brought a trembling hand to her face and was surprised to find it wet with tears.

"Oh, love, *there* you are! I've been searching all over for you!" It was Sallie rushing toward her. Her gown was torn and dirtied, and the auburn hair that fanned around her shoulders caught the bright glow of fire. "I was so afraid you had fallen asleep or something! I saw you head upstairs a while ago and—oh, here, love, you're in shock." The young woman wrapped comforting arms about her and squeezed her tight.

"Sallie! Thank God you're all right! You aren't hurt, are you? What about the others; Randolph, Fong? Did they— did they make it out safely?"

"Yes, love, they're fine. The minute Fong smelled smoke, he whisked me out the back door. As for Randolph, he's helping to keep the flames from spreading to the adjacent buildings. I think everyone made it out, love. Don't you worry now. You just take care of yourself. Look at you! You've a nasty burn on your leg! What happened?"

Catherine stepped out of Sallie's embrace and stared numbly down at her uncovered legs peeping from beneath the blanket. There was indeed a black area on her right leg now turning a nasty red, but she couldn't feel a thing, nothing at all. "I—I'm fine, Sally. I—my skirts caught on fire, but I'll be fine. Really. Have—have you seen my father? Did he come home tonight? Do you know?"

"I haven't seen him, love, but you know your father. He never returns home before the sun rises. Now don't go getting yourself all worked up. I'm almost certain he wasn't in the building."

Catherine, wondering if she could ever be certain about anything again, just pulled the blanket tighter about her and stared up at the angry flames shooting skyward. Jack

Reese. He had done this horrible deed, had destroyed the only bit of security she'd ever had in her life. He'd pay for this, she vowed.

"Catherine, look! Isn't that your Rory O'Shay coming this way?" Sallie was saying. "What is that he's leading?"

Catherine tore her gaze from the licking flames and focused on the tall, bare-chested figure heading toward them. It was indeed Rory, with Irish Fire trailing nervously behind him. The yearling, frightened by the chaos, was straining at his reins. He danced sideways as Rory brought him next to Catherine.

"Got him just in time," Rory said. "Flaming debris ignited his stall just as soon as we were out the door."

Catherine put a hand to her mouth. She'd forgotten about her horse. "Oh, Fire," she breathed, reaching to gently rub his nose. The colt threw his head back, his eyes wide, reflecting the flickering, chaotic scene. After a moment, he allowed himself to relax under Catherine's soft touch. Catherine's gaze met Rory's. He looked like an ancient Roman soldier standing there shirtless with sweat glistening on his chest and arms, his dark hair tossed wildly about his head. His blue eyes were like chips of ice, fiercely protective as he beheld the yearling.

"Thank you," she said.

He nodded, giving her a quick half-smile. He handed her Fire's reins, then headed back to help control the blaze. Catherine clutched at the leather strap still warm from his palms.

Sallie wrapped an arm about her friend's shoulders and led her away from the middle of the street toward a millinery shop where a group of spectators had gathered to watch the scene. But Catherine could not stand still.

"I can't just stand here and do nothing," she told Sallie. "There must be something I can do! Here, take the yearling—and, Sallie, don't let anyone near him. Do you understand? I—he's all I have now for the future." Thrusting the reins into Sallie's hand, Catherine shrugged off the coarse blanket and headed back across the crowded street.

"Catherine, be careful!" Sallie called after her, but Catherine wasn't listening. She joined the ranks of the volunteer firemen who numbered well over a hundred. The Knickerbocker 5, the Manhattan 2, and the Howard 3 Fire Companies were all there in full force and even now the clanging bells of the charging Tiger 14 could be heard coming down the street. Precise and efficient, working like a single, huge piece of human machinery, the men and some women, heaved buckets and directed the hoses from the hand pumps, and even the Amoskeag steamer pump, to douse the scorching flames. San Francisco was a city that had been plagued by many fires in its time and the volunteers knew their job well. In a little under three hours, they had the blaze under control. Only one other building, next to the Diamond, had caught fire, and thanks to the quick work of the firemen, only half of the structure had burned. As for the Diamond, it was totally lost. Everything gone. All that was left was an empty charred shell that smoked and hissed beneath the spray of water still being hosed onto it. Catherine could only stare at the blackened hull as silent tears streamed down her smudged face.

"Come," a deep voice said. "You're shivering and that burn on your leg needs tending." It was Rory who stood beside her, his own bared chest blackened from the soot. He had a nasty cut just above his right eye and his whole body was covered with a fine film of sweat. Catherine knew he had fought the blaze with every ounce of his strength. She'd seen him help the firefighters. He had stood in the foreground, fighting the fiercest part of the fire as though he had battled hundreds of blazes in his life. Gently, he wrapped one arm about her shoulders and turned her away from the ruined structure.

"I — I can't believe this has happened," she whispered. "It's a horrible nightmare. Do you know if anyone was — was caught inside?"

"No. As far as we know, everyone got out safely, Catherine. I spoke with Randolph a few moments ago and he's accounted for all the employees. Right now, he's making temporary living arrangements for those who occupied rooms above."

"I should be helping him. It isn't his responsibility; it's mine. Where is he, do you know?"

"Don't worry about Randolph, he can take care of things. You should be worrying about yourself now. I told him you were coming with me and that you'd contact him as soon as you were settled."

Catherine stopped in her tracks. "You told him what? You had no right to tell Randolph such a thing! What will he think? He —"

"Who cares what Randolph thinks," he cut in as he pulled her along. "You're coming with me. I know for a fact that fire was no accident. I heard you scream, Catherine, and I saw a man run out the window just as I entered your rooms. Who was it? Who set the fire?"

"I — I'm not sure," she said, forcing the lie past her lips. Her father was obviously involved in some sort of dangerous dealings with Jack Reese, and revealing too much to Rory might put Ned in further jeopardy. "I — he didn't let me see his face."

"But you know his identity. I know you do. All right, Catherine, have it your way. You and I will be spending the next few days together. There'll be plenty of time for you to come to your senses and tell me who was in your room."

Catherine skidded to a halt, staring at him. "What do you mean we'll be spending the next few days together? You must have suffered a blow to your head along with that cut to your eye, Mr. O'Shay. *I'm* not going anywhere with you. My saloon just burned to the ground leaving half a dozen employees homeless. I have a responsibility to see those people clothed and comfortably lodged."

"Randolph will take care of that," he said firmly. "As for your responsibilities, I'd say you should start worrying about yourself and the yearling. It's my guess Jack Reese is the one who torched the saloon, and if I'm right — which I see I am by the look in your eyes — then you won't be safe in the city. I'm certain Reese will come looking for you. He has ways of making sure that witnesses don't talk."

Catherine felt a thrill of fear down her spine. It wasn't her own safety that worried her. What would Reese do to her father? she wondered.

At that moment the sounds of a gun discharging from somewhere above their heads filled the air, and a bullet ricocheted on the cobblestones at Catherine's feet. She screamed, and Rory yanked her toward him, then headed for cover. The bullet was followed by another that just missed her head. "Someone's shooting at me!" she cried.

Before them, the crowd broke apart as people scrambled for cover. A few of the firemen pointed toward an abandoned two-story building. Immediately, several men charged toward the structure, intent on catching the gunman, but Rory wasn't about to let Catherine stand on the street to wait for the outcome.

"Is that enough proof for you, Miss Diamond? Do you now believe me when I say you're not safe in the city?"

"But why?" she gasped as he dragged her along behind him. They shouldered past murmuring pedestrians who had flocked to watch the fire and were now buzzing about the near-fatal shootings. Tongues would wag for days — months — about the catastrophe at the Diamond Saloon.

"I think you know why. Jack Reese leaves no loose ends. If he thinks you could incriminate him in any way — which you can — the man won't rest until he silences you."

Catherine felt another shiver creep along her spine. Rory was right. Jack Reese would come looking for her. "But where can we go? I—I have no money, no clothes—and the yearling, how are we going to keep him, feed him?" Catherine pressed her eyes shut, forcing herself to remain calm, to not lose what little control she had left.

"I know of a place," he told her, "outside the city limits. It won't have all the comforts of home, but it will do." They had now reached the place where Sallie stood with the prancing yearling. She was having the devil of a time keeping him under control and it was quite obvious the task had thoroughly upset her.

"There you are!" she exclaimed. "Take this beast before I swoon! Catherine, you know how I feel about these animals! I swear the creature tried to bite me!"

Catherine would have been amused by the sight of Sallie and Fire, but the events of the night had been too terrifying. She watched as Rory took the reins from her friend's hands and then soothed the frightened animal.

"Come, Miss Diamond," he said to her as he cast Sallie an appreciative smile of thanks. "We'd best hurry."

"But where are you going?" Sallie asked.

Rory was already pulling Catherine and the yearling away. Catherine turned to look back at her friend. "I—I can't explain right now, Sallie. If you see my father, tell him I'm safe and will contact him soon! And—and tell him to be careful!"

"But, Catherine, what is going on?" Sallie asked. "Where are you going with—with *him?*"

"You'll have to trust me!" Catherine called back, trying to yank herself free of Rory's tight grasp. He was unyielding as he led her and the yearling away from the melee. Catherine ran along beside him. "Please," she said. "Can't you at least pause long enough for me to explain things to Sallie?"

"So she can wag her tongue to the wrong person? It's best no one knows where you're headed or for what reasons."

"But surely you don't expect me to keep anything from my father?"

Rory slowed their fast pace, his dark head turning to glance up the street. He hailed a carriage for hire, and stood impatiently until it was beside them. "Until I'm certain of what's going on, no one is to know our whereabouts. Sallie will let your father know you are alive and well. For the time being, that will have to suffice. Now, no more talk. Who knows what this driver might hear and then repeat for the right price."

Catherine looked up at the tall, straight-backed driver. His hawklike features were pinched as he squinted his eyes to make out the scene down the street.

"Quite a blaze, eh?" the man asked.

Rory only grunted in agreement, then motioned for Catherine to get inside the conveyance. She quickly did so, more for the sake of modesty than anything else, for she hadn't missed the driver's quick appraisal of her uncovered legs. Suddenly she felt terribly vulnerable. She was glad the carriage was closed and no more prying eyes could view her immodest attire. Sliding along the cool leather seat to the far side, she huddled in the corner and stared out the window. A few people were still running down the street to catch a glimpse of the smoking ruin.

Rory hitched the yearling to the back of the carriage. He gave directions to the driver, then climbed inside and settled down beside Catherine.

Catherine looked at him. They made quite a pair, he without his shirt, she in only a torn and tattered dress, both of them covered with soot. They were lucky, she thought, to have been allowed inside the conveyance. As the carriage made a wide turn in the middle of the cobblestone street, she leaned her head against the cushion and let out a long, trembling sigh.

Rory glanced over at her. She looked tiny and vulnerable all curled up in the corner. He felt a queer feeling in his chest.

"You are a very brave woman, Catherine Diamond," he said.

She gave him a wan smile. "That's funny. I don't feel very brave."

Those were the last words that passed between them as the gentle swaying of the carriage and the clip clop of the horse's hooves lulled her to sleep.

Chapter Six

The carriage came to a grinding halt along a desolate dirt-covered road that appeared to lead to nowhere. The only light came from the faint rays of a moon that peeped from behind fast-moving clouds. There were no homes, no traffic. Nothing but an endless roadway, lined with towering pines, and nearly grown over with wild grasses.

"Are you sure this is where you want to get out?" asked the driver in amazement.

Rory assured him it was. He thrust a handful of coins at the man, then waited as he turned the carriage around and headed back toward the city, which was now only a pinpoint of light in the distant valley below. Catherine stood beside Rory, shivering in the cold night air. She'd been rudely awakened and ordered to climb out of the carriage while he untethered the yearling. Now, as she stood in the middle of nowhere, she felt every muscle in her body screaming with pain. Her head throbbed with a horrendous ache.

"Where are we we?" she asked in a flat tone.

Seemingly undaunted by the wilderness, Rory quirked an eyebrow as he peered down at her. "Outside the city," he replied easily.

"I can see that. *Where* outside the city? And where are we

going? Surely you don't expect me to sleep beneath the stars!" As she watched the departing driver become one with the dark shadows, it suddenly occurred to her just how alone she was with Rory O'Shay. There was no one in sight should she need assistance, no one to hear her scream for help. She moved to the center of the narrow roadway, wrapping her arms about herself and looking up and down the deserted road. She had been a fool, she decided. An utter fool for letting Rory lead her where he would.

He seemed to read her thoughts. "No need to fear for your life, Miss Diamond — or even your virtue for that matter. I've got more important things on my mind. We'd better start walking. We've a ways to go before we can rest for the night."

Catherine stood her ground. "I don't fear for my life," she said mutinously. "I only want to know where you're taking me. Surely no one *lives* out here."

"I don't know why anyone wouldn't want to live here. It's beautiful country in the light of day. Room enough for a person to breathe . . . but I wager a city woman like yourself wouldn't know of such places, nor would you know about sleeping beneath the stars."

"And what is that supposed to mean?"

"Come along, Catherine, I've a need for some sleep before the sun rises."

"Let me tell you something, Rory O'Shay," she said irately as she stopped in the middle of the roadway, arms akimbo. "I spent the first half of my life in utter poverty. My parents and I were fortunate if we had one decent meal a day and coal enough to keep us warm. Whatever luxuries I've enjoyed in the recent past, I've earned them. And I do not appreciate your implication that I've been spoiled and cosseted. My father and I worked hard to make the Diamond what it is — was — and I've not been wealthy so long that I've forgotten what it's like to be dirt poor!" She paused a moment to catch her breath, and was surprised to find tears moistening her lashes. She quickly brushed them away. Her memories of going to sleep hungry and scared were all too close to the surface. "I've slept more than a few nights on the hard ground and I can certainly do it again — with or without you!" She stomped over to the yearling and snatched up his reins. Without waiting for Rory, she headed off into the dark night.

"And where do you think you're going without me?" Rory called after her.

"I can take care of myself!" she flung over her shoulder.

"Can you now? And what will you do if a wildcat comes after you and Fire? Lash him with that tongue of yours? Come now, Catherine, this is no place for a woman alone."

"And this is no place for a woman to be alone with the likes of you either."

To her surprise, Rory laughed. "Touché!" he said. "Nevertheless, I'm here as your protector, and protect you I shall."

He said the words lightly, but Catherine wondered if he wasn't mocking her. He caught up with her, and together they set off down the narrow roadway with Fire moving along leisurely behind them. A misty fog, cool and damp, hovered waist-high above the ground, hiding the bottom portion of the towering pines that stood like ghostly sentinels in the night. Catherine strained her ears for any sound of prowling animals, but all she heard were the hollow clops of Fire's hooves along with Rory's footfalls and her own. The rest of the world was hushed, and waiting. Still, she could not shake the feeling that somewhere eyes were watching. She curbed the urge to move closer to Rory, chastising herself for being skittish. Had the sun been shining, she would not be so fearful of the woods.

They walked for a good hour before Rory paused a moment to check a landmark, a blackened hull of a tree stump rent apart by a lightning bolt. "This way," he said, directing her off the roadway.

"Where are we going?" she asked warily.

His pace didn't let up. "We're heading for shelter," he explained.

Although she couldn't imagine what kind of shelter there could possibly be in these woods, Catherine followed him. She'd give him exactly fifteen minutes before she turned around and headed back to the city.

She followed him along a narrow path overgrown with wild grasses and surrounded by eucalyptus trees that loomed grotesquely in the half-light. The weirdly shaped branches hung low over the path so that both Rory and Catherine had to duck beneath them. The path took them sharply to the right and then deeper into a wooded area. Catherine was startled by the sudden flapping of wings as an owl, disturbed from its resting place, sailed up into the misty night. Fire shook his head at the small commotion, then plodded on, stopping now and then to chomp on a clump of grass before Rory tugged at his rein.

The dampness clung to Catherine's skin, and with the breeze that soughed through the tree tops, she was becoming icy cold. The path finally gave way to a rolling meadow in which a small, square cabin nestled. In the dark, Catherine could make out only two windows and a small, sagging porch. An outhouse and a lean-to stood a few yards away. Rory headed in that direction, motioning for Catherine to go on ahead into the cabin. She waited for him near the steps, unsure of herself and not a little afraid of what she might find inside. After settling the horse for the night, he joined her.

"Why didn't you go in?" he asked, spurning the steps and making the porch in one bound. "It's perfectly safe here—for the time being anyway."

"I—I thought the door might be locked, or that we might be disturbing someone."

"No one here but us, lass. This place has been vacant for the past twenty years." The door creaked on rusty hinges as he pushed it open. "The last person to live here was a man named Albert Latham, back in the early fifties. He worked a gold claim a few miles from here."

"And where is he now?" she asked, stepping into the cold, dark interior. To her surprise, there was no musty odor, nor any scuttling of rats.

"He moved himself atop Rincon Hill after he struck it rich. Hasn't been back since. He went to work in his mine one day, dirt-poor, and walked out a millionaire."

"And you know this man?"

"No. Never met him, and I can't say as I ever want to meet him. Money has a way of bringing out the worst in some people. The newly rich can oftentimes be very good at making other people's lives hell."

Catherine made no comment, for both she and her father had fallen into that newly rich category when Ned had made his first successful investments. Instead, she said, "But wouldn't this Mr. Latham have us both arrested if he knew we were trespassing on his property?"

"No doubt he would, but I'm not going to worry about it tonight. Albert Latham doesn't dirty his shoes anymore; he leaves that to his underlings. The chances are very slim that he'll come up here."

The cabin was small, only one room with a wood stove, a single cot, and a chair and table. There was a small cupboard near the table that Catherine assumed held eating utensils, and on top of this was a pitcher and basin. She noticed water in the basin.

"I think someone has been here recently," she said, with a worried frown. As Rory bustled about, she didn't budge from her spot by the door. "I think we should leave," she said.

"And go where?"

"I don't know. Back to the city. I shouldn't have let you talk me into coming with you. I should be with my father; he'll be devastated when he learns of the fire."

"Your father will recover, I'm sure. From all I've heard, he's not a man to let something like this keep him down for long. And the city is the last place you should be. You'd be a sitting duck, my girl. That is, until Jack Reese is taken care of."

"And how can the authorities do anything about Reese when I haven't even alerted them to the fact he was responsible for the fire?"

"The authorities won't take care of him; I will. Now stop worrying. Here," he said, reaching for one of two shirts that hung on a peg on the wall, "put this on. I'll get some fresh water so you can wash."

Catherine caught the shirt he flung in her direction. She hesitated. "I — I can't wear this," she said. "Why, I've no idea who wore it before, or if it is even clean!"

"It's clean," he assured her as he headed out the door with the pitcher and basin in hand. "And as to its previous owner . . . you're looking at him."

Catherine stood there for a moment, nonplused. The shirt she held was Rory's shirt, the same one he'd worn on the night that he'd walked into the Diamond and pressed a revolver to Reese's throat. Glancing at the pegs lining the walls, she recognized his dark trousers, his hat, and of course the boots, which were placed on the floor beneath them.

"How long have you been staying here?" she asked when he returned.

"A few weeks," he answered, placing the rinsed basin and filled pitcher back on the cupboard. "The water is cold, but if you want to wait until I've built a fire, I'll heat it for you." He moved to a wood box and placed some dried bits of kindling into the belly of the stove. Within a few moments, the sounds of a crackling fire filled the room. She was glad when he closed the stove door and she could no longer see those dancing yellow flames.

"Cold water is fine," she answered. She felt self-conscious

as she walked the short distance to the cupboard where Rory had laid out a square of cloth for her use in wiping away the grime of the fire and smoke. She swished the cloth around in the water, then squeezed it out, and with slow strokes, wiped her bare arms. Quickly, she sponged herself off, finishing up with a cold splash of water to her face. The shock of it revived her a little.

"There's a good fire going now," he said, "and the water is heating. I'll make coffee in a moment. I'll step outside so you can change out of that dress and then we can see to bandaging your leg. That's quite a burn you've got."

Rory's shirt came almost to her knees and she had to roll the cuffs up in order to use her hands. Despite its generous proportions, the shirt did little to make her feel even partially dressed. She looked helplessly around for something else with which to cover herself. The only thing she saw was the coverlet on the cot, which she immediately snatched up and wrapped around her body. This done, she settled nervously onto the narrow bed, tucking the blanket securely around her legs.

After one quick rap on the door, Rory reentered the small cabin. He was still shirtless and Catherine felt a slight pang of guilt that he'd gone back out in the cold just to give her some privacy. He warmed himself in front the stove, quietly watching her.

Catherine could not help but note that his physique was magnificent outlined in the glow of the stove. The ruggedness of the mountain cabin seemed to complement his tall, lean frame. He looked completely at home in these surroundings, much more so than he had in the ornate splendor of the Diamond.

"Feeing better?" he asked.

She nodded, wondering if he'd noticed her perusal of him. "But I would like some of that coffee you mentioned."

"Ah, yes," he said with a smile, and set immediately to the task. Soon, he handed her a tin cup filled with steaming coffee. As she sipped the aromatic brew, Rory rummaged through the cupboard cabinets for a roll of white bandages and a jar of ointment. He pulled the chair up to the side of the cot.

"For your burn," he told her. When she made no move to uncover her leg, he added, "Come now, Miss Diamond, my intentions are quite honorable. You need only lift the blanket as far as your knee."

Again, there was something in his tone that made her bristle. Glaring at him, she nudged the blanket away and raised her right leg. Gently, he took hold of her bare ankle and propped her foot on his knee.

He was very efficient. She felt only a slight bit of discomfort as his large hand gently smoothed the ointment across her burned skin.

"Now it's time for us both to get some rest," he said, when he had finished with her leg. "You may sleep in the bed. I'll find a place on the floor. Good night, Catherine."

She said nothing, only eased down on the cot, clutching the blanket to her body. She lay on her back rigidly, staring up at the ceiling.

Sounds floated to her—Rory moving about the small room, the crack and pop of the wood fire. She heard a splash as Rory used the remaining water to sponge himself off, and she tried not to watch as the cloth—the same one she had used on her body—moved over the smooth contours of his muscled chest. She rolled to the side, her back to the center of the room, and stared at the wall. She had to grit her teeth, for as she changed position, her burn sent spasms of pain darting through her leg.

Rory extinguished the lamp and only the faint glow from the wood stove filled the room. Then she heard the undeniable rustle of clothing. Catherine's heart skipped a beat. He was removing his trousers! She mentally chastised herself: of course he was undressing; did she expect him to sleep fully clothed?

She was motionless, alert to every movement he made. She heard the gentle swish of air as he moved past the cot and then settled himself on the floor somewhere across the room. Within only a few moments — even before her heartbeat returned to normal — she heard his even breathing, punctuated by a soft snore now and then. He was asleep.

Catherine sat up, miffed that he had fallen asleep so easily with her in the room. He lay on the floor between the door and the wood stove, wrapped in a blanket identical to her own, his head resting on one arm. She fell back against the cot, sighing irritably. Slumber for her was long in coming.

Chapter Seven

Bright, late-morning sunlight filled the cabin when Catherine finally awoke. It took her a few seconds to realize where she was. Then, memories of the previous night came rushing back, leaving her with the same deep sense of loss she'd experienced while watching the saloon go up in flames. And her leg felt as though it were still on fire. Moving gingerly, she glanced once around the small space. Rory's blanket was gone from the floor and he was nowhere to be seen. Catherine kicked the covers from her body and went to the small basin to splash cool water on her face. Rory had thoughtfully filled it with fresh water and there was even a pot of coffee brewing on the wood stove. After running her fingers through her hair and securing it as best she could with a few pins left from the previous night, she poured herself a cup of coffee and moved to gaze out the window. It was then that she heard the voices. One was Rory's, the other definitely female.

"Jasper couldn't wait to see you," the woman said. "It's our little secret — his and mine — that you are here."

"He won't say anything to your husband, will he? You must make certain that he doesn't. All of my plans would go awry if Albert were to learn I was in San Francisco."

"No, no, don't you worry about that. Jasper is very good

at keeping our secrets . . . we have so many of them. I don't know how I would have gotten through the years without him. He—he is my link with the past." A moment of silence passed before she added, "I am so glad you're here, Rory. I've missed you terribly, and Jasper needs the guidance of a good man."

"Albert doesn't mistreat the boy, does he?" Rory asked, his voice low.

"Oh no, not—not in the physical sense, at least. He just doesn't talk with him, not like you do. You're good for Jasper, and he looks forward to these hours when we visit. I do, too, but then you know that, don't you? Yes, I know you do."

"Jenny, if I thought it would do any good, I'd go into the city right now and face Albert myself. I'd take you away from him without a moment's hesitation."

"But such a rash action would put your life in danger, Rory. Please, don't concern yourself with worry over Jasper and me. Our needs are well taken care of."

"A woman has more needs than just a fine house and proper food. A woman needs to be in love . . . and be loved in return. You deserve so much more."

Catherine heard the words Rory spoke so tenderly, and with them, came a tingle at the base of her spine. For Rory O'Shay, this tender moment with the mysterious woman outside seemed totally out of character. Catherine knew she should step away from the window or, better still, let the two know she was awake and could hear them. But something held her from making a move. She waited, and listened.

"I was so young when I gave my hand in marriage to Albert, but not too young to realize the vows that I made would be for my lifetime."

"But Albert is not Jasper's father—nor does he want any

part in his upbringing. I know your one true love has not diminished over the years, Jenny. Why should you go on denying yourself and your son what is rightfully yours? You care nothing for Albert. You never did and never will."

"Stop, Rory, such talk can only complicate matters."

A child's squeal of delight filled the air then, and the two figures moved away from the front of the cabin.

"Mama, look! The horse, he likes me! He kissed my hand, just like my puppy that Father took away! Can I ride him, Mama, can I? Please?"

Catherine had to part the curtains in order to see the small boy running toward the pair who were still out of her view. The lad was small in build, but lean and fit as any young boy who enjoyed physical exercise. Brown, gold-tipped curls tumbled over his forehead above huge brown eyes that shone with excitement. He wore a nut-brown, waist-length jacket, white shirt with a striped brown bow tie, knickers, hose, and buckled shoes; all well cut and immaculate.

Catherine heard Rory's laughter as he stepped toward the boy and gathered him up in his arms. "So you want to ride my colt, do you? Very soon he'll be ready for you to ride, but not yet. He's still too young."

"When he gets bigger, then?" pleaded the boy as he gazed adoringly down at Rory.

"Yes, most definitely when he gets bigger." Rory reached up and ruffled the boy's hair. "Speaking of getting bigger, you've grown at least an inch since I last saw you!"

"No I haven't. My father says I never get any bigger. He says I don't eat enough."

Though only the woman's back was visible to Catherine, she could see Rory turn to her with a slight frown. "You eat enough, Jasper. I know, because you're getting too heavy to hold. Here now, run along and feed Fire one of the apples you brought for him."

The boy's face shone with a wide grin that revealed a missing front tooth. "Can I, Mama?"

"Yes, of course, darling. You know where the apples are in the wagon. You'll be careful climbing in, won't you?"

Jasper wriggled out of Rory's hold, breaking into a run as soon as his feet touched the ground. "I'll have an apple, too, so I can grow big and strong just like Rory!" He darted away then, full of childish glee.

Catherine watched as the woman slipped her hand easily into the crook of Rory's arm. She was petite and fashionably thin, dressed in an elegant day dress of forest green. A shining mass of brown curls was caught up with a velvet ribbon at the back of her head and capped with a smart bonnet in a lighter shade of green. From the back, the woman was breathtaking. Catherine could only imagine how beautiful her face was. Standing beside Rory, her graceful head coming only to his broad shoulders, she had an unmistakable air of gentle breeding. Even the small movements of her gloved hands were artfully executed.

"Had I known of your guest, I would have packed more provisions," the woman said. "I do hope there's enough food. Jasper and I baked your favorite pie. My cook was beside herself when I shooed her out of the kitchen and proceeded to cover myself with flour!"

"So you remembered I love apple pie? Ah, dear Jenny, you don't know how long it's been since I've enjoyed such a treat."

She laughed, the light sound trilling across the air like tinkling bells. "Do you remember when we used to sit at your mother's table and eat apple pie, just the four of us? Oh, Rory, what I wouldn't do to have those precious moments back. . . ."

Rory nodded, bending his head to plant a gentle kiss on

her forehead. "I remember, Jenny. I remember."

Catherine let the curtain fall back into place feeling as though she had intruded on a very private moment. Her face burned with a deep blush as she moved quickly back to the center of the room. She was amazed at the odd feelings aroused in her by the chaste kiss that Rory had given the woman. Surely, she couldn't be jealous. She barely knew Rory, and there was no reason on earth for her to be jealous of someone who obviously shared many memories with him. Still, there was a strange unease within her.

"I am famished, that is all," she mumbled to herself. Resolved to dwell no longer on the intimate little scene, she quickly tied a blanket around her waist to form a sort of skirt, smoothed back the errant curls framing her face, and then marched to the door. It had been really quite rude of him not to introduce her to this Jenny, she decided—not acknowledging her own impropriety in eavesdropping.

She swung the door open and forced a tight smile to her lips. "I thought I heard voices," she said with false cheeriness. Startled, Rory and the woman both turned around. Each took a quick step away from the other, which Catherine pretended not to notice. "I wasn't aware anyone knew Mr. O'Shay made his home here," she called out boldly. Then, holding the homespun blanket just above her ankles, she stepped out onto the porch and moved down the rickety porch with an elegance that Sallie Burt might have envied.

The woman next to Rory was quiet for a moment as she took in Catherine's outlandish costume. Catherine forced herself not to feel foolish. With more spunk than she felt, she said, "If you'll overlook my attire, I'll excuse Mr. O'Shay's lack of manners in failing to inform me of early morning visitors. You see, my home burned to the ground last night and I have only the clothes I fled in."

Rory turned warm eyes upon her. He was thinking that even in an old blanket and his baggy shirt, Catherine Diamond was absolutely stunning. His blue eyes alight, he said, "Catherine, this is Jenny Latham. Jenny, meet Catherine Diamond."

Jenny Lathan smiled with a radiance that spread from her delicate lips to her fawnlike brown eyes. Her face was heart-shaped, her nose pert and turned up just so at the tip. Her lashes were thick and long, and her skin was as pure and unblemished as her son's. "How do you do, Miss Diamond? Please, you must call me Jenny. My son and I have only just arrived, but Rory has told me about your situation. I am terribly sorry about your misfortune. When I was a very young girl my family suffered a similar fate. You must let me know if there is anything I can do for you."

Catherine could only blink. She hadn't expected such warmth from a stranger, and certainly not from such a beautiful woman who had obviously, at some point in her life, been very intimate with Rory. Didn't it bother Jenny Latham to see her clad in Rory's shirt? Was it of no consequence to Mrs. Latham that she and Rory had spent the night, alone, in this mountain cabin?

"I — why thank you for your concern Mrs. — Jenny, but I need nothing. I can take care of myself."

"Of course you can. I'm certain you can see to your own needs, but as I said, my family lost a home once and I know how difficult it can be. Especially since your home was also your place of business. Please, do not hesitate to call on me should you find that you need some assistance."

Catherine murmured her thanks. At that moment Jasper came bounding up to them with an armful of green apples.

"I've one for each of us!" he exclaimed, tossing one apple to Rory as the others rolled from his grasp. "Don't tell

Father I dropped the apples, will you, Mama?" he asked, quickly gathering the scattered fruit.

Jenny Latham knelt to help him. "Of course I won't tell him, darling. It was an accident. Hurry now, we must be returning to the city. You've missed your morning lessons and I'm afraid there'll be no way of avoiding your afternoon tutor. We'll tell your father we went to the gardens this morning; he shouldn't mind that."

"Yes, Mama," the boy replied, clutching his apples. "Father cannot deny us a morning in the gardens!" With a wink, he placed a quick kiss to her cheek. "I wish we could live *here*, Mama, and then we would always be happy." He did not give his mother time to answer, but scooted away toward Irish Fire, who was grazing contentedly in the nearby field.

Jenny Latham gathered the last of the apples, dabbing quickly at her eyes before she stood. Her cheeks were flushed, and she absently shined the apples with a lace handkerchief, avoiding Catherine's gaze.

"That was Jasper, Jenny's son," Rory explained. There was a wistful note in his voice as he watched the boy feeding the colt.

Catherine became uncomfortable. "He's a lovely boy," she replied, feeling like an intruder. She felt the need to get away from the two of them. "If you'll excuse me, I've not had time to freshen up this morning." She bade them both good day and headed back inside the cabin where she shut the door and leaned against the cool wood.

It was obvious. Rory O'Shay and Jenny Latham had been lovers . . . and Jasper was their son.

Catherine wondered why this should make her feel so bitter. What did she care of Rory's past or the women who populated it? What was it to her if Rory chose to pursue a married society woman? It was clearly none of her affair, and after today, she planned to have nothing to do with Rory O'Shay. She would take herself and her horse back to the city to find her father and then the two of them would rebuild their life. She had only needed Rory to train Irish Fire, but now that she was penniless, there was no reason to see anything more of him. As for Jack Reese, she would take care of him on her own.

It was nearly three hours before Rory entered the cabin. He was alone.

"Where is Mrs. Latham and her son?" Catherine asked coldly.

"She's gone home to her husband," Rory answered.

In his hands, he carried two heavily laden baskets which he set down on the small table and unpacked. Fresh-baked bread, more apples, fried chicken, and salad greens appeared along with two golden apple pies. The aromas were mouth watering.

"Come," he said. "Help yourself to some food." He tore into a chicken thigh and consumed it with relish.

Catherine moved beside the table and took a piece of the chicken. Within a short time they had eaten all of the chicken and greens and had demolished half of one pie. Nothing had ever tasted so wonderful.

The sun was beginning to slant low on the horizon now, the line of trees on the mountain shadowing its warm rays. "It's getting late," Catherine commented. "I hadn't meant to stay here so long."

"Oh?" he inquired, lifting one brow. "And where had you planned to go?"

"I shouldn't be hiding here like a fugitive. I've done no wrong."

"Here is the safest place for you, Catherine. Jack Reese has no way of finding you."

"Am I to be on the run the rest of my life, then? The

man set my home on fire; I intend to see he pays for his deeds."

"And he will pay. I'll see to it. Until then, you're staying right here where I know you'll be safe."

"Really, Mr. O'Shay, you don't know me at all if you think I'll stay put just because you say so."

His gaze slipped down her meagerly clad figure, his brows lifting as his dark blue eyes came to rest on the blanket tied around her hips. "So you're heading back to the city dressed as you are? I assure you, you wouldn't get far in such attire. These woods are populated with ruffians who would not hesitate to lay claim to your favors—freely given or otherwise. Besides, I'd like to see you try to find your way back. A backwoodsman, you are not."

Conscious of the sight she made dressed only in the oversized shirt and threadbare blanket, she crossed her arms and forced herself to meet his gaze. "I have my gown," she said. "And this blanket. As for finding my way back to the city, I wasn't totally without my senses last night."

Rory snorted. "Don't overestimate yourself. And as for your gown, it was nothing but a tattered rag when you removed it."

Catherine quickly scanned the small interior. Her dress was nowhere in sight. Only her underclothes lay at the foot of her cot.

"It went into the wood stove," he replied, seeing her frantic search, "along with the kindling. Surely it's no great loss. My shirt and that blanket cover more of you than your gown did."

"How dare you burn my only garment—without my permission!" she gasped.

"I think you'll find me quite a daring man—when I see something I want."

Catherine flushed, as much with fury as with embarrassment.

"So I am to be your prisoner then?"

Rory's blue eyes hardened. "Let's just say you will stay here until I deem it safe to travel into the city."

She felt anger boiling inside of her. "And what makes you so sure that I wouldn't go back dressed just as I am, Mr. O'Shay?"

Rory reached out and jerked the blanket away from her, leaving her in only his shirt. She clutched at the table for support.

"Don't push me too far, lady," Rory said. "If I have to leave you in this cabin stark naked I'll do it."

Catherine, grabbed furiously for the blanket but he held her at bay, his left arm going easily around her slim waist while with his right hand he tossed the blanket behind him, out of her reach.

There was a grim smile on his lips. "Shall I prove it to you?"

"You wouldn't dare!" she hissed.

"Don't tempt me."

He held her so close that his breath stirred the tendrils of hair curling against the long column of her neck. Catherine shivered slightly.

"Catherine, listen to me," Rory said. "In truth, I feel I am partially to blame for your run-in with Jack Reese. If it weren't for me, you'd still have your saloon, and your life would not be in danger."

Catherine debated informing him that Reese hadn't torched the Diamond because of him, but because of his hatred for her father. Not knowing what her father was involved in, Catherine was hesitant to reveal too much.

"You can absolve yourself of any guilt on my behalf, Mr. O'Shay. The events of last night are my own worry. You need not concern yourself about my safety. I managed quite well before your arrival at my saloon, and will continue to do so without your interference. Now I'll thank you to release me!"

"A summary dismissal if I've ever heard one." He reached up with his right hand to toy with the buttons of the shirt. The deep neckline, made for a man's build, was low on her tiny frame and the fact that she had neglected to fasten all the buttons was an oversight she now greatly regretted. Her generous cleavage was in full view of his hungry gaze. He slipped open the fourth button, which was the first she had secured, and then dropped his fingers to undo the next. Catherine inhaled sharply, catching his hand between both of hers.

"Stop," she cried.

His fingers lingered over the closure. "But you've left me no choice. I can't let you escape so easily."

"But you cannot—"

"Just say the words, Catherine, and I'll stop. Tell me you'll not leave this cabin without my say so."

"I won't be tricked into giving my word."

He smiled, his chiseled lips parting as his gaze rested on the opening of the shirt. "Very well," he said. "You were given fair warning." The next button was slipped from its hole, and then the next.

Catherine stood rigid, too proud to admit she had lost the battle, and dreading what would come next.

"Rory..."

"Yes?" he asked, even as he undid another button.

The faint amusement in his eyes fueled her anger. "You're enjoying this, aren't you? You're deliberately provoking me, testing me to see how far I'll let you go with this charade!"

"And at what point will you stop me, Catherine? When the shirt is around your ankles? Will you then come to your senses and promise me you will not leave this cabin until I deem it safe?"

The remaining closures of the shirt fell away then. He parted the material and ran his warm hand across her flat naked belly.

Catherine drew a deep, unsteady breath, her cheeks aflame. To her chagrin, his touch was pleasurable.

His fingers fanned over her soft white skin, gently caressing their way up to the underside of one firm breast. Although she still held onto his wrist with both hands, she did not stop him. She shut her eyes, surprised and dismayed by her body's response. This man was a murderer, and here she was, letting him touch her! She must truly be a wanton, she thought in bewilderment.

His thumb rubbed lightly across one rosy nipple until it stiffened as Catherine felt a sharp, achingly sweet sensation sweep through her. The blood pounded in her veins, and her body was suffused with a delicious warmth—and an undeniable anticipation. He had meant for this act to humble her, she knew, to remind her that he was completely in control of her fate.

And he was right, Catherine realized, as he bent his dark head to her swelling breasts. His lips traced burning kisses across her flesh until he held one taut nipple in his mouth. Gently flicking, his tongue twirled over the now rigid, sensitive bud, sending shivers of delight racing through her. Unconsciously, she arched her body slightly to meet him. His left arm moved along her back to draw the shirt away from her and down the gentle curve of her shoulders. With a gentle swish, the oversized garment fluttered downward, to her elbows. She knew she should stop him. This was madness.

Rory's lips traveled up to place a feathery kiss on the wildly beating pulse in her throat. She smelled just the way a woman should, he thought. He loved the taste of her, too. True, it was her beauty that had at first attracted him, but it was the woman inside the body that drew him to her now. There was an indefinable quality about her that he hungered for.

It was when they'd walked along the early morning streets of the city that Rory knew he wanted Catherine Diamond, body and soul. The realization had shocked him. Never before had a woman affected him this way.

Catherine could not help the sigh that escaped her at his caresses. Surely a cold-blooded killer could not be so gentle. He kissed her mouth again, and Catherine felt her knees grow weak. Sweet heaven! What was wrong with her? Why did he have this effect on her?

She heard his sharp intake of breath, and felt his hesitation just before he swept her up effortlessly and carried her to the narrow cot. Perhaps he hadn't meant to go this far; perhaps he had originally intended to use only words to keep her from running. But once he'd discovered that satin skin, there was no turning back—for either of them.

She said nothing as he placed her gently on the cot. Within moments, he had divested himself of his shirt. His blue eyes were dark with passion as he knelt beside her, gently lifting her hands to place them against his chest. Catherine, frightened yet excited, felt the curling masculine hair there and reveled in the quivering response it evoked within her.

He hovered above her for a moment, drinking in her beauty, noting the touch of fear in her gray eyes. Carefully, he eased himself onto the cot beside her, drawing her supple body close to him as his mouth captured hers. With infinite tenderness, his lips moved against hers, slowly teasing them open so that his tongue could probe the moist recesses of her sweet mouth.

As his tongue met hers, Catherine felt the world tip crazily. An irresistible yearning crept over her. She was consumed by a need, a burning desire for some unknown goal. His hips pressed against her, and she stiffened as she felt the unfamiliar male hardness.

Her petal-soft skin was like velvet beneath his palms. With an easy grace, he drew away from her just long enough to remove his trousers and to strip away what shred of respectability his loose shirt, now twisted around her body, afforded her conscience. Then, he was beside her again, his lean, bronzed torso pressed tightly against her.

Beneath his practiced touch, Catherine came alive as his hands explored every dip and hollow of her body. Every wonderful sensation he brought forth was new to her, and with each touch of his hand, she wanted more.

By degrees, he caressed his way to the flat expanse of her belly and then to the dark triangle at the apex of her thighs. Almost unbearably intimate, his knowing touch there set her afire. Pure, sensual pleasure enveloped her, and she felt an aching fullness in her loins.

He poised himself above her then, and Catherine moved to accommodate him. Trembling, she ran her hands along the corded muscles of his upper arms as he nudged her legs apart.

He twisted atop her, grasping her hips with strong hands as his mouth sought hers in a deep kiss. Suddenly, she felt a piercing pain, and she cried out in surprise. She heard his muffled curse.

He hadn't wanted to hurt her. With a controlled effort, he held himself from penetrating deeper. Tenderly, he stroked the cloud of dark hair that spilled over the pillow like a skein of silk, kissed her eyelids, her temples, her cheeks, as he murmured soft, loving words that spread a delicious, soothing warmth through her. Then, with another twist of his hips, he pushed past her maidenhead and took her beyond the pain, into a realm of almost unbearable pleasure. She caught her breath and dug her nails into the hard sinews of his back as the liquid heat of ecstasy washed over her again and again.

As he moved within her, she lifted her gaze to meet his blue eyes. They were filled with passion, heady and powerful.

"Catherine, Macushla," he whispered, cradling her head in his hands as he buried himself deep within her.

Chapter Eight

Mrs. Albert Marshall Latham, Jenny to her few close friends, moved quickly up the winding staircase of her Rincon Hill home, a home that was far removed from her roots in Shenandoah, Pennsylvania. She had been fifteen years old—and four months pregnant—when she recited her marriage vows to her then fifty-two-year-old, impotent husband. But her fall from virtue had been a conscious decision that Jenny had never regretted, not even during the long and painful twenty-six hour labor she'd suffered bringing her only child, Jasper David, into the world.

Jenny had loved Jasper's true father heart and soul. And she still loved him, would always love him.

Every moment she'd ever shared with James David Hambleton was still poignantly alive in her mind. Even now, she could recall the touch of his hands, roughened and dried by coal dust, caressing her virgin skin. Every husky love word he'd ever uttered still echoed in her mind. J.D. Hambleton was a living, breathing part of her. His was the face she saw each night before drifting off to sleep. She would silently cry out his name as she buried her face in her pillow, seeking some surcease from the daily hell of her existence. His smile haunted her as every minute of the day she searched fruitlessly for him in the crowds around her.

But Jenny knew she wouldn't find him. She had left him far behind in the coal mines of Pennsylvania, left him alone to wonder what he'd done to make her leave, to wonder what had become of the child they had created when they themselves were but children—she only fourteen years old, he just turned seventeen. She remembered how proud and happy he'd been at the news. He promised to build her a home with a white picket fence and gingham curtains, and even before she was three months pregnant, he'd built a small cradle with their initials carved into the headboard and a space to add the initials of their child. Oh, how happy they had been during those stolen hours when he was able to get away from the mine. It didn't matter to Jenny that he was merely a coal miner, that he made only a pittance on each ton of coal that he managed to wrest from the unyielding earth. It didn't matter that he would have to support his widowed mother, as well as the baby and herself. All that counted was being with him. She would gladly have given up any chance at future riches just to be with J.D. But her tyranical father had discovered their secret.

He had learned she was pregnant on her fifteenth birthday, and instead of handing her a birthday present and his blessings, he had called her a whore and locked her in her bedroom with a Bible. Five days later, he dragged her to the train station in Philadelphia, with strict orders of what he expected from her. She was to travel to San Francisco, there to wed a man named Albert Marshall Latham.

She had not been informed that Latham was old enough to be her grandfather—nor did she know that he was impotent. She'd been told only that he would keep her in style and claim her illegitimate child as his own. She'd had absolutely no say in the matter, nor did she dare to beg her father to let her marry J.D. Her father was the owner of the Trenton mine, where J.D. was employed, and it was only by agreeing to her father's wishes that Jenny could protect his job. Had she disobeyed her father, J.D. would have been immediately dismissed—and blackballed from every other mine within three hundred miles. She could not jeopardize her lover's future, and, at fifteen, Jenny still lived in fear of her father's wrath. She'd suffered more than one beating at his hands.

So Jenny had gone to San Francisco and had become Mrs. Albert Marshall Latham. At first, she was grateful to her new husband for accepting her with no questions asked, but as the years passed and her son, Jasper, grew, it became painfully clear that Albert Latham disliked the child. Nothing Jasper did was ever right, and Albert was constantly correcting the boy's behavior. Soon, Jasper grew wary of the man he believed to be his father, and he clung to his mother's skirts, which was just one more thing for Albert to find disfavor with. Jenny protected the youngster with a ferocity she hadn't known she possessed. She would never leave her son alone with Albert, nor would she give in to Albert's demands that she send the child away. Jenny trusted Jasper's care to very few people.

Jasper's handsome looks came from his father. He had J.D.'s laughing brown eyes and bouncy, golden curls. He was quick and almost frighteningly independent. He was a child who enjoyed his moments alone. As he grew, Jenny detected many more likenesses of J.D. in him. Some days, it was all she could do not to break down into tears whenever she looked at her son. He was J.D. all over again, and it tore at her heart to see Jasper's lighthearted spirit crushed beneath Albert's insensitive, oppressive manner.

The first time that Jasper had asked, "Why doesn't Father love me?" Jenny had not known what to say. She had assured him that Albert did love him, in his own way, but Jasper was much too intelligent to be taken in by her words of comfort. After a few weeks, he had never again asked that question. In fact, he took great pains to avoid Albert altogether. Soon, there was an unspoken pact between Jenny and her son to keep out of Albert's way.

Jenny sighed, putting aside these burdensome thoughts for the moment. Peeking into the child's bedroom, she found Jasper's nanny, Claire, sitting in a chair with her needlepoint. The woman gave Jenny a smile, whispering that Jasper was well and had been asleep for an hour. Jenny nodded, then quietly shut the door. She usually tucked Jasper into bed herself, but her visit with Rory in the countryside had put her behind schedule, and she'd had to spend some time with Albert before he went out for the evening.

She moved down the long hall to the bedchamber she slept in alone. A grandfather clock ticked loudly in the cavernous hallway, and Jenny once again felt a wave of loneliness wash through her. She cared nothing for Albert's wealth, nor for his social position. She would have gladly exchanged this grand home for the one-room dwelling J.D. had shared with his mother so many years ago. . . . What had happened to her young lover, she wondered? What story had her father given him when he came looking for her as he must have done?

Jenny crossed the spacious chamber to her wardrobe from which she withdrew a sheer nightgown and wrapper. Sitting down at her vanity, she combed out her long brown tresses and then began to undo the buttons of her dress.

Suddenly, she heard the click of the latch on the balcony door, followed by the stirring of cool night air around her ankles. Brush in midair, she stared wide-eyed into the mirror before her. She thought about screaming, but what good would it do to scream? Only she, Claire, and Jasper were in the house. The Chinese servants were all day workers who left after dinner, riding the cable cars down to their homes in Little China.

She sat there, frozen, watching in the mirror as a shadowy figure stepped into the room.

"Jenny?" The voice that spoke was hauntingly familiar.

Shock waves ripped through her body and the brush toppled from her nerveless fingers. She dared not utter a word, fearful that the image in her mirror would vanish as it had so many times in the past. He was tall, so much taller than she remembered, and his voice was deeper, huskier. Gone was the lanky figure she remembered and in its stead she saw a powerful, lean frame dressed in expensive, custom made clothing. He stepped forward slowly, and the glow of the bedside lamp fell on the golden brown curls she had so often run her fingers through. He was handsome, far more handsome than anything she had imagined over the years. And he was here now.

"James?" she whispered huskily, tears stinging her eyes. "J.D., is that you?" She turned then, one hand covering her mouth in disbelief as her delicate shoulders shook with mingled joy and sadness.

"Jenny . . ." he whispered again, crossing the distance between them so slowly it pained her. "God, how I've longed for you! Jenny, sweet Jenny, the only love of my life . . ." His arms were around her before she could breathe again, and his hot kisses rained down on her hair, her cheeks, and her lips, which parted slowly, hesitantly, almost as if she feared he would dissolve once they touched. "Oh, Jenny," he murmured against her lips, bruising her, thrilling her. "Why did you leave me, baby? Why did you go away when we were so happy?"

She was speechless, stunned into silence by his presence and drowning in a sea of pent-up longing. He'd been the first man to make love to her — and the last. Twelve years. She'd gone twelve long years without the touch of a man's hands on her body, twelve long years of denial. And now, a dream come true, J.D. was with her once again. He was a man now, no longer the youth she had known. There was unleashed power in him now, a finally realized potential she'd always known he possessed. He was forceful and passionate, his kisses just as burning and hungry as she remembered. Her senses whirled at the touch of his lips. Even the scent of him was as she remembered it. Oh, how cruel life had been and how wonderful it was now.

"James," she whispered. "How I've longed for this moment! How—how did you find me? What took you so long to come to me?"

He silenced her with a long, deep kiss that reminded her of long ago stolen moments in a woodland cove; of dewy nights with crickets chirping and the hard ground beneath her back; of the scent of coal grime and sweat on his hard body as he thrust deep within her. She reveled at the feel of his hands upon her body once again. He was ripping her clothes away, but she didn't care. Tiny buttons popped and flew, falling silently onto the carpet. Feverishly, he pushed the gown over her shoulders, drawing it down until her suddenly overheated flesh was exposed to his hungry eyes. Her creamy white, blue-veined breasts gleamed in the lamplight, and she arched her back as she helped him strip her naked. He drew her up then, sighing heavily as he grasped her slim waist with both hands. His brown eyes were intense as he beheld her upturned face. "Where is your husband?" he asked in a raspy whisper as he pressed his hips against hers.

Jenny gasped at the force of his hold. "He—he's gone . . . for the night."

"Are you certain?" he demanded, his fingers digging painfully into her skin.

"Yes! But—" She was going to say it didn't matter, now that he was here with her nothing mattered, but J.D. didn't give her a chance. Placing one powerful hand at the back of her neck, he covered her mouth with a penetrating kiss, plunging his tongue into the honeyed recesses that no other man had ever explored.

Jenny melted against him, moaning with pleasure. Wrapping her arms tightly about his neck, she gave herself to him with total abandon. She couldn't get enough of him, nor he of her.

Swiftly, J.D. removed his own clothing and carried Jenny to the bed that had never been shared with her husband. He flung the covers aside, tossed her down and then covered her body with his own, forcing himself inside her with a savage possessiveness.

She met him thrust for thrust, her nails raking his skin, from his back to his buttocks, where she pulled him into her. Time and place dissolved. She only knew only one thing—she needed him, burned for him, and would not deny herself.

It was over within moments, a shattering, all consuming assault on their senses. For Jenny, the joy was tinged with a certain sadness, a lingering hunger. Their mating was just as it had been ten years before—passionate, overwhelming, but always too quick.

He stroked her hair then, cradling her face as he kissed her deeply, murmuring softly as his seed spread through her. "Ah, Jenny," he whispered, "why did you leave me?"

"But I didn't leave you," she answered, tears in her eyes, "not by my own choice. My father made me leave. He—he forced me into this sham of a marriage."

"What of our child?" he asked.

She was crying again, unable to stem the tide of emotion. "A boy," she whispered. "as handsome and brave as you."

She thought she heard him moan then, but it might have been the soughing of the wind through the trees outside the window. He pulled himself out of her gradually, then rolled to the side. Jenny lay still, suddenly fearful, though she didn't know why.

Finally, he spoke. "What is my son's name?"

She turned her face toward him, wondering at the tight sound of his voice. "Jasper," she replied. "Jasper David." She did not add Latham to the name.

He stared straight up at the ceiling, his face unreadable. She wanted to reach out and touch him, but some inner voice told her not to. Suddenly, the twelve years they'd been apart sprang up between them.

"Soon, I'll be taking my son home with me," he said at last. "He belongs with his father."

Jenny went rigid, every muscle suddenly tense. *Take her son away? But what of her? Did he not want to take her away also?* "Wh—what do you mean?" she asked aloud.

"Just what I said. The boy belongs with me. I've been denied twelve years of his life; I'll not be denied anymore." J.D. pushed himself up to a sitting position, running one hand through his golden curls. With quick, efficient movements, he stood and began dressing. Jenny felt a terrible sinking in the pit of her stomach.

"And what of your son's mother? Where does she belong?"

J.D. looked at her as he slung his topcoat over his shoulder. "She belongs right here, playing whore to the highest bidder." With those stinging words, he took a step toward the open balcony door.

Jenny lunged toward him, teetering naked on her knees at the edge of the bed as she reached to grab his arm. "No!" she gasped. "You cannot take him from me, J.D.! Never that! You must take us both. I love you, I've always loved you. *Only you*—no one else."

His handsome face twisted with an ugly grin as he grabbed her roughly by the shoulders and pulled her close to him. "Don't worry, sweet Jenny, I'll be back," he told her, his mouth a hairsbreadth from her own. "Whenever and wherever I feel the need for you, I'll have you. I'll take you in the parlor, or in your husband's bed. If I want, I'll take you right beneath Albert Latham's nose. I'll let him watch while I strip you naked and have you every way possible. And you'll squirm with delight and cry out for more, won't you, baby? Because it's good between us. It always was good between us." He kissed her savagely then, bruisingly, but Jenny didn't care. She clung to him, needing him more than ever.

"Do not lock your doors, Jenny," he whispered against her mouth. "There is nothing that can keep me from you now. I'll be your phantom lover who will take you at any hour of the day, in any place I find you. Just utter my name, and I will appear."

She squeezed her eyes tight, hating the hard tone of his voice, dying inside with every harsh word he spoke. "Oh, James, please don't do this to me—to us. Take me with you, now! Jasper and I will go away with you. I—I have money of my own that I've saved over the years. We can have all the things we always dreamed of—"

Her words were cut off as he pushed her down on the bed, leaving her sprawled there, shivering in terror.

"You think I have need of your money?" he thundered. "Do you think I'm still the dirt-poor coal miner you left for a wealthy old man? I've come up in the world, dear Jenny. I've enough money to buy this dump and your old man besides! I could ruin your husband financially with just a stroke of my pen." He glared at her. "No, Jenny, you keep your whore's wages. I've no need of them." His eyes raked over her nakedness then, branding her. Then, with an abrupt, insolent lift of his shoulders, he turned and left the same way he had come.

In shock, Jenny mutely watched him depart. Then, curling up into a ball, she clutched the sheet to her body, letting the grief wash over her, drowning in misery. "Oh,

James," she cried over and over. And even though he had wronged her grievously, she could not altogether blame him. She was the source of his anger; she was the reason he had grown into a cold, uncaring man. No matter that she'd acted unwillingly, she had planted the seed of his terrible vengeance.

And God help her, but already she yearned for their next encounter . . . .

Chapter Nine

The rhythmic pounding of a horse's hooves brought Catherine sharply awake. Confused, she sat straight up on the narrow cot. For a moment, she didn't know where she was, and then, suddenly, she remembered—everything. Especially the loss of her innocence.

She was alone in the tiny cabin, just as she had been the previous morning when she awoke, and already the late-morning air was warm. She wondered how Rory had managed to dress and slip out without disturbing her. As she once again donned the oversized shirt, she decided it must be the clear mountain air that enabled her to sleep so soundly, and so far into the morning. The sun was shining brightly, all traces of fog long ago burnt away, and the world was alive with bird calls and buzzing insects. She was hesitant about facing Rory after last night. Certainly, she'd enjoyed the passionate moments. And that was the problem—no respectable lady would have enjoyed such intimacies.

She pressed the palms of her hands to her eyes, trying to blot out the embarrassing images. Sweet heaven! Had she actually let him do . . . those things . . . to her? Her face turned crimson.

Rory's voice floated in to her, firm and commanding as

he directed the yearling through a series of trots and canters. Well, Catherine thought, she might as well get the inevitable over with. The sooner she said good-bye to Rory O'Shay, the sooner she could forget what had happened between them.

She left the cabin and crossed the high grass to the back where she could see Rory and the stiff-legged colt going through their paces some distance away. Seating herself in a sun-dappled patch of grass, she wrapped her arms around her knees, and watched the pair. Absorbed in his work, Rory did not notice her presence, which, she thought, was just as well. But the frisky Thoroughbred was very much aware of an appreciative audience. Tossing his sleek head spiritedly, Irish Fire gamboled this way and that, tail flying, legs kicking.

Catherine smiled at his capriciousness, feeling a thrill course through her. Fire was indeed a born racer, capable of commanding attention in any crowd. He was a showpiece, fully aware of his own worth and ability. There was an exciting future ahead for the yearling, and it was obvious that Rory O'Shay was the perfect trainer. The two worked well together, like old friends.

That thought brought Catherine up short. Immediately, she suppressed her nagging conscience and waved shyly to Rory, who had finally noticed her. He nodded, smiling in the early morning sunshine. He went on with Fire's training for another fifteen minutes, then left the animal to run about on his own, while he took a break and dropped down beside Catherine. "Good morning," he said.

Catherine murmured a cordial greeting but averted her gaze. Had she really let this man hold her and make love to her? What had come over her, to let him take such liberties with her body? Yet, she knew, she had been a more than willing participant in what had passed between them. What must he think of a woman who allowed—indeed encouraged—such intimacies? The need to know was strong, and before she could stop herself, the words were out.

"About last night . . . I—I must tell you that I, well, what I mean to say is that I don't usually—" She faltered, confused, unable to get straight in her mind what she wanted to say.

Rory heard the tremor in her voice and looked over at her, barely able to keep from stroking her cheeks, which were now suffused with a deep blush. It was obvious that she was having trouble trying to explain that she didn't fall into bed with every man that she met. It was equally obvious that she was deeply ashamed of what she had done.

Inwardly he cursed himself—perhaps for the hundredth time that morning. Ever since he'd awakened beside her and gazed at her innocent, slumbering form, he'd been regretting his actions of the night before. He had been surprised to discover she was a virgin; there had been moments when her actions led him believe she was an experienced woman. And the fact that she lived and worked in a saloon, surrounded by tough, hardbitten men, reinforced this assumption. He should not have made love to her, he knew, should have kept his distance—as he'd planned and striven to do since first meeting her. She was both child and woman—crying out to be protected, then suddenly rallying to take care of herself with admirable independence.

He had a bitter taste in his mouth as he recalled how he'd taken advantage of her half-dressed state. He had never meant for things to go so far, but when he'd seen her so vulnerable—and simultaneously spitting fire—he was consumed by uncontrollable desire.

"Hush," he said soothingly, not liking to see her so distraught. "You needn't explain anything. It is I who should be explaining—even begging forgiveness." His words were low and tinged with regret. He could never be the man she deserved. He was wanted for murder. He had no home, no security to offer her. He could be nothing but trouble for her, and in truth, her life was in danger because of him.

Catherine turned toward him, her gray eyes clear in the morning light. "You needn't apologize. I—" She wanted to tell him she'd enjoyed what they'd shared, that it had been the most joyous experience of her life. But the words wouldn't come. To admit that she'd found pleasure in his arms would be to label herself a harlot. No respectable woman would talk of such things, let alone do them. She was shameless, she told herself bitterly.

"Perhaps," Rory said, cutting into her miserable thoughts, "we shouldn't try to analyze what happened last night. I think it would be wisest, and best, if we both left what is behind us in the past, where it belongs."

And never repeat the performance. He hadn't said the words, but that he meant them was painfully clear. Catherine was hurt to the core. Her fall from virtue had been swift—and immensely pleasurable. Living with what she'd done was another matter.

Rory stretched out on the grass, hands clasped beneath his head. In an attempt to help them both to forget the events of the previous night, he turned the conversation to other things. Whenever he was troubled, he turned to thoughts of the one thing in life that gave him the will to go on. That he now wished to share these thoughts with Catherine was something he didn't stop to ponder. Quickly, before the moment was gone, he said, "I could lose myself in country like this. I've always dreamed of owning rich, fertile land with room enough to let my horses roam. I can't remember ever wanting anything else. All my life I've been searching for the perfect spot, a place where I can build stables, huge stables, and a home as a grand as these pines."

Catherine caught the unguarded, wistful note in his voice. "And you think this is the place you've been looking for?" she asked.

"Yes, I think it is. Can you picture it, Catherine, right over there on that knoll? A two-story house with a wide verandah across the front. Nothing ostentatious like the homes on the hills in the city. What I want is something big and airy, with plenty of room for my children to romp about, but cozy, too. I want it filled with children—boys and girls, whatever—I have no preference just as long as I have at least one of each. And I want stables, lots of stables, to house the finest racers. This land will be my family's private paradise. Solid roots, that's what I want to give my children. I want them to know that they always have a place to come home to."

He was quiet for a moment, and Catherine chanced a glance at his face. He was gazing up at the sky, his blue gaze dark in the bright light. Yes, she could see his home—proud and solid, just as he was. She could see the stables and the horses. She could see all his dreams—and she didn't have to look at the surrounding land to picture them. It was all in his eyes.

A sudden emptiness spread through her, so profound she had to turn her own gaze skyward. Was it regret that she could not be a part of his future? Of course not, she told herself. She barely knew the man.

"What is your dream?" he asked. "Is there something you've always wanted in life, something you would give anything for?"

His question, asked so easily, took her by surprise. Oh yes, she had her dreams, but compared to his, hers were not so lofty. There were those who might even consider hers ambitious, selfish and unworthy. Dare she share her innermost wishes with him, the man to whom she had given her innocence?

"Catherine?"

She nodded, brushing the soft petals of a wildflower against her cheek. "Yes," she replied slowly. "I have a dream . . . but I'm afraid it is not as grand as yours. I have no desire to create a dynasty—although, like any mother, I would want only the best for my children. But there is something I've always wanted, desperately—ever since my father brought me to San Francisco."

"And that is?" he gently prompted. "Come, you can tell me."

"Well, I—it's hard to tell you. You'll think I'm silly—or worse—selfish."

He rolled onto his side, and brought his hand up to brush a stray wisp of hair from her forehead. "Tell me, what is it you dream of when you close those beautiful eyes at night? What is the one thing in this world that would warm your heart and bring a true smile to these lips?" His fingers trailed down to softly caress her mouth, and Catherine felt a small shiver.

She gave him a shy smile. "Well—all right, I'll tell you. I—I have always wanted to be treated like a lady. A real lady, I mean. You see, when my father and I first came to San Francisco, I was just a child and we didn't have much money. I used to do laundry and mend clothes to help pay the rent. I used to dream of going to a proper school—a finishing school—to learn all the things a young society woman would be taught. I wanted to be sought after, to attend the balls and the theater, go to teas, and wear the latest fashions. When my father made his fortune, he was finally able to outfit me in style and introduce me to young ladies of social standing . . . but they never had time for me. I—I was a social outcast to them. They took great pains to ignore me, and even though my father was accepted in those circles, the girls my age turned their backs on me." She gave a small laugh in an attempt to hold back the tears. It seemed only yesterday that she had stood alone at a society tea. "My father did his best but, well . . . it was never enough. My mother died when I was very young, and since then, it has only been my father and me. I love him dearly, but there have been times when I wished he knew more about raising a young lady."

There, she had told him; she had shared her innermost desire with him. She was pleased that he wasn't laughing at her.

"And if you were given one night to live as a 'real' lady, what would you wish to do?"

She gave him another shy smile, and closed her eyes. Indulging herself, she let her mind take flight. "Mmm," she said, thinking aloud, "I should like to go to the theater; I've never been to the theater. And I should like to sit in one of the private boxes."

"And then?"

"Then I would like to go to a ball and dance into the wee hours of the morning, until just before sunrise, when I would sit on some terrace in one of the beautiful homes on the Hill. I'd drink champagne and eat strawberries while I watched the sunrise."

She opened her eyes, surprised at herself. "It's just a silly daydream," she whispered quickly. "Something that could never come true."

He had moved his head closer to hers, and now his lips were just a breath away. "But sometimes dreams do come true," he told her, his gaze intense. He brushed his lips gently against hers. "Let us each hold fast to our dreams; we shall let them be the well from which we draw our strength to face the darkest hours; they will be the shimmering light that guides us to our paradise." He took her face between his strong hands, threading his fingers through her hair as he pulled her close and set his mouth on hers in a hungry, achingly sweet kiss. Gently his tongue skimmed the pouty swell of her lower lip, and Catherine opened to him like a flower to the sun.

Did she suddenly feel a bond between them because she'd shared her secret, something she'd never told to anyone else? Or was it some deep physical need for this man that made her feel their souls were connected? Perhaps it was just a need to be comforted that drew her to Rory O'Shay. Her life had been in turmoil since the day she'd met him, and in just a few short hours, Rory had somehow become her pillar of strength.

Catherine gave up trying to reason it out. Logic was meaningless when the heart took over. She was here with Rory O'Shay, and there was no place else she wanted to be. Thoughts of fleeing alone to the city vanished. She had given him her innocence, and in return had been awakened to a part of herself she hadn't known existed. Did it really matter what tomorrow would bring when right here and now they shared such warmth — and the mutual gratification of intense physical need? What did it matter if Rory — or she, herself — might be gone on the morrow? She had this moment with him, and her soul would be nourished by the memory of it through eternity.

Catherine rested her head on his shoulder.

Rory felt the tension leave her limbs, felt her body relax against him. He felt touched by her trust. Lately, his life had been filled with too many cynical, hardened people. It had been years since he'd been near someone as sweet and innocent as Catherine. Someday, he vowed to himself. *Someday I'll make your dream reality, Catherine.*

The remainder of the day passed quickly in the performance of small household tasks. Catherine swept the floor of the cabin, washed out their clothing, and then took a long, leisurely bath in a small tub Rory found tucked away in a corner. While she bathed, Rory chopped wood, and by the time he returned with the fragrant logs, she'd already donned her sun dried shirt — along with the threadbare blanket, for modesty's sake. She spent the next half hour sitting on the porch steps, drying her still damp hair, enjoying the last of the sun while Rory prepared a rabbit stew. He'd shot the rabbit earlier in the day, and had even unearthed some sprouting potatoes to add to the stew.

As Catherine ran her fingers through her long, dark tresses, listening to Rory rattling pans and humming to himself, she was surprised to find herself so much at ease. When was the last time she had felt so relaxed? she wondered. Ever since she'd learned the saloon was in financial trouble and that her father was rapidly depleting their reserves, she'd been nervous and on edge. How was it possible for her to sit here now, calmly enjoying her surroundings, when the saloon was burned to the ground and she had yet to find out how her father was? Again, she blamed her curious lassitude on the mountain air.

That air was now filled with the scent of wild roses, pine trees, and sweet grass, and it was turning cooler as the sun dipped slowly below the horizon. Birds chirped and twittered as they folded their wings and settled in for the night, and a great horned owl, who was just beginning his day, whoo-whooed into the still air. Leaves rustled, fanned by a slight stirring of wind. The sounds were not altogether unfamiliar; Catherine had spent many nights sitting outside her family's coal town shack in Pennyslvania. There, she'd also heard the croaking of peepers—calling for rain, as she'd been told—although it was never explained why they confined their chorus during downpours. And there had been the constant tap-tapping of the great kingfisher on the oak and cherry trees.

The sounds around her now were comforting, transporting her back in time to another, long ago dusk. Her mother had been alive then, and when her father returned from a long day in the mines, the three of them would sit outdoors, talking quietly with other families who shared their hardships. The bonds that were forged in the coal towns were bonds of life, and friendships ran deep.

Thinking about this, Catherine wondered again why her father had not kept in touch with their old friends and neighbors. Catherine had thought that after he'd made his fortune, he would send money back east to help ease the burdens of those still there. But, to her knowledge, he had not. He'd closed the book on that chapter of their lives the minute they'd settled into the saloon. Ned had even changed their last name. No one in San Francisco was aware that Catherine Diamond was in truth Mary Catherine McGuillicuddy. There were times when even she forgot where her roots lay. Not until she and Rory had arrived at this mountain cabin, had she been reminded of sleeping beneath the stars.

At the sound of Rory banging with a spoon on a frying pan, Catherine put aside her reflections and reentered the cabin. Dinner was served, he announced, and the two of them sat down to eat.

As they ate their stew, they spoke of the yearling — with Rory doing most of the talking. He described the rigorous training schedule he'd set up for Irish Fire, and told Catherine how important it was that he spend the major portion of each day with the horse. Talk turned then to the land on which the cabin stood. It was rich and fertile, the perfect place for the colt. Seeing the enthusiastic gleam in Rory's eyes, Catherine decided not to remind him that the property was not theirs to do with as they pleased. Somehow, being there with him — even knowing they were trespassing — was still occasion for joy.

Together, they rinsed and dried the few dishes, then lingered over coffee until Catherine had to stifle a yawn.

Rory saw how tired she was, saw also her reluctance to end the day. He knew that she did not want to be the first to speak of going to sleep. She was wondering, as was he, how they would spend this night. Although he longed to take her in his arms again and make long, lingering love to her, he knew better. He had wronged her once. He would not do it again.

Rising and taking her cup, he told her to go ahead and turn in for the night, adding that he had to check on the yearling and tend to some other chores before he retired. Feeling her eyes on him, he fixed a bedroll for himself, halfway between the woodstove and the door, letting her know with this gesture that they would be sleeping separately. He then bade her good night and went outside.

The cool air was exactly what he needed to clear his head and subdue his rising passion. Just being in the same room with Catherine—clad only in his shirt and threadbare blanket, with her long hair loose and falling about her shoulders in soft, silken waves—was enough to drive even a monk crazy. A man could only take so much.

It was a long time before he reentered the cabin, and when he did, Catherine was already asleep on the cot. She was curled up into a tight ball, her face toward the woodstove, bathed in the rosy glow of the fire. Her breathing was soft and deep, and did nothing to help Rory fall asleep.

Chapter Ten

By the next morning, Catherine knew her conscience would not allow her to stay another day in the wilderness with a man her father had labeled a murderer. Even though she'd enjoyed her moments with Rory, she knew she was a fool for doing so. That she felt a stirring of desire whenever Rory was near her was shameful. She was extremely upset to find herself fantasizing about spending another night of physical pleasure in his arms. What had become of her in just two days' time? Her moral fiber had somehow weakened in the gentle hands of a man wanted for murder. Was this moral laxity caused by the man—or was there some fraility in her own nature that robbed her of all reason when he held her?

Gentle hands. The words echoed in her mind. It was true, Rory had never given her any reason to believe he was a killer. And yet, her father would never have said such a thing unless he had good reason to believe it.

Seated on the narrow cot with a blanket wrapped around her shoulders to keep out the morning chill, Catherine watched as Rory entered the cabin carrying a load of wood. The kindling clattered into the woodbin.

He glanced over at her, smiling as he said good morning. It was then that he noticed how tightly she clutched the blanket to her chest. "What is it?" he asked quietly, straightening and brushing his hands on his trousers. "You look troubled."

Catherine could not stop the words that tumbled from her mouth. "I should not be here."

Feeling somewhat relieved, Rory's smile deepened as he tried to reassure her. "We've been through this, Catherine. You're not safe in the city, not until Reese is taken care of. This is the best place for you."

"But . . . am I any safer with you?"

He stared at her for a long, considering moment. Of course she was referring to that night of passion, of her lost virginity, and most likely wondering when he would force himself on her again. The fear in her voice stabbed at him, and once again he was filled with remorse at having initiated her into the rites of lovemaking. She was so young and vulnerable, filled with proper dreams of making a proper marriage. And now, because of his impulsive desires, he had stripped her of the one thing a gentleman wanted most in his bride: her innocence.

Quietly, he said, "I am sorry, Catherine. It pains me to see the fear in your eyes. Believe me, I will not force my attentions on you again. I promise you."

Catherine averted her gaze, a deep blush spreading across her cheeks. "I am not speaking of . . . of the other night."

"Then what?"

She tipped her face up toward him, her gray eyes clear. "Murder," she said. Even in the face of his suddenly guarded manner, she continued in a rush, "It seems your reputation precedes you, and there are those who label you a—murderer." Her voice was flat, not accusing but not forgiving either. In her heart, she wanted him to deny the accusations, to explain away the allegations. But he did not. He merely stood there, holding his powerful arms at his sides, fists tightly clenched.

He saw the stricken look on her face, the silent plea in her eyes. He felt the age-old, guilt-honed knife in his belly twist a little deeper. He knew he should explain things to her, should tell her that it had been a case of kill or be killed. But what was the use of trying to explain?

He turned away so that she couldn't see his face. Catherine Diamond was suddenly making him feel more vulnerable than he ever had in his life.

"My father says you murdered a man," she continued, letting the blanket drop and coming to stand beside him, clad only in his shirt and blanket-skirt. "Tell me, Rory, are you guilty or not?"

"Are you to be both jury and judge, then?" he asked softly, with narrowed eyes.

"Is what my father told me true? Did you really leave your family in their darkest hour and then return home only to murder a man in cold blood?"

He gave a low grunt. "So that's what Ned told you. I'm surprised he didn't round up a lynch mob to string me from the nearest tree. It would be an unendurable hell for him if he knew his daughter was here with me now. It seems I've brought you and your father nothing but misery since I first stepped into your saloon. You would do well to turn and run from me, as far and as fast as you can."

"If you'll recall, I wanted to do just that and you wouldn't let me go."

He turned to face her, his mouth set in a grim line. "True. Even now, I must wonder if I'd ever willingly let you leave."

Why? she wanted to ask him. Was it because of the threat Jack Reese posed, or was there some deeper meaning to his words? She desperately wanted some answers, but before she had a chance to speak again, the quiet of the mountain hideaway was shattered by the sounds of an approaching carriage.

Rory stepped away from Catherine and moved quickly to

the window, parting the curtain to see who was coming. "It's Jenny," he said. He opened the door and waved to her. Here was his chance. If he let Catherine go back to the city with Jenny, he'd no longer have to fight the temptation to take her in his arms again. He could simply let her ride away with Jenny, and he could follow at a distance to make certain Catherine got back safely. After that, he would be free to seek out Jack Reese.

His decision made, he said to Catherine, "You will be delighted to know your ride to freedom has just arrived." With that, he stepped outside the cabin.

Catherine did not move. She stood rooted to the spot, conflicting emotions coursing through her. Suddenly, leaving Rory O'Shay and their mountain retreat was the last thing she wanted to do.

But there was nothing she could say. Certainly she couldn't announce she didn't want to return to the city, for she did. Still, there was a part of her that regretted having to leave the comfort—and undeniable excitement—of Rory's presence. Also, there was the matter of the yearling. Since she had no home to return to, taking the colt with her was out of the question. Fire would have to be left behind and entrusted to Rory's care.

The ride back to the city passed by swiftly and easily enough, with Jenny in a talkative, somewhat nervous, mood. She had brought Catherine a steamer trunk filled with clothing, bestowing it with such graciousness that Catherine could not refuse. A day dress, which Catherine had immediately donned, was a bit snug but all the other garments fit her perfectly. The subject of fashion occupied them for much of the trip.

Catherine found her mind wandering more than once. The urge to ask Jenny about Rory and his past was too great to be ignored, and it was a difficult task indeed to keep from blurting out indecorous questions. Somehow she managed to keep up her end of the polite small talk, and before too long, they were in the streets of San Francisco.

"If you'd like, we can go to my home where you can freshen up while I send one of the servants to find your father," Jenny had offered. "Rory mentioned that he would feel much better about your returning to the city if you stayed at my home. I don't know what kind of trouble you've encountered, nor do I know why Rory insisted you stay with him at the cabin for the past two days. I have no wish to appear intrusive in any way, but I do want you to know that you are more than welcome to stay with my son and me for as long as you like. We've more than enough room."

"Thank you, Jenny. You've been too kind already. I couldn't possibly impose."

"You wouldn't be imposing! Far from it, Catherine. Truth be known, Jasper and I get lonesome at times and your company would be good for both of us. Do say you'll stay with us . . . it would mean so much to Rory to know you are safe."

Obviously, Rory had given Jenny specific instructions while Catherine had been dressing. That he could ask his former lover — the mother of his child, no less — to house her was outrageous!

"I appreciate your offer, Jenny, and I hope you'll forgive me for saying this, but I do not see where Mr. O'Shay's desires enter into anything concerning me. My proper place right now is with my father and the other employees of the Diamond. I can hardly move in with you and enjoy such comforts while my friends are homeless. If you'll just deliver me to Montgomery Street, I'll take care of myself."

Jenny, who had chosen to drive the carriage herself, suddenly looked very small and forlorn. The woman was a study in contrasts, Catherine thought. Tearing about the countryside on her own, when her husband was wealthy and socially prominent; boldly visiting an outlaw, who had apparently been her lover; then suddenly losing her composure where Catherine showed her displeasure with Rory's attempted manipulations.

Seeing her discomfort, Catherine quickly added, "It isn't that I don't appreciate your concern; I do. But my father and I have always taken care of ourselves in the past, and we shall continue to do so."

"Of course. But I would hate for you to let pride stand in the way of a safe haven for yourself and your father. Surely if Rory is worried for your safety, he has good cause. I'm not prying, not at all. Just, please, remember you are welcome in my home."

"Yes, I'll remember," Catherine replied gratefully as they neared the burnt-out shell that had once been the Diamond Saloon. The sight pained her beyond belief. There was nothing left, nothing at all but a few charred beams and knee-deep, blackened rubble.

Catherine pressed a hand to her mouth, fighting back the tears.

"I'm sorry," Jenny whispered from beside her. "I should have warned you. Please forgive me for chattering on and on about nothing." She reached out a gloved hand to touch Catherine's arm. "Look. Who is that kicking through the rubble? Is it anyone you know?"

Catherine looked past the debris to where the back of the building had once been. Her father and Randolph were there, their heads bowed as they searched for anything they might be able to salvage.

"Pa!" Catherine cried out. "It's my father, Jenny! Thank God he's all right!" In a moment, she was off her seat and running blindly toward the men. The acrid smell of damp smoke stung her eyes, and the sound of crunching debris beneath her feet sickened her, but nothing mattered now except seeing her father alive and well. As she flung herself into his tight embrace, she cried and laughed at the same time.

"Katie! Ah, Katie, my girl! Where have you been? I've

been sick with worry! Sallie and Randolph told me you were dragged away from the fire by that murdering scoundrel O'Shay, and I've been turning the city upside down for you!" Then he stepped back to look at her, demanding, "He didn't harm you, did he, Katie?"

Catherine could only shake her head, as tears of relief coursed down her cheeks. "No, I—I'm all right, Pa. But what about you? I was so worried about you. Nobody had seen you before the fire began and then, afterwards, I couldn't find you in the crowd. I was so afraid you'd—"

"Hush, child," he soothed, wiping her tears away with his hand. "I'm just fine, and no little fire is going to keep me down for long. Now stop your crying, lass. We're all alive, no one was hurt in the blaze. It's just another setback, that's all, and the good Lord knows we've had one or two of those in our lives. Did you hear me, Katie?"

Catherine nodded again, unable to control her tears. She clung to her father a moment longer before she stepped away, brushing the wetness from her cheeks and forcing a tremulous smile. "I'm sorry. I'm just glad to see you—both of you," she added, turning to smile at Jake Randolph.

He gave her a familiar wink, reaching out to squeeze her arm. "I sure am glad to see you in once piece, Miss Catherine," he said. "I had no idea what a blackguard O'Shay was until your father filled me in. Are you sure you're all right?"

"Oh, Randolph, he didn't hurt me—he just—"

"Just what?" Ned boomed. "Dragged you away and kept you for two days, leaving us to wonder what in the world had happened to you! What *did* happen, child? By God, if that man laid one hand on you I'll see him die at my own hands! Come, Catherine, we're heading right to the proper authorities. We'll see that O'Shay is behind bars before the day is through. Why I hesitated to inform the police of his whereabouts I'll never know!"

"No, Pa!" Catherine exclaimed, digging her heels into the

you my gratitude for seeing to my daughter's welfare in our time of need."

"You are most welcome," Jenny replied easily. "And I'll be certain to relay your thanks to Mr. O'Shay also. After all, he did escort your daughter from the burning building and then give her over to my care."

"Yes, of course," Ned muttered, turning his gaze back to Catherine.

Catherine felt uneasy under his stare, but pushed such thoughts aside as she looped her arm through his. She was just thankful he was alive and well. She would deal later with any problems resulting from her stay with Rory.

"Thank you, Jenny," she said with meaning.

Jenny merely nodded. "No need to thank me, Catherine. But before I leave, there is the matter of the clothes trunk. Where would you like it delivered?"

"Clothes?" Ned asked.

"Oh, yes, Jenny has given me some clothing she no longer needs. A trunkful, in fact. Where are you staying, Pa? We can have it delivered there."

Ned once again nodded his thanks to Jenny, then gave her the address of a boardinghouse near the Chinese Quarter. The address was not a prestigious one, but neither was it disreputable. Jenny, maintaining her gracious demeanor, took note of the address and then bid the three of them good day, promising to stop and visit them soon.

Catherine watched her leave, wondering why Rory didn't spirit Jenny and her son away just as forcefully as he had her . . . She was still mulling over the odd relationship between Rory and Jenny, when Ned decided to leave the rubble of the Diamond saloon and head for the boarding house, situated near old St. Mary's Church. The Roman Catholic cathedral marked the southern edge of the Chinese Quarter. The Quarter comprised only eight city blocks but supported a population of anywhere from ten to thirty thousand Chinese. No one was actually certain how many people lived in the Quarter, for the numbers constantly fluctuated, depending on the season. In the winter months, when out of work laborers flowed in from the northern canning factories, Little China was filled beyond capacity, and it was said that many of the Chinese burrowed three stories underground to find living quarters.

Without a spare nickel to ride the horsecar, Catherine and Ned had to walk the many blocks to the boarding house. Randolph, it seemed, would not be joining them, for he was staying with a friend who lived on nearby Kearny Street. Catherine was not fooled. She knew very well that Randolph's "friend" was a woman. Although the fire at the Diamond had blazed away Randolph's income, just as it had Catherine's and her father's, Jake still maintained his jaunty, amiable air. No matter what obstacles life threw in Jake Randolph's way, he would always manage to come out on top.

Catherine's spirits lifted as she said good-bye to him and she and her father went on their way. No matter that their business was ruined and they were in debt over their heads, they were all alive and that's what counted. Life was sweet, and things would get better, she told herself. They had to.

She took in a deep, sweet breath of air, then tucked her hand in the crook of her father's arm, smiling up at him. "You don't know how good it is to see you again, Pa," she said.

"If it's anything like as good as it is to see you, then I know just how it is. You're a sight for sore eyes, you are."

Together, they made their way up Kearney Street, which teemed with activity. Shops, theaters, cafés, and gambling halls were filled with patrons coming and going. Fashionable ladies dressed in smart, colorful garb, strolled the cobbled walkways, escorted by equally stylish gentlemen attired in conservative broadcloth, many sporting the popular beaver hats. Vehicles of all descriptions clattered by: privately owned carriages, some opened to the day air, others enclosed; for-hire rigs; elegant caleches; and even a rickety grindstone-on-wheels whose owner shouted, "Oho, get your razors ground!"

Snatches of conversation floated around Catherine's head—women talking of fashions and family; men swapping jokes and tips on mining stocks, gossiping in whispers of corrupt politicians and bets placed on the next winner at Menlo. Catherine's heart swelled at the cacophony of voices, and her pulse raced in time to the throbbing beat of the burgeoning young city. Yet, something deep inside her ached for a quiet cabin in the lush, green countryside. Her spirit yearned for that sense of peace and comfort she had only hours before enjoyed, and she wondered what Rory O'Shay was doing and thinking at that moment.

By the time they reached the humble boardinghouse, Catherine's feet ached and burned with the blisters she'd acquired from her too-tight borrowed shoes. The only thing she wanted to do was climb into a hot tub. Ned immediately ordered a bath for her, and within an hour, Catherine had scrubbed herself clean and was seated in the only chair their small quarters offered. The room was merely that—a room with one double bed, a chair, washstand, and a wardrobe. Jenny's trunk had been delivered and Catherine wasted no time looking through the contents for fresh attire. Along with a pretty, sprigged muslin dress, she found toilet articles, and even a small cut-glass perfume bottle with her favorite scent, California flowers. She would have to remember to thank Jenny Latham for her thoughtfulness.

Ned, returning to the room, which he had vacated to give Catherine privacy, now stood with his shirt sleeves rolled up, shaving at the washstand. With a somewhat shaky hand, he skimmed the blade across one cheek, being careful not to cut into his mutton-chop whiskers. Watching him, Catherine was reminded once again of their destitute condition. Ned had always gone to the Bank Exchange, a popular establishment for businessman, for a professional shave and manicure.

"I have something to speak with you about, Katie," Ned said as he finished up and rinsed the blade.

The graveness of his tone pricked the hairs on the back of Catherine's neck. She watched as her father returned the articles to his shaving kit with trembling hands. "What is it, Pa?" she asked. "Is something wrong? It isn't your health, is it? I do wish you'd go and see a physician—"

"No, Katie," he interrupted, "it has naught to do with my health. Now, I want you to listen closely, girl. What I'm about to tell you cannot be repeated to anyone. Do you understand?" At her silent nod, he continued. "The reasons we left Pennsylvania and came to San Francisco are complicated, but I've go to try and explain them to you now, for I need your help. You remember the Molly Maguires, don't you, Katie? I always told you and your mother I would have nothing to do with that lot of lawless men, and I tried my best not to, I did. But sometimes a man's best is just not enough. I became deeply involved with the society and, against my wishes, I was made privy to many of their dirty dealings. I was soon in over my head. I couldn't stay with the group because of my conscience, but I couldn't just leave the circle either, because of my knowledge." He paused for a moment, pacing, then sat down on the edge of the bed. "I decided to leave the society and put all the terrible deeds behind me. I knew it was risky, for once a man joins the Mollies, he's a member for life—or else. I took you out of Pennsylvania and we came west. Once I made my fortune here in San Francisco, I began sending money back east to help other families break away from the society and start new lives elsewhere."

"So that's where all the profits from the saloon were going!" Catherine was enormously relieved to learn her father had not just squandered away their money as she had previously believed.

"That's right, girl. But all of this was done very secretly, and I cannot express strongly enough how important it is that you not breathe a word of this to anyone. I'm still helping men who want to get away from the Mollies. That villainous band's thirst for revenge grows stronger each day, and people are still being murdered in the coal towns. Things are very grave back east."

"I—I must confess, I thought your were throwing our money away on wildcat investments. Tell me how you've helped the men and their families. Where do they go once they leave Pennsylvania?"

"They're scattered all over the country, Katie. When I first started this underground operation, I used to arrange for escaping families to come out west. But now, I'm proud to say, there's a nationwide network of helping hands so that people may settle where they wish. Others, who are not actively engaged in the escape operations, pool their money to help the cause."

"I see. So that means that even though the saloon is gone, there is still money available to those who need it."

"That's right. But we've a problem now, girl. A man named Jack Reese has gotten wind of my business." Catherine's eyes widened at mention of Reese, but Ned seemed not to notice. "I've a hunch this Reese fellow is working for someone wealthy who has a bone to pick with one of the mine superintendents. Reese has masterminded a sabotaging operation at one particular mine, which brings me to the point of why I'm telling you all this. There's a young man named Connor, who's come west via the underground. He's wanted by the Mollies something fierce. It seems Connor knows more than he should, and Reese is out to silence him. Connor's testimony could put Reese behind bars for life."

"Connor O'Shay? The man you were planning to hire to work at the saloon?"

"Yes, he's the one. I've taken him under my wing for the

158

time being. It is my goal to travel back east with him and make sure he lives to tell his tale to the Pennsylvania authorities. He should be here any minute."

"Here?" Catherine questioned. "In this room?"

Ned nodded, and rose to begin his pacing anew. "This young fellow is in a heap of trouble. Unlike his brother, Connor did not commit the murder he is accused of. Reese framed him. But I don't really know why, not yet. Connor will be staying here with us. Since we're so short of funds, we will all have to share the same quarters. I'm sorry for the inconvenience, Katie. I'll do my best to see you have as much privacy as possible. I need you to be strong, girl. There's a rough road ahead of us before this mess comes to an end."

Catherine came to her feet, stopping her father with a touch to his arm. "I'll help you, Pa, you know I will. I don't mind sharing what little we have."

Ned Diamond gazed with loving eyes at his only child. "That's my girl," he said affectionately, ruffling her hair just as he'd done when she was a small girl.

Now that her father had shared his confidences with her, Catherine felt greatly relieved. Together, they might be able to work things out. She was about to tell her father that Jack Reese had been the one to torch the Diamond, when there was a light rap at the door.

"That must be Connor," Ned said. Quickly, he moved to open the door, and a young man stepped into the small room. "Did anyone follow you?" Ned asked in a low voice. Receiving a negative response, he nevertheless checked the narrow hall, then shut the door.

Catherine stood rooted to the spot, thoughts of Jack Reese momentarily forgotten as she stared at the young man before her. Connor O'Shay was not tall—in fact he was an inch or so shorter than Catherine—but he had a muscular build. His jet-black hair spilled in silky waves over his forehead, framing china-blue eyes that were hauntingly familiar. The smoothness of his fair skin was broken by two tiny half-moon scars on his left cheek, and there was a slight crook in his nose where it had obviously once been broken.

Ned made quick introductions, which the young man acknowledged with only a nod, shy and totally endearing. Then, he turned his full attention to Ned, who fired half a dozen questions at him concerning his movements and the present whereabouts of Jack Reese. Connor O'Shay answered slowly and precisely, his deep voice contrasting sharply with his youthful appearance. Catherine continued to stare at him, no doubt in her mind that this was Rory's brother. She had known the minute he stepped into the room. Though Connor's eyes were not yet overlaid with the cynicism that Rory had acquired over the years, he was, in many ways, a younger version of his brother. There was a certain self-assured air about both men, a dangerous aura tinged with the wariness of an animal who has been too long caged. The sense of power each projected was frightening in its intensity, and while Rory had learned to leash that force, Catherine had the distinct feeling that Connor had not yet acquired the same self-control. She wondered anew at the circumstances that could shape such men.

Ned Diamond was too wrapped up in his own thoughts to observe his daughter's reaction to Connor. In a few terse sentences, he ordered them both to stay in the room until he returned with the evening meal. Then, shrugging into his waist coat, he left the two of them alone.

Catherine stood motionless, completely fascinated by the young man. She wanted to ask him a hundred questions about Rory's early years, then sharply reminded herself of the vow she'd made to have nothing more to do with Rory O'Shay. But watching Connor was like seeing Rory as he might have been nine or ten years before, and the sight was not unpleasant.

"Please," she said, breaking the silence, "have a seat. We

haven't much room here, but what we do have is yours as well."

Connor glanced up and nodded his thanks, then took a seat on the edge of the bed since Catherine was standing in front of the only chair. He ran his palms nervously over his thighs, then abruptly stopped, and stared down at the worn, flower-patterned carpet. His unruly, windblown hair was blue-black in the lamplight. *Just like Rory's,* Catherine thought, remembering the night she'd run her fingers through Rory's fine hair . . .

"Do you mind?"

Catherine shook off her reverie and directed her attention to the cigarette in Connor's work-roughened hand. "Oh, no, of course not. You may smoke if you like, I don't mind. It's thoughtful of you to inquire."

"Thanks," he muttered, then struck a match to his boot and lit the hand-rolled cigarette. Acrid smoke curled upward to the high ceiling.

Another difference; Rory did not smoke. She watched Connor, noting the way he studiously avoided her gaze, looking around at the dingy surroundings. Catherine could not recall such shyness in Rory. Trying to put the young man at ease, she seated herself and smiled at him warmly. "My father tells me you are from the east," she began. "I suppose you know that my father and I are also from Pennsylvania."

"Yeah, I know," came the gruff reply.

"Schuylkill County to be exact," she continued, determined to ferret out some information about Rory's background. When Connor made no comment, she realized she would have to be more direct. "Where in Pennsylvania is your home?" she asked.

He lifted his head, arching one dark brow — a gesture of Rory's she'd often seen him make when he was confronted with her persistence. After taking a long drag on his cigarette, Connor replied. "Also Schuylkill County. I lived in Shenandoah. I worked in the Trenton mine, that is, until it was blown. My father is still there, along with my baby sister. With your father's help, I aim to go back and get them out. That coal town isn't fit even for the mules that haul out the coal."

"Yes," she agreed softly, "I well remember the hardships we endured while living in a coal patch." Pausing a moment to gather courage, she then asked, "So you have a father and sister . . . any other relatives?"

"None to speak of," he replied flatly. "My mother passed away of consumption a few years back. My father hasn't long to live, either—if he continues to work in the mines. That's why I came to Ned. Your father is the only man I know who can help my family."

"I see." She was glad she hadn't mentioned anything about Rory. Obviously, there was a rift between the brothers. But then what had she expected? Rory O'Shay was a confessed murderer. She suddenly felt a deep compassion for the young man sitting across from her. He had been left alone to care for his small family and to also deal with the Molly Maguires, two monumental tasks for a man of Connor's age. That Rory had abandoned his needy family and left them to bear the weight of his sins was unforgivable.

Impelled by a desire to help alleviate Connor's distress in whatever small way she could, Catherine rose and moved slowly toward the bed, stopping to stand beside him. At the touch of her hand on his shoulder, he glanced up uncertainly.

"I want you to know," she began, "that my father and I will do everything in our power to help you and your family. You need not carry this burden alone any longer."

Before Connor had time to answer, the door swung open and Ned Diamond stepped into the room, balancing a large tray in one hand as he tried to manuever the door shut again. Connor bounded to his feet to help him, and the quiet moment between Catherine and the young man vanished.

After they'd devoured the meager meal prepared for them by the landlord's wife, they discussed their plans for the next few days. If Connor was to clear his name, he had to go back to Pennsylvania. The trouble was that none of them had the money or the means to make the trip back east.

Catherine fell asleep mulling over their financial problems. There was only one thing in her possession that could help them now: Irish Fire. Even though Rory claimed the beast as his own, she could not afford to believe him. She would have to use the Thoroughbred as collateral for a loan.

She needed to find a bank willing to extend her credit without proof of the colt's ownership. That, she knew, would be a problem.

Chapter Eleven

After seeing personally to the delivery of the trunk for Catherine, Jenny Latham turned her horse and carriage toward home. She dreaded returning to the huge mansion atop Rincon Hill, and if not for Jasper, she thought ruefully, she would not return at all.

Although Albert's constant carping at the boy gave her plenty of reason for wanting to leave—Jasper didn't hold his fork properly, he talked too much, he deliberately lisped in Alberts' presence—Jenny paradoxically stayed on for the boy's welfare. If she left Albert, where would she and Jasper go? How could she manage to bring up the boy without the security of a home and unlimited funds? She was not skilled enough in any profession so that she could seek employment, and, from childhood on, there had always been a male figure at the center of her life—first her father, then J.D., and now Albert. Jenny had never had to make a decision on her own. Even now, Albert saw to the running of the household, along with all his other business and social duties. For Albert, there could be no other way, for he was a perfectionist and absolute master in his own home—a position Jenny never attempted to usurp.

As she considered her lifestyle and all the restrictions that went with being Albert Latham's "perfect" wife, she found herself making comparisons with Catherine Diamond. She admired Catherine's determination to shape her own destiny, her strength in the face of adversity, and the freedom she enjoyed. No wonder her good friend Rory O'Shay had taken such a keen interest in the young woman. Catherine was dynamic, beautiful, and possessed of a fiery independence. How glorious it must be to know that the decisions you made were entirely your own. Beside Catherine, Jenny felt colorless and meek. At twenty-seven, she felt old beyond her years, and the future stretched before her dark and lonely.

What would her life have been like had she defied her father that long ago day? What would Jasper be like if he'd had J.D.'s sturdy guidance?

With recent memories of J.D., Jenny's thoughts became darker as she turned into the circular drive that led to the main entrance of the house. Alighting from the carriage, she left it to one of the servants who appeared instantly.

She found her husband in his study, seated in his favorite leather wing chair close to the bay windows, which overlooked the drive and the street beyond. His white head was bent over a ledger spread across his lap. At his side was a decanter of brandy and a half-empty crystal snifter. Over his black breeches and pristine white shirt, he wore a knee-length, red velvet smoking jacket with slim, garnet lapels. Hearing her enter, he closed the book and looked up.

"Where have you been?" he asked, his watery blue eyes taking in every detail of her attire.

Irritated by his failure to give her a civil greeting, she closed the door rather more sharply than she meant to. Had she been a business associate or one of the many wives whose husbands he did business with, he would have immediately risen, gushing pleasantries as he offered a chair. But she was merely his wife, a woman who had fallen from virtue even before he'd first laid eyes on her. In all their years of marriage, Albert never let her forget her past.

"Good afternoon, Albert," she said in a toneless voice. She wished she had the gumption to walk over and pour herself some brandy, but Albert would not allow her to even touch the decanter. She maintained her position near the door, ready to flee should his beady gaze and cold manner become too unbearable. "I did not expect to find you home so soon," she ventured.

"Obviously. Where have you been? I'm told you left some time ago, giving no one any indication of where you were headed or what you were about. You know I disapprove of any excursions without a proper escort."

Even now, after all these years, Albert Latham feared his young wife would return to her scandalous ways. Did he think she would take a lover? She smiled to herself, thinking of the night J.D. had made love to her in this house, right beneath Albert's glittering roof. She wished she had the courage to fling the details of her adultery in his hateful face.

"I was visiting a friend."

"Who?" he demanded.

"You—you don't know her. She is an invalid," she lied, "who lives in a part of the city where you would never be seen. She has no family and—"

"And you took pity on this wretched soul. Really, Jenny, can't you find something more uplifting to do with your time?" he complained. "The way you personally cater to every stray in this city is sickening. It isn't proper. There are missions whose sole purpose is to care for the sick and needy. You certainly don't need to be dirtying your own hands in their affairs. If you insist on helping unfortunates, then let us make a contribution to one of the churches or missions and be done with it. You've enough duties right here in your own home."

"I enjoy visiting those who are house-bound. And as for my duties here, you know very well it is you, not I, who sees to the management of this household. I've barely enough to keep me occupied each day!"

"Do not raise your voice to me, Jenny. You have duties aplenty, and the fact that Jasper is running wild again only convinces me that you are not properly discharging those duties."

Jenny was instantly alert at mention of Jasper. "What do you mean 'running wild?' What has Jasper done to make you say such a thing?"

"What hasn't he done?" Albert roared, tossing his ledger onto the table and coming to his feet all in one motion. "That whelp has been carrying on all day in your absence. I allowed him to join me at my midday meal, and not five minutes had passed before he spilled his milk and began sniveling like a girl five years his junior. I've told you time and again he belongs in a strict school where the people in charge are accustomed to such behavior. I'm having someone check into such a school this very moment. No longer will I tolerate such behavior under my roof!"

"No! Albert, you can't—I won't allow you to take Jasper away from me!"

"If you can't handle the child on your own, Jenny, I see no other solution to the dilemma."

"What dilemma? He spilled his milk, Albert, that is all! It isn't every day you allow him to join you in the dining room."

"And for good reason! The boy has a lisp that makes my skin crawl! No child of twelve should stutter and carry on so; it's abnormal."

Jenny clenched her fists, keeping her arms at her sides as she desperately tried to control her emotions. It would be a mistake to tell Albert that Jasper only became nervous and acquired a lisp in his presence. That would only affirm Albert's domineering control of his little family, and if there was one thing Albert enjoyed in life, it was power over others. For Jenny to wallow and beg now would be a tactical error. They had had this conversation about sending Jasper away on more than one occasion, and the only reason Jasper still remained in the house was because Jenny always reverted to her role of meek little wife.

"I'm sorry he upset you, Albert. I'll have a talk with him."

Albert seemed satisfied with her quick apology. "See that you do. As to your outing today, I'll no longer tolerate such excursions. Is that clear?"

She nodded. "Very clear."

He walked across the room then, stopping briefly to bestow a cold, dry kiss on her temple. He did not touch her with his hands; there was only the fleeting touch of those dry lips. Jenny repressed a shiver of revulsion, tilting her head just so, as she had always done throughout their marriage. The only time Albert had held her hand was during the wedding ceremony, and that had only been to place the cool band of gold on her finger. Other than that, he kept his distance, limiting their physical contact to a chaste kiss on the forehead — once in the morning before he left for work, and again in the evening before they retired.

"I'm meeting some associates at the Bank Exchange this afternoon. I will not be home for dinner and will most likely be out late tonight. The staff has been informed of my plans, and a light meal is being prepared for you and your son."

Your son, never *our* son. Jenny nodded in docile agreement. Albert moved to the door, and stepped out into the hall, leaving the door open. That he had not shut it, was a pointed reminder that he expected her to promptly leave his private domain. Jenny was happy to do so; she had never been comfortable in the study, which seemed to symbolize everything she detested about her husband.

As soon as Albert made his exit for the night, Jenny sought out her son and found him alone in the nursery. Actually, the room was no longer a nursery, but she continued to think of it as one. She reminded herself that she must stop thinking of Jasper as her "baby." At twelve, he was wise beyond his years, with a surprisingly realistic view of the world around him. In this respect, as in many others, he was much like J.D.

She found him sprawled on the floor playing with two hand-carved wooden dragons one of the Chinese servants had given him. One was dark and menacing; the other was golden and radiated goodness. Between the two dragons, lay another figurine, a delicate Chinese Princess. Jasper hadn't heard the door open, and Jenny stood for a moment listening to the make believe words he gave to each of the dragons.

Holding the golden dragon in his right hand and raising it high, he proclaimed, "If you hurt the princess again, old dragon, I'll slay you! You are old and mean and I have the power to destroy you!"

"Ha!" Jasper continued, now lifting the ugly dragon with his other hand. "You are only a young dragon. Your powers are useless against me, for I will merely send you far away and you'll never see your princess again."

Jenny closed her eyes, pressing back the tears. The heartbreaking little drama was all too clear. She was the princess and the dragons were Jasper and Albert.

"Jasper," she said quietly, opening her eyes.

Jasper dropped his toys, looking up. "Mama!" he cried. "You're home, finally you're home!" In a minute, he was on his feet and bounding across the room to her, his arms outstretched.

Jenny knelt and gathered her son to her in a tight embrace, stroking his golden brown curls. "Yes, I'm home, darling. Next time I go on an outing, I'll take you with me, I promise."

Jasper clung to her. "I hope so, Mama. I don't want to stay here alone ever again. Father was—he was mean to me today. He yelled at me and told me he was going to send me away. You won't let him send me away, will you, Mama?"

"No, darling, of course not. Your father just had a great deal on his mind today. He's not going to send you away, so I don't want you worrying about such things. There now, don't cry. I'm home now." She rocked him gently until, very bravely, he backed out of her embrace and wiped his eyes with his shirt sleeve. Jenny smiled and gave him a wink. "That's a good boy. No more tears and no more sad thoughts. Shall we read a story together?"

He looked down at his shoes. "No, I'm too old for stories," he replied quietly.

"Oh yes, I'd quite forgotten. Very well then, what would you like to do?"

He tilted his boyish face up to hers and said brightly, "I want to go and visit Rory. I want to ride his horse, Mama. Can we, please?"

She shook her head. "Not today, darling. But soon, baby, very soon."

He shoved his hands deep into his pockets. "I'm not a baby," he said sulkily.

Jenny reached out to smooth a stray curl that had fallen across his brow. "I didn't mean to imply that you're a baby, darling. It's just that to me, you'll always be my baby. Even when you grow to be a man, you'll be my baby."

Jasper screwed his face into a grimace that soon changed

to a smile beneath his mother's loving gaze. Impulsively, he flung his arms around her neck, and said simply, "I love you, Mama."

Jenny held him tightly. "I love you, too."

With all her heart she wished J.D. could be with them to share the embrace.

Night fell swiftly, and darkness cloaked the world beyond the gaslit windows of the stately homes on Rincon Hill. Jenny, her elaborate toilette completed, paced restlessly up and down her bedchamber. Attired in a flowing pink satin robe and filmy nightgown that brushed sensuously against her skin, she felt nervous and vulnerable. Albert had not yet returned home and it was already very late. She didn't expect him now until morning. In truth, she did not care if he ever returned home. At the moment, she thought only of J.D. Would he come to her this night? Would he take her in his arms and make slow, savage love to her once again?

She waited anxiously in the silence, every nerve jumping at the commonplace sounds of the night. With every tick of the clock, every creak of the big wood house, she imagined J.D.'s approach. Would he come through her bedroom door or the window? Both were unlocked, and she had even left the balcony windows open wide, hoping J.D. would come through them into her arms.

She waited in vain. By the stroke of midnight, he still had not come. Frustrated, she leaned over to extinguish the gas lamp on her nightstand. Her long, unbound brown hair brushed against the table top, shining brightly in the lamplight for a moment before the room grew dark. She pushed the strands away, wishing it was J.D.'s hand running through her tresses.

Dear Lord, she wondered, what was to become of her? How could she carry on a normal life while she waited each night for a phantom lover? This was total surrender, she realized with a start, this longing to be touched, this yearning to have her passionate needs satisfied—and this was exactly what J.D. had intended for her! He wanted her to lie awake at night and wonder if he would ever return. He wanted her to experience the same anguish he had gone through.

He was cruel, she decided. So very cruel. And yet, she wanted him. Would always want him.

Barefoot, she moved to the balcony overlooking the circular drive and the deserted street beyond. A misty, gray fog hovered above the ground, rolling in gently from the bay to cloak the dewy night. Jenny stared into the darkness, trying to discern human movement where there was none. A dog's bark echoed faintly in the distance, followed by the clatter of carriage wheels. Before her own home, nothing stirred. She stood for a long moment, leaning against the cool wood frame of the window, her nerves taut from the strain of waiting.

A sudden movement on the opposite side of the street caught her attention. A man in dark clothing stepped out of the shadows to lean sinisterly against one of the lampposts. He was tall and lean, with a wide-brimmed hat slanted low on his forehead, shielding his face. Jenny inhaled sharply. It was J.D. who stood there, casually smoking a cigar while he watched her home. She felt certain he knew she was standing near the window, watching him, waiting for him to come to her.

Jenny clutched her robe tightly as every nerve jumped and tingled with anticipation. Soon he would come to her, would ease the terrible ache in her heart with tender lips and soothing hands. Soon, she told herself . . . and this time she would not let him leave without her and their son.

She leaned forward, watching, waiting, going over and over in her mind what she would say and do once he stepped into her room.

J.D. continued his vigil for a full half hour, smoking his cigar, maintaining his casual, arrogant pose, lifting his face now and then to stare directly up at Jenny's bedroom windows. Then, abruptly, he moved away from the lamppost and strode away, swallowed up by the darkness.

"No!" she whispered, as she stretched to catch another glimpse of him.

But he was gone. There would be no comfort in his arms this night, nothing but the same mental torment she'd endured for so many years.

Depressed and frustrated, she moved listlessly to her bed and lay down, not bothering to remove her robe. Sleep was long in coming.

Once asleep, disconnected, disturbing dreams swam through her mind. Strange black shapes bobbed around her, brushing her thighs, moving upward until they covered her face. At first, the sensation was pleasureable, like silk against her bared skin, but then the pressure increased and became suffocating.

Jenny snapped her eyes open, a scream rising in her throat. A firm hand, clamped tight to her mouth, muffled any outcry as a man's body moved on top of her, crushing her against the mattress. Terror seized her, catapulting her into frenzied movements, thrashing desperately to free herself.

"Don't be frightened," a familiar voice crooned as the hand was removed from her mouth. "It is only me."

"J.D.! Are you mad? Wh—what are you doing?"

James Hambleton laughed insinuatingly, his fingers trailing over the fastenings of her dressing gown, undoing each one as he went. "What do you think I'm doing, dear Jenny?" he whispered huskily. "Have you so soon forgotten my promise of coming to you when you least expect me? Say you haven't for if you have, I do not know what my reaction will be."

Her robe, as well as her nightgown, were fully opened now, the swelling globes of her breasts bared to his view in the crystal clear light of dawn that filtered through the open windows. Jenny lay motionless, her chest heaving. "It was you standing across the street. Why didn't you come then, when it was dark?"

He skimmed his knuckles across her dark-tipped breasts, smiling as her nipples puckered into tight, tiny buds. "I'm no thief in the night. I've nothing to hide, nothing to fear."

"B—but it's morning. Soon the house will be filled with servants, and my husband—"

"To hell with your aging husband and his domestics." His gaze centered on her lush breasts as he bent his head, kissing them lightly, and said, "I couldn't care less whether or not he finds me in your bed. In truth, I hope he does."

Despite her fear, Jenny found herself warming to his caresses. The treacherous longing she'd felt the first night he'd entered her room was once again seeping through her body. "And—and what of the consequences to me and our son? Don't you care what happens to Jasper?"

J.D. immediately ceased his exploration, his head snapping up, his gaze hard and unrelenting as he looked into her eyes. "Are you saying the old man would dare harm my son because of something you did?"

Jenny lowered her lashes, afraid her eyes would tell all.

"Are you?" he demanded.

"N—no, of course not," she whispered, hating the lie. Why couldn't she just tell him the truth? Surely J.D. wouldn't take Jasper away, leaving her alone with Albert—

would he? "I — I only meant we would be scandalized and Jasper would naturally be hurt by the gossip."

A protracted silence hung between them, during which Jenny was acutely aware of J.D.'s weight atop her, his left leg intimately entwined with hers, and the not unpleasant pressure of his right hand as it clutched the tresses at the crown of her head. She brought her gaze up to meet his.

Hesitantly, she whispered, "I've missed you, J.D. Terribly."

For a moment, she thought he'd been moved by her blunt admission, for the hard light in his eyes wavered. But in the next instant, he had collected himself. Once again, he became the wary, unapproachable predator.

"Yes," he replied in a flat voice. "These past twelve years must have been hell for you as you floated from one gala to the next, adorned with gems and silks, a wealthy man at your side, ready to give you anything your heart desires. I suppose now you'll have me believe you fell asleep each night with thoughts of me lingering in your party-dazzled mind."

Although the words were cold, there was undeniable pain laced through them, and Jenny was hurt to the quick. Tears spilled over her lashes, coursing down her cheeks in warm rivulets. "I did," she whispered truthfully. "You have been the object of my every dream, the bright beacon in my dreary world."

"Empty words, Jenny. The truth is, you never attempted to contact me. Never. And yet you say you pined for me. Shall I be a fool again and believe you now, as I believed you when you plighted your troth to me so many years ago? I doubt you even recall that night."

Oh, God, how she remembered! It had been the happiest day of her life. The memory was blindingly clear to her even now. She had known then for certain she was carrying

J.D.'s baby, and the two of them had met at their favorite spot; a tiny, intimate clearing skirting a grouse covert, dotted with sumac cones and gray-mossed boulders amid a bed of lush fern. They had made love in those ferns, and much later, as J.D. had lovingly stroked her flat stomach, they had recited their own version of marriage vows to each other. And Jenny had honored those vows. To this day, Jenny had never given herself to another man, had never loved anyone, except Jasper, with such passion and commitment.

"I remember, James. I remember . . ."

Her use of his given name triggered some inner feeling he clearly did not want to acknowledge. With more force than was necessary, he tightened his hand in her tangled mane of hair, pulling so hard her neck was arched and bared to his hungry mouth. "Enough words," he said, his lips descending on that long, slim column. "I did not come here to talk."

Jenny's hands reached up to pull him to her as he fitted his body perfectly to hers. Even after the passage of so many years, even in the face of tragic misunderstandings, they still came together as truly as a magnet to steel, and their union was no less powerful. The potency of that attraction triggered passions too long suppressed, and Jenny soon abandoned any notion of talking through their misunderstandings.

Later, she told herself. Later, they would span the chasm of presumed betrayal that kept them apart. For now, they would grasp and cling to the glorious bond of mutual desire.

Garments were swiftly removed in a blinding torrent of naked lust that shook them both to the core. Then, with endless energy and infinite finesse, J.D. made love to her; with his hands, his mouth and his body. Slow and tender at times, fierce and passionate at others, he took her to heights she had never scaled before, leading her to the very brink of fullfillment, then letting her tumble back to full rationality before taking her once again along the hot, dizzing path to ecstasy.

Jenny writhed beneath him, digging her nails into the hard muscles of his back as she met him thrust for thrust. She moaned in unabashed pleasure, totally abandoning herself to the moment, with no feelings of guilt or regret.

"Feel good, baby?" he asked in a ragged voice as his hot tongue flicked the lobe of her ear.

"Yes," she panted. "Oh, yes!" She was almost there; one more touch, one more stroke, and, free of all constraints, she would plummet into that wondrous, uncharted region where only the spirit could enter, soaring to unimagined heights.

Together, they reeled over the edge in a primitive magical rhythm. At that moment, Jenny was sure that J.D. truly loved her, and the knowledge freed her to savor every nuance of their achingly sweet ascent into ecstasy.

He plunged into her a final time, spilling his seed deep within her, and then, they were both still, their heavy breathing and racing hearts gradually slowing to normal. Jenny, enjoying the weight of J.D.'s body, felt suddenly abandoned as he rolled off her. He did not reach to pull her close as he had always done after their lovemaking near the grouse covert. Instead, he clasped his hands behind his head and stared moodily upward, not saying a word.

Outside, the dawn's rays had spread to completely banish the darkness. Even now, the sounds of servants moving about the house could be heard from beyond Jenny's chamber. Jasper, his child's voice loud in the early morning stillness, could be heard pleading with his nanny. He was begging to be taken for a walk before breakfast, but

Claire would not agree to such an excursion at this hour.

Jenny felt J.D. stiffen at their son's voice. She chanced a look at him beneath her lashes. His features were harsh in the clear, telling light of dawn. Though the years had taken their toll, he was still more handsome than any man she had ever seen. She wanted to reach out and touch him, to assure him that Jasper had flourished in his absence. But she could not, for there had always been nagging doubts in her mind as to how well Jasper had really fared under the roof of her tyrannical husband.

"Jasper loves to be outdoors," she said in an attempt to explain something of the boy's day-to-day existence. "This is a daily argument he has with his nanny."

J.D. had a murderous look in his eyes. "Then why not let him take a walk in the morning?" he demanded. "Is there any reason to keep the child locked in this pathetic household?"

Jenny did not know how to reply. Albert had established the child's rigid schedule — breakfast promptly at seven each day, with lessons immediately thereafter.

"I — I suppose it could be arranged," she said.

"You suppose?" he thundered, pushing himself up to a sitting position. "Exactly what stands in the way of Jasper's going outdoors in the morning? See that he has a walk each morning, Jenny, as well as anything else he desires." Agitated, he bowed his head and drew a deep breath, exhaling slowly.

Jenny rolled toward him, propping herself up on one elbow, covering her breasts with the sheet. "Please, don't raise your voice. Albert might hear you."

J.D. snapped his head up, his gaze bright with anger. "I don't care if the whole damned world hears me. That's my son out there!"

"I — I know, but — "

"Then, you see to it he has whatever he wants! If not, I'll take the boy with me and the matter will be settled."

At those terrifying words, Jenny reached out and touched his shoulder. "J.D., don't talk like that. Jasper is my life! I couldn't bear to be without him! If you must take him, then take me, too—don't leave me here alone."

He shrugged away from her touch, at war with his emotions. Abruptly, he stood and began dressing, slipping into his clothes with quick, jerky movements. When he was finished, he moved toward the windows. Just before exiting, he said, "If I take you anywhere, Jenny, it will be because you came to me, not because I came to you."

Chapter Twelve

For Catherine, the night spent at the boardinghouse seemed endless. She did not get much sleep. She was too consumed with worry over finances and the threat that Jack Reese posed to her and her father. Every time she closed her eyes, she would see Reese's squinty eyes and hear his raspy voice. Rather than risk crying out from a nightmare, she passed the wee hours of the morning staring up at the ceiling. The sounds coming to her from beyond the makeshift partition — two quilts which Ned had hung wall to wall — told her that the two men had not fared any better through the night. The small room was heavy with the tension created by strangers sharing such cramped sleeping quarters. Catherine hoped she could obtain a loan soon, so they could leave the boardinghouse behind them.

As soon as the sun rose, Ned and Connor were up and about. Catherine stayed abed, knowing the men had risen early only to leave the room and give her some privacy.

"We'll be downstairs, Katie," her father called out to her. "Join us as soon as you can."

As soon as she heard the door close behind them, Catherine arose and began to dress. She had just started to brush her hair when there was a knock at the door. Her hands froze in midair. "Who — who is it?" she called. Worries about Jack Reese, coupled with lack of sleep, had left her nerves jangling.

"It's me, love. Sallie. I saw your father downstairs and he told me to come up."

"Sallie!" Catherine dropped her hairbrush and ran to the door.

Sallie Burt stood before her, shockingly lovely in a low-cut crimson gown that hugged each voluptuous curve. The auburned-haired beauty gave Catherine a wide smile, then wrapped her in a warm embrace.

"I can't tell you how good it is to see you, love! I was worried sick about you after that O'Shay fellow spirited you away. You must tell all, Katie. Where did he take you?"

Catherine pulled her friend into the small room, and said excitedly, "Oh, Sallie, how I've longed to talk to you since that night. So much has happened. I—I hardly know where to begin."

"The beginning is a good place."

Catherine felt herself blush, and she turned her face away, hoping that Sallie wouldn't see her embarrassment. But Sallie had noticed, and she immediately forced her friend to look at her.

"Why, Catherine Diamond, if I didn't know better, I'd say I was looking at a woman head over heels in love!"

"Don't be absurd."

"Don't you! You're positively *glowing!*" She laughed throatily, thoroughly enjoying the moment. "The first moment you spoke of Rory O'Shay, I knew he would be the man to win your heart. If you weren't so dear to me, I might find cause to be jealous. Come now, love, tell me all about him."

Catherine glanced up, hesitant at first. After days of emotional ups and downs, however, the relief of being with an old friend won out, and she began to tell Sallie all about the days—and nights—she'd spent with Rory. She left out no details, and even included her suspicions about Rory and Jenny once being lovers. Catherine knew she could trust Sally. Whatever was said between them would go no further. So the words tumbled forth—about Rory and herself, Jack Reese, Jenny and Jasper—even about Connor and his reasons for being in San Francisco. Forty minutes had passed before she was finished.

"Well, well . . ." Sallie said, sitting down on the edge of the narrow bed, digesting all the news. "So that's why your father has been acting like a cat on a hot tin roof for the past few months. Goodness, I had no idea."

"No one did. You know my father. He can be very secretive when he wants to."

"So all the Diamond profits have been used to help destitute families back east?"

"Yes, and there is no end in sight. My father is determined to help Connor clear his name. And I'm afraid he's just as determined to see Rory strung from the nearest tree."

"I see. And how do you feel about that?"

"I . . . I'm not sure, exactly. I can't believe Rory could ever murder anyone. He was so—so gentle with me, and—"

"And you're in love with him."

"I never said that."

"You didn't have to."

Catherine let out an exasperated sigh. "How can I possibly be in love with the man? I just met him. Besides, he—he obviously has feelings for Jenny Latham."

"But Jenny Latham is a married woman. I've heard of the Lathams, Catherine. The old man has more money than Croesus. As for the little boy being Rory O'Shay's son, I can hardly believe it. Albert Latham has been married to Jenny for *years*."

"But Rory knew Jenny when they both lived in Pennsylvania. From what I can gather, they were very close. Perhaps Jenny was carrying Rory's child when she came here."

"Perhaps," Sallie said thoughtfully. "But if the manner in which O'Shay claimed his colt is any indication of how he protects the things he cares about, I doubt he would have ever allowed the woman he loved to leave him—especially if she was carrying his child."

Catherine brought her gaze up to meet Sallie's. "My goodness," she breathed, feeling an odd sense of elation. "I hadn't thought about it in that light. Do you know, Sallie, you just may be right."

"Of course I am, love. Think of how he spirited you and the horse away the night of the fire. His actions spoke volumes. I've learned people are not what they say but what they do, and your Rory O'Shay is a perfect example. Neither hell nor high water could have kept him from protecting you and the colt that night. Make no mistake about it, Rory O'Shay couldn't possibly be the father of Jenny's son. He wouldn't stand for another man raising his child."

Hope bubbled up in Catherine's heart, and she smiled. "Oh, Sallie, even if your assumptions aren't correct, and Rory is Jasper's father, I feel much better than I ever have since that morning Jenny rode up to the cabin and talked with Rory. I'm glad you came here today."

Sallie reached out and gave her friend a hug. "Don't you worry, Katie. If you have your heart set on Rory O'Shay—which you do—then you'll have him. After all, you're Ned Diamond's daughter, and the Diamonds always get what they want."

No, Catherine thought, we don't. But she didn't say the words aloud. For once, she would let herself believe that all her dreams could come true.

Another knock sounded on the door then, and Catherine moved to open it. She was startled to find Jenny Latham standing in the darkened hall.

"Jenny!"

"Good morning, Catherine," Jenny replied. "Forgive me

for coming unannounced, but I did want to see how you and father were getting along and to ask if there's anything you need."

"I—no, we're fine. But how kind of you to inquire. Please, come in." She motioned Jenny inside, cringing inwardly at the shabbiness of the rented room. Quickly, she moved to clear away her father's overcoat, which was draped over the back of the only chair. As soon as Jenny was seated, Catherine introduced her two friends.

If Jenny was shocked by Sallie's attire or conspicuous make-up, she never let on. Seeing this, Catherine's respect for her rose.

Jenny, dressed sedately in a dove-colored day dress complete with matching gloves, smart hat, and pearl-trimmed reticule, gave Sallie a gracious smile. She appeared completely at ease in the dingy surroundings, and immediately gave her two companions her full attention.

She actually looks pleased to be here with us, Catherine thought. As the awkward moments passed, and Jenny opened a linen napkin filled with fresh-baked croissants, Catherine felt herself warming toward the young society matron. As the three women nibbled on the buttered, still warm pastry, Jenny asked endless questions about Catherine and Sallie's days at the Diamond Saloon. She seemed genuinely amused by Sallie's quick wit and outrageous stories. She especially enjoyed hearing about Sallie's encounters with the Chinese cook Fong.

"What is Fong doing now?" Catherine asked Sallie. "I hope he's been able to find employment."

"Oh, he has, love. He's working in a teahouse in Little China."

"And you?" Catherine asked. "How have you fared since the fire?"

Sallie gave Catherine a quick wink. "Don't you worry about me, Katie. I saved enough of my tips to see me through any dark days. Of course, that's what any smart girl would do. In fact, all of the girls who worked for you and your father are doing quite nicely. But keep in mind, if your father ever reopens the Diamond, we'll all come back straightaway."

"I will keep that in mind, Sallie. Thank you."

There was another knock at the door. "Katie?" her father called.

"Yes, Pa. Come in. The door is unlocked."

Ned Diamond stepped into the small room, followed by Connor. With five people crowding the chamber, it was near to bursting, but Catherine didn't mind. She was surrounded by people who meant a great deal to her, and she included Jenny Latham in that list. Catherine suspected that, for all Jenny's wealth and her sweetness, the young woman had very few friends. She could see the loneliness in Jenny's eyes, could hear it in the soft tones of her voice. And Catherine wondered again at Jenny's past, and the woman's reasons for living on Rincon Hill with a man she obviously did not love.

Ned Diamond offered his hand to Jenny. "Mrs. Latham, how very nice to see you again. The things you had delivered for my Katie are lovely. As soon as we're able, we'll repay you."

"Oh no, you won't," Jenny replied. "Consider them a gift. I insist."

Connor stood apart, leaning against the doorjamb, with his hands deep in his trouser pockets. For a moment, his blue gaze lingered on Jenny, recognition lighting his eyes. Then, he turned his attention to Sallie, who gave him a sly wink and a sloe-eyed smile. Connor acknowledged the flirtatious look with a nod and a slight quirk of his lips.

"Connor," Catherine said, noticing Sallie's interest. "You've met Sallie, haven't you?"

"Briefly," he replied. "I was downstairs with Ned when she came looking for you this morning." His gaze did not leave the auburn-haired beauty's animated features.

"And my other guest?" Catherine inquired, wondering if Connor would remember Jenny from days gone by.

Connor reluctantly pulled his gaze from the saucy Sally. "Hello, Jenny," he said, looking straight into her pale face. "How have you been?"

"Connor," she whispered. "I—I've been well. And you?"

"Fine," he answered softly. Tension between the two ran through the air like lightning.

Braving the brooding look he gave her, Jenny asked, "What brings you to San Francisco?"

"For the moment, I'd rather not say," he replied.

Catherine, growing uncomfortable, stepped into the breach. "Connor is staying here at the boardinghouse."

"I see," Jenny said, rising. To Connor, she said, "I hope we can meet sometime soon and talk. It . . . it has been too many years since I've seen you."

Connor nodded slowly, making no comment, and Catherine had the distinct feeling that the last thing Connor wanted to do was spend time alone with Jenny Latham.

"I must be going now," Jenny continued.

Before she left, she and Catherine arranged to meet for lunch the next day.

Sallie was next to make her exit with a rustle of red silk.

"May I see you downstairs?" Connor asked from his post by the door.

Sallie tilted her head, her burnished curls glistening. "You may escort me to my *door* if you're good," she replied, tucking her arm in his. As the two made their way through the hall, her laughter floated back to Catherine.

"I should have warned Connor about Sallie," Ned said, closing the door.

"Warned Connor?" Catherine repeated, shocked. "I'd say it is Sallie who should have been forewarned. Did you see the scowl on Connor's face at the sight of Jenny? I thought the poor woman would wilt."

"I'd say Mrs. Latham is made of sturdier stuff than either

of us can imagine. As for Connor, I believe his guilt is getting the best of him. He knew Jenny years ago, and if not for his recent past, I think he would have been glad to see her."

"What do you mean?"

Ned hesitated. "Do you remember I told you Connor was involved in sabotaging a mine back east?"

"Of course I remember."

"Well, it was the Trenton mine he blew. Jenny's maiden name was Trenton. The mine Jack Reese forced Connor to sabotage belonged to Jenny's father. The operation was a small one, and the explosion put the man right out of business. It will be years before he ever gets himself back on his feet. I'd say what Connor is feeling now is pure guilt."

"But what reason could Jack Reese have for wanting the Trenton mine out of business?"

"I don't know, Katie. Something about the whole affair isn't right. It's possible one of the Mollies might have been engaged in a vendetta with Samuel Trenton, but I doubt it. Even when we were living in Raven Run, Samuel Trenton ran a smooth operation. He was shrewd enough to recognize the Brotherhood and their growing strength. No, I think Reese framed Connor for a different reason."

"Such as?"

Ned shook his head. "I don't know. I just don't know."

"Do you think Connor ever intends to tell Jenny about the explosion?"

"Unlike his older brother, Connor O'Shay is a good man. He'll confess to Jenny and explain the circumstances. And in the meantime, I'll be trying to find a way to get us back east. Perhaps then, I'll be able to figure out what Jack Reese is up to. Soon, this whole mess will be behind us, Mary Catherine, and we'll be able to get on with our lives."

Yes, Catherine thought as she watched her father move about the room, preparing to go out for the day, soon our lives will return to normal. But not until she had acquired the money they so badly needed. She could not ask Jenny for a loan; the woman was far too generous and would, Catherine had no doubt, insist on *giving* the money to her. Catherine would take no charity.

Snatching up her empty drawstring purse, she told her father she would see him later, then darted out the door.

Chapter Thirteen

"I am sorry, ma'am. Surely you understand you haven't sufficient collateral. If in the future your financial situation changes, I will be more than happy to reconsider. As things stand, I'm afraid I cannot help you."

The bank officer droned on and on, and Catherine, seated across from him in a straight-backed chair, listened with only half an ear. She had heard the same story from nearly every banking institution along Montgomery Street. She had been sure that the people at Wells Fargo would be able to help her. After all, her father had done business with them for many years. But it was now painfully clear that even this bank would not loan her money while there were debts still outstanding on a property that had burned to the ground.

Moreover, stories of the suspicious fire had been printed in the *Call, Chronicle,* and *Examiner.* Each of the newspapers had mentioned that Ned Diamond had let his fire insurance lapse, and no reputable bank was willing now to have further business dealings with the Diamonds.

The man rose, nervously waiting for Catherine to depart. Perhaps he thought she might make an ugly scene, ranting and raving that he give her the funds she needed. But she was too weary and depressed to do more than mutter her thanks.

She clutched her small drawstring purse and headed toward the door. She had taken only two steps before the elderly loan officer was beside her, handing her a sheet of paper.

Catherine glanced up at him, noting the look of pity on his wrinkled countenance. That he should feel sorry for her made Catherine uncomfortable. "What is this?" she asked, her voice wary.

The man quickly pressed the paper into her palm. "It is the name of a person who may be able to help you. You see, Miss Diamond, I know your father and consider him to be a good man. I truly wish I could lend you the money you need, but since I cannot, you might find the name on this paper helpful. There is a man, J.D. Hambleton, who has recently arrived in San Francisco. He is president of the Hambleton Bank in Philadelphia, and has business interests here. It is my understanding that Mr. Hambleton sometimes extends personal loans to businessmen in San Francisco. Now mind you, I cannot promise that Mr. Hambleton's business ethics are anywhere near those of Wells Fargo. Nevertheless, your father might be able to strike a deal with him. It is my belief that Mad Ned can handle his own with the likes of J.D. Hambleton. Of course, I am not suggesting you seek out Mr. Hambleton on your own. I strongly advise you to let your father handle this business transaction."

Catherine looked down at the scrawled name and address. "Thank you," she murmured. "I appreciate your assistance."

The man appeared vastly relieved. "I only regret that

Wells Fargo cannot be of more comfort in your time of need. Please, give my regards to your father." He held his office door open for her and then returned to his desk.

Catherine moved quickly across the main floor of the bank, and once on the street, she headed up the throughfare toward the offices of Hardle and Hardle, hoping she would be able to have a private audience with J.D. Hambleton immediately. She didn't want to involve her father in this transaction. She wanted to surprise Ned with the train fare to Pennsylvania—and some extra money to pay their most pressing bills. Besides, she reasoned, her father had enough worries to contend with, and though J.D. Hambleton's business practices might not be strictly aboveboard, she was certain she could keep the situation under control.

The huge plate glass windows of Hardle and Hardle's offices were papered with money from all nations, from the white notes of the Bank of England to the greenbacks of the United States. Sunshine streamed into the large main room, which was furnished with two massive desks, floor-to-ceiling bookshelves, a large globe of the world, several chairs, and a brass spittoon. The room smelled of ink and glue and stale cigar smoke.

Catherine stood still for a moment, unsure of how to proceed.

Suddenly, a door between the two desks was opened, and a tall, powerfully built man, strode into the room. In his large hands he carried a sheaf of papers, and his interest in them kept him from glancing up and noticing her. Dressed in black frock coat and breeches, with a pin-striped vest, white shirt, and gray ascot, he appeared every inch a businessman. A shock of brown-gold hair spilled over his forehead as he bent to read his papers.

"Excuse me," Catherine said. "I'm looking for a Mr. J.D.

Hambleton."

The man looked up, the expression in his brown eyes distracted until he took in her curvaceous form. "I'm Hambleton," he replied, his sensuous lips forming a slow smile. As he straighted his lean figure to its full height, Catherine saw that he was even taller than she'd thought. He sported long sideburns that were neatly clipped, but his chiseled upper lip and firm, square jaw were clean-shaven. Catherine felt a moment of déjà vu, as though she had seen his face at another time. But the feeling instantly vanished, leaving her rudely staring.

His deep voice cut into her perusal of him. "How may I help you? I don't recall that we've met."

Finding her own voice and composure, she said, "Forgive me. My name is Catherine Diamond." She extended one gloved hand. "One of my business associates gave me your name and suggested I speak with you."

"Business associate?" he asked skeptically. "What kind of business are you in, Miss Diamond?"

Catherine was not unaccustomed to the male viewpoint that a woman's place was in the home, and so she did not allow his tone of voice to upset her. "My father and I run a saloon. I've come to you because we are in need of a loan, and I've been led to believe you might be able to help us."

J.D. Hambleton raised his golden eyebrows. "I see. You do, of course, have collateral?"

"Of course."

"Very well then, now much money do you wish to borrow?"

Catherine took a deep breath. "Two thousand dollars," she said quickly. To her surprise, the man did not bat an eyelash.

He stood for a moment studying her, measuring her actually, and then, as if suddenly reminded of his manners, he said, "Please, have a seat, Miss Diamond. Would you care for something cool to drink?"

"No, thank you." She sat down and clasped her hands in her lap.

J.D. Hambleton remained standing, leaning casually against the doorjamb. "Two thousand dollars is a great deal of money. Why did you come to me? Am I correct in assuming no other bank would deal with you and your father?"

Catherine realized he had chosen to remain standing in order to maintain the upper hand in their dealings. But she was determined not to let this man cow her.

"I'll be candid with you, Mr. Hambleton. I've approached other institutions who have turned me away, but that does not mean I am a financial risk. Quite the opposite. My father and I were owners of the Diamond Saloon, which, before a recent fire, was a thriving business. Together, we built the Diamond up from just a drinking place into one of the most successful eating and gambling establishments in this city. My father and I are hard workers. Any loan we receive will be promptly repaid."

He nodded, maintaining an insufferable insinuating grin that grated on Catherine's nerves. "And the collateral you speak of . . . what is it?"

"A horse."

"Oh?"

"A Thoroughbred racer, to be exact. He is just a yearling and even now in training. I expect to race him within the next five months—and I expect him to win."

"Bold words. I don't know of many loans that have been made with an untried horse as collateral. Surely you have something more to offer."

His words, though easily spoken, seemed to have a deeper meaning. One that was not lost on Catherine. "No," she replied. "Only my Thoroughbred. Is it possible for us to do business, Mr. Hambleton?"

He did not give an immediate answer. Instead, he reached inside his frock coat and pulled out a slim, hand-rolled cigar. Rolling the slim stick between his thumb and forefinger, he stared at her, still smiling. "With a man like me, Miss Diamond, anything's possible." He stuck the cigar in his mouth, lit it, then blew out the match with a puff of smoke. "Tell me something, does your father know you're here?"

Catherine quelled the urge to avert her gaze. "That's entirely irrelevant. I'm my own woman, and was often left in complete charge of the Diamond Saloon. Any amount I borrow from you, I will repay in full."

"Yes, you will, I'll see to that. But there are those who would say a pact with me is a pact with the devil."

"A simple business deal is all I seek."

"Anything worth two thousand dollars could never be simple."

The man was frightening, and arrogant beyond belief. Suddenly, Catherine realized she had been a fool to visit J.D. Hambleton on her own. She had been warned. Standing, she said, "Forgive me, then, I believe I've come to the wrong man."

"I'll not deny that fact. You can turn and leave as any proper young lady would do—or you can stay. I've two thousand dollars in gold. It's yours, Miss Diamond. All you have to do is sign for it."

Catherine wanted to turn away, to walk out the door and never look back. But she needed the money . . . and she had come this far. She lifted her chin, gazing squarely at the man across from her. "And what are the terms?"

"No terms, other than your horse as collateral and you pay me whenever I demand."

"I could hardly agree to such an indefinite contract. We would need to set a specific time, a predetermined rate of payment."

"No. You pay me whenever I request payment."

"And if I haven't the money to pay you then?"

"Then I suppose I would be the proud new owner of a racer." He laughed, blowing a ring of smoke up toward the ceiling. "Really, Miss Diamond, didn't your daddy teach you never to look a gift horse in the mouth?"

"Not if the beast is a Trojan horse. You must think me mad to agree to such a deal."

"No, I think you're desperate. Here," he said, pushing away from the doorjamb and kneeling beside a small safe that stood next to one of the desks. He twirled the dial. "Let me see if I can't persuade you." After several spins, he opened the door and withdrew two cloth bags clinking with coin. He plunked each one down on the desk. "Two thousand dollars. Take it or leave it."

The temptation was great—too great.

"All you have to do is sign your name." He dropped a sheet of paper to the desktop, flipping it over and pushing it toward her.

"The page is blank," she said.

"Of course. Our agreement is a verbal one."

"Then why do I need to sign my name?"

"Only so I can remember where my money has gone."

Catherine hesitated, her hands still clasped in front of her. She eyed the bags filled with money, thinking of the dingy boardinghouse. She *would* be able to pay the loan back, she told herself. She would.

Quickly, she scrawled her name on the blank sheet of paper. Her clear gray gaze met his bold one. He took a long drag on his cigar, exhaling lazily, and again Catherine felt as though she should recognize him . . . and fear him.

Hastily, she pulled the heavy bags toward her.

"My best to you and your daddy," J.D. Hambleton drawled. "I trust you'll keep in touch."

Catherine said nothing. She merely nodded as she walked out of his office two thousand dollars richer.

Chapter Fourteen

Dusk was closing in on the city as Catherine left J.D. Hambleton's office. She'd spent all day seeking a loan. Now that she had the gold in her hands, she wasn't as happy as she thought she would be. Perhaps once her father used the money to pay off some of their debts she would feel better.

She tucked the bags securely under her arm and quickened her pace. Ned would be wondering where she'd been all day. She hoped that he'd be pleased when she showed him the bags of gold.

Preoccupied with what her father's reaction would be when he learned about the loan, Catherine did not hear footsteps close behind her. She jumped as a meaty hand gripped her elbow.

"If you value your life, then you'll do exactly as I say," a familiar voice rasped in her ear. Jack Reese tightened his hold as he directed Catherine off the near-deserted street and into a narrow alley littered with debris. "That's it, lady, just keep walking and you won't get hurt."

Catherine, her senses numbed by sheer panic, finally collected her wits when she realized they were headed away from any passersby and into the labyrinthine back alleys leading to the Chinese Quarter. Digging her heels in, she tried to wrest herself from his grasp.

But Reese merely twisted her arm behind her back and pushed her along roughly. "I said keep walking!"

Once again, panic swept over her. This was the man who had torched her saloon, and she was the only one who could testify to that fact and put him behind bars. There was absolutely no reason in the world why Jack Reese should allow her to walk out of the alley alive; he had every reason to want her dead. Moreover, she was carrying all that gold. By murdering her, Reese would not only ensure her silence, he would also net himself a handsome profit.

The tip of a sharp blade pricked the side of her neck, and Catherine felt herself growing faint. Something warm and wet trickled down between her breasts—blood! In another moment, she realized, with an odd sort of disbelief, it would all be over.

"Please," she heard herself whisper, "don't kill me."

"And why not?" Reese asked viciously, shoving her deeper into the alley. Although the bright lights of the city had now flickered on, the narrow, screened-off alley was cloaked in darkness. Two drunks, clutching near empty bottles, lay sprawled in the shadows, but when they saw the struggle between Catherine and Reese, they merely lowered their bleary-eyed gaze. There was no one else in sight to keep Jack Reese from slicing her throat from ear to ear.

"Goddamn little bitch," he hissed. "Do you think I'm going to let you live so you can turn me into the police? I been following you around all day, and I also know what you got in them bags." He laughed malevolently.

"You—you can have the gold," she said, trembling, feeling trapped and totally helpless. If she tried to move, the blade at her neck would plunge into her throat, spilling her life's blood. What a fool she'd been to leave herself so vulnerable to Reese's attack. Why had she decided to walk back to the boardinghouse? She certainly had enough money to have taken a horsecar.

"Please," she begged him in quavering tones. "The police don't know it was you who torched the saloon. I—I won't ever tell them, I promise. Just—take my money and go."

"Shut your mouth, bitch! You think I need Hambleton's filthy gold?" He laughed again, unable to keep from boasting, careless now about what he disclosed since he meant to kill her. "Hambleton paid me a fortune to have the Trenton mine blown sky high, and I didn't have to lift a finger. Connor O'Shay did all the dirty work for me!" He tore the sacks of gold from under her arm and threw them onto the cobblestones.

The bags split open, and the shiny gold coins rolled toward the two drunks, who suddenly came to life, scooping the gold up with greedy, grimy hands while Catherine watched in horror.

"No!" she managed to scream before Reese clamped a hand atop her mouth.

"So much for your precious gold!" he said, yanking her away from the drunks and pushing her deeper into the alley. "Your death, bitch, will be the bait to bring O'Shay out of hiding. That murdering lover of yours killed my best friend—and I'm gonna make him pay. I've a score to settle with Rory O'Shay."

"Rory?" she gasped, surprised even as she trembled under Reese's knife. "I—I thought it was Connor you were after."

"Connor is only a pawn in my plan to get his brother. When I'm through, Rory O'Shay is gonna wish his mama never spread her legs for his pa. I'm gonna kill everyone dear to that murdering son of a bitch, and while he's weeping over your dead bodies, I'm gonna put a bullet through his ugly heart. Yeah, that's what I aim to do. And you, missy, you're gonna be the first to go." Releasing her arms, he grabbed a handful of hair and jerked her head back savagely, nearly snapping her neck.

Catherine yelped in pain and renewed terror, seeing nothing now but the dark canopy of the sky. Her mind whirled, wildly seeking some way to escape what now seemed inevitable death. Instinctively, desperately, she brought her hand up and dug her sharp nails deep into the beefy arm that held the knife at her throat. Cursing loudly, Reese brought his fist up to clip her had beneath the jaw. Catherine's teeth clamped together with sickening force, the sharp edges biting into her tongue, instantly drawing blood which filled her mouth. She cried out, gagging on the hot, salty flow that seeped down her throat and out one corner of her mouth.

And then, miraculously, she heard a familiar voice behind her. "Let the lady go," Rory said with deadly calm, "or I'll shoot you where you stand." He cocked the gun he held at Reese's back, the metallic click loud in the deserted alley.

With lightning speed, Reese whirled around, placing Catherine as a shield between him and Rory.

Rory stood motionless. He had vowed never to kill again, but he was ready to do so now for the woman he loved.

Except that she stood between him and his target.

Rory's keen eye searched for some flaw in the picture, some vulnerable spot on which to train his gun. There were two possibilities — one between Reese's ugly, squinting eyes, the other his temple. Rory had always been a crack shot, and if he was forced to fire, he thought he could wing Reese without hitting Catherine.

"Let her go, Reese," Rory said again, playing for time. "You've a score to settle with me, not the lady."

"But she's part of the score," Reese retorted. "I'm gonna snap her neck just like you snapped Big Pat's. And you're gonna watch her die . . . just like I watched Pat die. I wanna watch you suffer while you listen to her pretty little bones snap and break. I wanna see the look in your eyes as you watch her fall listlessly to the ground . . . just like I watched Big Pat fall."

Rory scowled darkly then, and his fist tightened on the rosewood grip of his gun. He itched to pull the trigger and send Reese's ugly bulk toppling over backward. Steadying himself, he said in an even voice, "If I hadn't killed Pat, he would have killed me. Catherine is innocent. Let her go."

"Only when she's dead!" Reese spewed a stream of tobacco juice onto the ground before Rory's booted feet. "She ain't nothing but a whore," he sneered. "I'll let her go when she's dead!"

Those were the last words Jack Reese had a chance to utter. In the next instant, Rory's finger pulled back on the hair trigger of his gun, releasing a bullet that found its mark on Reese's left temple. The powerful impact sent Reese flying, arms and legs jerking spasmodically. As his body landed with a sickening thud, Catherine fell to the side, screaming in terror. Jack Reese's blood spattered her neck, chest, and arms. She wiped viciously at the warm, sticky liquid, crying uncontrollably as the gore covered her hands in long red smears. "Oh, Lord!" she cried. "Oh, Lord!"

And then Rory was beside her, pulling her to him in a hard embrace, letting her bury her face in his neck. "Hush," he soothed, his strong arms enfolding her, steadying her. "It's over," he whispered. "It's all right, Katie. You're safe now." He rocked her gently, squeezing her tight, murmuring comforting words.

Gradually, Catherine quieted, her sobs slowly diminishing until finally she was able to speak. "Is—is he dead?" She could not bring herself to turn around and view the body.

"I don't know," Rory answered, his voice flat. "He can't

harm you now, though. Are you able to walk?" he asked then. "You have to go home now, Catherine. I want you to go back to the boardinghouse." He pressed a coin into her hand. "Hire a carriage to take you back home. Don't talk to anyone, do you hear? Just go home and bolt the door behind you." He took a big checkered handkerchief from his pocket, and moistening it with the tip of his tongue, he dabbed at the splotches of blood on her face.

Catherine stared up at him with frightened wide eyes. "What are you going to do?" she asked.

He shook his head, still wiping away the telltale blood. "Don't worry about me, Catherine. You just take yourself far away from here."

"But if he's dead, we can't just leave him here!" She moved to look over his shoulder at Reese's body.

Rory stopped her. "Don't," he said. "I'll take care of the matter. Promise me you'll go directly home. If you must confide in someone, tell your father what has happened, but no one else. Do you hear?"

She nodded. "Y—yes. But what of you? Shouldn't we go to the authorities and tell them—?"

"Listen to me, Catherine," he said sternly. "I'm wanted for murder back east. No lawman is going to give me a chance to explain what happened here. They'll have me bound and gagged before I can even utter a word in my defense."

She was silent for a moment as the full impact of what had happened hit her. Rory O'Shay had just killed a man in her defense. Although he'd had the opportunity to shoot Jack Reese before this day, he had not. He had killed only for her sake. *For her, Rory had taken another man's life.* The realization was unnerving.

"I—yes, of course . . . I understand. I'll go back to the boardinghouse. But what of you, Rory? What if someone witnessed the scene?"

"No one saw," he replied, his blue gaze hard. He had wiped her face clean of the blood and there were now only small stains on the fabric of her gown. He handed her his handkerchief, closing her fingers atop the cloth with his own hands as he gazed deep into her eyes.

He wanted to say more to her, so much more. But now was not the time. And, he wondered, would there ever be a right time after today? He had killed one man, possibly two—the first in self-defense, the second in defense of the woman he loved. Now, even more so than before, there seemed to be no future for him. He would be running from the law forever. He could not tell Catherine that he loved her, could not take her in his arms and carry her away as he longed to do. He would be nothing but trouble for her, just as he had been nothing but trouble for his family. It seemed that wherever he went, he brought nothing but grief to those he held dear.

Shackled to cruel circumstance, he said only, "Get out of here, Catherine. Leave before anyone comes."

Catherine wanted to reach out to him, bridge the widening chasm between them. But the terrible note of desperation in his voice stopped her from saying anything further. She stood then, and turned her back on Rory and the man he'd killed for her. She ran out of the alley, toward the thoroughfare. The loss of the saloon and her father's debts suddenly seemed inconsequential compared to the sacrifice Rory O'Shay had just made for her.

"Mary Catherine! What is wrong? What happened to you?"

Catherine stood on the threshold of their rented room, her breath coming in ragged gasps as she stared up at her father. "Oh, Pa," she cried. The tenuous hold she'd had on her emotions suddenly broke in the face of her father's concern. The dam burst and she began to sob violently.

Ned Diamond moved to shut the door behind her, then gathered her into his arms. "What is it, Katie?" he asked again, awkwardly stroking her hair with one large hand. "What has happened to upset you like this?"

Catherine could not speak as she pressed her face against the rough material of her father's frock coat. Her tongue was swollen, and her mind was still reeling with the sound of the shot that had felled Jack Reese. Rory had *killed* a man for her. And now he was alone, seeing to the disposal of the body with no one to help him. Guilt and fear washed over her. Why had she listened to Rory and fled like a frightened schoolgirl? She should have stayed with him, should have insisted on giving him her support.

"Oh, Pa," she finally whispered. "It — it was horrible. I — I was walking along the street and the next thing I knew I was being dragged into an alley. He — he was going to murder me! He said he would kill me for all the trouble I'd caused him."

"Who? Who threatened you?"

"J — Jack Reese. He — he said he would have to kill me because I'm the only one who knows he set fire to the saloon. I — I meant to tell you about this before, but I — I didn't. Reese frightened me so."

"That swine!" Ned muttered, holding Catherine tight. "I'll see he pays for this! How dare he touch my little girl. I'll — "

"No, Pa! He — he's dead," she blurted. "Rory shot him."

"What?" Ned pulled Catherine away, holding her at arm's length, his gaze incredulous. "O'Shay shot Reese?"

Catherine nodded. "It was terrible. He — he had a knife to my throat, and Rory saved my life, Pa!"

"What was O'Shay doing there? I told you to stay clear of that man, Mary Catherine. He's a murdering rogue, not fit to walk the streets with law-abiding citizens!"

Catherine shook her head, stepping away from her father. "Don't, Pa. Don't be angry with Rory. He—he's not the man you believe him to be. If he hadn't killed Jack Reese, I would be dead."

"He *killed* the man?" The full import of Catherine's story finally sank in. "Good Lord, Mary Catherine, what has that O'Shay involved you in?"

Catherine closed her eyes, not able to bear her father's anger.

"Where is he now, Katie?"

Her eyes flew open. "I—I'm not certain. Why? What are you planning to do? You're not thinking of going to the police, are you? Promise me you won't, Pa. Please!"

"A man's been murdered. I have no choice but to contact the authorities and report the incident."

"To what end? So you can finally have Rory behind bars where you want him? No! I won't let you. Rory shot Jack Reese only to save my life. You can't go to the police. They—they'll put Rory in prison, perhaps worse!"

"It's where the scoundrel deserves to be," he replied. "Here. Dry your eyes and lie down. I'll send for a physician to look at you."

Catherine batted away the damp cloth he picked up from the washstand. "No, I don't need a doctor, and I will not let you go to the authorities. Hear me, Father, I *will not* let you condemn Rory. If you go to the police, I'll leave and you'll never see me again. Make no mistake, I mean what I say."

Ned Diamond shook his head, giving his daughter a sympathetic look. "You're distraught, Katie. O'Shay has put you through a terrible ordeal."

"Rory saved my life! It was Jack Reese who harmed me

and it is Reese whom you should be denouncing, not Rory! You should be glad Reese is dead and can no longer menace our family."

"I could never be joyous over a man's death and neither, young lady, should you."

"Well, I am," she spat out, crushed by her father's reaction to Rory's bravery. "I'm glad he's dead. He set fire to our saloon and nearly killed me in the act. If not for Rory coming into my room that night, I might not be here now. And if Rory hadn't intervened today, I most assuredly would be dead." She wiped vigorously at her tear-stained face, determined not to cry any more as she stood defiantly before her father.

Ned was silent for a long moment, his eyes narrowed. "I had no idea it was Reese who torched the saloon. Why didn't you tell me?"

"I—I was afraid for you. When it happened, I didn't know what you were involved in. All I knew was that the profits from the saloon were not being used to pay our debts. I—I wanted to help you, Pa, not worry you. I was afraid if I told you Reese had set the fire, you would confront him. I couldn't stand for you to be hurt."

"Ah, Katie," he said, his features softening. "Such a headstrong girl."

"You won't go to the authorities?"

A sad smile touched his lips. "Not if it means losing the only thing I hold dear in this life. I suppose if O'Shay sent you home, then he most likely had decided what he will do with the body. I'll leave this mess to him. But I warn you, if there's an investigation and your name is mentioned, I will not care a whit about O'Shay. It is you I am protecting here, no one else."

"Thank you, Pa," she whispered.

"Reese didn't harm you, did he?"

"No. I'm just a bit shaken is all. I—I think I would like to lie down now." She moved to the bed and lay down, allowing her father to pull a light cover over her shaking limbs. He picked up the damp cloth again and pressed it to her forehead. Catherine closed her eyes, whispering her thanks once again.

Ned merely grunted as he pulled the chair alongside the bed and sat down, taking his daughter's hand in both of his. He stayed there all night as Catherine slept.

Chapter Fifteen

Jenny's private carriage, drawn by two-in-hand and maneuvered by a skilled and straight-backed groom, pulled up before the dilapidated boardinghouse at precisely eleven in the morning. Catherine was waiting for her new friend, happy at the prospect of an outing. She couldn't stand to be cooped up in the boardinghouse worrying about Rory. Ned had fussed over her throughout the night, damning Rory again and again for "putting his little girl through such a trauma." She was dressed smartly in one of the gowns from Jenny's trunk, a printed silk and satin creation with a cuirass bodice and tieback skirt trimmed with pleats and bows. A delicate white lawn collar provided a pleasing contrast to her dark hair, which was swept up at the back and secured with a single blue ribbon. On her feet she wore a too-tight pair of Jenny's boots, black kid leather, adorned with blue and black ribbon rosettes.

The groom jumped down and helped her into the handsome, enclosed carriage.

"Catherine, how splendid you look," Jenny said as Catherine settled into the cushioned seat opposite her. "That outfit never looked so stunning on me. I'm glad you chose to wear it."

Catherine managed a smile, not wanting to discuss

clothing or any other trivial topic. "You're just being kind," she replied, wishing she could tell Jenny the whole sordid story about Rory and Jack Reese. But she could not. For Rory's safety, she had to keep her mouth shut.

Jenny's own ensemble was the very latest fashion—a smartly cut, medium-brown faille suit with single-breasted jacket trimmed in camel's hair, braid and fox fur. Atop her brown curls was a white felt hat adorned with brown feathers and faille drapery.

"No, I'm being honest," Jenny persisted, not noticing Catherine's somber mood. It was as if Jenny was bent on enjoying herself this day, and Catherine wondered if she, too, had moments she wished to forget. "It's really grand to be with you today! I've done nothing but pace the floor this morning. I'm so glad you accepted my invitation. An afternoon with a friend is just what I need."

"I'm looking forward to our outing, too," Catherine replied honestly. "How is Jasper?"

Jenny's lashes dropped at the mention of her son. "He is good," she said, a shade too quickly. "My husband decided to spend the day with our son, so he has taken Jasper with him. I suppose they will have lunch somewhere in the city—Albert did not give me any details."

Catherine ventured a personal question. "I see . . . does that upset you, Jenny?

The young woman answered, "Yes, the fact that Jasper is alone with Albert does bother me. I—I am rather worried about Jasper. He does not enjoy the time he spends with his father. Albert is a very demanding man; a little too demanding when it comes to Jasper."

"Perhaps today will be a turning point for them," Catherine suggested.

Jenny lifted her gaze to Catherine, her doelike eyes filled with pain. "I have little hope of their ever getting on, Catherine. Their relationship, at best, can only be described as stormy."

"I'm sorry," Catherine said into the silence that followed Jenny's candid words. "Jasper is such a sweet, well-behaved boy, it's a shame his own . . . father cannot accept him the way he is." Inwardly, she winced when she said the word "father."

Jenny turned to stare absently out the window. "Yes," she agreed softly, "it is a shame Jasper's own father cannot accept him."

From that moment until they arrived at the What Cheer House, near the wharves, Catherine became increasingly depressed. Even after hearing Sallie's sensible opinion on the matter of Jasper's paternity, Catherine still had reservations. *Rory.* What had he gone through last night after the shooting? Suddenly, she didn't want to think about Jasper, Jenny, or Rory. She didn't want to think at all.

Both women were relieved when the carriage pulled up to the small restaurant that was fast becoming famous for its à la carte meals. Catherine was somewhat surprised that Jenny would choose to dine in a place that was so popular with working-class people and tourists. But the petite, quiet Jenny seemed to be full of surprises.

The What Cheer House was located in a five-story building adjacent to the Original House. A favorite with out-of-town visitors, the charming little inn offered such amenities as wood burning fireplaces in all its public rooms, and even a thoughtfully selected library for guests to browse through. Robert Woodward, owner of Woodward's Gardens, a favorite haunt of San Franciscans, had amassed a small fortune from the House.

After the two women had been seated in the cozy dining room and ordered their meal, their conversation turned to very light topics, such as the theater engagement Jenny had that evening.

Catherine ate her hearty lunch with gusto. She had not enjoyed a meal so much since the rabbit stew she'd shared with Rory in the mountain cabin. Thinking about those precious moments they'd spent together, she had to mentally shake herself when she thought she heard his voice.

Looking up, she realized she had indeed heard Rory O'Shay. He now stood beside their small table. There was concern in his eyes as he looked down at Catherine.

"Good afternoon, ladies," he said. Although he spoke to both women, he did not take his eyes from Catherine.

"Rory! What a pleasant surprise," Jenny exclaimed, her brown eyes suddenly alight with mischief. "Catherine and I were just about to have dessert. Won't you join us?"

"If Miss Diamond doesn't mind."

"Of course I don't mind," Catherine murmured. "Please, sit down." He looks pale, she thought, wondering again what he must have gone through to take care of Reese's body. Oh, Rory, she said to herself, I should have stayed with you. I should have been there to help you last night.

Pulling out a chair for himself, Rory called to the waiter to bring him a slice of apple pie and a cup of coffee. Catherine noticed that he used the waiter's given name. Obviously, he was a familiar face at the What Cheer House. As the waiter brought their desserts, he asked about Rory's health and whether or not he was enjoying his stay in the city.

"Mmm," Jenny said, tasting the hot apple pie. "This tastes almost as good as the pies your mother used to bake, Rory. Do you recall how the four of us would sit around the table, devouring a whole pie, and how your mother would scold us for being so greedy!"

"I remember," Rory replied. "Those days seem so long ago."

"Yes, they do. I wonder whatever became of Margaret. Do you know?"

Rory shook his head. "I suppose she's still in Pennsylvania. I'm surprised the two of you didn't keep in touch over the years. As I recall, you were inseparable."

"Inseparable, indeed!" Jenny replied with a laugh. Then, turning to Catherine, she said, "Forgive us for talking of times past. How terribly rude of us."

"I don't mind," Catherine assured her. "Please, continue. Who is Margaret?"

"Margaret was my closest friend from—well, from the time I could talk, I believe. I can't remember a day we didn't spend together."

"Until you met Jimmy," Rory said.

A soft radiance suffused Jenny's face. "Yes," she murmured, "Until I met J.D." To Catherine, she explained, "J.D.—Jimmy to his boyhood friends—was my first and only beau before I met my husband." Here she paused, her lashes lowered over sparkling eyes. "He and Rory were close friends and worked together in my father's mine. The four of us—Rory, Margaret, J.D., and myself—could always be found together after the men were finished working in the mines."

"And our favorite pastime was eating my mother's apple pie," Rory added.

As she listened to their nostalgic recollections, Catherine felt a heavy burden being lifted from her heart. Jenny had been in love with someone called J.D.—and not with Rory—as Catherine had mistakenly assumed from the conversation she'd overheard at the cabin. Rory was not Jasper's father! She felt giddy with the revelation.

How absurd to have ever thought that Jenny and Rory had been lovers, conceived a child, and then chose to live apart!

Her face must have registered her happiness, for Rory said, "I see the apple pie is to your liking, too. Does the taste perhaps bring back special memories for you as well?"

He was referring, she knew, to the day they'd eaten apple pie at the cabin. "As a matter of fact," she replied before putting the last bite in her mouth, "it does."

They lingered over their coffee as most of the lunch patrons filtered out and a hush settled over the room. Catherine sat back, wishing she could ask Rory what he'd done after she'd left the alley the night before.

It was then that James David Hambleton entered the restaurant.

Only Catherine could see him as her chair faced the front entrance. As soon as he stepped over the threshold, their eyes met, and Catherine froze in her seat. What was it Reese had said about him? She couldn't remember. The trauma of the night before had blocked out all but the shooting and the loss of the gold.

Dressed in a black business suit complete with black bowler and cane of Madagascar wood, James Hambleton loomed larger than life. Looking neither left nor right, he immediately headed in the direction of their table.

Oh, Lord, Catherine thought to herself. He's come to demand full payment of the money I borrowed! Her palms began to sweat. How in sweet heaven's name was she going to handle this? She owed the man two thousand dollars and there was no way in the world she could pay him back! A wave of nausea swept over her.

"What is it?" Rory asked, seeing her white face. "Is something the matter?"

"N—no, nothing is wrong," she said, her voice no more than a whisper. "I—I believe I overindulged myself, that's all. Would you excuse me, please? I feel the need of some air." Rising before Rory could get out of his seat to assist her, she pushed her chair away from the table, intending to intercept James David Hambleton before he could create an ugly scene. She had no doubt that Jenny would immediately offer to repay the loan, and Rory, she knew, would not allow Hambleton to harass or threaten her. But Catherine wanted neither of them involved in her dealings with the shady banker. She had walked into the man's offices of her own free will, and she would not — no matter how grave the consequences — allow anyone else to suffer because of her poor judgment.

James David Hambleton neared their table, his stride bold and purposeful, his brown eyes narrowing with anticipation.

Catherine stepped forward, ready to greet him, then steer him away from the others and out the door. But before she could speak, he had walked right past her and put his hands on Jenny's slim shoulders. "Jenny, dear," he drawled. "Hello."

She whirled around to face him. "James!"

He ignored the stricken look in her eyes. Nonchalantly, he pulled out the fourth chair at the table, motioning for Catherine to return to her seat before he settled himself beside Jenny.

"What have we here?" Hambleton asked. "A reunion of sorts? If so, it's a shame I've walked in on the tail end of it. I would have liked to reminisce with the two of you. How are you, Rory? How many years has it been since I've seen you?"

Rory O'Shay leaned easily back in his chair, unperturbed by Hambleton's sudden appearance. "It's been a long time," he replied quietly. "I've heard you've done very well for yourself over the years."

James Hambleton smiled ruthlessly. "I have. But I understand you have not fared as well. While the passage of years has brought me a fortune, you've met with nothing but misfortune . . . I always said you were hell-bent for trouble."

"James," Jenny admonished. "Please, not here."

Hambleton ignored her. "For a wanted man, O'Shay,

you're certainly careless about where you're seen. Murderers should lie low. If I had a mind to, I could put the entire police force of San Francisco on your tail."

Nonplused, Rory replied, "I suppose you could, but I don't think you will."

Catherine, confused by this strange turn of events, sat stiffly in her chair. James David. J.D. The two men were one and the same. The man she'd borrowed two thousand dollars from was none other than Jenny's childhood lover! Jasper's father. And—at one time, Rory's close friend. But now, there was a palpable animosity between the two men. At some point in their pasts, before Rory had fled the coal fields of Pennsylvania, something had apparently happened to put the two men against each other. And now, with both men in their prime—one enormously wealthy, the other on the run, wanted for murder—fate had thrown them together. Catherine feared the outcome.

"Why shouldn't I report you to the police?" J.D. asked. "I've nothing to lose and everything to gain by acting the honorable, law-abiding citizen."

Rory leaned forward, his elbows on the table. J.D. leaned forward to meet him, and their faces nearly touched. "I think," Rory said in low, dangerous tones, "handing me over to the authorities would not get you the vengeance you seek. You want to plunge the knife into my back with your own hand. Were I in jail, you'd never have that chance."

"The fact is, I could kill you right now and be done with the matter."

Jenny came to life then, throwing out her arms to push the two men apart. "Stop this, the both of you," she declared, in hushed but urgent tones. "You're acting like children!"

J.D. straightened, laughing maliciously at Jenny's concern. Settling back in his chair, he withdrew a cigar from the inside pocket of his coat, struck a match and slowly lit up. Acrid smoke curled lazily upward, over their heads. "Don't worry, dear Jenny, I've no intention of slaying our good friend in the presence of ladies."

Jenny turned to him, her brown eyes blazing with anger. "I'll not tolerate such talk from you, James!" she said forcefully. "I've no idea why you're tormenting Rory, and I insist that you stop right now." To the stunned and silent Catherine, she said, "Come, Catherine. It's time we left."

Catherine, although reluctant to leave Rory alone with the formidable James Hambleton, nodded agreement.

J.D. shook his head, grasping Jenny's right arm with one hand. "You're not going anywhere until you hear what our good friend did to incur my wrath. Both of you ladies will please remain where you are and listen." He paused a moment, waiting for Jenny to get settled, his gaze never leaving Rory's face. "Go on, Rory, tell Jenny what you told her father so many years ago. Tell her how you ran to the righteous Samuel Trenton with stories of how his only child was seduced on the cold, hard ground by a filthy, no-good miner. Admit now it was you, our best friend, who told Samuel that I'd got Jenny pregnant. It was you who told him of our clandestine meetings, you who ultimately pushed the unstable, vengeful man over the edge."

Jenny, her face the color of parchment, turned to confront Rory. "Oh, my God," she whispered miserably. "Is this true, Rory? Were you the one who told my father?"

A muscle twitched in Rory's jaw as he muttered a curse and shook his head. "Of course not. I'd never betray you, Jenny—not in the past, and not now."

For a moment, she appeared uncertain, and then relief flooded her liquid brown eyes. "I believe you. Of course, you didn't tell my father; you'd have had nothing to gain by doing so."

"Nothing but a promotion at the mines," J.D. interjected.

Quick as a bolt of lightning, Rory came to his feet. His

chair went over backward, clattering to the floor as he reached across the table and grabbed J.D. by the lapels of his frock coat. He shook him once, roughly. "Listen to me, Jimmy. I never betrayed you and Jenny. Never, to anyone, have I disclosed your secret. To this day, I've not told a soul, and I never will. As for any promotion that might have been gained by such deceit, I never received one. In fact, on the same day that Trenton fired you, I left Shenandoah. Whoever told you I was the one who went to Samuel is a liar, and I'll be damned if I'll allow you to menace me and my family because of such lies."

With that, he released his hold, then stepped back, trying to calm himself.

Although Catherine had no idea what they were talking about, she believed Rory's story, and ached to reach out and support him. In that moment, she felt a fierce sense of kinship with this man who stood so proudly and bravely before his enemy. Once again, he was facing impossible odds. Life had indeed dealt Rory O'Shay a tough hand.

Finally in control of his emotions, Rory bade them all good day. After a long glance in Catherine's direction, he headed for the door.

Jenny pressed one hand to her mouth, stifling a cry. "Oh, James, how could you say such horrid things about Rory? He loves you like a brother!"

J.D. leaned back in his chair, legs sprawled carelessly beneath the table. "The man's a murderer, Jenny, and he's the reason we're not together now. I intend to even the score."

"But he said he didn't tell my father about us, and I believe him!"

"And I suppose you also believe he didn't murder a man."

Jenny pressed her lips tightly together without comment.

Catherine, impulsively leaping to Rory's defense, said heatedly, "Of course he didn't murder anyone! Rory O'Shay could never murder a man in cold blood." Images of Jack Reese's death flashed through her mind. She forced the picture away. Rory had killed for her. *Only* for her.

J.D. turned to Catherine, raising his brow in surprise. It seemed as if he'd almost forgotten her presence. "Is that an educated opinion, Miss Diamond, or one that stems from some tender feelings for this blackguard?"

"James," Jenny intervened. "I'll not have you badgering my guest. Catherine is defending Rory because she, as well as I, believe in his innocence. Your unfounded accusations against Rory are shocking."

"Ah, dear Jenny, I'm sure you find more than that about me shocking these days. I'm no longer the easily intimidated young man you knew so many years ago, am I? It is my deep regret that you weren't with me during those years when I was fighting my way to the top. We could have had such wonderful times . . ."

Jenny did not reply, but her face clearly showed how much she wished she could have been with him, rich or poor. "Come, Catherine," she said, "We should be on our way. My husband is doubtless awaiting me."

The three of them stood as one, but when J.D. glanced toward the entrance, he immediately sat back down. "Look who's here," he said, gesturing toward the door. "It seems your husband has grown tired of waiting. Here's the peacock himself, looking for his errant wife."

Jenny froze as she turned and saw Albert in the doorway. "Oh, my God," she whispered, sinking back in her chair. "James, *please*, do not confront him. Just let me leave quietly with him."

J.D. shook his head, once again assuming an arrogant pose. "There is no possible way I'm going to let that old man walk out of here with you on his arm, dear Jenny. I'd say this is the day of reckoning—and I intend to come out on the profit side of the ledger."

Catherine watched in fascinated horror as the prestigious Albert Marshall Latham walked slowly into the restaurant, his stocky frame clothed in sedate impeccably tailored gray. As he caught sight of his wife, his rotund face mottled with red, and his tiny, water-blue eyes widened in anger.

Jenny rose shakily, hands outstretched as she called a greeting to her husband. All the spunk she'd displayed in admonishing J.D. vanished at Albert's approach.

Albert ignored her courteous greeting. "What is the meaning of this?" he demanded. "You were expected home two hours ago."

"I—I'm sorry, Albert. Catherine and I were just having a bite to eat. We totally lost track of time. Do forgive me."

"I will not!" he thundered, glaring now at Catherine and J.D. "What are you doing in this place with these people? When you told me you were having luncheon with a friend, I assumed you meant you were dining on the Hill, with someone from our own circle."

"I'm—I'm sorry, Albert," she repeated wretchedly. "We—we just decided to have lunch out and, well, we came here."

Catherine quickly moved to Jenny's side, placing a protective hand on her friend's arm. "Mr. Latham, I'm Catherine Diamond. It was my decision to come to the What Cheer House. I'd heard about their wonderful meals, and I practically begged Jenny to join me here for lunch." Catherine lied without conscience, ready to say anything that would keep this man from publicly chastising his wife.

Albert Marshall Latham looked Catherine up and down with shocked rheumy eyes. "Diamond?" he repeated. "Diamond? *Ned* Diamond's daughter?"

Catherine stiffened defensively. "Yes. Ned Diamond is my father."

"Good God, Jenny!" Albert hissed under his breath. "What are you doing, running about the city with a woman who operated a gambling parlor?!" Roughly, he yanked

Jenny away from Catherine, and pulled her toward the exit.

Jenny's yelp of pain was all that it took for James Hambleton to jump into action. In one fluid movement, he was off his seat and standing in front of Latham.

"Take your hands off her," J.D. warned, with intent.

"Out of my way, man, this woman is my wife and my property!"

J.D. didn't flinch an eyelid. "I'll tell you one more time, Latham. Release the lady."

Albert's eyes bulged in his round, overfed face and he tightened his grip on Jenny's forearm. Seeing her wince, J.D.'s arm shot out, and his powerful fist connected with the older man's jaw. Albert groaned, and collapsed like a rag doll.

"Oh, James, you fool! You've killed him," Jenny screamed hysterically. "Why didn't you just leave us be?" Kneeling, she cradled Albert's head in her lap, patting his heavy jowls, crooning words of comfort through the tears that streamed down her cheeks.

Catherine was horrified. "You've best leave," she said to J.D. before she knelt beside Jenny to help her revive the old man.

"The hell I will," J.D. replied. "I'm not finished with him."

As it happened the old man needed no reviving. In a moment, he had pushed himself back on his feet, his face livid as he spewed out a string of angry words.

"I'll have you behind bars for this!" he shouted. "How dare you attack me! The authorities will be notified of this outrageous behavior. I'll see you're thrown into prison!"

J.D. was unimpressed. "Try to put me behind bars, Latham. I've a whole army of politicians under my thumb in this city. I doubt, despite your outward prestige, you have the same clout. Stand and fight me like a man, Albert. To the victor, go Jenny and her son."

At the mention of Jasper, Jenny started to tremble. Catherine moved beside her, taking hold of her hand.

"He'll kill him!" Jenny said in an urgent whisper. "J.D. will kill Albert."

The maître d' had rushed to the scene, but when his repeated pleas for order went unheeded, he backed away, frightened. Even the waiter was reluctant to get between J.D. and Albert. A violent exchange of blows seemed inevitable. The quaking Jenny stood stubbornly by, and Catherine had to forcibly pull her out of harm's way. Sniffling about Albert's safety and J.D.'s craziness, Jenny allowed Catherine to move her back near the table they'd recently vacated. After that, Catherine noted, Jenny did not again voice any concern for her husband.

J.D. stood arrogantly before the older man, taunting him to make the first move. Albert, seething with suppressed rage, carefully removed his coat and rolled up his sleeves. The two adversaries, so unequally matched, began to circle each other warily. J.D. towered almost a foot above Albert, and his eyes shone with a strange, mad light. He seemed to have taken complete leave of his senses as, totally unmindful of his opponent's age and frailty, he prepared to fight him to the death.

Albert made the first move. Closing in with his head lowered, he charged into J.D.'s middle, throwing the younger man off balance, and sending both of them crashing against a table. Recovering swiftly, J.D. wrapped his hands about Albert's neck and squeezed hard. Jenny screamed, lunging forward out of Catherine's grasp.

It was then Rory appeared in the doorway. Without hesitation, he strode to the middle of the fray, grabbing J.D.'s hands and prying them from Albert's neck. Albert staggered away, the wind momentarily knocked out of him. Jenny rushed to his side.

J.D. lit into Rory then, coming at him with both fists.

Rory ducked the blows, sending a right and then a left into J.D.'s unprotected middle. As J.D. doubled over in pain, Rory wrapped one arm about his neck and yanked him up, hard.

"What's gotten into you, man?" Rory demanded, his voice close to J.D.'s ear. "Think what you're doing! Do you want to endanger both your son and Jenny? Fighting Latham is not the way to go about helping Jenny. She needs your cool thinking now, Jimmy, not your hotheaded temper. You're a damned fool if you think she cares about Latham. She's stayed with him only because you never made any effort to contact her after she came to San Francisco. She didn't want to marry Latham. Her father turned her out of the house when he learned she was pregnant. He forced her into marrying Albert, and the only reason she did his bidding was for your sake. She was afraid Trenton would fire you and have you blackballed."

"How do you know so much?" J.D. wheezed, trying to pry Rory's arm from his windpipe.

Rory did not relax his hold. "Because I took the time to ask, that's why. And I assure you, old friend, I'm not the one who told Samuel Trenton about your relationship with his daughter. Swallow your pride, Jimmy, and forget your quest for vengeance. Jenny and Jasper need you now, more than ever. You've got the money and the power to get her peacefully away from Latham. You don't need to resort to such tactics. I suggest, for the benefit of Jenny and your son, that you apologize to the old man and make a hasty exit." With that, Rory released his grip.

J.D. stumbled, then righted himself. He glared at the trembling Jenny, who stood beside her husband. Reluctantly, he extended his hand to Albert.

The older man ignored the gesture. "I'll see that you pay for this scandalous conduct," he said with venom.

J.D. shook his head, and withdrew his hand. "You have

my apologies, Mr. Latham. Beyond that, do as you wish." With one last look in Rory's direction, he headed out the door, not looking back.

Catherine quickly moved to Rory's side. "Are you all right?" she asked.

He nodded. "Yes, I'm fine. And you? Were you hurt? If I'd known Jimmy would turn so violent, I would not have left. I only came back because I saw Albert's carriage pull up. I was certain there would be trouble."

"I'm glad you came when you did, Rory. Poor Jenny must be so filled with guilt at this moment. It's clear she loves J.D., but I believe she is truly frightened by Albert. I think she fears Albert will in some way harm her son."

"Is that what she told you?" Rory asked, concerned.

"No, not in so many words . . . it's just a feeling I have. Do you think it could be so? Would Albert deliberately hurt Jasper?"

Rory gave a quick lift to his shoulders, shaking his head. "I don't know. It's possible. Jenny has told me Albert has very little to do with the boy. For Jasper's sake, though, I guess we better believe the worst." He hesitated for a moment, then continued, "Perhaps you could stay with Jenny for a few days. Could you do that, Catherine? I don't want her to go home alone with Albert, not after this incident."

"I—yes, I suppose I could. But I don't think Jenny would allow me to help. She is so independent at times."

Rory gave a rueful smile. "Only in Jimmy's presence is she independent," he said. "With Jimmy, Jenny has always let her emotions rule her. With all others, I'm afraid she is too often influenced by the rules of polite society."

Catherine nodded in agreement. It was a shame Albert Latham held such sway over Jenny, for on her own, the young woman had a dynamic personality. Catherine was proud to claim such a woman as her friend, and she vowed to help Jenny extricate herself from the difficult situation. Surely, she thought, there had to be some way of dissolving the loveless marriage. If Albert disliked Jasper so much and thought so little of Jenny, wouldn't he be glad to be rid of them both?

Catherine looked over at Jenny and her husband, who was still ranting angrily. Jenny stood beside him, quiet and meek.

"I intend to go to the Chief of Police about this," he growled.

Jenny only nodded, absently patting his arm as she stared at the door from which J.D. had just exited.

"I want you to get in the carriage and go home," Albert continued. "Your son has been asking about you all morning."

"Jasper? Is he all right, Albert? Did he enjoy your morning together?"

"Thunder and damnation! Of course he didn't!" Albert snapped. "The boy never appreciates special treats. He's incorrigible, Jenny—" He stopped a moment, breathing hard, then went on in a lower voice, "we'll discuss the matter when I get home."

Jenny nodded spiritlessly. "Yes, of course," she said. "Perhaps you should see a physician, Albert. You've a nasty bruise on your neck."

"Yes, yes. But I want you to go home now. Don't worry about me, and do not wait up. I've business to attend to. I'll see that Hambleton character run out of the city on a rail if it takes until dawn!"

Jenny looked at her husband blankly. "Yes, of course," she murmured. "You do remember I have a theater engagement tonight?"

He nodded agitatedly, shooing her out the door. "Go and enjoy yourself. As I said, I'll be taking care of that blackguard Hambleton . . . " He moved away toward the bar then, motioning the owner to pour him a stiff drink.

Jenny left her husband behind and stepped into the afternoon sunshine. "What a nightmare," she groaned as Catherine and Rory came to stand beside her.

"It's over," Catherine said gently, "and no one was hurt. Let's just try and forget the whole incident."

"But I can't forget," Jenny said. "Neither J.D. nor Albert will let the matter drop. They'll each work to see the other's ruin. Oh, Rory," she said. "What have I done? I love J.D. I've always loved him. How could I ever have married Albert? How can I stop those two from killing each other?"

"Don't blame yourself," Rory said. "You did what you thought was best. For the time being, though, you can allow Catherine to stay with you."

"What? No, no," Jenny said immediately. "I couldn't ask her to step into the middle of such a situation."

"But I don't mind," Catherine broke in. "I want to help you, Jenny, and if my presence in your home will ensure your safety and your son's, then I want to be there."

Jenny looked relieved. "Thank you," she whispered. "I *would* feel better if you were with us."

"Fine. Then it's settled," Catherine replied. "Let me go back to the boardinghouse to tell my father and pack a few things."

"Yes, do," Jenny said, allowing Rory to help her into the carriage. Once seated, she looked out at Catherine, and asked, "You will join me at the theater tonight, won't you?"

The theater? After everything that had happened? At any other time, Catherine would have been thrilled to go to the theater, but the idea held little interest for her at this moment.

"Are you certain you want to go, Jenny?" she asked.

Jenny nodded, glancing briefly at Rory, who stood beside Catherine. "Yes, I'm positive," she said firmly. "Please, say you'll come. Albert will not be home until late. I hate going to the theater alone, and I dread the prospect of sitting around worrying about what he and James are up to."

"Well, I . . . yes, of course. I'll join you if that's what you truly want to do."

Brightening considerably, Jenny sat back on the seat while Rory helped Catherine into the carriage.

Rory's hand was warm on Catherine's elbow. She glanced up at him. How she wished they could have a quiet moment alone. She wanted to know how he was coping with the previous evening's traumatic events.

"Soon," he whispered as though he could read her thoughts. "Go to the theater tonight. You might enjoy yourself."

As the carriage pulled away from the curb, leaving Rory in its wake, Catherine felt her spirits lift with an odd sort of anticipation. Suddenly, she could not wait to get back to the boardinghouse so she could dress for her night at the theater.

Chapter Sixteen

Six hours later, Catherine and Jenny were seated in one of the ornate, private boxes of the California Theater. Opened just five years earlier, the theater was now a showcase for San Francisco's elite.

"I'm so very glad we came this evening," Catherine said, just before the curtain rose. "I can't tell you what a thrill it is for me to be here."

Jenny smiled and nodded distractedly. Her attention was directed not to the stage below but on the door directly behind them. "Yes, it will be fun," she agreed absently. "Catherine, would you excuse me for a moment? I—I seemed to have misplaced my purse. Perhaps I left it in the lobby—I'll just go take a look. I won't be but a minute."

Catherine turned toward her friend. "Your purse? Why, Jenny, I didn't notice you set it down anywhere. No, I'm quite certain you had it with you when we were seated. Are you sure it's not here? It's so dark, maybe you just can't see it." Catherine started to rise to help look for the bag.

"No, no," Jenny said, stopping her with one hand. "I—I'm quite certain I left it in the lobby. Not to worry, I'll go and retrieve it. I'll be right back."

"I'll come with you," Catherine offered.

"No, I insist you stay here. Look, the curtain is rising."

She patted Catherine's gloved hand. "Enjoy yourself," she whispered, then left the secluded box.

Catherine settled back into her seat and was soon caught up in the play, Dion Boucicault's *The Octoroon*. When nearly half an hour had passed and Jenny still had not returned, Catherine began to worry.

Just then, the door to the private box opened and Catherine breathed a sigh of relief.

"Oh, there you are," she whispered, her eyes still fixed on the stage. "I'm glad you've returned. The performance is simply wonderful."

"I'm glad you are enjoying yourself," a male voice said. "This night was planned with only you in mind."

Catherine's heart skipped a beat as she whirled around to discover Rory. He was dressed in a black claw-hammer coat and silk top hat. In one gloved hand, he carried a silver-topped cane. He smiled, and in the dim light, his teeth were startlingly white.

"Rory!" Catherine was dumbfounded. "You—you are the one who arranged this?" she asked. He'd remembered her special wish, her dream of spending one night like a lady of quality!

"Guilty as charged," he confessed. "Are you pleased?" His gaze was expectant, filled with boyish charm.

"Of course I am," she whispered, so softly he barely heard.

He settled himself onto the seat beside her, removing his hat and gloves and placing them on the rail before them. His cane made a small click as he placed it on the floor near his chair. "You look beautiful tonight, Catherine."

Catherine smiled shyly. "Oh, Rory . . . you shouldn't have. You and Jenny must have gone to great lengths planning this. Especially after all that has happened in the past twenty-four hours."

"Ssh," he said, shaking his head. "No sad thoughts tonight." He beamed with pleasure at having delighted her so.

Catherine studied his profile for a moment, feeling an odd tightness in her chest. How thoughtful he was. In the span of just a few short days, she had been witness to a side of Rory O'Shay she imagined few others had ever seen. He'd whisked her away in time of trouble, had tended to her burn, and had even killed a man to protect her. How many other men would have done for her the things Rory O'Shay had?

"Thank you, Rory," she whispered.

"Hush now," he whispered back, "you are missing the performance."

The play was fast-paced and, at times, hilarious. San Franciscan audiences enjoyed taking part in the entertainment. During the scene in which a lovely slave is placed on the block and auctioned off to the highest bidder, a man in the adjacent box shouted, "Damn the law! I bid $30,000!" Everyone had applauded thunderously.

When the curtain fell and the house lights came up, Rory asked, "Did you enjoy the play?"

"It was wonderful, Rory. This is truly a night I'll never forget."

"But you speak as though the evening has ended."

She cast him a curious glance, thinking how handsome he looked now that she could see him fully. But he was not merely handsome; Rory had a rugged individuality, a powerful inner presence, which asserted itself even in his elaborate, tailor-made evening clothes. He was a man who could never melt into a crowd.

He stood, and she looked up and asked, "Are you saying the evening is not yet over?"

"That is exactly what I'm saying, Miss Diamond. Come now, surely you remember the rest of your wish?" He reached for his gloves and hat, and then offered her his arm. "As I recall, there is dancing ahead, and of course, a special breakfast at sunrise." His last words were low and held a certain promise.

Catherine was overwhelmed. "You would do all of this for me?" she asked.

"I would," he whispered. "And much more."

His reply sharply reminded her of Reese's death. A troubled frown creased her brow.

Noticing her change of mood, Rory added lightly, "You need only ask. Your wish is my command. Tell me, where does the lady wish to dance this night? Atop Rincon Hill? Nob Hill? Or will it be Russian Hill? I hear Senator Sharon is entertaining this night. Shall we grace his home with our presence? Or do you prefer something more prestigious?"

Was he teasing? She wasn't quite sure. "Surely you haven't an invitation to any of those places. Do you?"

"Who needs an invitation? We need only enter to be welcomed. The secret is in how we carry ourselves." He leaned to whisper against her ear. "Also, I've this cane with me. If any man tries to bar our way, I shall simply bop the lout on the head."

Catherine laughed then. He had arranged this night to help her forget the horrible ordeal with Reese, and the recent skirmish between J.D. and Albert. His thoughtfulness was moving. She decided to indulge his lighthearted mood, and put aside her worries, at least for this night. "I'd rather not be the cause of any lumps on the head," she said, only half-joking.

"Very well then, we shall make our own entertainment." He patted her gloved hand, then escorted her out of the private box.

"But where?" she asked.

"You will see." And that was all he would say.

He led her through the bustling theater crowds and onto the street where a stately enclosed carriage awaited them. With a deep bow, Rory ushered her into the dimly lit, white satin interior. Once they were both seated, he produced a bottle of fine French wine, and opened it with a grand flourish. He poured the sparkling amber liquid into two long-stemmed glasses, and placed one in her hand.

"To us," he said, lifting his glass. "To a night of dreams. May all your tomorrows be as golden as this wine."

"Yes," she murmured. "To golden tomorrows." For a brief moment, she believed she could see her future in his eyes. The warmth and bright hopes reflected there could get her through a thousand dark nights. They both drank to the future.

Too soon, the magical ride was over. As Rory helped her to alight, Catherine was surprised to see that he had taken her, not to her boardinghouse nor Jenny's mansion, but to a secluded knoll overlooking San Francisco Bay. Beneath the spreading branches of a huge cypress tree, a picnic basket had been set out on a blanket. Rory waved the driver away, then escorted Catherine to the tree.

Together, they watched as the carriage lights disappeared into the darkness. "I hope you don't mind," he began, "but I've taken the liberty of arranging a private picnic. I thought a few hours away from the city would do you good."

"I guess I haven't much choice," she murmured teasingly. "Seeing as how you've sent our transportation away."

"I could run after him," Rory offered in the same playful tone.

Catherine smiled. "I don't think you really want to do that . . . nor do I want you to."

He reached out then, to take her hand in one of his, while his other hand circled her waist. "May I have this dance, Miss Diamond?" he asked softly.

"Rory." She felt suddenly shy, alone with him on this moonlit, windswept knoll. "There's no music."

"But there is," he insisted. "I've music in my heart. Can't you feel it?" He placed her right hand over his heart.

She felt the sure, steady rhythm beneath her palm, each beat vibrating through her senses. "Yes," she whispered. "I can feel the music."

"Then dance with me, Catherine. Let this be our own private dance, for us alone. Let me be a part of your dream—tonight, and for however long you may wish. For now, let us enjoy the moment and not think of tomorrow, or what is past." He lowered his head to her upturned face, waiting for her response.

She tilted her face slightly and let him brush her lips as his body began to sway to the strains of an unseen orchestra. She moved with him, her cheek against his, his words echoing in her mind. The urge was strong to throw caution to the winds and yield to his allure.

Cold reason stepped in and broke the spell. What real future could she possibly hope for with an accused murderer, someone who would always be on the run?

It would be best to let things end here, now. She should leave while she had the strength to do so. She was almost angry that he had given her this dreamed of night, breaking her heart, raising hopes that could never be realized.

It was obvious that Rory had planned on more than just a picnic and an innocent dance under the moon. Although her body ached for him, she knew that she should not allow herself to be drawn any deeper into an illicit relationship. To do so was dangerous, a serious threat to the independence she valued so highly.

"No, Rory, this—this is wrong," she whispered, wincing inwardly at the pain these words caused her. "I should not be here with you. To indulge my senses and lose myself in your arms is a risk I cannot afford."

His blue eyes were filled with anguish. "Do not let thoughts of the future intrude on this one timeless moment. I do not deny that I can make you no promises for a safe tomorrow—my own future is too uncertain and dark." He paused, looking into her eyes. "But over the past weeks I have learned to cherish each moment graced by your presence. Can you fault me for wanting to give you one night of exquisite pleasure, a night in which time ceases to exist? For now, that is all it is in my power to give you, though I yearn to lay the world at your feet. Please, *macushla*," he whispered, releasing her and bringing both hands up to hold her face. "Do not refuse the only gift I am, at the moment, capable of offering."

"And if, by accepting such an offer, I lose a part of myself?" She spoke in a barely audible whisper.

"I would never ask of you what you cannot give. Trust me . . . and yourself. Please, stay." His hands tightened on her face, and he brought his mouth down on her sensuous, partly open lips. He deepened the kiss, letting it linger for the span of a heartbeat before he drew away, his gaze questioning.

In the end, she could not refuse him, could never refuse him. She reached up and twined her arms about his neck. "I will stay," she said, relief washing over her as she joined him in their enchanted dance.

Under the pale light of the moon to the accompaniment of the soft breeze that sighed through the boughs overhead, they danced atop the grassy knoll overlooking San Francisco Bay.

They danced on and on, until gradually he brought her

to a halt, pressing her close.

"Catherine," he whispered, "you are the most breathtaking dance partner I have ever held in my arms."

She felt giddy, and smiled but did not speak.

"No laurels for me?" he asked. "No laurels at least for all the effort I put forth?"

Emboldened by a sense of growing excitement, she lowered her lashes and replied, "Laurels may be awarded later — if you have not overtaxed yourself with dancing."

"No fear of that," he assured her, and then suddenly serious, added, "Remember, Catherine, I will take nothing from you unless it is freely given."

In response, she took a small step back and began to undo the buttons of his coat. She heard the sudden catch of his breath, felt the tightening of his muscles. "What is this?" she whispered playfully. "Has my phantom lover had a change of heart? May I remind you that this is my fantasy — and I shall orchestrate it."

He smiled then, and helped her remove his coat. Even as it fell to the grass, Catherine was unfastening his vest and shirt. Soon, they were peeled away, and she was running her palms over his naked chest, glorying in the feel of his smooth, hot skin.

He bent to nuzzle her neck, murmuring, "Very brazen you are within the freedom of your fantasy."

She checked herself, momentarily taken aback, then relaxed as he said, "It is my delight."

Then, one by one, he undid the fastenings of her gown while he placed feather-light kisses across her forehead and cheeks. What Catherine had begun, Rory now continued, with mounting desire.

With deft hands, he stripped the gown from her shoulders and worked the sleeves over her gloved arms. Then, bending, he lifted the hem and very slowly drew the garment up and over her head, leaving her clad in only her silken undergarments. With the rush of cool air on her fevered skin, her nipples puckered and jutted out beneath the light chemise. She shivered and Rory quickly enfolded her in a close embrace.

Murmuring soft endearments, he rained passionate kisses down the slim column of her neck to that vulnerable spot where her pulse throbbed. "I've waited so long to give you this night," he said. "Had I the power, I'd give you a lifetime of them, each one followed by a glorious morning. Your face has been the sunshine of my days, Catherine, and I cannot put into words how the short time we've spent together has sustained me. Rejoice with me, *macushla*, for there may never be a tomorrow for us — only this moment."

Catherine clung to him, trembling. He had not said he loved her, but he had said enough. She would take whatever he offered, seize the moment and let it nourish her through the difficult days to come. He was right. There was no past, no future, only tonight. She loved Rory O'Shay; she realized that now, with heart-stopping certainty. Despite everything he was accused of, despite all that he could never give her, she loved him.

"This moment is all I need," she told him, her voice ragged with emotion. "You are all I need, Rory."

He kissed her deeply then, and as his tongue gently touched the still-tender spot on her own tongue, she was sharply reminded of Jack Reese's death. Despite her resolve to put it aside for tonight, she could not forget it.

He sensed what she was thinking, and drew back for a moment. "Don't think of Jack Reese," he whispered, "the man isn't dead, Catherine." He felt her stiffen in surprise, then hastened to explain. "The bullet only grazed his head. I took him to a physician's home in the city where he will stay until he recovers. Last I knew, he was still unconscious."

Catherine was stunned by the news. "I—I thought you'd killed him," she replied softly.

"No," he answered. "Jack Reese is very much alive and will be delivered to the authorities when he's well enough. I've made certain of it. There's a fugitive warrant out on him, and the physician tending him knows this."

A great wave of relief washed over Catherine, and when Rory kissed her again, she responded with less hesitation.

"Let me love you," he whispered huskily as he drew her down on the blanket. "Let me make you forget the past days . . ."

As he spoke, he caressed her, swiftly removing the few remaining garments that kept her satiny skin from his touch—her silk chemise, and then her garters, which he undid with a flick of his wrist; then her filmy stockings, which he rolled down her legs and tossed over his shoulder. She trembled with anticipation as she watched the white silk flutter to the ground. Then he stripped off his own clothing, and they lay together, naked, in the moonlight.

Bending his head to her firm young breasts, he took one pouting nipple in his mouth, sucking hungrily, until it grew rigid and she squirmed with pleasure. From there, his mouth moved to her other breast, then downward to her smooth white belly, while his hand sought the moist heat of that most sensitive place between her quivering thighs. He stroked her there, slowly, skillfully, until she thought she would go mad with excitement. She pulled him closer, needing to have him inside her—now.

"Please," she cried. "Don't wait any longer! I cannot bear it."

He hovered above her for an instant, then spread her thighs wide and entered her, thrusting so deep it made her gasp. Catching her breath, she smoothed her hands down his muscled back to his lean haunches where she pressed hard, drawing him deeper inside her, closing tightly around him. This time, there was no pain, only sweet relief as they moved together in a frenzied, heart-pounding rhythm.

Together, they soared, two beings lost in another dimension, souls touching and clinging, free of all restraint. Their pleasure in each other was so intense, it hovered near pain as they spiraled upward to the ultimate ecstasy.

Exhausted, replete, Catherine snuggled against Rory's chest while he gathered her close, pulling the blanket around them. Cozy and content, listening to Rory's deep, easy breathing, Catherine slept.

Chapter Seventeen

Jenny hurried away from the California Theater, thinking about the lovely, enchanting evening that Rory had planned for Catherine. She was so happy to have played a part in orchestrating the surprise, helping Rory to choose the performance and obtain the private carriage that would spirit the two of them away to the secret trysting place overlooking the Bay. Oh, how Jenny wished it were she and J.D. keeping that rendezvous.

As though conjured up just by her thoughts, J.D. walked out of the shadows and stepped up beside her.

"Hello," he said, and the sound of his deep voice sent shivers up Jenny's spine.

"James! Wh—what are you doing here?"

"Escorting you home. You shouldn't walk unescorted through the streets at night."

"I—I'm not alone. My carriage is waiting for me."

"I know," he said. "And so am I."

Jenny glanced up and down the street, fearful that one of Albert's business associates might see her conversing with

J.D. Hambleton.

"We shouldn't be seen together," she whispered as she quickened her pace. "Someone might tell Albert."

"I don't give a damn about that bastard. Right now, he's occupied in plotting my financial ruin, gathering all his resources, calling in favors. What a fool that pompous old goat is! While he's busy trying to ruin me, I shall be busy seeing to his wife's . . . needs."

"You've become a heartless cad. Is that all I am to you now, a source of revenge against Albert?"

"The sweetest revenge I could ever hope for," he replied, halting her hurried steps with one hand to her arm. Before Jenny could protest, he kissed her full on the mouth while his other hand brushed across her full breasts.

Jenny backed away, outraged.

He gave her a slow smile. "Go straight home, Jenny love," he whispered. "I'll be waiting for you." He turned away then, losing himself in the crowded street.

Jenny didn't know whom she hated most: J.D., Albert—or herself. Agitated and miserable, she climbed into her carriage and headed for Rincon Hill. Once home, she went into Jasper's room to check on him. The boy was lying awake in bed.

"Hello, mama," he said as she stepped into the room and sat down on the edge of his bed. "Did you enjoy your evening out?"

"No," Jenny answered honestly. "I didn't. I missed you."

Jasper smiled, then reached up and gave his mother a tight hug. They spent the next forty-five minutes talking quietly. Jenny would have liked to spend the entire night in the safety of her son's room, but Jasper soon fell asleep, his small hand clutching hers. Over the past few days, she had observed a significant change in Jasper. He seemed extremely anxious, but also happy. It was as though he had a secret he could not share with anyone. Dropping a gentle kiss to his forehead, Jenny placed his hand on his chest and pulled the covers up to his chin, tucking him in lovingly.

"Good night, my darling," she whispered, then turned and walked from the room.

She was startled to find J.D. waiting for her in the hall, lounging arrogantly against the wall. He was drunk.

Jenny closed the door to her son's room, her heart racing with fear. "I want you to leave," she told him flatly. "You shouldn't be here. Albert will be home soon. He—he cannot find you here in this condition."

"To hell with Albert," he said, his words slurred. "I want what's rightfully mine, baby, and I aim to get it." He moved toward her slowly, like some feral animal stalking its prey.

Jenny wanted to run, to scream, but she was transfixed by the dangerous glimmer in J.D.'s eyes. With sudden clarity, she saw exactly what he'd become—a brutal male animal consumed by a thirst for revenge. The realization was strangely exciting, thrilling. J.D. wanted *her*, he wanted Jasper. And he would have them both.

"Come," Jenny said huskily, yielding to him, accepting the fact that she loved him—would always love him. She led him to her bedchamber, closing the door soundlessly behind them.

Their lovemaking was frenzied and violent, both in the thrall of a raw, primitive lust that drove them wild. He moved over her, on her, and in her, and Jenny met him thrust for thrust, over and over again until, spent, they lay motionless.

"Jesus . . . you're good baby," he whispered hoarsely in her ear. And Jenny smiled, sighing, loving life once again.

But her mood was abruptly shattered when J.D. moved

off her roughly, standing to yank his trousers on.

"What are you doing?" Jenny asked, wanting him to stay.

J.D. did not even look at her. "I'm leaving," he replied. "And I'm taking my son with me. I know why you left me for Latham; your father told me a long time ago that you thought I wasn't good enough. Well, baby, I'm here to show you who's the better man. I should have done this years ago."

Jenny was horrified. How could her father have told J.D. such a terrible lie? No wonder J.D. had stayed away for so long. And now he was going to take their son away from her because of her father's lies. No! He couldn't! She sprang off the bed, unmindful of her nudity. "You can't!" she screamed. "My father lied to you. Don't do this, James, please! Take me with you, I beg you! Jasper and I will go with you, all of us, together. We'll be a family, James! We'll be happy. We'll—"

J.D. wasn't listening. He swung the door open wide and stepped out in the hall, heading for Jasper's bedroom. Frantic, Jenny took a moment to yank the top sheet from the rumpled bed, quickly wrapping it about her body as she scrambled after her lover.

J.D. was already in Jasper's room and to Jenny's astonishment, her son was not frightened by his presence.

"You came!" the boy cried joyously. "I knew you'd come back, Daddy. I just knew you would!"

"Of course I came back for you, son," J.D. replied, and there was an odd, tender note in his voice, the same loving tone she'd heard only once before—on that long ago night when he'd asked her to be his wife. J.D. scooped the boy up in his arms.

"No, James!" Jenny said, moving to block his way before he could walk out the door with their son. "I'll come with you. Wait while I dress. Please don't leave, not without me."

Jasper clung to his father, but there was a frightened look in his eyes as he stared at his mother, who clutched only a sheet to her naked body.

J.D. said only, "Get out of my way, Jenny. It's too late for us. You wanted better things and so you left me, taking our child. Now it's my turn."

"No!" she cried brokenly. "You're wrong. I never wanted to leave you."

He didn't reply, he merely plowed forward with the child in his arms while Jenny watched helplessly.

Jasper gave his mother a quivering smile. He didn't understand what was happening; he only his knew real father had returned for him, just as he'd promised to do several nights ago, when he'd appeared, out of nowhere, in Jasper's bedroom. The two of them had played games and whispered stories to each other, and Jasper had been overjoyed. But now he was troubled to see his mother so worried and frightened. He tried to reassure her.

"Don't worry, Mama," he said, clinging to J.D. "Daddy will take care of me. He told me he would."

Jenny stood there, trembling, unable to think or move. Part of her wanted to rip her son from J.D.'s arms, but another part of her was thrilled to see father and son together at last.

They were at the top of the staircase now, leaving her, walking out of her life. Jenny finally forced herself to move. "Wait!" she cried out, running toward the stairs. "Let me come with you. I'll leave Albert and never see him again. Please, James, you are the only man I've ever loved. I don't love Albert, I hate him. Don't you understand? It is you I love, James. You! Only you!" She tripped on the trailing sheet, lost her balance, and had to grab for the banister to keep from tumbling down the stairs. By the time she had righted herself, J.D. was out the door, with Jasper still held tightly in her arms. Jenny sank to the stairs, tears streaming down her face. It was this scene Albert Marshall Latham came upon. He had heard Jenny's screams as he'd come up the walk, and the awful words she said about him. And just as he walked into his own home, he had been passed by the towering figure of James Hambleton. Hambleton had said only, "She's all yours, Latham. Just like she's always wanted to be."

Albert was livid as he looked up at his young wife, a silk sheet falling loosely around her body, exposing her breasts, which were still flushed with J.D.'s lovemaking. There were even red marks along the delicate column of her throat where J.D. had nipped her fair skin. The sight made Albert's blood boil.

He bounded up the steps and grabbed her long mane of hair in one powerful hand. He yanked her face up toward his. "You whore!" he spat, and then slapped her hard.

Jenny stared up at him numbly as again and again he lashed out at her. Soon, her whole face was on fire as he continued to slap her. Then, something inside her snapped. No more, her mind screamed. She would not be tormented anymore—by Albert or anyone!

With sudden, brute strength, she pushed hard against Albert. He lost his balance, arms flailing as he groped for support he could not find.

Jenny looked at him with cool detachment as he teetered on the top step, beseeching her to help him. She merely put her hands behind her and drew back, watching with an odd sort of fascination as he fell backward, tumbling down the whole flight of stairs.

He landed at the bottom, his neck bent at a queer angle,

watery-blue eyes opened wide, staring sightlessly upward. Blood trickled from the corner of his mouth.

Chapter Eighteen

It was just before dawn when Catherine awoke. The chill morning air was gloriously reviving, although overlaid with a lingering gray fog. Nestled beneath the blanket next to Rory, Catherine was snug and warm. She lay still for a while, listening to the birds welcoming a new day.

"Sleeping Beauty awakens," Rory murmured, greeting her with a soft kiss to her forehead. "I tried not to wake you. As you can see, there'll be no watching the sunrise for us."

"Ah, well," she replied, raising herself on one elbow, peering toward the east. "I'll have to settle for watching the fog lift. I don't mind . . . as long as we do it together."

He smiled, inching himself away to reach for the picnic basket. Noticing her shiver slightly, he grabbed his shirt and handed it to her. "Here," he said. "Slip this on. I don't want you catching cold." As she shrugged into the shirt, he stood and stepped into his dark trousers, then settled back down beside her.

Catherine watched as he opened the picnic basket and withdrew a silver bucket brimming with ripe, red strawberries. "You remembered," she exclaimed with delight.

"Of course. You should know by now that every word

you utter is instantly branded in my memory." He brought one berry to her mouth, holding it as she took a bite.

"Hmm," she said. "That's heavenly."

"So, too, are you, my angel." He kissed one corner of her mouth still moist with strawberry juice.

Catherine was just about to reach for another strawberry to feed to him, when the thundering sound of a horse's hooves shattered the peaceful morning. Rory stiffened. Instantly alert, he peered through the fog, trying to make out the rider.

"Who knows we're here?" Catherine quickly asked.

"No one else but Jenny. I can't imagine that she—" But his words were cut off as the rider came into view.

It was indeed Jenny Latham, riding sidesaddle with her long, unbound hair flowing behind her. Her face was an anguished mask as she maneuvered her sweating horse to an abrupt halt just at the foot of their blanket.

"Thank God I've found you!" she exclaimed, breathless as she slid off the saddle. She did not appear at all surprised or shocked to find Catherine and Rory half undressed. Indeed, she appeared far too upset to notice much of anything. She looked frightful, wrinkled and soiled, dressed in the same gown she'd worn the night before. There were nasty bruises darkening her fair cheeks.

"Jenny, what is it? What's happened?" Rory demanded. In one fluid movement, he stood and reached to take Jenny by the shoulders.

Trembling, unable to speak past her tears, Jenny threw herself into Rory's arms, clinging to him as she sobbed. "Oh, Rory! My son—Jasper, he—he's gone!"

"Gone? Where? Jenny, you must tell me what's happened. Where did Jasper go? Did someone take him?"

Jenny nodded, her fingers clutching at Rory's arms. "It was J.D.! He came to the house last night. He—he was drunk and he wanted to see Jasper. My husband came home and there was a horrible scene. Oh, God, Rory, it was so awful! You must help me! I—I don't know what to do!"

"What happened?"

"My husband . . . he—he's dead! I *killed* Albert!"

Catherine gasped, shocked at Jenny's words. Kicking away the blanket, unmindful of her nudity beneath Rory's shirt, she quickly moved to place her hand on Jenny's shoulder. "What should we do?" she asked, looking at Rory.

Rory's brow furrowed as he held the weeping Jenny away from him. "Tell me exactly what happened, Jenny. Did Albert strike you? Who gave you these bruises?"

Trembling, choking on her tears, Jenny clapped her hands to her face. "I—I don't know!" she wailed. "It—it all happened so fast. When I left the theater J.D. was there, waiting for me. Later, he came to the house and took Jasper. I—I didn't mind letting him take Jasper, truly I didn't. But I wanted to go with them—and J.D. didn't want me. When Albert came home and found me on the stairs, he went wild with rage. He hit me over and over. I—I just couldn't take his abuse any longer. I pushed him away . . . and—and he fell down the stairs. Oh, God, Rory! What am I going to do! They'll arrest me and I'll never see J.D. or Jasper again!"

"I don't know what to tell you," Rory said, thinking. "Are you certain Albert is dead?"

Jenny shook her head, trembling as she ran her fingers through her tumbled hair. "I don't know! I just panicked and left. I didn't know where else to come but here. You two are the only friends I have. I'm sorry to have involved you, but I—"

"Hush, Jenny. You were right to come here. Now listen to me," he said in a slow, deliberate tones, "I'm going back to your house. If Albert is still alive, I'll summon a physician. If he's dead, then I'll take care of the matter. You stay here with Catherine until you've calmed down." He eased Jenny down on the blanket, then grabbed the wine he and Catherine had opened hours ago. After filling a glass and making certain Jenny had taken a healthy swallow, he turned to Catherine.

She put her hands out to him, clasping his in a tight squeeze. Her clear gray gaze locked with his dark blue one. "Be careful," she whispered.

He nodded. "Don't let her leave here until she's calmed down. Can you find transportation back to the Hill? Or should I send a carriage for you?"

"No, no. There might be too many questions if someone is sent here to pick us up. Don't worry, I'll get her back safely."

"Very well. I'll take her mount. Here," he said, reaching into his trousers and pulling out a handful of gold coins. "The two of you will need money. I'll leave my coat for Jenny. We don't want her going about the streets in such a state." As Catherine took the coins, Rory suddenly gathered her in a bone-crushing hug. "I'm sorry our night had to end like this, Catherine."

"Don't say anything more," she whispered, suddenly terribly afraid. "There'll be other nights for us, more sunrises."

He did not comfort her by agreeing, and his silence filled her with a dark foreboding. In the next instant, he released her, then gathered up her clothes, which were strewn on the ground. "You can dress behind the tree," he told her. "I'll need my shirt."

"Yes, of course."

The cold realities of dawn had thrust them apart. Had Jenny's tale taken Rory back to that fateful day when he had been forced to kill a man? Catherine was certain it had. The past was intruding once more, haunting Rory and driving a wedge between them. She dressed quickly, not bothering with all the fastenings on her gown. When she stepped from behind the tree and handed Rory his shirt, he was already astride Jenny's horse. Shrugging into the garment, he buttoned it, then turned the horse toward the city and urged it into a fast trot.

Catherine watched as the fog gathered him in its gray cloak. Not until he was out of sight did she realize he'd not said good-bye. We *will* be together again, she told herself sternly, trying to chase away the inner, lingering doubts.

It was a full hour before Jenny had calmed down enough for them to leave. Catherine folded the blanket and packed the picnic basket, then helped her friend into Rory's tail coat, trying to make her as presentable as possible. Then, the two women headed down the hill to the street where they boarded a horse car back to Rincon Hill.

"Something's gone wrong, I can feel it," Jenny whispered, on the verge of tears again as they left the car and started walking toward her house.

"Hush," Catherine scolded. "You're just nervous; the events of the night have been too much. Rory is at the house and will put things right. Don't worry, Jenny. Whatever you did, you did in self-defense. You must remember that."

"But look!" Jenny cried, pointing to the carriages lining the drive in front of the mansion. "The authorities have already arrived! They must not see me! They'll arrest me!"

Catherine saw the uniformed men standing on the steps leading to the front door. Fighting down her own alarm, she took Jenny by the arm and pulled her along. "You'll have to face them sooner or later, Jenny. Let's get the questions over with now. Trust me, Rory is not going to let anyone arrest you."

But as they made their way up the drive, Catherine wasn't so certain Rory *could* help Jenny. After all, Rory was wanted by the state of Pennsylvania for murder. What if the San Francisco authorities knew this and had already arrested Rory?! What if the police had somehow learned that Rory had shot Jack Reese?

She forced herself to cling to the small hope that all would be well. She had to be strong, for Jenny's sake—and for Rory's.

She greeted the officer who seemed to be in charge, while Jenny stood beside her, mute and trembling.

"Good morning, ladies," one officer said, removing his hat. He was a big man, with sandy-blond hair and sympathetic green eyes that he turned on Jenny. "Mrs. Latham?" he asked. "You *are* Mrs. Albert Latham, are you not?"

When Jenny didn't respond, only widened her reddened eyes, Catherine spoke up, "Yes, this is Jenny Latham." She wanted to say more, to act as if she were surprised to see all the policemen. But the words wouldn't come.

The man straightened, then spoke in an official tone. "I regret to be the bearer of bad news, Mrs. Latham, but it is my unpleasant duty to inform you your husband has been killed." Jenny slumped against Catherine as the man continued, "Your husband's neck was snapped, Mrs. Latham. My men are even now in pursuit of the murderer."

"What?" Catherine asked in a low voice, thinking she hadn't heard correctly. "You know who killed Albert Latham?"

"Yes, ma'am, we do. We were alerted to a disturbance here earlier this morning and when my men arrived, they found him standing over Mr. Latham's body."

"Him?" Catherine repeated, feeling suddenly weak.

The man nodded, his eyes, filled with concern, darting back to Jenny. He shifted uncomfortably. "The man's wanted for a similar killing back east. We almost had him in custody, but he put up quite a struggle. I—I'm sorry to say he escaped, but as I said, my men are searching for him even as we speak."

The world tipped sickeningly and Catherine had to close her eyes for a moment. Rory had snapped a man's neck back east . . . Albert had fallen down the stairs and broken his neck. Oh, no! Finally, she was able to ask, "Who—who is the man you're searching for?"

"Rory O'Shay, ma'am. And not to worry, my men will have him in custody before the day is out."

Catherine's mouth dropped open. *No!* her mind screamed, it's all a terrible mistake! She turned to Jenny, tightening her hold and giving her a quick shake. "Jenny! Say something! Did you hear what this men said?!"

But Jenny said nothing; she merely stared at the officer, her eyes wide and vacant.

"Jenny!" Catherine persisted.

Jenny's mouth moved, but no words came out.

"I'm sorry, Mrs. Latham. I know this must be a terrible shock. Come, there's a physician inside who tried to save your husband. He should have a look at you." The man reached for Jenny, taking her gently by the arm.

But Catherine would not release her hold. "Jenny!" she urged. "Did you hear what this officer said? Tell him it's all a misunderstanding! Tell him!"

The policeman gave Catherine a stern look of disapproval, prying her hand from Jenny. "Mrs. Latham is obviously suffering from shock, ma'am. I suggest you let me lead her to the doctor before she swoons."

"Let her swoon!" Catherine shouted, disgusted with Jenny's reaction. She brushed the officer away and grabbed Jenny by both shoulders, shaking her. "Jenny, speak to me! Tell this officer Rory did not kill your husband! Tell him Rory is no murderer!" She wanted to slap her, to rattle her until her teeth shook. But Jenny, face white, eyes staring straight ahead, did not seem to comprehend anything that was happening. It was horribly clear Jenny would be of no help to Rory now.

"Ma'am, I insist you release Mrs. Latham," the policeman said in a louder voice, finally penetrating Catherine's panic-stricken mind. "And if you know anything about this Rory O'Shay character, then you're going to have to answer some questions. Please wait here while I see to Mrs.

Latham." He pried Catherine's hands away, then talking in low, soothing tones to Jenny, he escorted her into the house.

Catherine stood there, her mind whirling. She had to find Rory—but where could he have gone? And then she knew. Of course! She glanced around. The other officers were talking amongst themselves, assuming she was just a friend, apparently unaware that the officer in charge had asked her not to leave. She began to move down the steps, very slowly, so as not to arouse suspicion. She would not stay to be interrogated by the authorities. How absurd of the officer to think she would.

Not until she was halfway down the drive did she pick up her skirts and run. She had to get to the cabin in the hills; she had to be with Rory. *I'm coming, Rory,* her mind chanted, trying to span the miles. *Hold on, my darling. I'm coming.*

The fog-shrouded morning gradually gave way to a clear day as the sun climbed higher in the sky. It was nearly noon before Catherine reached the small cabin in the hills. She'd rented a buggy with the money Rory had given her— something she hadn't wanted to do, but she'd had no choice. It was imperative she reach Rory before the authorities found him. Pulling hard on the reins, she brought the rickety vehicle to a quick halt in front of the cabin. She scrambled from the seat. Even before the horse had calmed, she flew across the damp grass and up the few stairs, thrusting open the door and stumbling inside.

He stood in with his back to the door, windblown and unkempt. As he heard her enter, he whirled about, his face grave as he saw that it was Catherine.

"Rory! Thank God you're safe!" she cried, then flung herself into his welcoming arms.

"You shouldn't have come," he said softly, holding her tight.

Catherine tried not to cry, tried not to give into the terrible fear knotting her stomach. She had worried all along that the authorities would eventually catch up with Rory for the killing in Pennsylvania. Now that he was wanted for a second murder—of a prominent San Francisco businessman—she saw little hope of his escaping, despite the fact that he was completely innocent of this crime.

The bitter tears came, and she could not stem the flow. "There's no place I'd rather be," she whispered.

"But you could be held as an accessory. No matter how much it pains me to say the words, I must insist that you leave. Go now, before you are brought down with me. Please, *macushla*, I could not bear for you to be hurt further because of me."

"No. I'm staying. You need me, Rory . . . and I won't leave you. Ever," she said as she stepped out of his embrace. That he should ask her to go at such a time was a bitter pill. Angry now, she said, "Your unflinching sense of responsibility is admirable, but you didn't kill Albert! And you shouldn't bear the blame!"

He shook his head sadly. "My avenging angel. My dear, sweet Catherine. You don't know the crimes of which I *am* guilty. I abandoned my family when they desperately needed me; I left my father and brother to break their backs in the Pennsylvania coal mines, making pennies a day, so that I could travel the world, free of care, coming and going as I pleased." He ran a nervous hand through his hair, his gaze agonized. "I have never lived up to my responsibilities. Now I must. Jenny cannot face a murder charge. She has a son to raise, someone who needs and depends on her."

"And what of you?" Catherine asked. "Do you think you have no one who depends upon you?" When he didn't answer, she whispered, *"I need you, Rory."*

For an instant, he looked shattered, then the shutters

closed on the pain in his eyes. "And that is where I have wronged you, *macushla*," he replied. "I should never have taken you that first night here in this cabin. I should have left you alone as my conscience dictated. I am sorry, Catherine, if I've raised your hopes with deceptive actions and pretty words. You knew from the beginning that I am a wanted man. Surely you must have known this day would come. What did you expect? That I could run from the law forever?"

Catherine looked away, confused. What *had* she expected? Certainly not this, not to be torn apart from him just when she had discovered how much she loved him. When she again returned her gaze to his, hers was frank. "The fact remains that you didn't kill Albert. You shouldn't go to prison for a murder you didn't commit."

"I don't intend to go to prison, but neither do I intend to inform the authorities of Jenny's involvement. I'm a wanted man in one state already. What does it matter if I'm now wanted in two?"

His words, said so coldly and carelessly, sent a shiver down Catherine's spine. He was planning to leave California, to be on the run for the rest of his life. He planned to leave behind the land he loved, his dreams . . . and her.

"Where will you go?" she asked, forcing the words out.

He shrugged and grinned. "Who knows. Forget me, Catherine. I've been nothing but trouble for you since the day we first met." He reached out a hand and gently brushed his fingers along her jawline.

"Stop," she said, moving her face from his touch. "Please, Rory, don't force me away from you now. We'll find some way to clear your name. Or I'll go away with you! We'll— we'll build our dreams somewhere else, someplace where the law will never find you—"

"Hush, you're speaking nonsense now." He pressed two fingers to her mouth, silencing her rush of words. "The only place I can go is out of the country. I cannot ask that of you, Catherine. I will not ask you to leave your home and family for an uncertain future with me. Your dream is living the life of a fine, wealthy lady. How could you do that with me, with an outlaw? No," he finished, shaking his head, "we have no future, only cherished memories. Go now, Catherine, before I . . . Just go. There is nothing you can do to help me."

"Before what?" she insisted. "Before you ask me to stay? That is what you were going to say, isn't it? Oh, please, Rory, there must be something I can do!"

"There is nothing. Go. Now."

Hearing the harsh tone of his voice, Catherine stepped away. The hardness in his eyes chilled her.

"I'll be back," she whispered. "I won't let you face this alone." With those words, she turned and walked out the door, her head held high. She felt Rory's gaze on her back.

Chapter Nineteen

Catherine raced back toward the city, not slowing her lathered horse until she was once again back at the boardinghouse. Taking the steps as fast as her legs would carry her, she raced up the narrow, dimly lit stairwell. Her mind whirled with confusion and fear. She had to keep Rory from leaving the country! If he fled now, to South America or Europe, she could never see him again. She had to find a way to clear his name in San Francisco so that he would stay here.

She burst through the door and ran directly into Connor.

"Whoa, there," he said, in a voice hauntingly like that of his brother. He reached out to stop her mad dash. "Where are you headed in such a hurry?"

Catherine stared up at him. The moment of truth had come; she had no alternative but to tell Connor of Rory's plight and hope the younger O'Shay would help his brother.

"It's Rory," she said, breathless. "He—he needs your help, Connor."

Connor's eyes narrowed at mention of his brother. Immediately, he released his hold on her, then swung away, saying, "I have no brother."

Catherine hadn't the time to argue with this stubborn young man. With every passing minute, the chance of the authorities finding Rory increased tenfold. Grabbing Connor's shirtsleeve, she forced him to look at her.

"Don't do this, Connor. Don't turn your back on Rory now, not when he needs you more than ever before."

"Rory's never needed me! He needs no one. He deserves whatever has happened to him."

"To be thrown in jail for a murder he didn't commit?"

There was a flicker of emotion in Connor's blue eyes, and then, suddenly, it vanished. "If you are speaking of the murder in Pennsylvania, Rory is guilty."

"No! A man was killed last night, right here in the city . . . and Rory has been wrongfully charged with the murder. He didn't do it, Connor! He—he is protecting someone by letting the authorities believe he is the murderer. Please, Connor, go to Rory and help him."

Connor was not easily persuaded. Agitated and nervous, he reached into his shirt pocket and withdrew a hand-rolled cigarette. He fingered the slender stick for a moment, staring intently at Catherine. "How do you know Rory is not the murderer? He has killed before; he could do so again."

"I know," Catherine said evenly, "because he was with me the entire night. He was holding me in his arms at the time the crime was committed. I will stand before any judge and jury and testify."

"Why?" he asked viciously. "Because what you say is true, or because you have foolishly succumbed to my brother's charm, as so many women before you have?"

"Both."

Connor shook his head, laughing without mirth. "Ah. My legendary brother can add yet another notch to his belt." He struck a match, watching as it hissed into a sputtering flame. Lighting his cigarette, he inhaled, then spoke through the smoke. "Killer of men and debaucher of virgins . . . is it any wonder I hate my brother as much as I do?"

Catherine itched to slap his face, but she held herself in check. "Your brother is a good man, Connor O'Shay. You would do well to take a few lessons from him."

"As you, no doubt, have."

At this, Catherine lost her tenuous hold on her temper. Her open palm met his cheek in a stinging blow. His face turned to the side with the impact, and an ugly red mark quickly spread across his cheek. Catherine stood motionless, shocked by her own impulsive action.

Immediately, she regretted what she'd just done. "I'm sorry," she said stiffly. She knew Connor's strong emotions were probably rooted in deep sibling rivalry—and love. Whatever words he hurled out now were motivated only by anger and pain.

The fury that had distorted Connor's features was gradually dissipated. "Don't be sorry," he said. "I'm the one who should be sorry. Your relationship with my brother is none of my affair. You say Rory is in trouble. Where is he?"

Catherine brightened "Then you'll help him?"

"I didn't say that. I asked where he is."

"I won't tell you that unless you give me your word you'll help to keep him from fleeing the country."

"Fleeing the country? Is that what he's planning to do?"

"I—I think so," she replied. "And we've got to stop him, Connor, make him see that he's got to stay in San Francisco and fight the wrongful charges brought against him here. Please help me convince him. He can't keep running."

"I agree with that," Connor said thoughtfully.

"Then you'll help me make him stay and fight these charges?"

"I will definitely keep him from leaving the country," Connor replied firmly. "Now, where is he?"

"Thank you, Connor," Catherine said, grateful and relieved. And then she told him where Rory was hiding.

Connor and Catherine rode the rented buggy out of the city and back toward the cabin. The going was too slow for Catherine. She wished they could have just taken two fast horses, but Connor had been adamant about using the buggy. The reason remained unclear to her. When at last they reached the path leading to the cabin, Connor jumped down from the buckboard and told her to go on ahead.

"Where are you going?" she asked, puzzled.

"Trust me," he said. "I know what I'm doing."

She opened her mouth to protest, but Connor had already disappeared into the woodland.

Catherine picked up the reins and slapped the horse into motion. When she pulled up to the cabin, Rory was just walking out the door. Both horses were out in front, Bess all saddled and ready to ride.

"Rory!" she called, jumping off the seat and hurrying toward him. "Wait!"

Rory turned at the sound of her voice and watched as she sped toward him, her skirts fluttering in the breeze. She was beautiful. His chest constricted as she came to stand breathlessly before him, her clear gray eyes bright with worry.

"You're leaving the country, aren't you?" she demanded.

He paused near her for only an instant. Any longer, and he would succumb to the overpowering urge to take her in his arms, and to hell with the law! He moved toward Bess, fastening the saddle bags and testing her saddle.

"I told you not to come back," he said, too gruffly. He couldn't be weak now. No matter what was in his heart, he had to let her go. He had to let her build a decent life, one untainted by his sins.

She moved to his side, reaching out to touch his hand that lingered near the saddle. "Wait, Rory. Please listen to me. There's no need to leave San Francisco. I—I've thought of a way to help you!"

"I don't need your help, Catherine. I've told you that. Go on home now. Forget me. I can take care of myself." He shrugged away from her touch, then placed one foot in the stirrup, ready to swing himself up in the saddle.

Catherine panicked. Where was Connor? What was he doing? In another minute, Rory would ride off, out of her life. The thought left her weak and trembling.

"Of course you can take care of yourself," she blurted. "But who will take care of me?" The words were out before she realized their implication.

With one hand on his saddle horn, ready to mount, Rory halted abruptly at her words. They cut him to the quick. He'd heard those words before . . . Even now, after all these years, the bittersweet sound of his mother's voice echoed in his head . . . *Don't go, son. Don't leave us. Who will take care of us when you're gone?* And the young man had answered, *I'm no good to you here, Ma. I need to set my life in order and then I'll be back. I'll take care of you then, Ma. When I'm able* . . . That day had never come. He'd returned home to find his mother dead and buried. He'd had greenbacks in his pocket then, but they were of no use to his mother.

Rory gazed down at Catherine whose heart was in her eyes. He cursed fate, cursed the tide of events that had swept Catherine Diamond into his life at this time. If only the law weren't on his tail, if only he weren't wanted for murder, if only he didn't have to work things out with his family. *If only* . . . He stopped himself abruptly. Such regrets were for weaklings and fools. His bleak future held no hope for such a bright and beautiful woman as

Catherine. She deserved far better.

Slowly, he let go of the saddle horn and took his foot from the stirrup. He turned to face the only woman who had ever touched his soul. Summoning all his will, and assuming a mask of indifference, he said quietly, *"You* will take care of yourself, Catherine—as you have always done. You don't need me. You never have. I told you once that all we had was the moment at hand. That moment has passed. It's time to move on."

"No," she whispered, tears welling up in her eyes. "I won't let you go, Rory."

"You have no choice."

Oh, but she did! As they spoke, she could see Connor coming toward them, moving up behind Rory. She fixed her gaze on Rory's eyes. The task was not difficult. She could drown in those blue eyes, could let herself go, let herself forget the tomorrows that might never come.

Beside them, Bess munched contentedly on a clump of grass. But Fire, skittish as always, sensed Connor's presence. He snorted, shuffling his hooves as Connor drew closer to Rory.

Something in Connor's movements made Catherine uneasy. What in the good Lord's name was he going to do? She had a sudden, chilling feeling that something had gone wrong, but she dismissed it. She'd asked Connor to help, and now she had to trust him to handle the situation in his own way.

Connor made his move then, quick as lightning, leaving Catherine stunned as she watched Rory crumple to the ground, knocked unconscious by the butt of Connor's revolver.

"Rory!" she screamed, kneeling beside him, cradling his head in her lap. Blood oozed onto her hands. "What have you done!" she shrieked at Connor.

"It's just a knock on the head," he assured her. "He'll be right as rain in a few hours."

Catherine looked at the blood on her hands, reminded of the night that Rory had sent a bullet winging into Jack Reese's temple. Blood! Everywhere. "You've killed him!" she screamed.

Connor immediately sank to his knees, pushing Catherine away so he could inspect Rory's wound. He felt for the pulse in Rory's neck, then pulled out a torn handkerchief to stanch the flow of blood. "He's not dead," he said. "You think I'd kill my own brother!" His gaze was fierce and possessive as he glared down at Rory with an odd mix of love and hate. Roughly, quickly, he brushed a hand across Rory's brow. A long moment passed in which he just stared down at his brother.

"Did you have to hit him so hard?" Catherine asked. "I had no idea you intended to harm him, Connor. Had I known, I would not have led you to him."

"And if you hadn't, Rory would be on his way out of here," Connor stated plainly. "I'll put him in the back of the wagon. You hitch up the other horses."

"Be careful," Catherine instructed, grimacing as she watched Connor struggle with Rory's big frame. She moved to help him, and together they finally succeeded in getting Rory into the wagon.

The ride back to the city was a nightmare for Catherine as she sat beside Rory, watching the horrifying flow of blood from his head. Connor assured her that most head wounds bled profusely. But surely not this much, she thought. Just outside the city limits, Connor ordered her to sit up front with him, telling her it would be better for appearance' sake. Reluctantly leaving Rory unattended, she climbed to the buckboard beside Connor. The carriage rumbled on. Even Catherine was bothered by the jolting

and bumping. What must Rory be going through?
Oh, Lord, she prayed. Please don't let Rory die.

Chapter Twenty

Jenny lay on her bed staring sightlessly up at the ceiling. Albert was gone. She'd killed him. She felt only the barest remorse. For twelve long years her husband had verbally whipped both her and Jasper into submission. He'd excoriated her, called her a whore, and treated her like one. And Jasper, the poor boy, had suffered greatly under the tyrannical rule of the vengeful Albert Marshall Latham. Not a day had gone by since Jasper's birth that Albert had not reminded both mother and son that Jasper was not from his loins. Even if he had not told Jasper to his face that he was not his father, he had gotten the message across in many indirect, underhanded ways.

No. Jenny did not regret killing Albert. Her only regret was that she'd waited so long.

"Oh, Jasper," she cried aloud. "How I miss you!" Her only comfort lay in knowing Jasper was with J.D. James would never harm the boy. He would care for him and protect him, shower him with love—just as he had once done with Jenny.

Oh, how she longed to turn back the clock twelve years. If she'd the power to relive her life, she would have defied her father and not married Albert. She would have run away with J.D. and married him. But she could not turn the clock back. She had to deal with her life as it was.

Jenny dried her eyes and rolled on her side. She had decisions to make.

An hour later, she ordered her carriage brought to the front of the house. *Her* carriage. Not Albert's. All of Albert's wealth now belonged to her. She was a woman of independent means. She could have anything in the world she wanted.

She wanted James David Hambleton. And by God, she would have him.

Jenny's carriage came to a halt before the offices of Hardle and Hardle. The thoroughfare was crowded with people, bustling about in the gas light that streamed from the windows of the still open shops. Men and women floated by, sporting expensive, fashionable clothing, smelling of exotic scents. San Francisco was a city of doers and dreamers. This night, Jenny Trenton Latham was both.

Boldly, she entered the building. J.D. was there, sitting behind one of the desks, his back to her as he fiddled with the combination of the safe. Hearing her enter, he whirled around.

"Hello, James," she said.

He was speechless for a moment and then his eyes narrowed. "What are you doing here?" he asked, his voice gruff.

Jenny ignored his tone. She didn't care what he thought of her. If he thought her a whore, then she'd be a whore, *his* whore.

"What do you think I'm doing here?" she asked, unflinching beneath his cold stare.

"I've no idea. I thought I made it quite clear Jasper was coming with me."

"Oh, yes. You did. But now it is my turn to take what I want. I've come to lay claim to the only man I've ever loved—ever will love. I've come to fetch the true father of my son."

J.D. straightened, forgetting the safe and all the riches it held. "You would come to me now, when the body of your husband is not yet cold?"

"I would have come to you twelve years ago had I not thought my father would take his anger out on you."

"That's a lie. You father told me you wanted nothing to do with a dirt-poor coal miner."

"He lied," she said. "He lied, and you know it. My father *forced* me to marry Albert! I was afraid that if I didn't, he would fire you and have you blackballed. I—I was young and frightened, you must understand that."

J.D. turned away as though he couldn't bear to see the truth in her eyes. "And what makes you think I'd take you now?" he asked. "You're a fallen woman, Jenny Latham."

"No," she whispered huskily. "Never was I a fallen woman. I was madly in love when I gave you my virginity at fourteen . . . and thirteen years later, I'm still in love with you. Never has another man touched my naked body, never has another man touched my heart. Only you, James. Only you."

J.D. stepped away from the desk, moving quickly to stand before her, his face a mask of rage. He clutched her shoulders, his grip hard. "Are you telling me your own husband never made love to you? Do you think me such a fool that I would believe those words?"

Jenny forced herself not to tremble. She faced J.D.'s towering anger, faced the raw hurt she saw in his eyes. For James D. Hambleton, she would face hell, and the devil himself.

"Yes," she said quietly. "That is exactly what I am telling you."

"I don't believe you," he whispered, tightening his grasp, hurting her.

Jenny closed her eyes, reveling in his touch, not caring

how badly he hurt her. "It's true."

"You're lying."

His fingers were digging into her flesh, sending painful spasms through her body.

"No," Jenny breathed, tipping her face up to his. "I'm not lying. I love you, James. I always have. I always will."

"Oh, Jenny," he murmured at last, bringing his face close to hers. "Can you ever forgive me? God, how I wanted to hurt you when I first came to San Francisco. I wanted to hurt you as badly as I was hurt all those years ago."

"My father did us a terrible injustice," she whispered. "But, please, let us try and put the past behind us. It doesn't matter now. I love you, and we're together now." As he slowly drew her to the floor of the silent office, Jenny offered him her lips, her body, everything that was hers to give. "I love you, James," she whispered.

He did not speak of love, but his body told her all she needed to know. In the glow of a single gas jet, they tore at each other's clothing and made love with a passion Jenny had not known since she was fourteen. She *felt* fourteen again, renewed, and ready to savor all that life had to offer. Oh yes, this was what she had been waiting for all these long, hurtful years. This moment, with J.D., was all she'd ever dreamed of. Jenny was insatiable, moving beneath him with fevered intensity, giving herself with total abandon.

And J.D. returned her outpouring of love, with every caress, every burning kiss to her eager body.

Some time later, with the curtains of the windows drawn against the eyes of passers-by, Jenny and J.D. lay in each other's arms. Jenny was the first to speak.

"Where is Jasper? How is he? Is he safe?"

"Of course he's safe, Jenny. He's in my hotel suite, awaiting my return. We leave for Pennsylvania in the morning."

"You—you're going back east?"

"Yes."

"And—and taking Jasper?" she asked softly.

"Yes." He kissed her hair. "And Jasper's mother, if she'll come."

Jenny felt her heart swell as her eyes brimmed with unshed tears. "Of course she'll come," she whispered. A while later, she asked, "How did you hear of Albert's . . . death?"

"I have my connections," he replied. "As you must realize, I was planning his ruin, long before he ever toppled down the stairs."

"Yes, I guessed that," she said. "I suppose you also know that Rory O'Shay is being charged with Albert's murder."

J.D. nodded silently.

"I cannot let him go to prison for me."

"He won't," J.D. assured her. "O'Shay's too smart to let the law catch him."

"But whether he's caught or not, I cannot let him take the blame for my crime.

"And why not? He's wanted for the murder of a man back east. What's one more murder?"

Jenny sat up, stunned. *'I* killed Albert. I am the one who should be punished, not Rory!"

J.D. pulled her back down beside him, kissing her neck with slow, flicking kisses. "You didn't kill anyone, and forget O'Shay. Who cares if he lives or dies? He betrayed us once—a betrayal that led to our separation. I, for one, hope the man rots in some squalid prison."

Jenny pushed his face away. "No," she said. "I'll not do that to Rory. He—he has been too good to both Jasper and me. It was Margaret who told my father of our meetings. Not Rory."

"Forget O'Shay," he repeated.

And Jenny almost could. Almost. "No!" she said emphatically. "I killed Albert. I am the one who must be punished."

She moved away from James, fired now with a determination to tell her story to the authorities immediately. But

J.D. grabbed her, holding her in a tight embrace.

"If you leave me now," he told her, his voice a husky whisper, "You will never see me again. O'Shay has been charged with Albert's murder. Let it be. You have our son to think about. What would Jasper do without his mother?"

"But—" Jenny tried to protest, but J.D.'s lips came down on hers, hard, smothering her words.

"Forget it," J.D. said again, when he released her. "I want my wife and son with me . . . forever."

Jenny's heart melted with those words. Never again would she jeopardize her future with J.D. Never. *I'm sorry, Rory,* she said to herself. *I am sorry.*

And J.D.'s kisses soon vanquished any lingering doubts. He had said, "forever." J.D. would be with her and Jasper forever! At last, Jenny's dreams had come true.

Chapter Twenty-one

For Catherine, the night seemed to last forever. Her trust in Connor had been misplaced. He had duped her, never intending to help Rory stay and fight the murder charges in San Francisco. Instead, he was planning to drag him back to Shenandoah, to face the murder charge there! Ned had won some money in a poker game the night before, enough for them to take the trip back east that he and Connor had planned. There was only one bright spot in the whole wretched situation. Although Ned had forbidden her to have anything to do with Rory, he had agreed that she could accompany them to Shenandoah. He had, in fact, insisted on her going with them. He was greatly concerned about her possible involvement in the shooting of Jack Reese.

Guilt weighed heavily on Catherine, especially over the injury Rory had sustained because of her gullibility. He had not yet regained consciousness.

When a red-streaked dawn finally appeared in the sky, she rushed to Rory's side. The bleeding had long ago stopped, and there now remained only a huge lump, encrusted with dried blood. Shortly after she rebandaged the wound, Rory opened his eyes.

As he tried to focus his eyes, the first face he saw was Catherine's. He opened his mouth to speak to her, but Ned Diamond's tall frame suddenly came into his line of vision, followed by a face he hadn't seen in years. His brother, Connor, stepped up to the bed.

"Where am I?" Rory asked, addressing Catherine, although his gaze was fixed on Connor.

"You—you are at the boardinghouse," she replied, relieved to see him awake, but consumed by guilt over what she'd done.

"The last I recall," he said groggily, "I was getting ready to leave San Francisco. What am I doing here?"

Catherine averted her gaze, toying absently with the moist cloth in her hand. "I—we brought you here."

"We?"

Before Catherine could answer, Connor spoke up. "I brought you here, after Catherine came to me for help."

Rory looked up at his brother, an odd light flickering briefly in his eyes as he studied Connor for a long moment. "I see," he finally said.

"No, I don't think you do. You've a hell of a lot to answer for back east, and I aim to take you back there—willing or not."

Rory laughed mirthlessly. "By the size of my headache, I'd say you stooped pretty low to get me here. Cracking me on the skull was unnecessary, Conn. I would have come with you willingly had you only asked."

Connor shook his head, obviously angered by Rory's answer. "Nothing I've ever done can compare to the sins of your past, brother. You should consider yourself fortunate that I find killing abhorrent. I might have given you more than a whack to the head."

271

"That's enough," Catherine admonished. She was startled and upset by the harsh tone of Connor's voice. "Rory is in no condition to be badgered."

"I'll be fine, Catherine," Rory said, his eyes still on Connor's face. "It is apparent my brother and I have unfinished business. I've been searching for you, Conn. In fact, you are the reason I came to San Francisco. I heard you were in trouble. I came to help you."

"I don't need your help," Connor shot back. "I never have, and I never will. The day you walked out on our family was the day I disowned you as my brother. You're dead to me, Rory. The only reason I'm standing here now is to see justice served. Beyond that, I want nothing more to do with you."

Catherine whirled on the younger O'Shay, her eyes flashing with anger. "That is enough, I said. I'll not have you speak to your brother in such a manner. Had I known your true intent, Connor O'Shay, I would never have come to you for assistance!"

"Calm down, Mary Catherine," Ned interrupted, sensing that things were getting out of hand. "This is none of our affair. Let them settle their own differences."

"I will not," she said hotly. "Rory is not the heartless individual everyone seems so quick to paint him. I'll not stand here and let Connor browbeat him."

"It's all right, Catherine," Rory said in a low voice. "My brother has a right to his opinions, and the fact is, his opinions aren't so far from the truth. I came to California to try and mend the bonds I severed years ago."

"Well, I want no part of it," Connor broke in. "No part at all." With that, he bent to pick up some of their baggage for the journey. "Get up, *brother*. The eastbound train departs in an hour, and by God, you'll be on board." He headed out the door to load the parcels and to check on Irish Fire and

Rory's mare. Both horses would be making the trip east with them.

Shaking his head, Ned watched Connor leave. To Rory, he said, "The day I saw you in my saloon, I knew there'd be trouble."

"Pa, please," Catherine said. "Let's just leave and say no more."

For Catherine, the journey on the Central Pacific Railroad was at once exciting and nerve-racking. She feared for Rory's safety once they were in Pennsylvania, and her worry grew with every mile of track behind them. Rory himself did not appear as concerned about his fate. For some unfathomable reason, he seemed to be enjoying the journey. Sitting in the seat directly behind Catherine and her father, he made repeated, unsuccessful efforts to engage his brother in conversation. Not until the train had steamed into Utah did Connor's stony silence begin to melt. Catherine, ostensibly absorbed in reading a newspaper, listened intently to the two men. Guilt at having gone to Connor for help still weighed heavily on her conscience. She did not want her impulsive actions to cause a permanent rift between her and Rory. Once, when he leaned forward to direct her attention to the passing scenery, she felt a burgeoning of hope.

There *is* hope, she told herself. Perhaps by the time they reached Pennsylvania, Connor and Ned would no longer be so bent on dragging Rory to the authorities. Her hopes were dashed though, when Ned turned in his seat and ordered Rory not to have any further conversation with his daughter. Catherine held her tongue—out of deference to her father and because she did not want to create a scene in front of the other passengers. Rory acquiesced in a gentlemanly manner and sat back in his seat. Catherine was not fooled by his apparent passivity. She had a gut feeling that Rory would soon cast off all restraint and let neither his brother nor Ned monitor his every movement. She dreaded that moment.

Her anxiety ebbed at times as she was caught up in the camaraderie that developed among the other passengers who shared the cramped, second-class accommodations.

The nights, however, were torture. Although the cars grew hushed after the many noisy children on board were finally bedded down, Catherine could sleep only for an hour or so at a time. The upholstered seats, also used for sleeping, were stiff and smelled of cigar smoke, and the thundering sounds of the train wheels seemed somehow louder at night. Having to share the confined space with her stiff-necked father, did not add to Catherine's comfort.

Late one night Catherine sat awake, huddled beneath one of Jenny's quilts she had brought aboard. Beside her, Ned snored softly.

"Can't sleep?" a voice asked from behind.

Catherine turned in the seat, leaning against the cold window pane. It was Rory who spoke. Connor was sound asleep beside him.

"No," she whispered in the dim yellow light cast by the few oil lamps that had been left burning.

"It is a wearing journey, I know," Rory said, speaking softly. "You should try and get some rest, though. We've a hectic day ahead of us."

Catherine nodded, welcoming the private moment. She had not had any chance to speak with Rory since the train had stopped briefly at Cape Horn, out of Sacramento, just above the American River. While the passengers were given ten minutes to view the historic spot where the gold rush fever had begun, Ned had stayed close to Catherine, conveying with just a stern glance his determination to keep her and Rory from conversing.

"What about you?" she asked. "Have you been able to rest?"

"Now and then," he answered.

"I wish there'd been enough money for first-class fare," she told him. "A sleeping car would have been much more comfortable."

"I don't mind. I'm just glad to be away from San Francisco, for the time being, anyway."

"Then you're not—not angry with me for bringing Connor to the cabin?"

"I didn't say that."

Catherine averted her gaze. "I—I thought, at the time, I was doing what was best for you. I had no idea Connor would react the way he did."

"How could you know? I never did explain to you my . . . situation with Connor. To my regret, there is a great deal I never explained."

Catherine looked up, her clear gray eyes filled with sympathy. "Are you really going to allow my father and Connor to cart you off to the authorities when we reach Pennsylvania? The submissiveness you've shown so far seems so out of character."

"Submissiveness?" He laughed softly, his gaze never leaving her face.

"Well, you have been very . . . quiet."

"Only because I've been admiring the woman seated in front of me."

Although inwardly pleased, she passed over his flattery, and continued in a serious vein. "Connor is determined to see justice served. He—he is very bitter."

"I know that."

"Then what are your plans? Surely you don't intend to let

him go on with this—this madness?" Because of their proximity to the other passengers, Catherine was careful to avoid any mention of the murder charge.

Rory shook his head, reassuring her. Leaning forward, with his arms folded on the back of her seat, he whispered, "I don't want you to worry about me, Catherine. Promise me, no matter what transpires, you'll stay by your father's side."

A sense of panic filled her. "Why?" she asked. "What are you planning?"

"Just promise me."

"I'll do no such thing!" she returned in a fast whisper. "You've a plan, haven't you? Tell me!"

"I can't. I've already jeopardized your safety, and I don't wish to be the cause of a rift between you and your father."

"My father is being unreasonable, appointing himself judge and jury! If a rift arises between us, it will be due to his own pigheadedness."

"Hush, Catherine, don't talk about your father that way. His reasons for keeping you at arm's length from me stem from his worry for your safety."

"But if not for you, I wouldn't even be alive! Jack Reese would have killed me."

Rory shook his head once, compressing his lips as he brushed the back of one hand lightly along her jawline. There was sadness in his blue eyes. "I'm sorry you had to witness what happened between Reese and me."

"None of what happened was your fault. You did what you had to do."

He wasn't listening. "If I could," he continued, "I would erase the memory of it from your mind."

"But you cannot. And I don't know why you and my father insist upon sheltering me as if I'm an innocent schoolgirl." She grasped his hand in both of hers. "You needn't feel you have to protect me from everything. If you've some plan to get away from Connor and my father, please tell me. I want to help."

"I know," he whispered. "That's what concerns me. I don't want you following me, Catherine. After what happened at the Latham home, there will be a price on my head. Make no mistake about it, Latham's moneyed friends will not let the matter rest until I'm found."

"But surely Jenny will—"

"Will what? Confess? I don't think so, not if Jimmy has any say in the matter, which he will."

"You think J.D. will come to Jenny's aid?"

"Of course he will. He loves her; he always has."

"Even so, you're not guilty! Jenny could not allow you to go to—"

"Ssh," he whispered, his gaze flicking across the crowded car as he leaned closer. "Take care what you say aloud. Those who seem to be asleep may be only pretending."

Catherine herself had wondered if her father was truly sleeping. "But you're innocent," she insisted.

Ned stirred then, opening his eyes. Licking his dry lips and taking a moment to focus on his daughter, he said, "Katie?"

Catherine immediately let go of Rory's hand, feeling a stab of longing as he eased back into his seat. Fighting down the emptiness she felt without Rory's touch, she said, "Yes, Pa?"

"What? Oh. Good night, Katie," he muttered groggily, then turned his head to the other side and was soon fast asleep again, his breathing deep.

Catherine turned to look back at Rory. He had put his hat on, the brim pulled low on his forehead, covering his eyes and nose. She waited a moment, thinking he might resume their conversation. When he made no move to do so, she laid her head against the rough upholstery and tried to sleep.

"Good night," she heard him whisper.

For Catherine, it could hardly be a good night. Knowing now that Rory was planning to slip away she had to guess when and where he would do so. When he did make his move, she vowed to be right behind him.

Chapter Twenty-two

Transferring from the Central Pacific Railroad to the Union Pacific line at Promontory, Utah, was time consuming and hectic, with first-class passengers switching from Silver Palace cars to Pullman accommodations. During the layover, many passengers traveled the short distance to Salt Lake City to see firsthand the unusual lifestyle of the Mormons. Since polygamy was accepted, even encouraged, among the Mormons, Salt Lake was a popular attraction for tourists traveling east and west.

For Catherine, Promontory held no interest. It was just a place where railroads met, a dreary little town with canvas-roofed business establishments along one side of the tracks, and the railroad station on the other. She was thankful when the whistle blew and they left Utah far behind.

As the miles fell away, Rory became quiet, seemingly content to ride in silence beside his brother. Ned and Connor seemed much relieved by Rory's silence. Catherine perceived it as only the calm before the storm. At every tank and whistle stop, she feared Rory would make his move. While hurriedly forcing down horrid meals, mostly greasy meat, boiled potatoes, and day-old bread, she would watch him closely, always prepared to dart after him should he wander away.

At one way station, just west of the Missouri River, she had a chance to walk back to the train alongside him. Her father and Connor were lost in the sea of bodies moving behind them, all eager to be aboard the train before it pulled away with a racehorse start as this engineer was wont to do.

In a hurried whisper, she asked, "When?"

Rory, surprise lighting his blue eyes, gazed at her for a moment, then said, "Soon. But you're not to follow, do you hear?"

"But where will you go?"

"The only place I can go."

Catherine was left to ponder that cryptic answer as Ned caught up with them and slipped her gloved hand through the crook of his arm, steering her away from Rory. After that, Catherine was not given another moment alone with Rory.

At Council Bluffs, just after crossing the muddy Missouri, the train stopped, and the foursome sought rooms for the night at the Union Pacific Hotel. After unpacking and washing away the travel grime, Ned and Catherine went down to the hotel dining room. They had just been served when Connor joined them at their table.

"Where is Rory?" Ned asked in alarm. "You don't plan to leave him alone for any length of time, do you?"

Connor shook his dark head. "Don't worry about Rory. He won't be going anywhere. Since his saddle and gun are in your room, and his horse is out of reach, I don't think he'll attempt to flee. Besides, he has no money. Anyway, if Rory is planning to escape, he'll wait until we're closer to Pennsylvania. But I don't think he'll try."

"And why not?" Ned asked.

"I believe Rory *wants* to return to Shenandoah. In my opinion, he's looking forward to seeing our father and baby sister. I actually believe he's anxious to see them again."

Ned gave a grunt of disbelief. "Even so, I wouldn't relax

our vigilance." Dismissing the subject of Rory, Ned motioned to the vacant chair opposite him. "As long as you're here, Connor, sit down. I want to talk with you. I've a friend in Philadelphia who will be meeting us. We will stay the night with him and learn what has transpired since you were last seen in Shenandoah. Once we learn what is going on, we'll decide whether or not you should go directly to the authorities with your side of the story or whether we should lay low and wait."

Catherine, seated beside her father, listened to their exchange. She watched Connor carefully. He seemed far more nervous than he had at any time during their trip. She wasn't sure what worried him more: facing the authorities and admitting that he had indeed blown a mine shaft, but only under duress—or seeing the outcome of his plan to take Rory forcibly back to Pennsylvania. She watched as he stuck an unlit cigarette in his mouth, then pulled it back out and tossed it on the table. She decided Connor feared his brother more than any justice system. And rightly so. When all their troubles with the Molly Maguires were resolved—if they were *ever* resolved—the O'Shay brothers would have to confront each other. It was inevitable. And given the volatile nature of both men, coupled with Connor's deep-rooted resentment of Rory, the clash was bound to be ugly. Catherine only hoped she would be able to intervene. She wanted a happy ending for the O'Shay family and would not allow herself to believe the outcome could be otherwise.

"I just want one meeting alone with John O'Reilly," Connor said to Ned, his face in grim lines. "I'm going to give that man his due."

"Hold on, boy," Ned said quickly. "I, just as much as you, want to see O'Reilly brought to justice for all the murdering and mayhem he's instigated, but I don't truly believe O'Reilly had anything to do with the men who set you up."

Connor's green eyes flashed. "What the hell do you

mean? Of course O'Reilly was involved. He's at the bottom of this whole rotten business! Reese was acting under O'Reilly's orders when he forced me into blowing that shaft, and I'll be damned if I'm going to let him get away with ruining my life."

"Think what you're saying, boy," Ned pressed, his voice low. "You say Reese told you of O'Reilly's involvement. How can you credit anything Jack Reese might have said? I think Reese acted under the orders of someone other than O'Reilly."

"And what makes you think that? Who else but the Mollies would want another mine out of business, and who else besides O'Reilly gives the members their instructions?"

"That's just it, boy, I don't think the Mollies had anything to do with this."

Connor looked puzzled, and irritated. "I don't follow you," he said.

Ned Diamond gave an uneasy grunt of laughter. "I'm not sure I follow myself sometimes, but hear me out. After listening to your side of the story, I made some inquiries on my own and from all the information I've garnered, it just doesn't make sense that O'Reilly would have to blow the Trenton mine. I have it from a reliable source that both the foreman and the colliery supervisor were Molly sympathizers. O'Reilly's a smart man; he knows that in order to keep his organization on an upward climb, he needs men in positions of power. There's no way he would've had anyone touch the Trenton mine with both the foreman and supervisor backing the organization."

Connor digested this bit of news. After a moment of contemplation, he said, "If what you say is true and Reese is working for someone else, who could that someone be? Who could want me dead, and why?"

"That's what I am to find out, boy. Sure as I'm sitting here though, it isn't O'Reilly. The fact that Reese followed you all the way to California is a good indication that his superior, whoever he may be, is first, still desperate to see you silenced, and second, has the funds to pay a man to follow you clear across the country." Ned held up two fingers to emphasize both points. "Now, I suggest you start thinking real hard about who you might have angered in the past."

Connor pressed his lips tightly together as he shook his head. "I don't know, Ned. I just don't know."

"You think on it, boy. For now, we'll worry about clearing your name with the authorities." Having had his say, Ned set himself to the task of eating while Connor ordered his own meal.

"And what about Rory?" Catherine asked. "Has he eaten?"

"I'll take something up to the room for him later," Connor replied, suddenly moody. "It will do him good to have to wait on others for once in his life."

"And his head wound? Is it healing properly?"

Connor shrugged his shoulders. "I haven't inquired. My brother's health is his own concern. I'm only taking him back to Pennsylvania, that's all." His meal came then, and Connor, preoccupied with his own problems, gave Catherine no more information concerning Rory.

Shifting the conversation to other things, Ned said, "Did you hear of the card game tonight, boy? A few of the passengers are setting up a game to take place within the hour. What do you say we join them and see if we can't win some greenbacks to tide us over until we reach Philadelphia?"

Connor nodded, shoving a spoonful of beans into his mouth. Catherine wrapped the fried chicken that was left on her plate into her linen napkin along with her uneaten roll. If Connor and her father were going to play cards, she knew well enough not to expect them back in their rooms before sunrise. Once involved in a game of cards, her father would play for hours. It was more than likely that

Connor would forget to bring Rory any food.

Napkin in hand, Catherine excused herself, saying she was weary from all the train travel. "I look forward to spending the night in a proper bed," she told them.

Both men wished her goodnight, unaware that she intended to check on Rory before she went to her own room.

Catherine approached Rory's door with growing hesitation. No matter how innocent her errand, it might enrage her father and cause more trouble for Rory. Uncertain, and nervous about being found out, she decided to go to her own room and think the matter over.

Once inside, she paced indecisively, went to the door and opened it, then closed it and returned to her bed where she unpinned her hair and brushed the long tresses.

She fidgeted for nearly an hour. Then, deciding Rory must be famished, she stole out into the hallway, cursing Connor for his indifference.

Chapter Twenty-three

As she stood before Rory's door, Catherine's palms were moist and her pulse was racing. In her heart, she knew that her reason for being here was not just to see that he didn't starve. Once she entered, there might be no turning back. Finally, she opened the door and stepped inside.

The chamber was small and sparsely furnished, with a single lamp that threw reflections on the windows, which had not been curtained for the night. Rory lay stretched out on his back on one of the two bunks, his right arm bent behind his head. Even supine, he radiated great, leashed power. Under his red plaid shirt, the sleeves of which were rolled to his elbows, Catherine could see the well-defined shape of his muscled chest and his slender tapered waist. He looked every inch the caged beast who, content for now to let his captors rest and enjoy their victory, would soon rise up to reap vengeance. Catherine felt her heart trip at the thought.

Rory glanced up as she entered. Lord, but she was a vision as she stood hesitantly just inside the door, her gray eyes wide and filled with indecision. In that instant, she appeared far lovelier even than he had remembered. Her hair, loose and falling about her shoulders like a dark cloud, shone like silk. His desire for her suddenly sharpened; he ached to run his fingers through those luxuriant tresses.

"I wondered if I would see you alone before we reached our destination," he whispered.

"I am only here to check your wound and to bring you some food," she said quickly.

He lifted one dark brow, amusement glimmering in the depths of his blue eyes. "At this hour?" he questioned.

"And why not?" she rejoined, although a blush crept up to her cheeks. "I've only just eaten, and it is obvious you've been awake for some time."

"I could have been resting."

"But you were not."

"Still, I could have been asleep. What would the ministering angel have done then?"

"In that case, I would have quietly checked your wound, left the food, and then returned to my own room."

Rory gave her a rakish smile, settling back against the headboard of his bunk. "Would you now? I somehow doubt it."

"Oh? And what is it you think I might have done had I found you sleeping?" She should not have posed the question, she knew, but the words seemed to leap from her lips of their own accord.

His gaze darkening, he waited a moment before saying, "Since you are the nightingale stealing about while the rest of the world makes ready for bed, you tell me."

Catherine pressed her lips tightly together, giving him a quelling look as she brought forth the napkin filled with food. "I did not come here to be interrogated, Mr. O'Shay. I am here only to see to your welfare. How does your head feel?"

"Like I've been whacked on the head with the butt of a revolver. But you needn't worry yourself over me, I have suffered worse—if you recall."

She did indeed recall. A bullet had grazed his leg the

night Jack Reese had opened fire in the Diamond Saloon. That he should remind her of the incident, only heightened her sense of guilt. If not for her, Rory might not have been shot by Jack Reese and would certainly not be now at the mercy of his brother.

"Regardless, I would still like to check your wound. May I?"

Plumping up the pillows behind him, Rory motioned her to come forward. "Seeing as how my comfort means so much to you, how can I refuse?"

Ignoring his teasing, mock formal manner, Catherine stood beside the bed and examined him. His hair was damp and sweet smelling, and she realized he must have ordered a bath while she had been dining. The dark strands were silky and soft in the pale light. Gingerly, she parted the curls at the back of his head, finding an ugly lump the size of an egg. The cut that zigzagged across the bump had formed a scab and was, as far as she could tell, healing as it should be.

Throughout her gentle ministrations, Rory sat quietly, watching her from the waist down through lazily hooded eyes. The snug fit of her striped, cream-colored gown accentuated her slender waist and the curve of her rounded hips. Rory remembered vividly how it felt to span that tiny waist with his large hands. He recalled with clarity the petal smoothness of her ivory skin. He wanted to caress her nakedness again, wanted to once again make her his own. Her long hair, black and sleek as a raven's wing, fell like a swath of rich silk against Rory's bare forearm. Rory swallowed hard. It was only with great effort that he refrained from reaching out to grasp those silky strands and guide her toward him. He wanted nothing more than to have her lie beside him and to give to her the myriad pleasures she had so willingly given him on that windswept knoll above the bay.

Despite his earlier, bantering manner, he felt that she was

here now mainly out of pity for his present circumstances. Would she ever be able to come to him again, freely, for love's sake only? He wanted her love, not her sympathy.

Her task completed, Catherine gently let Rory's damp curls fall back in place. Her fingertips tingled from touching him, and she was uncomfortably aware of his body heat radiating toward her.

"Are — are you hungry?" she asked, turning quickly, trying to cover the awkward moment. I brought some chicken and a biscuit for you."

Rory smiled to himself, watching her skirts swish about her ankles. "No, that won't be necessary," he replied. "Connor was here just a short time ago. Despite his underhanded methods of getting me home, he has been seeing to my needs well enough. Perhaps he is feeling some guilt."

Surprised, Catherine then noticed the newspaper and the bottle of bourbon on the bedside table. Connor's harsh words in the dining room had evidently been spoken to cover up a real concern for his brother's welfare.

"I see," she replied, feeling foolish now for having come to his room. Obviously, he was fine. She readied herself to leave. "I — I guess my worry for your welfare was unnecessary. You appear to be in good health, and now that I've seen for myself that Connor isn't neglecting you, I can —"

". . . return to your own chamber and continue the journey with a clear conscience," he finished for her. "But there's one thing you've forgotten."

Warily, she asked, "And that is?"

"My emotional state, of course," he replied, his blue eyes completely guileless. "The worst torture for prisoners is solitary confinement."

"Solitary confinement? That hardly describes your situation."

"Oh, but it does," he replied. "Other than my brother, you are the only person I've seen in, oh, about two hours. Can't you stay with me for a while? I am desperately in need of companionship."

She sent him a quelling look. "I don't think you will expire from lack of company if I leave. Besides, it—it's late. You need your rest."

"I'm not tired."

"Still, we are in a public hotel. It would be inproper—perhaps even dangerous—if I remained here alone with you."

Rory smiled. "Dear Catherine, what has propriety to do with us—or with the way in which my brother abducted me? Besides, any hotel guests who might pass judgment on your being here, are by now fast asleep. And, as for any danger of discovery by Connor or Ned, they are playing cards and will not return until dawn.

His reasoning was nearly flawless, but he had not taken into account her own turbulent, conflicting emotions. Every time she thought about him—and she thought about him every waking moment—she was torn by both shame and regret; shame that she had given herself so wantonly to him, regret that there might never come another time when she could do so again. Even now, her hunger for him was mounting.

"I shouldn't stay," she whispered.

Rory heard the pain in her voice, saw the conflict in her eyes. He had done this to her, had made her afraid of her own healthy instincts. Swiftly, he rose from the bunk and reached to grasp her by the shoulders. "Stop, Catherine. Stop torturing yourself with needless guilt. There is no reason for you to feel so tormented.

"Isn't there?" She didn't look at him, couldn't. "What I've let pass between us isn't right. And yet—even though I know I should not—I crave your touch, your kiss." The words tumbled from her lips. "You can't imagine what thoughts have been swimming through my mind since I stepped into this room!"

"Oh, but I can," he said hoarsely. "For the very same

images have been setting me aflame. Your incredible beauty, your proud, fiery spirit have driven me wild since that moment at the saloon when I first saw you. You're a witch, Catherine Diamond, and I am completely under your spell."

There were tears shimmering in her eyes when she finally lifted her gaze to his. "Yes, I *am* a witch. I am wicked and—"

"Stop," he ordered, pulling her close, his lips closing on hers in a fierce, possessive kiss. He plundered the honeyed recesses of her mouth like a man snatching at treasure which might soon be out of his reach. And when Catherine fought him, he dropped his arms to encircle her waist, holding her tightly against him. "I didn't say you're a *wicked* witch," he murmured against her mouth. "I meant only that you're a full-blooded woman with more passion than any conventional, priggish matron. You are life itself, Catherine. My life. *Never* be ashamed of what we've shared." He bent his head to sear kisses along the slim white column of her neck.

Catherine felt her knees grow weak, felt that familiar treacherous longing spread through her like hot, flowing lava.

Rory's kisses grew bolder as he dipped his head toward the top closures of her gown. One by one, he undid them, his tongue flicking at her satiny skin as he went.

With trembling limbs, she moved her hands across his chest, slipping free the buttons of his shirt as her clear gray gaze met his.

Rory saw the sweet surrender in her eyes. *"Macushla,"* he murmured, then dipped his head to claim her mouth with his own a tender kiss that deepened, became searing. His hands trailed atop her shoulders, slipping the material of her bodice and chemise down her arms and over her elbows, baring her pink-tipped breasts. His hands, and then his mouth, moved hungrily over the stiffening peaks, warming her entire body with deliciously hot sparks.

Catherine arched toward him, letting her garments drop to her waist and working quickly to undo the remaining buttons of his shirt. Rory took one step back and then another, holding her to him, his kisses never ceasing. He turned her in a slow circle, and then eased her down atop the narrow bunk where he pressed his naked chest against her eager breasts.

Reaching up with one hand, he yanked the window curtain partly closed, then extinguished the light near the bed. Catherine barely noticed. Not even the night air that came in at the open window could cool the fever that rose in her with every intimate caress of his mouth, his hands. The shriek of a distant train whistle, noises from the street below, all went unnoticed as they explored each other's bodies.

Slowly, skillfully, Rory slipped the bunched up bodice and chemise down over her hips and legs, stripping her naked. Then, beginning at her smooth, taut belly, his hands and tongue moved downward. There was no place he did not touch, no inch neglected. When he rose for a moment to gaze into her eyes, Catherine reached frantically to undo his breeches, unable to endure the sweet torture another moment. She wanted to be one with him, to appease the hunger that only he could satisfy. Rory moved away briefly, just long enough to shed his shirt and trousers. She smiled up at him, lifting her arms to pull him back down beside her.

Their lovemaking rose to fever pitch then, each of them straining toward the other, touching, tasting, reveling in the sheer, utter joy of such intimacy. Parting her thighs, he thrust inside her, filling her with his manhood. Catherine caught her breath, squeezing his muscled shoulders in an agony of pleasure. His movements were slow at first, his rhythm controlled and even. Then, they were each caught up in a spiraling ecstasy. He drove more deeply within her, brushing her eyelids with tender kisses, then ravaging her mouth with a deep, probing kiss that swept her to the razor's edge. Catherine's eyelids fluttered open and she gazed up at him.

"Catherine . . . my witch, my love . . . do you know what spells you weave about me?" He plunged deep, then pulled back, only to plunge again. His opened mouth against hers, he whispered roughly, "I want you with me— *always*. Damn the hangman's noose in Pennsylvania. I'll outfox them all just so I can have you every night."

Catherine clung to him, nodding as she returned his kisses, swept up in a tide of pure sensation. Together they soared, two beings mindless of consequences, bound together by the inexplicable magic of love. Finally, at the apex of their flight, release came—tumultous and agonizingly sweet. They rode the crest together, sharing the blinding joy, exulting in the power that was the sum of their spirits.

Catherine, pressed tightly to Rory, her breath coming in ragged gasps, knew what it was she craved, yet could not have. She wanted Rory, all of him, forever. She wanted more than just brief, stolen moments of pleasure. She wanted to lie beside him as his wife, wanted to bear his children, share his life completely. She did not want the threat of prison hanging over them like a raised sword that could descend at any moment to sever their tenuous bond.

Catherine was still for a long while, savoring the slow drift back to sanity. When the sounds of their breathing had evened, she spoke.

"You don't really intend to let Connor drag you back home like this, do you?"

Rory rolled to one side of the bunk, gathering her close to him and stroking her hair. "Do I have a choice?"

"I think you have a plan," she replied, running her fingers lazily through the crisp hairs of his chest. One ear was pressed against his body and the steady thump of his heart filled her head. "If you wanted to, you could break down the door of this room and head out of Council Bluffs. I don't believe your wound is serious enough to keep you bedridden."

A faint smile touched his lips. "Connor seems to think so."

"And that is exactly what you want him to believe, isn't it? You want him to think you're not well enough to escape. Tell me, Rory, what are you waiting for?"

He planted a light kiss to her forehead. "Not only are you beautiful, dear Catherine, you are also quick. You are quite right. I could have long ago evaded Connor and your father. But there are many reasons I decided to stay on the train, you being one of them."

Her heart skipped a beat. She moistened her lips, then said, softly, "But I thought, after our last conversation at the cabin, you wanted nothing more to do with me . . ."

"I don't believe I used those exact words. I felt then, as I do now, you would be better apart from me. I've been eternally damned by a checkered past, a past that is even now catching up to me. To involve you in my sins is something I will not do."

"I am already involved."

"Yes," he agreed and his voice was tinged with remorse.

Catherine lifted her lashes. "Surely you must realize by now that I will stand by you, no matter what. I will do whatever it is in my power to—"

He pressed a finger to her lips. "Hush, he whispered. "I know." He dropped his finger to the tip of her chin, tilting her face up to his. He planted a feather-light kiss on her lips as his other hand softly stroked the naked small of her back. His lips lingered for only a moment before he pulled away, saying, "Gather your clothes. I want you to get dressed and go back to your own room."

"Now?"

"Yes, now. And I don't want you to return. I tried saying good-bye to you at the cabin, thinking then I had severed the bond between us. But now here you are in my bed once again, and we've come full circle. Nothing has changed, Catherine. I'm still a wanted man, with no future."

He pushed himself up and moved to sit on the edge of the bunk, raking one hand through his tousled hair in a frustrated gesture. Catherine lay still for a moment, drawing the sheet over her breasts. The silence lay heavy between them, underscored by echoing voices and laughter that floated up from the street below.

Quietly, she said, "Perhaps my dream of one day being a lady of quality ensconced in a proper house with a proper gentleman has been a child's vision . . . perhaps that is not what I want at all. I've matured since I've met you, Rory. In your arms I find I no longer need the approval of a judgmental society. I know exactly what I want, Rory. To hell with the rest of the world . . . I want to stay with you."

He looked over his shoulder at her, surprised at her choice of words. "Christ," he muttered, shaking his head, giving her a wry grin. "What have I done to you, Catherine? Now you're even beginning to sound like me!"

She sat up, boldly letting the sheet fall away as she laid her head against his shoulder and wound her arms about his neck. "You've done nothing to me that I didn't want to have happen. Face the truth, Rory O'Shay. Whether or not you want me by your side, you've got me." She gave a teasing nip to the bronzed skin of his upper arm as her grey eyes flashed with mischief.

Rory watched her from the corner of his eye. "You are a witch, Catherine Diamond."

She smiled, feeling more relaxed than she had in days. "Since I am being so very candid," she said softly, "I must confess and tell you my name is not Diamond. I was born Mary Catherine McGuillicuddy. Only when I arrived in California did I become Catherine Diamond. I guess San Francisco was just not ready for a McGuillicuddy Saloon." She laughed at the cumbersome name and was pleased when Rory laughed too.

"Ah, but here I have you, for I've known of your true name almost from the beginning. Come now, don't you recall a time in your childhood when a young fellow and his mother came calling on your small family?"

"You visited my home?" she asked incredulously. "No, you didn't. I would remember."

He laughed again, and reached up to place his hands on her arms. "Yes, I did. Let's see," he said, narrowing his eyes, remembering. "I was only seventeen then, but definitely believed myself to be every inch a man. I remember the time well, for it was the first and only journey my mother and I made alone. You were only about five years old at the time. A little girl with long dark braids and a spotless dress. I thought you were the prettiest thing I'd ever seen, quiet as a church mouse, though. Surely you remember, Catherine."

She didn't, although the story her father had told her, just weeks before—about Rory's background and his family's friendship with hers—came back to her now. But she hesitated to mention it since that was also the night on which her father had branded Rory a murderer. "Why did you come?" she asked. "And where was the rest of your family?"

"Home. My father stayed behind since he couldn't afford to miss even an hour of digging coal. Neighbors cared for my brother and baby sister. Connor was about seven or so, and my sister, Cally, had just been born. Our mothers were close friends, and one day when my mother received a letter from yours we made plans to visit. I was working in the mines, too. I was what they call a 'trapper,' opening and closing the doors in the mines to keep the ventilation working properly. But my father decided I should travel the miles to accompany my mother on her visit."

Catherine nodded, trying to recall that long ago time when she was just five years old.

"You were wearing a white dress, pure white. There were even white ribbons in your hair," he continued softly.

"Yes," she replied, staring at nothing and seeing the past. "I remember that dress. It was my mother's favorite. She used to call me her little angel . . . and I *felt* like an angel whenever I wore it—which was nearly every day."

"Do you remember when my mother and I came to stay?"

"I—I think so. My mother had just suffered a miscarriage, hadn't she?"

Rory nodded, patting her one arm as he leaned his head against hers. "Yes. That was the reason we came. My own mother had feared the worst when she learned your mother was expecting another child."

Catherine closed her eyes. Even after all these years she was still moved to tears whenever she thought of her kind, gentle mother. "There were so many miscarriages, Rory. And after every one, I felt I had to be even more the perfect child. Tell me about your visit. I only remember the pain and fear."

"You don't remember the walk we took?"

She concentrated, letting her mind take flight back through time. "I—I think so. Yes . . . yes, I do. You led me to a field, didn't you? I remember now. It was summertime and we walked out of the coal patch to a field filled with wildflowers."

"You picked a handful of black-eyed Susans for your mother. There were daisies and forget-me-nots galore but you picked only the yellow flowers with the brown centers. Even then, you were meticulous, Catherine. Every stem had to be the same length. If you picked a flower too short, you left it on the ground."

Catherine smiled, seeing the past as though it were projected by a magic lantern. "My mother loved black-eyed Susans. She was very pleased with that bouquet."

"Of course she was. You were the apple of her eye, her

most precious treasure. Do you remember what you said to me after you had fallen and skinned your knees and dirtied your dress? You had been running along the road, eager to reach home and present the bouquet to your mother, when you tripped. I picked you up and brushed away your tears, and you said, 'Now my mother will be angry because I fell and dirtied my dress! Young ladies don't fall and they never, ever run.' You were positively horrified."

Catherine tried to laugh but the sound came out like a strangled cry. Yes, she remembered—vividly. Hot tears burned the lids of her eyes.

"You know, Catherine, as I held you in my arms then and stroked your braided hair, I wondered what would become of all of us living in those miserable coal patches. You were trying so hard to grow up to be a real lady. But I knew, even then, only the very rich could be proper ladies, only the wealthy could get through a day without getting dirt and coal dust on their hands. And yet, there you were, dressed all in white, the picture of innocence in a filthy black town where fathers could sweat and bleed to death and still never see their young ones receive better than they got. It was at that moment the injustice of our lives hit me with full force. It was then I vowed that I would get out of the coal mines before I suffered more hardship."

Catherine felt him stiffen, felt his muscles tense. "I had no idea," she whispered. "I was just a little girl crying because I'd gotten dirt on my favorite dress . . . Life was harsh then, Rory—it still is for the people who remain there. Did you—did you leave soon after?" Somehow, she felt responsible.

He nodded. "Yes, I left. I woke up one morning to realize that I was seventeen—almost a man—and I was still following my father into the mines, my belly aching with hunger and my clothes reeking with the smell of my sweat from the day before. I was sick of my life then. I hated every sunrise, for it meant only one more descent into the bowels of the earth, picking at hard coal in near total darkness, with mine water sometimes a foot deep and chilling me to the bone."

"So you left it all behind you. I can't blame you for that; no one should. Tell me, where did you go? Where could a young man of your age go to find a safe haven in such a harsh world?"

"Everywhere . . . anywhere. A year passed and then another. I soon found myself in Baltimore—and in the bed of a very willing widow. She owned land and horses, and we made a deal; I'd be her companion at night, and in return, she'd teach me all there was to know of horse breeding and managing a vast estate. We both accepted our relationship for what it was—a mutually convenient arrangement. Neither of us had any illusions; we were both too hardened by the realities of life. I stayed on until the day she died. I was twenty-seven when I took the brood mare she bequeathed to me and I set my sights for home. I had money in my pocket, and my mare was going to foal a Thoroughbred that January."

Irish Fire, that was the foal he spoke of. "And what happened when you returned home?"

He straightened, shrugging out of her loose hold. "The same damned thing that always happened. I ran into trouble."

"You mean . . . the murder?"

He let out an anguished sigh. "If that's what you want to call it. I walked into O'Reilly's, a shebeen that I knew was a favorite of the Mollies. I was feeling reckless that night, and I confess that I was indeed in the mood to knock a few heads together. I had just been home to see my father, who informed me my mother had died of consumption and that my brother was thick as thieves with the Molly Maguires. He blamed me for everything; my mother's death, my brother's bad judgment—everything. I had come home to help him, to buy him out of his misery, but he didn't want my help. He wanted nothing to do with me. So I just left, determined to find my little brother and do what I could for him. Connor wasn't at the saloon, but some of his pals were there. They were planning Connor's downfall and I overheard them. I just walked up to the man nearest me and told him if they intended to bring harm to any O'Shay they had to deal with me first."

Catherine wanted to reach out to him, but knew better. "What happened then?"

Rory gave a short laugh. "They came at me, that's what. All of them. All twelve of those bastards jumped me. I guess they didn't figure I could take them all on at once. They didn't know what devils were screaming inside of me. I went wild with rage, blinded by guilt at having left my needy family and by the horrid news that my mother was dead. I was inhuman that night, invincible only because my pride wouldn't let me be beaten down again.

"They formed a circle around me, and one by one I fought them. By the time the last man came at me, I was bloodied and near passing out. But something in me wouldn't give up. They saved the strongest man till last. He came at me with a knife, and I knew then that I had to kill him or he would kill me . . ."

"Oh God, Rory, I'm sorry—"

"Don't be. I'm not."

"But you killed the man in self-defense! The authorities believe you killed him in cold blood with no provocation! You're innocent, Rory! Doesn't Connor know the truth? My goodness, he's dragging you back to Pennsylvania to stand trial for murder!"

"That's right. And if the powers that be have their way, I'm going to hang for that murder."

"No!" she nearly screamed. "I won't let them do this to you! You're innocent. You had no choice but to kill the man!"

He turned toward her then, his blue eyes as cold as a

299

Sierra snow. "And who is going to believe me when there are eleven men who will testify that I just walked into that shebeen and broke the man's neck? It's over, Catherine. My fate was sealed the night I walked into that saloon." He motioned with his head toward the door, his mood suddenly ominous. "You've heard my story, now get dressed and go. You shouldn't be here, and Lord knows, I should have kept my hands off you from the start. Go on, get. And if you're smart, you'll head back to San Francisco and forget you ever knew me."

Chapter Twenty-four

"No," Catherine said flatly. "I won't leave you. Not now, not ever."

Rory's only response was to turn away and gather up her clothes. He tossed them to her, and then began dressing himself. She watched as he yanked on his trousers, then shrugged into his plaid shirt, his movements quick, jerky. Her own clothes lay in her lap.

"There must be something we can do," she persisted. "Surely there must have been other witnesses that night, someone who will speak up and tell the true story. Please, Rory, don't give up! You can't go on running from the law for the remainder of your life. Think! Wasn't there someone in that saloon who saw what happened? What about the owner, the bartender, an employee?"

"Mollies, all of them," he answered grimly. "Everyone there is somehow attached to the Molly Maguires."

"But are they all so loyal to the organization that they would let an innocent man go to prison? Isn't it possible that one of the men in the saloon that night would be willing to tell his story now? Perhaps someone there was an unwilling member, just as your own brother was."

"I don't know, Catherine. It's possible. I've considered

what you're saying, but I can't for the life of me remember anyone else besides those twelve men."

"All right, then let's consider the possibility that one of those men might be willing to help you. Do you remember who they were? Could we seek them out and ask them for their help?"

He met her direct gaze. "What do you mean 'we'? There is no way I'm going to let you walk into that coal town with me. Emotions are high. I don't want you involved."

"But I'm already involved. I want to help you, Rory. Perhaps I could find answers where you could not. People might be willing to talk to me."

"I don't see why they would. You're an outsider, just as I am."

"But we could try! What have you got to lose?"

"My life . . . *your* life."

Catherine lifted her chin defiantly, undeterred by the black look in his eyes. "The way matters stand, your life is in jeopardy even if we don't do anything."

"But your life isn't."

She swept the clothes from her lap and stood, her naked skin gleaming in the lamplight, as she said, "And what is my life without you?" She took a slow step toward him and then another until she stood beside him. Running her palms provocatively along his forearms, she caressed her way to his shoulders. The corded muscles there were taut and she began to massage them, kneading them gently. Looking up at him with her clear gray eyes, she said, "I've told you once how wretched my days and nights have been since we've been apart. Must I tell you again?"

He stared down at her lovely upturned face, his whole body tense as he fought the urge to drag her back to the bunk and do indescribable things to her young body. "It isn't right," he told her gruffly, reaching up to grasp her slim hands. "Our being together can only bring you grief."

She rubbed seductively against him, placing a kiss on the

tip of his chin. "Grief is not what I'm feeling at the moment." She pressed her body against his, chest to chest, leg to leg. Eyes stormy with passion, she placed her parted lips on his mouth, her tongue teasing, courting, as her body undulated against him in that ancient rhythm Rory could not resist.

He could not deny her—could never deny her. He wanted her with him, always and forever. And though he knew they might well be damned in the end, he led her back to the narrow bed, guiding her gently down atop the tangled sheets. Once again, they entered that magical realm that helped make the real world bearable. . . .

An hour later, Catherine slipped back to her own room. Ned had not yet returned from his card game. Gratified and feeling warmly content, Catherine swiftly undressed and got into bed. Sleep came quickly, her dreams filled with lovely images. By morning, she felt utterly refreshed and ready to face the last leg of their journey.

As the foursome boarded yet another train, Ned and Connor were in high spirits, despite their weariness and wrinkled attire. They had won heavily at the all night card game, and now, with money in their pockets, looked forward to completing the long, transcontinental journey. Both men soon drifted off to sleep as the train chugged across the network of track that crisscrossed the eastern portion of the United States.

Catherine had hoped she and Rory might steal a moment of private conversation while Connor and Ned slept, but Rory was seemingly absorbed in a well-thumbed copy of the *Police Gazette*, purchased from the train's newsboy—or "candy butcher" as he was sometimes called—who also sold sweets, cigars, and sundries. When Rory seemed content to let the miles pass in silence, Catherine wondered if he perhaps regretted their shared moments of the night before.

If so, she was prepared to remind him that she intended to stick by his side, no matter what the consequences.

Their aisle seats faced each other, and Catherine was just about to tap his leg with her shoe, when Rory folded his newspaper and stood.

Catherine looked up at him with lifted brows. With a finger to his lips, he cut off any questions. In silence, she watched as he moved through the aisle toward the conductor. The two men spoke at some length in low tones, then moved to the back of the car, near the potbelly stove, where Rory unobtrusively slipped some folded greenbacks to the conductor. Rory then returned to his seat and once again opened his newspaper.

"What was that about?" Catherine whispered.

Rory glanced at her over the top of the paper. "I think you know," he whispered back.

"I'm coming with you."

"Yes," he replied. "You are."

She sighed with relief. She had feared that Rory would somehow prevent her from following him. "When? Where?"

"Soon. When I make my move, you'll know. It will be up to you to get away from your father and Connor," he whispered. "After that, I'll find you."

She nodded, excited by the prospect of what lay ahead. When Rory again returned his attention to the *Police Gazette*, Catherine no longer minded. She was content in the knowledge that she and Rory would soon be together again.

A great cloud of steam issued noisily from the tall black smokestacks as the train pulled to a grinding halt in Philadelphia. As the other passengers bustled about, gathering up their belongings, Catherine stood and brushed off the black skirt of her riding costume. The outfit was too warm for the heat of the day, but if she and Rory were to travel through the coal regions, it would be the most practical attire.

"Are you ready, Catherine?" Ned asked, touching her elbow.

She looked up, nodding, but her reply was cut off by the conductor, who strode purposefully through the aisle, coming to a halt beside Rory.

"Mr. O'Shay? Rory O'Shay?" he asked.

Rory looked at the man with a great show of surprise. "Yes. I'm O'Shay."

"Excuse me, sir, but you'll have to come with me. I've orders to see you personally off the train."

Catherine stiffened, apprehensive. She hoped this was all just part of Rory's plan.

"What?" Connor intervened, his voice harsh. "What are you talking about? Whose orders?"

"I'm sorry, sir," the conductor replied, nonplused as he grabbed Rory firmly by the arm. "This is official business. I'm not at liberty to say." He began to lead Rory away.

"Now see here," Ned thundered. "You just can't take this man. He's traveling with us and—"

"I'm sorry," the conductor interrupted. "You'll have to speak with my superior. I'm just following orders." With that, he whisked his unprotesting prisoner away. Other passengers, eager to disembark, filed into the crowded aisle, and soon Rory and the conductor were out of sight.

"Superior?" Ned echoed. "Hell, that man answers to no one but himself. I smell a rat, here. Come on, boy," he said to Connor. "Let's go after them." To Catherine, he said, "Stay with our baggage, Mary Catherine, and do not move from the station, do you hear?"

Catherine nodded, frightened by the force of her father's anger. He would be even angrier, she knew, when he learned she'd fled with Rory. She watched the two men shoulder their way through the crowded car. When there was an opening, she too stepped into the aisle and headed for the exit.

Once on the platform, waiting for their bags, she looked

for some sight of Rory among the crowd of people. Jostled by the hurrying throng, their noisy shouts ringing in her ears, she became suddenly nervous and unsure of herself. All these people—fashionables and working people alike—were on their way to ordinary, everyday pursuits. And what was she walking into? The thought of what might lie ahead made her shiver, and she felt very alone.

With all their bags firmly in hand, Catherine deposited Connor's and Ned's at the ticket counter, hoping her father would check there when he didn't find her. Hastily, she pinned a note to Ned's valise. The note read: "Please don't be angry, Pa. I've gone with Rory to help him clear his name. He's no murderer, and I'm perfectly safe with him. Do not worry about me. I love you, Katie."

Her own bag was heavy as she made her way out of the station. The crowds had thinned now, and when she failed to spot Rory among the few remaining people, she became increasingly anxious. She dropped her bag to the ground and began to pace up and down, the clicking of her heels loud in the stillness of the now almost deserted area. Suddenly, she stopped stock-still, deciding that she must have been mad even to have considered running off like this. Picking up her valise, she was starting back for the depot, when a powerful hand grabbed her shoulder. Her heart lurched. She whirled—and looked up into Rory's face.

"Going somewhere?" he asked in a deep voice, gathering her tightly against his solid chest.

"Rory! Wh-what are you doing?"

His eyes, a startling blue in the midmorning light, smiled down at her. "That's what I was about to ask you. Why are you headed back toward the depot? I thought we agreed that you would stay clear of Ned and Connor."

She pushed hard against his chest, angry because he had frightened her unnecessarily. But she was also filled with relief.

"Well?" he inquired, waiting for an answer. His arms

went around her slim waist. "Have you decided to abandon me and return to your father?"

"Certainly not! I just thought—"

"You thought I hadn't gotten off the train in time," he finished for her. "Tsk, tsk, Katie dear, you had better have more faith in me if you intend to venture by my side deep into Molly territory." He dropped a chaste kiss to her forehead, releasing her then as he stooped to retrieve the bag she had dropped.

Catherine took a moment to collect herself before she said, "Connor and Ned are looking for you even now. We haven't much time to spare."

"We haven't any time to spare," he corrected. "Come," he said, taking her gloved hand. "The horses are over there, beyond that warehouse. Fire is still skittish from the train ride, so we'll both have to ride on the mare until he calms down."

"And how did Bess fare?" she asked, taking two steps to each of his long strides.

"Beautifully, as always. She's a calm one, Bess is. And that's the only reason she can never be a fine racer, as Fire one day will. No racing silks for Bess, only foals."

The two horses stood side by side, Bess patiently awaiting her master's return, and Fire, spirited as always, nickering softly as he beat a fidgety rhythm with his hooves. Rory helped Catherine astride Bess, then climbed up behind her. He gathered the reins in his hands and they headed out of the city.

The road they traveled took them through lush, rolling countryside—vast fertile fields and snug, gray stone farmhouses which had been handed down through generations of families dating back to the early years of Pennsylvania. Everywhere, the landscape was dotted with lacy white picket fences and ancient gnarled apple trees whose fragrant boughs were heavy with fruit, some of which had fallen and rolled onto the dirt road. When allowed to, the horses would briefly break their gait to dip down and munch on a treat.

As verdant farmland gradually gave way to the outskirts of anthracite coal country, Catherine grew nostalgic. Everything, from the heady fragrance of goldenrod to the tinkling murmur of roadside streams, seemed to trigger some memory. Vivid images of her childhood—many of them forgotten until now—flashed before her eyes. Each sound and scent brought back some treasured moment.

Home, she thought, I am finally home. The glittering excitement of San Francisco began to fade, diminished somehow by compelling images of her girlhood in a coal patch, harsh but cherished images that were closer to the core of her soul:

They stopped to eat beneath a dogwood tree, on a velvety, sweet smelling carpet of white teardrop petals. Their meal consisted of leftovers which each had tucked away before leaving the train.

"If we keep our pace, we should be able to catch the night train to Mahanoy City," Rory said. He was seated across from her, his back against a sagging brown fence, one leg stretched out before him, the other bent at the knee with his arm resting atop it.

"And then?" Catherine asked as she fanned her face with her black beaver hat. Her heavy riding habit had become stifling and uncomfortable, even in the shade of the tree.

"Then we'll head for Shenandoah and find lodging. Tomorrow, I'll begin my search for any witnesses who can testify to my innocence."

"Have you remembered anything?" she asked. "Is there perhaps someone who can testify, but may be unwilling to do so?"

He grunted with mirthless laughter, tossing away one of the apples they'd picked during their long ride. "You're too perceptive, Catherine. I should know by now there isn't much I can keep hidden from you."

She smiled. "Now, who is it that you think may be able to help you?"

Rory shrugged his shoulders, staring off into the distance. "There is someone . . . but I can't believe he'll testify. He was in O'Reilly's shebeen the night the Mollies came after me. Actually, he threw a few punches too, only because he couldn't risk angering the other men. He had joined the Mollies, not realizing that their crusade for workers' rights included mayhem, and worse. I think he wanted out then, just like Connor. But unlike Connor, Murphy just kept quiet. There's no way he'd stand up against such a powerful force."

"Murphy?"

"Yes. John Murphy's his name. We all call him Murphy since his father's name is John, too. His sister, Margaret, was Jenny's closest friend."

"Oh yes, I remember Jenny mentioning her. She . . . she was infatuated with you, wasn't she?" Catherine had made another perceptive guess.

Rory smiled. "Yes, I suppose she was, and the two of us were too often left to ourselves while Jenny and J.D. slipped away. Back then, I figured I owed Jimmy something because he'd helped me pull my injured father out of a crumbling mine shaft. I was willing enough to spend time with Margaret, so Jimmy could be alone with Jenny. But I made the mistake of confiding in her and telling her of my plans to leave town. Much to my surprise, she was heartbroken. Until that moment, I hadn't realized how deeply her feelings went. To me, the hours we'd spent together were just a smoke screen, so Jenny's father would think she was with Margaret. But somehow, Meg fancied I was in love with her. She went running home with tears in her eyes. Undoubtedly, Murphy got an earful of what a beast I had been to her."

"But that was years ago—surely, this Murphy would now be willing to help an old friend," Catherine said.

"It's possible. We'll see soon enough. There's one more thing, though. Soon after I left Shenandoah, Margaret married O'Reilly's son. When the old man died, she and the younger O'Reilly took over the shebeen. There cannot be much love for me in the bosom of that little family."

The last leg of their journey was not as pleasant as their first. After leaving the train at Mahanoy City, they again traveled by horse, toward Shenandoah. As night descended, the air grew damp and chilly, and Catherine, who had been so overheated the day before, now began to shiver. Rory stopped and dug out wraps for them both from their valises. Now, the roadway narrowed, and the meager light diminished as a deep wood sprang up around them.

The night was filled with sounds; a chorus of peepers chirping from beneath their cover of cool, wet leaves; bullfrogs belting out their hoarse songs; and even the snorting of a buck could be heard now and then from beyond the thick line of trees skirting the roadway. Huddled in her cloak, Catherine leaned back against Rory.

His right arm snaked about her waist in a comforting embrace. "Frightened?" he asked.

Catherine nodded. "A little."

"Don't be. There's nothing in those woods that's going to harm you. For me, they are like an old, welcoming friend." He dropped a warm kiss to her temple. "Look. Up ahead. See that dot of light?"

Catherine squinted into the darkness. "Yes . . . yes, I do see a light. Is that Shenandoah?"

"None other." His voice was low, cautious.

Catherine clasped a hand to his wrist and felt his pulse quicken. "You're finally going home," she whispered, and unexpected tears welled up in her eyes.

The coal dust and grime of Shenandoah were covered by the blanket of night, dotted here and there by the pale glow of gas lamps. The stillness was broken only by muffled voices drifting across the cool night air, and the sound of a child's hungry wail from one of the many houses lining the main thoroughfare. Catherine and Rory were both silent as they made their way down the middle of the dusty street, passing the crudely built homes that were spaced only a few feet apart. From all, came the pungent smell of anthracite coal used to fuel the small stoves within. The ghostly shapes of laundry flapped on a clothesline that led from the front of one house to a scraggly, budding tree. A lone, tired man sat on the stoop of another house, a peaked cap pulled low on his forehead.

Rory did not turn in the man's direction. He looked straight ahead, nerves taut, every sense alert.

"Where are we going?" Catherine whispered. "Is it wise for us to come right through the center of town?" It was common knowledge that Cass Township and Shenandoah were the wellspring of the Mollies, and only now did Catherine realize the full import of what she might have let herself in for. True, she had wanted to come here with Rory, but now that she was actually here, her fears were beginning to mount.

"O'Reilly's shebeen is just up ahead. Let's get safely past it, and then we'll talk of lodging."

They passed the saloon as quietly as they could. O'Reilly's shebeen, one of the principal meeting places of the infamous Mollies, was a shadowy gray shape in the darkness, its windows aglow with a soft yellow light. Catherine tensed as she imagined an angry mob bursting through the doors, intent on attacking Rory. But this night, O'Reilly's was quiet, seemingly peaceful as a churchyard. Nevertheless, Catherine did not relax until the saloon was behind them and Rory had drawn both horses to a halt in front of a dark, deserted building. He dismounted, then reached up to help Catherine to the ground.

"What is it?" she asked, noting the grim set of his face,

the muscle that twitched above his lean jaw. He was in the grip of his private demons again.

"Catherine," he said, gesturing to the empty building. "This is where I thought we'd find lodgings, but as you can see, the proprietors have evidently given it up and moved on. The only other boardinghouse in town is above the shebeen—and Margaret and John O'Reilly run it. We can hardly go there, nor would we be welcome."

"What will we do, then," she asked in a tight voice.

He looked at her evenly. "Catherine," he replied in firm tones, "I'm going home. It's time my father and I had a long talk."

Chapter Twenty-five

The O'Shay home was a small, shabby, slapped together structure made of scrap lumber. It was one of many such "homes" thrown up by the mine owners many years before for the Irish immigrants who were wooed away from their homeland with exaggerated promises of good paying jobs and housing for all. Catherine was aghast to think that a family of five had once all lived together beneath the sagging roof. She said nothing, however, as she followed Rory up the uneven path to the house.

The more populated part of town had been left behind, and they walked in total darkness, closer now to the tipple of the Trenton mine where so many coal miners had once labored from dawn to dusk. The surrounding landscape was bleak, bare of any vegetation, and even in the darkness, Catherine could sense the noxious presence of the coal dust that clung tenaciously to everything. Behind them, the horses snorted nervously, impatient to be rubbed down and fed for the night. Absently, Catherine wondered where fresh feed could be found for the animals.

Ahead of her, Rory paused before the dilapidated door, breathing deeply of the cool night air before he knocked once and then yanked on the rusty handle. Catherine hung back, not wanting to intrude on his first moments with his family. She waited anxiously in the silence that followed, her heart beating erratically. There was no sound from the small house. The only thing she heard was the chirping of peepers, the lonely hooting of a distant owl, and the occasional soft snorts of the horses. Fear of the elder O'Shay's wrath made her hesitant to venture farther.

Finally, concern for Rory's safety propelled her to the threshold. The heavy smell of cooked venison wafted to her, mingled with the pervasive odor of damp, rotting wood. She peered into the dark interior.

"Rory?"

A moment passed before he answered. "Here," he said softly. Somewhere a match was struck, its flame hissing, then glowing bright yellow in the inky darkness. Rory's hand moved the wavering flame to the wick of a stubby candle that sat atop a crude table.

In the meager light, Catherine could see that Rory was holding a little girl. A cloud of dark hair covered her face, which was pressed to Rory's shirt front. Her muffled sobs filled the air. Holding her tightly, protectively, Rory stroked the little girl's long, tangled curls. He looked up at Catherine with haunted grief-filled eyes.

"This is Cally," he whispered. "My baby sister."

Catherine nodded, her heart breaking at the stricken face of the man she loved. The demons within him were gathering force. It would not be long now before he erupted violently. Terrible trouble lay ahead.

"And your father?" she asked, dreading the answer.

"Out. On a drinking spree. Cally hasn't seen him in

hours." Gently, he lifted the little girl's chin, saying softly, slowly, "Cally, this is Catherine. She is . . . she is here to help you. You can trust her, Cally. She won't harm you. I'm going to find Pa and bring him home."

Cally nodded, wiping grimy hands across her tear-stained face as she looked up at Catherine with wide, frightened eyes. She was a miniature of Rory, with clear translucent skin and eyes the same startling shade of blue, framed by thick black lashes and dark, winglike brows. Her red gingham dress was rumpled—and badly in need of washing, as were her bare feet and long, skinny legs.

"Hello, Cally," Catherine said, moving to kneel on the dusty floor before the child. She reached out to lift a lock of tangled black hair from the girl's shoulder.

Cally smiled tentatively. "Hullo," she replied, suddenly done with crying. "You're pretty. Are you my brother's wife?"

Catherine felt herself blush. "No," she answered. "I'm not."

Cally nodded, then said to Rory, "You'll probably find Pa at O'Reilly's shebeen. But you'd best take care if you're heading over there. O'Reilly's always telling everyone you're a murderer. I told 'em you ain't, but no one listens—not even Pa."

Catherine looked up at Rory, concern shading her clear gray gaze.

Rory had pulled himself together, and the haunted look was gone from his eyes now. He gave his baby sister a cheery smile and ruffled her hair. " 'Ain't' is not a word, Cally. And don't you worry about me. I've dealt with O'Reilly in the past and I'll deal with him now. While I'm gone, I want you to clean yourself up and get ready for bed."

"Are you going to shoot him, Rory?" Cally asked excitedly, gazing up at her brother with innocent, adoring eyes.

Rory shook his head, giving her a stern look. "Certainly not," he replied. But as he walked out the door, Catherine was swept by fear and uncertainty.

Through the closed door, Catherine heard the whirr and click of his revolver as he spun the six-shot cylinder, then snapped it back in place. She winced at the sounds.

"Don't worry," Cally piped, surprising Catherine with her perceptivity. "Rory ain't — *isn't* going to get himself into any more trouble. He promised me."

In the hour that followed, Catherine wondered where she'd gotten the notion that Cally was a shy child, given to brooding and crying. Chattering happily about a dozen different things — from Rory's homecoming to a new dress she was making from fabric given to her by a neighbor — Cally moved busily about the little house.

"They all feel sorry for me," she said, screwing up her face in an unbecoming grimace. "I don't know why, though. Me and Pa ain't anything what they think we are. Pa works hard during the day and it's only at night he sneaks out for a drink or two. Lately though, since Connor left, Pa doesn't come home at night sometimes. I think he's lonely."

"He leaves you here all alone?" Catherine asked.

Cally nodded, her eyes going wide. "But I don't mind. Besides, now that Rory's home, all the talk about taking me away from Pa will die down and things will be right as rain."

"Who's talking about taking you away, Cally?"

"Some of the women in town. They say it ain't right for me to be raised without a woman in the house. But they don't know Pa, and like I said, now that Rory's home . . ." Her voice trailed off as she began to get undressed in the bedroom next to the kitchen.

Catherine moved to the little room and sat down on a narrow bunk, listening to Cally chatter on about Rory in adoring tones. Catherine was amazed that the little girl could feel so close to a brother who had left home when she was just a baby. Soon though, it became apparent that Cally's affectionate feelings for Rory were based entirely on what Connor had told her of him. Through Connor, the little girl had formed a deep respect and admiration for her oldest brother. Though he would deny it now, Connor had idolized Rory. Catherine smiled to herself. There might be hope for the O'Shay brothers after all.

After tucking Cally into bed, Catherine went back into the kitchen to wait for Rory. Two hours later, he still had not returned. Impatient and edgy, Catherine drummed her fingers on the crude wooden table, wishing she could go out and see what had happened to him. Unable to sit still any longer, she went to check on the sleeping child. Cally was still awake.

"Are you going to find Rory and Pa?" she asked.

Catherine smiled down at the sleepy-eyed girl. "I was going to. But I don't want to leave you here alone."

"Oh, don't worry. Pa leaves me alone all the time. He says I'm old enough to take care of myself. And I am. Please go. I'm getting worried about Rory. There's too many men in this town who would like to see him dead."

"Cally! Where did you hear such a thing?"

"I hear it all the time," she said. "They want Connor, too, since he was the one who blew up the Trenton mine. Please, Miss Catherine. Go find my brother. I don't want to lose him just when he's come back home to me. I promise I'll stay right here in bed until you get home."

Catherine smoothed the covers on Cally's bed. "All right,"

she said softly. "I'll go to the saloon and see if Rory is there. Will that make you feel better?"

She was rewarded by Cally's nod and bright smile.

Chapter Twenty-six

Patrick O'Shay sat alone at a small table near the back of O'Reilly's Place. There were only a few patrons still clustered around the bar. The rest of the men who had recently crowded the room, nearly fifteen in number, had all gone upstairs to the second floor where a secret meeting of the Ancient Order of Hibernians was now taking place with John O'Reilly presiding.

Patrick O'Shay was not fooled. He knew the men were all members of the Molly Maguires and that they used the fraternal organization as a smoke screen for their nefarious activities. He himself was a member of the AOH and of the Mollies, but the other members had long since ostracized him from actively participating in any of their gatherings. He didn't care. Lately, he cared only for his drink. He had little interest in anything else these days, ever since the town doctor had told him he hadn't long to live. He had acquired "miner's lung," or "miner's asthma" as some called it, and his physical condition was deteriorating rapidly. His lungs, ruined by the noxious air of the mines, could not get enough oxygen and so, neither could his other vital organs. His body was failing him, one organ at a time—including his liver, which was being eaten away because of his heavy, long-time consumption of alcohol. It would not be long until he was dead, he knew. And he was glad.

Pouring himself another shot of whiskey, he sat back in the chair, his eyes focused on nothing. This night, as every night, he thought of his dead wife and all the harsh years they had shared together in Pennsylvania. He had brought her to America, hoping to give her a better life, but once they arrived in the coal country of Pennsylvania, he found that he had been sadly deceived with the promise of greener pastures. There was only back-breaking labor in the mines, frequent layoffs, illness, and grinding poverty. At first, they held on to their dreams, hoping always to improve their lot in some other coal town. But with each move, they found the same appalling conditions.

They lived a hand-to-mouth existence, and although his son, Rory, had gone to work in the mines as soon as he'd turned seven, three years later there was another mouth to feed when a second son, Connor, was born. When Rory was twelve, however, things took a turn for the better. He was then able to earn a man's wages in the mines, and the family was assured of keeping a roof over their heads and food on the table. Hope for the future rose once again.

And then, just five years later, when Rory was seventeen, he wanted nothing more to do with the mines. Patrick O'Shay remembered that day well.

As usual, Rory and Patrick had risen before sunrise, and they had eaten their breakfast together. "I'll not be going to the mines with you today, Pa," Rory had announced.

"Oh?" Patrick O'Shay had replied. "And why not? Are you ill, son?"

"No, Pa. I'm only sick of working in the mines. There's no future here for me. You've worked in the mines all your life, and today you're no better off than when you first went down into those hellish pits. I'm leaving, Pa. I'm going to some big city to find better work."

Patrick O'Shay had been filled with an odd mix of anger, pride, and jealousy as he'd watched his son walk down the snow-covered road, out of Shenandoah. He wished he could walk away from the life he led, but responsibility for his wife and little ones chained him to his fate. With Rory gone, their livelihood once again became precarious. Seven-year-old Connor had just begun to work in the mines, and there was another child now, a baby daughter, Cally.

Rory's mother, Kathleen, had cried herself to sleep every night for five days after Rory's departure. Once she'd dried her eyes, she was never again quite the same woman. It was as though a part of her had left with her son. And Patrick O'Shay began to wonder if his wife didn't wish *he* had had the nerve to leave the coal mines and seek better employment.

It was then that Patrick began to drink steadily, often reeling home blind drunk. But he never missed a day in the mines, and in the early 1870's, when conditions were at their worst, with mine owners cutting wages and importing scab labor, Patrick joined the Molly Maguires—a secret society which sought to combat oppressive working conditions. But as time went on, the big companies grew more powerful—some even had the police in their pay—and it soon became apparent that it would take more than just talking if the Mollies were to make any progress. Soon, the secret society took harsher measures to gain their ends. Determined to obtain positions of power for their own members, they began to threaten mine bosses and superintendents with physical violence. A reign of terror began as the Mollies drew closer together, each member sworn to avenge the wrongs done to all. Although the Mollies were not, in truth, responsible for all the maiming and killing in the hard-coal country, journalists were quick to attribute most of the mayhem to the society. The resulting notoriety made the Mollies even stronger.

Patrick O'Shay loved the notoriety. His participation in the lawless activities gave him back a sense of his own manhood. His wife, who had long been ill with consumption, said not a word to him. Every Sunday, the two of them would take themselves and their two children, Connor and Cally, to church where the priest would preach sermons directly to members of the Mollies. Patrick listened with only half an ear. If he could not pick up and leave the hated mines as his oldest son had done, then he could at least derive some satisfaction from knowing he had helped create chaos for his employer.

But then, on one cold December day, just a week before Christmas, he'd come home to find his wife dead. Although she had suffered dreadfully from consumption for many years, Patrick was shaken to the core. He had never believed that she would go before him. She had been their little family's pillar of strength, never complaining even through two miscarriages and the loss of a newborn. Patrick could still remember the day their fourth child had died, after living only forty-three hours. Even though weak and drained by the ordeal, Kathleen had insisted on walking the long distance to the Catholic cemetery, where they laid their infant to rest in the plain wooden coffin he'd built with his own hands. She'd cried only once that day, when the first shovelful of dirt had been tossed on the tiny coffin. Afterwards, she'd dried her eyes and went back home to care for her three living children. *Kathleen*, he thought. *My beautiful Kathleen. I'll be joining you soon* . . .

He looked up at the sounds of the men coming back down the stairs. There were ten of them, and all but two headed out the front door, going home to their families. O'Reilly and his brother-in-law, Murphy, remained, each pouring themselves a draught of ale. That left five men still conferring upstairs. Murphy sat at the bar, leaning his back against the rough wood as he lifted his mug in Patrick's direction.

"Buy you a drink?" Murphy asked the older man.

Patrick O'Shay shook his head, then drained the glass in

his hand.

"Guess you're wondering what the meeting was about," Murphy continued. He was a good-looking fellow, who was employed in the same mine as Patrick, where he worked as his own father's "butty" or partner. Patrick had nothing against the young man, but he knew Murphy was a talker and tended to create trouble wherever he went.

"Just you never mind," John O'Reilly said to Murphy. "Finish your drink and head home, Murph. Margaret is going to close up soon."

John O'Reilly, a man in his late twenties, had inherited his father's shebeen on the old man's death, and he and his wife, Margaret, ran the bar, and a boardinghouse upstairs for miners who lived alone. Patrick O'Shay knew Margaret well. She was Murphy's sister and had, at one time, been close to his own son Rory. But Rory had left Shenandoah, as well as Margaret, for a better way of life. And Margaret, filled with grief and humiliation, had immediately accepted O'Reilly's marriage proposal. Since that time, Margaret had always been very cool toward the entire O'Shay family.

As soon as O'Reilly left the barroom to return to the meeting upstairs, Margaret appeared, heavy with child and looking bone-weary. She took one look at Patrick O'Shay and gave a grunt of disapproval.

"I'll be closing soon," she told him in a wooden voice. "I suggest you take your bottle and leave."

Murphy turned on his bar stool to smile at his sister. "I was just going to tell the old man what our meeting tonight was all about. I figured, since it involved his sons, he'd be mighty interested."

Margaret gave her brother a quelling look. "Hush your mouth, Murphy."

Patrick O'Shay looked at the boy through bleary eyes. "What about my sons?" he demanded.

Murphy sipped at his seidel of beer, then smiled. "Oh, nothin'," he said innocently. "Nothin' other than they're gonna get their hides blown off if they show their faces in town."

Patrick ignored his empty glass and instead lifted the half-filled bottle to his lips. Anger seeped into his eyes as he took a long guzzle, then wiped his lips with the back of his hand. "I have only one son and he's miles away. Only over my dead body is anybody gonna shoot my Connor."

Murphy shrugged his shoulders. "I suppose that will be the way of it then. The boys are hopping mad at Connor. He blew up a good mine and there are more than a few of our brothers out of work. Lots of families are going hungry because of Connor's actions."

"Murphy," Margaret interjected. "That's enough. Finish your ale and leave. Ma's probably waiting up for you."

"Let her wait," Murphy replied, annoyed at his sister's intervention. He turned his attention back to O'Shay. "We all know you got two sons, O'Shay. One's a mine saboteur, the other's a murderer . . . and their old man's a drunk."

Patrick O'Shay had to restrain himself. "You looking for a fight, boy?"

"Maybe. Maybe not. You'd best take care, old man, or else the womenfolk of this town will see to it your little girl's taken away from you. Ain't that right, Margaret?"

Margaret did not answer as she picked up a damp rag and began to wipe down the top of the bar.

"No one's going to take my Cally away from me," Patrick O'Shay said.

"Seeing as how your boys fared, someone *ought* to take the girl away. Knowing you, the girl will be forced to go flat on her back for a day's pay."

Murphy never had a chance to say another word. With one sweep of his arm, Patrick O'Shay sent his whiskey bottle flying through the air. He stood up then and lunged across the barroom toward the younger man. In an instant, his meaty hands were around Murphy's throat, squeezing tightly as he roared, "I want an apology, boy! You hear me? No one slights my baby girl. No one."

Margaret looked on in alarm as her brother gurgled and gasped for air. "Stop it!" she yelled, running around the bar to grab at Patrick O'Shay's heavy body. "Stop! Let him go! Let him go!"

Patrick O'Shay wasn't listening. His mind was foggy with drink and his heart heavy with remorse. The only thing he could think of was what Murphy had said about his children. *One son's a mine saboteur, the other's a murderer* . . . It was true. His sons had gone bad and he was to blame. He wasn't squeezing the life from young Murphy's body; he was trying to squeeze out all the pain of his own hard life. He'd wronged his young wife by bringing her to America; he'd wronged his children by forcing them to live in the squalid coal patches. Only Rory, his eldest, had been brave enough to walk away from it all. And this was the very reason he hated Rory. Suddenly, it was Rory's young face he saw, Rory he was choking. *This is for leaving your mother,* he thought. *This is for breaking your mother's heart.* . . .

As Catherine approached the saloon, she heard the screams from within, and her heart skipped a beat. Thinking that Rory was inside, she feared the worst. Cautiously, she eased the door open and stepped across the threshold. To her surprise, and relief, Rory was not there. There were, however, two other men engaged in a violent struggle. One was young, and the other—an older man who bore a strong resemblance to Rory—she guessed to be Patrick O'Shay. A plain young woman with long brown braids, very agitated and obviously several months pregnant, was attempting to separate the two men. This must be Margaret, Catherine thought. Wanting to help, but hesitant to interfere in Rory's absence, she stepped to one side where she hoped she wouldn't be noticed.

Suddenly, Patrick O'Shay's face grew very red, and he

was seized with a fit of coughing. Gasping for breath, he released his hold on the younger man's throat and staggered back against a table.

"You'll pay for this, O'Shay," the young man said, retreating to a bar stool, rubbing his neck. "You're just a drunken bum! I'll tell the brothers what you did, I will! No man strikes a Molly and lives to tell about it!"

"Hush, Murphy," Margaret said. "Can't you see the old man's sick and drunk?" Catherine realized then that this was Margaret's brother, Murphy—the man whose aid Rory had hoped to enlist. Under the circumstances, that possibility seemed more remote than ever.

Where *was* Rory? Catherine wondered as the sound of heavy footsteps was heard on the stairs. The man who came into the room was tall and powerfully built, brutelike, with beady, feral eyes. Could this be O'Reilly? The man's forbidding appearance sent a shiver through Catherine, and she shrank farther back into the shadows. If this was John O'Reilly, Catherine thought, how could the fragile-looking Margaret endure sharing his bed?

"What's going on here?" the newcomer demanded of Murphy.

Murphy sat straight up on the stool, wiping his mouth with his shirt sleeve. "The old man just tried to choke me, John, that's what!"

O'Reilly turned to Patrick O'Shay who, seated now, was still coughing and rasping. "Is that true, Patrick?" he demanded.

"It's none of your affair, John," the old man wheezed. "Just stay out of it. You know how Murphy lets his tongue wag. I think you should bar him from any more meetings. He talks too damn much."

Murphy jumped off the bar stool, lunging at O'Shay with his fists. "He's lying! I said nothing to stir him up. He just came at me for no reason!"

Margaret screamed as her brother's right fist flew straight

for the old man's face. Patrick managed to duck that blow, but wasn't quick enough to avoid Murphy's left fist, which came up and clipped him hard on the jaw. Patrick grunted once, then doubled over and fell flat on the floor.

At that moment, the front door burst open, and Catherine's heart leaped as Rory stepped into the room. Windblown and rumpled, his clear blue eyes took in the scene at a glance: His father lying on the floor, Murphy and O'Reilly hovering over him menacingly, Margaret standing a few feet away, wringing her hands—and, to Rory's dismay—Catherine, half hidden at the far end of the bar. Cursing softly, he did not acknowledge the pleading glance she sent him. What in the good Lord's name was she doing here? He didn't want her involved in any part of this.

O'Reilly, Murphy, and Margaret all whirled around as the door slammed shut behind Rory. Margaret turned pale, and Murphy, fists still clenched, stood motionless. O'Reilly, a look of disbelief on his face, advanced a few steps toward Rory. His eyes were filled with hatred. Rory tensed, ready for an attack. John O'Reilly had good reason to hate him. Big Pat, the man Rory had killed in this very shebeen, had been O'Reilly's henchman, the man O'Reilly had assigned to do all his dirty work—including one or two killings.

Seeing the look that passed between the two men, Margaret gasped. "Leave now," she said to Rory in an urgent voice. "Please go before there's worse trouble here."

John O'Reilly gave his wife a push in the direction of a door behind the bar. "Go on, get! This doesn't concern you."

Margaret nodded, nervously wringing the bar rag in her hands. Then, with a final, warning glance at Rory, she hurried out of the room.

O'Reilly turned then to Rory. "You've got your gall, walking into my bar, bold as brass. What's to stop me from turning you in to the authorities for murdering Big Pat?"

"I don't think you'll do that," Rory replied evenly, "considering that Big Pat himself was wanted for murder—and I'll be glad to tell the authorities where his orders came from. It should clear up a lot of loose ends for the police."

"I'll take my chances," O'Reilly replied brashly. "The police can't prove my involvement in anything, but I can prove that you killed Big Pat. There are at least a dozen witnesses ready and willing to testify against you."

"Do as you wish," Rory shot back. "I'm in town to stay, and your threats can't make me leave."

O'Reilly hesitated a moment. "Bold words, O'Shay," he said, finally. "Go on, take your drunken father and get out of here. I'll deal with you when the time's right."

Still unnoticed by anyone except Rory, Catherine grew increasingly nervous. How much longer would Rory be able to restrain himself? Catherine knew he was carrying a loaded revolver. To her relief, he turned from O'Reilly, and knelt beside his father, who had come to, and was now nursing his jaw. Looking up at Murphy, who stood nearby, Rory said softly but firmly, "Murphy, I'm going to let this incident pass. But in the future, take care not to provoke my father. He's hardly fair game."

Murphy puffed out his chest, still ready for a fight. "I didn't do anything to rile the old man," he argued. "Your father's dealing with half a deck. He's in here every night, drinking himself into a stupor, neglecting his little girl—"

At those words, Patrick was up off the floor in a flash. Slamming his head into Murphy's midsection, he sent him reeling backward, knocking the breath out of him. The two men crashed against a table, arms flying, shoving and punching.

Out of the corner of her eye, Catherine saw O'Reilly reach behind the bar and seize a double-barreled shotgun. He took aim directly at Patrick O'Shay's back.

Before Catherine could shout a warning, Rory had moved swiftly to the bar and wrested the shotgun from O'Reilly's hands. Snapping the gun open, he spilled the bullets into his open palm, then tossed the weapon back to O'Reilly, whose face was a mask of rage. Then, turning back to the two men, who were still locked together, grunting and grappling, Rory grabbed hold of his father's collar and yanked him upright.

"It's over, Pa," he said quietly, sending Murphy a warning look. "Let's go home now."

Murphy scrambled to his feet, knowing the brawl was finished. He gave Rory an odd, quick look of respect, then turned away swiftly, seemingly nervous that O'Reilly might have noticed. Without another word, he strode out the door.

Patrick O'Shay was not as easily persuaded to calm down. "Home? *Home?*" he roared drunkenly. "You've got no home here, boy! You got nothing here. Nothing!"

To Catherine's surprise, Rory let the harsh words pass. Patiently, he said once again, "Come on, let's go home. Cally's asking about you."

At this, Patrick shoved his son away. "Christ!" he shouted, "she's been asking about you for years! Not a day's gone by that Cally hasn't asked where you were! Get your hands off me! I want nothing to do with you. You're dead to me, boy. Do you hear? Dead!"

Swaying, he walked out the door, leaving Rory staring after him, pale and shaken.

Oh, Rory, Catherine thought, her heart breaking for him. *It was nothing but the liquor talking. Don't let his words hurt you, my love.* Moving out of the shadows then, she walked up to him and laid her hand on his arm.

O'Reilly, who had been watching everything from the bar, saw Catherine for the first time. A look of bewilderment came over his face, and then he laughed, malevolently, as Catherine and Rory left the saloon together.

They walked back to the O'Shay house in utter silence. When they arrived, they found Patrick asleep at the kitchen table. His loud, raspy snores filled the small room. Wordlessly, Rory picked his father up and carried him off to his bed.

When he returned to the kitchen, he still had nothing to say. Moodily, he headed for the door.

"Where are you going?" Catherine asked in alarm.

He didn't answer. He just closed the door soundlessly behind him.

Chapter Twenty-seven

Catherine followed Rory out of the small house, lifting her skirts to better keep up with him. His pace was fast, unrelenting, as though the demons were closing in fast.

"Rory!" she called softly. "Wait. I'll walk with you. You shouldn't be alone tonight."

"This night is no different from any other night," he called over his shoulder. "I'll be fine. You go back inside. It's late and you must be exhausted from all we've been through."

"So must you," she said, determined not to let him put any more distance between them. She followed him out of the sleepy town, keeping close behind as he strode swiftly down from the hummock on which Shenandoah was built, into the valley, and then up toward the dark mountain known as Bear Ridge. Here he paused, waiting for Catherine to reach his side.

When she did, he started walking again, unmindful of the enveloping darkness and the wild growth that made walking dangerous.

"Where are we headed?" she asked, concerned and short of breath. She winced as she tripped over a rotting, moss-covered log.

Rory caught her elbow, steadying her, and saving her

from a nasty fall. "Careful," he said. "You must lift your feet high when you walk in these woods."

"What is out here that you're so determined to reach? Come, Rory, let us go back to the house. We shouldn't leave Cally alone."

"My father is with her."

"Your father is in a drunken stupor."

Although her words were unquestionably true, it pained Rory to hear them spoken aloud. He quickened his pace, still keeping hold of Catherine. They came to a small stream hidden by wild grasses, rhododendron, and hemlock. Only the sound of the mountain water rushing atop moss-covered rocks gave any indication of the stream's presence. Placing his booted feet atop the slippery rocks, Rory led the way, guiding Catherine across. On the other side, the land steepened, becoming more rugged.

Soon, they came to a sheltered spot surrounded by a thick growth of sumac and flowering mountain laurel.

It was here Rory finally came to a halt. Stripping the shirt from his back and letting it flutter to the ground, he motioned Catherine to sit beside him. She did so without hesitation, understanding now that this lonely spot afforded him a special kind of solace. They were quiet for a moment, listening to the night sounds.

Finally, he spoke, slowly and reflectively. "Years ago," he told her, "I used to hunt for game along this ridge. I burned my first powder on this land. There used to be a grouse covert here. As a young boy, I would come here often just to sit and think. Life seemed so simple then."

"Yes," she replied. "Rory, I'm so sorry about what happened tonight. I—I'm sure your father didn't mean the hurtful things he said."

"Didn't he? You don't know him as I do."

"But I know you. You're a good man. Your father will come to his senses soon enough. Time is all he needs. The passing of years has made him bitter."

"He's not the only one who is bitter."

Catherine waited a moment, choosing her next words with care. "You've every right to be, Rory. But the fact that you're here now, once again in Shenandoah, is proof that you are willing to mend your differences with your father. You've had a three-thousand mile journey to prepare yourself for this moment. Your father has not. He is shocked but, I think—if he would only admit it to himself—he's secretly pleased you've returned home."

Rory shook his head, as though he doubted her words. Then, turning to look at her, he whispered, "Enough of morbid thoughts. I came out here to clear my mind, to find an hour's peace."

"Then perhaps I shouldn't have followed you. I did so only because I thought . . . because I didn't think you should be alone this night."

"I'm glad you're here."

"Are you? It seems sometimes that I've done nothing but compound your problems."

His only response was to reach up and tenderly caress the curve of her jaw.

Catherine lowered her lashes, her body suddenly warm and tingling with his touch.

Hesitantly, as though he feared she might vanish like the mountain mist, Rory cupped her chin in one powerful hand and drew her face to his. His kiss lingered, deepened—and Catherine's blood surged with desire for him.

Her hands went to his naked chest, exploring the silken mat of hair there, marveling at the symmetry of hard muscle and tendon beneath. Dipping her head, she trailed kisses from his chest to the throbbing pulse at the base of his throat.

He groaned as he ran his hands through the dark curtain of her long hair. He lifted the satiny tresses, then let them cascade gently to her shoulders. He eased his body back, down upon the cool, hard ground, drawing Catherine with him until she lay half on top of him. His fingers sought the fastening of her skirt, found it, and then released the confining band in one quick movement. The cool night air caressed Catherine's bare skin as slowly, carefully, he peeled away each layer of her clothing. With every garment shed, searing kisses covered her body, nipping, teasing, enticing.

As she helped him remove his own clothing, she marveled once again at the lean hardness of his body. The harsh reality of what awaited below in Shenandoah, gradually receded as they explored each other's bodies. In the darkness, surrounded by sheltering woods and the clean, fresh scent of mountain laurel, they entered another world. The sense of freedom was heady, like a powerful narcotic seeping into their blood. Intoxicated, they both grew bold.

Languidly, Rory's hand moved along the creamy, smooth contours of her body, blazing a path from the underside of one full breast, down to her waist and around the gentle swell of her hip. His hand kneaded and caressed, making its way slowly, tantalizingly, to the apex of her thighs where, after a moment's pause, he stroked the satiny moistness there. Gently at first, a mere brushing, and then, as she strained toward him, his fingers plundered the honeyed recesses. Catherine gasped with pleasure, her own hands seeking to arouse and give him pleasure. Their passion mounted, making them dizzy, sweeping them into a whirling vortex of pure sensation that spun them higher and higher.

With a muffled groan, Rory rolled to his side, placing Catherine on her back, then moving atop her. His mouth closed over hers, hard, demanding, as if he could not get enough of her. His tongue ravished the sweetness within as he rubbed the hard length of his manhood against her thighs, her belly, her breasts. Catherine's blood boiled, and she shook with delicious tremors that could only be eased by him.

"Now," she whispered urgently against his lips.

Breaking the kiss, he lifted his head and looked down into her lovely face. Then, he pushed himself inside her, slowly, slowly, until he filled her. "*Macushla*," he murmured, bending his mouth to hers once again, kissing her tenderly as he made slow, mind-shattering love to her.

Later, they lay beside each other, Rory's arm cradling Catherine's head as they both gazed up at the night sky visible through the canopy of trees.

"We should get back," she told him, hating to break the spell, but knowing they must.

Rory nodded, his hand toying absently with one of her tumbled curls. "I've a feeling we'll have guests by sundown tomorrow," he said reflectively. "Sooner perhaps, if they took the night train from Philadelphia."

"You mean Connor and my father?"

He nodded again, and Catherine fell silent. She hadn't given her father much thought since they'd reached Shenandoah. Events has moved too quickly. Ned would be furious with her, she knew. She shuddered to think what he might do should he ever learn that Rory had taken her innocence. Perhaps if Rory had mentioned marriage, or at least some plans for the future, her father would be appeased. But how could Rory talk of a future that remained so bleak and uncertain? A wave of despair washed over Catherine.

"Come," Rory said, as if detecting her miserable thoughts.

He pushed himself up and began dressing. Catherine did the same, slowly, reluctant to leave the covert. Fully clothed, they headed back down the side of the ridge, following the same overgrown path. Although Rory held Catherine's hand, his grip strong and steady, he did not speak to her again.

Peering back over her shoulder at the ridge that now

loomed like a specter behind them, Catherine wished she and Rory could hide in that wild land forever.

"Come, Catherine," he said, again guessing her thoughts. "Soon, perhaps. But I can make no promises."

Catherine looked up at him in surprise. He knew; yes, of course he knew. She saw the same longing in his dark blue eyes. But in those eyes she also saw a fierce determination to vanquish the demons that held him in thrall. She straightened then, and lifted her chin. Whatever Rory had to face, she would face it with him.

Together, they walked up the slight incline toward Shenandoah. Together, they would meet the dawn and all that it might bring.

Chapter Twenty-eight

By sunrise of the next day, Patrick O'Shay had emerged from his drunken stupor and was up and about the small house. He was in a murderous rage, bellowing at Rory the minute he walked into the kitchen.

"So the prodigal son has returned, eh? What makes you think you're welcome here? I told you the last time I saw you never to return."

Rory, his face harsh in the cold light of dawn, looked levelly at his father. "I'm here to help you," he said. "I'm staying."

"The hell you are! Where were you when your mother was lying sick in bed and Connor and me had to head off to the mines, leaving your baby sister to tend to her? Where were you then, boy?"

Rory shook his head once, his lips compressed, a muscle twitching along his jawline. "I'm sorry, Pa, I truly am. I would have come straight home had I known mother was so ill. In her letters, she always said everything was fine."

Patrick snorted his disbelief, sitting down at the crude kitchen table. He put his head in his hands, running his fingers agitatedly through his hair. "I should be at work," he grumbled. "Why didn't anyone wake me when the whistle blew at the colliery?"

Before Rory had a chance to answer, Catherine spoke up. She was also seated at the table, brushing out Cally's long hair and working it into a thick braid. "I was the one who decided you should sleep," she said. "You were exhausted, and Rory told me you weren't working today, because of the big parade and picnic."

"That's right," Patrick admitted sheepishly, remembering now that this was the day of the annual parade and picnic sponsored by the Rescue Hook and Ladder Company for all the people of Shenandoah.

Patrick looked up at Catherine through bleary eyes that narrowed in grudging admiration. "I must be quite a sight to a gently bred lady such as yourself. Why you're here now with Rory is a puzzlment to me. You remind me of your mother, Miss McGuillicuddy."

Finished with Cally's braid, Catherine patted the girl on the shoulder. "My name is Diamond now, Mr. O'Shay. And I'm not here to pass judgement on you. But I do wish you'd give your son a chance to . . ."

Rory cut in before she could finish. "Pa," he said, "holiday or no, I think it best if you didn't go out today. After last night, it could be dangerous."

"I know how to take care of myself," he replied, not taking kindly to their intervention on his behalf.

"But there's serious trouble brewing, Pa," Rory said.

"There's always trouble brewing. Not a week goes by that someone isn't murdered in one town or another. A man just has to know how to protect himself is all."

"And you do?" Rory asked.

The elder O'Shay turned on his son, pointing a finger in his direction. "That's right I do. Ain't no son of a bitch

338

going to put a bullet in my back." He took a huge gulp of the hot coffee Catherine had placed before him, wincing as he did so. Pride and sheer obstinacy would not allow him to let his wayward son back into his life. Catherine didn't wonder that Rory had formed a protective shell about himself over the years. She also knew that underneath that calm façade, he was hurting.

"Pa," Rory said very patiently. "Do me a favor and stay put in the house today."

Patrick O'Shay was not about to let his son tell him what he should and should not do. "The hell I will!" he roared. "That is exactly the kind of attitude the Mollies expect. If other citizens of our counties want to be terrorized, then let them. But I'll not be cowed. Cally wants to see the parade today and I'm going to take her!"

"I'll take Cally to the celebration," Rory said in a low voice.

Catherine's eyes widened in alarm. "Rory, no. You can't be seen in public. The townspeople will have you clapped into prison before the day is through."

He shook his head. "It isn't the townspeople who want me, Katie, it is the Brotherhood. I came here to face them and face them I shall."

"But not with Cally at your side," she argued. Rising, Catherine directed Cally away from the table and toward her room. "Go and get dressed now," she told her. "*I* will take you to the picnic."

Cally squealed with delight. "Oh what fun we'll have!" she piped. "Thank you, Katie," she said, hugging her new friend tightly. She skipped off to her room to dress.

Catherine turned back to face the disapproving looks of both men.

"I will not let you go out on the streets alone," Rory said. "You don't want the child to miss the celebration, do you? And since both you and your father are targets for the Mollies, it is plain that I'm the logical one to take her. Besides, what can happen on a crowded street?"

What indeed? While Cally was getting ready and Patrick moved off to his own room, Catherine sat back down at the table and read through the Shenandoah *Herald*. She was appalled by the front page stories which told of murders committed in broad daylight throughout the hard coal region. Rarely were there any witnesses to the crimes. Catherine began to wonder if it was wise to take the girl out at all.

"I don't want you going alone," Rory said again, seeming to sense her sudden apprehension. "I'll join you."

"No, it's too risky. I think you should stay here with your father. This might be a good time for the two of you to talk."

"If you haven't already noticed, my father is a very difficult man to talk to. He always has been. I wonder why I let it bother me."

"It bothers you," she said softly, "because you love him, and I'm certain that in his own way he loves you too. Be patient with him, Rory. He's not had an easy life as you well know."

"And which of us *has* had an easy time of it? That's no excuse. He's always taken his anger and frustrations out on me. I never knew why. He never treated Connor with the same hostility. My mother used to cry herself to sleep after our fights. And the more she yelled at him to leave me be, the worse his beatings became. I think my father hated me from the day I was born."

She reached across the table to gently touch his large hand. "He doesn't hate you. If he did, he wouldn't bother to argue with you. If you want my opinion, I believe he is very proud of you, but just cannot tell you."

Rory sat back in his chair, shaking his head. "He's not proud of me. He believes I'm a murderer. Jesus! I *am* a murderer!"

"No," she said swiftly. "Don't say such a thing. You're a good man, Rory O'Shay and I . . . I am proud of you." She'd almost said she loved him. Why she couldn't get the words past her lips, she didn't know. But her love was in her eyes as she rose and walked around the table to stand behind him. She placed her arms about his neck, feeling a tightness in her chest as he reached up to put his hands atop hers. Resting her head against his, she held him loosely as he stroked her forearms with both hands.

"I'm ready!" Cally announced, stepping into the kitchen. Dressed in a pretty but worn red gingham dress and sporting a big red bow at the end of her long braid, she looked the picture of untroubled innocence. Seeing Rory and Catherine in an embrace, she quickly moved toward them and flung her arms about Rory. "I wish you could come with us," she said, her face pressed against his chest. "Maybe when it gets dark you and Pa can sneak out and watch the shooting crackers. Katie and I will wait for you, won't we, Katie?"

"We'll see," Rory answered, lightly brushing the top of her head. "You'd better hurry or you'll miss the parade," he said.

Cally nodded and stood on tiptoe to give him a quick kiss. "I'm glad you're home," she told him. "Connor always said you'd come back someday; I only wish he was here, too. Then we'd be a real family again."

Catherine saw the flash of pain in Rory's eyes. She knew he blamed all of the family's troubles on himself. She wished she knew how to ease the heavy burden of his guilt.

"Come along, Cally," she said quickly. "Help me with this food for our picnic." Catherine took two bowls from the larder, one filled with baked beans, the other with boiled potatoes. To Rory, she said, "We'll see you tonight."

Rory walked them to the door. "Be careful," he whispered just before they left.

Catherine nodded. "You, too," she replied, then stepped out into the bright August morning.

The parade was not nearly as grand as some of those Catherine had seen in San Francisco, but the populace of Shenandoah loved it. Heading the procession was the Fire Company's brass band, its proud members in full regalia, bright red uniforms and shiny helmets, trumpets and trombones sounding loud, clear notes in the brilliant summer sunshine. As the band passed by to the cheers of the townspeople lining both sides of the street, Cally's face was wreathed in smiles, and she clapped her hands joyfully in time to the stirring music. The excitement was contagious, and soon, Catherine and Cally joined the crowd that formed a line behind the firemen to march up and down the principal streets of the town. Singing and laughing, the gay procession wound its way to Heckscher's Grove where the picnic was to take place.

In the grove, huge barrels of beer with spigots had been set up for the men to quench their thirst, fires had been laid for cooking food and brewing coffee, and a nearby creek had been dammed for those who wished to go swimming on this lovely August day. Throughout the afternoon, musicians played for the enjoyment of many of the younger men and women, who twirled about in a grassy area that had been cleared for dancing.

Cally spotted one of her school friends with her family, and at Cally's urging, she and Catherine joined them for the afternoon. Thomas and Mary Franklin had three children, two toddlers and Matilda, the little girl who was Cally's age. While they watched the children, who had entered one of the many burlap bag races, Mary Franklin and Catherine chatted amiably. Although Mary asked many questions, mostly why Catherine had come to Shenandoah and how she had come to stay with the O'Shays, Catherine said only that her father had at one time been close to Patrick and Kathleen O'Shay. Sensing Catherine's reluctance to discuss anything too personal, the other woman contented herself with talking about the town, its people and Cally.

"She needs a mother, she does," Mary said. "I've never seen her as happy as she looks today. I do hope your stay in Shenandoah will be a long one. It appears you've done Cally a great deal of good in just a very short time."

Catherine was thinking the very same thing. She had always regretted being an only child, and now, she felt as though Cally might be the younger sister she'd wished for.

The day wore on with more festivities: three-legged races, tugs of war, a chase after a greased pig, and even a climb up a pole covered with lard — a difficult, slippery feat attempted by many of the young bucks in hopes of dazzling their lady friends.

During the course of the afternoon, Catherine was startled to notice John O'Reilly, Margaret, and Murphy, milling around with the rest of the crowd. Although apprehensive at first, she was relieved to see them apparently just enjoying themselves, laughing and joking harmlessly with the others.

As the sun dipped below the horizon and dusk fell, Cally began to yawn. She was quickly restored, however, with a good supper and the prospect of the fireworks, which would start as soon as it was completely dark.

"Do you think Rory and Pa will come?" Cally whispered to Catherine as they seated themselves on the grass some distance away from the Franklins.

"I don't know," Catherine replied. Although she had been worried about Rory's showing up at the picnic, she now yearned for his presence. Everything seemed calm enough; there had not been even the slightest hint of violence throughout the day.

Whistling and crackling, the first of the fireworks appeared in the night sky to the excited oohs and aahs of the onlookers. Cally's face, tilted upward, was a picture of pure joy as she watched the starburst of brilliant colors. At that moment, Catherine heard someone stirring beside her. She looked up to find Rory.

"Hello," he said, sitting down on the grass next to her. "Have I missed anything?"

"Rory!" Cally squealed. "You came."

"Ssh," he said. "Look, you're missing the prettiest rockets." He laughed as she quickly turned back to look at the display.

Catherine's heart raced as Rory's shoulder brushed hers. Watching the young couples dancing beneath the summer sun had left her wishing that she and Rory could also have twirled along to the fiddler's lively tunes.

"Enjoying yourself?" he asked.

She smiled. "Your little sister has been a very lively companion."

"I can imagine."

"Where is your father," she asked on a more serious note.

Rory shook his head. "I don't know. He left the house a short while ago. I thought he might have come here."

"You—you didn't have an argument with him, did you?"

"One argument? No. We had several."

"Oh, Rory." It was then Catherine noticed his holstered revolver beneath the light vest he wore. "Do you think it's wise to be toting that thing?" she asked, motioning with her head to the gun.

"I think it would be very unwise if I didn't," he answered simply. "Any trouble today?"

"None. In fact, I find it hard to believe this quiet town is the home of so many cutthroats."

"Looks can be deceiving."

"Indeed. Where do you think your father went?"

"No doubt looking for trouble and a stiff drink. I don't know what's come over him these days. He's bitter and angry and . . ."

"And you're afraid for him."

There was a long pause before Rory replied, "I aim to get him out of this viper's nest as soon as I can."

"Just, please, don't get yourself into more trouble in the process. Did you see Murphy? He and Margaret are here."

"Yeah, I saw him."

"Do you think it would do any good to talk with him? Perhaps he'll come forward and tell the authorities that you killed that man in self-defense."

"I don't know. After last night, the last thing Murphy probably wants to do is aid an O'Shay.

Catherine fell silent, depressed with their conversation. As much as she loved having Rory here at her side, she knew it was risky for him to be out in the open. Even if the law abiding townspeople were screaming for justice against Rory, the Mollies knew he was here, and as John O'Reilly had said the night before, they would "deal" with him when the time was right.

The last of the fireworks were sent into the air, and shortly thereafter, the women began gathering up their children and heading back home. By tradition, the men stayed on after the fireworks display — for some serious drinking, while the women tucked the children into bed.

"You aren't considering staying?" Catherine asked Rory as the three of them stood.

"I think I should," Rory replied. "I've a feeling my father will be making an appearance soon, and he's bound to be reeling drunk."

"I wish I could stay with you," Catherine said, worried about leaving him alone.

"I'd rather you got Cally safely home. When the heavy drinking starts, there could be trouble."

"That's why I hate to leave you alone with this bunch."

"I'll be fine," he insisted. "None of the Mollies has confronted me yet."

"Exactly," she replied. "They've probably been waiting for the cover of darkness to make their move."

"Believe me," he said, reaching out to take her hands in his. "The Mollies wait for nothing. When they want to strike, they strike. It doesn't matter if their victim is alone, or if it's broad daylight, or the middle of the night. I'm as safe here as I am in my father's house."

"Be careful," Catherine said, still not convinced.

"I will," he assured her. After saying good night to her and Cally, he walked away from them, heading for the crowd of men who stood drinking near the barrels of beer.

Catherine left Heckscher's Grove with a deep sense of foreboding. As Cally skipped away from her to join Matilda Franklin, who was walking with her parents several yards ahead, Catherine noticed a lone figure on the other side of the road. It was Margaret, walking by herself, her shawl pulled tight over her swollen belly. Catherine watched her bent head for a moment, remembering how she'd meekly retreated from the bar the night before when her husband had ordered her to get out. How could any woman live with the likes of John O'Reilly? Catherine shivered—and then, something significant about that scene occurred to her. Was it possible that the seemingly obedient Margaret had not closed the door behind the bar completely? If so

346

. . . On a sudden hunch, she crossed to the woman's side.

"Hello," she said in a cordial voice. "I'm Catherine Diamond. I'm a friend of Rory O'Shay."

Margaret looked up and nodded. "I know," she said carelessly. She seemed in a black mood, and Catherine guessed that she'd probably had a quarrel with O'Reilly, perhaps also with her brother Murphy.

"I guess you know who I am from seeing me with Cally today," Catherine ventured, trying to draw the woman out.

"I saw you last night at the bar," Margaret replied in icy tones. "You were hiding in the shadows, weren't you? And then, when the brawl was over, you left with Rory. I know you heard my husband tell me to get out of the bar, but rest assured, Miss Diamond, I am not the browbeaten little wife you may think me. I saw everything that happened afterwards, from the back room. There's little that goes on in this town that I don't know about." Her mouth set in a grim line, she plodded heavily on.

Catherine's heart leaped. Looking down the road to be sure Cally was still safe with the Franklins, she ran to catch up with the unhappy Margaret.

"Margaret," she began tentatively. "I know you were once very close to Rory. You, of all people, should know he's a good man. Surely you don't believe he killed Big Pat in cold blood?"

Margaret glared up at her. "And now, *you're* Rory's girl, aren't you?" she said in a bitter tone. "Well, you may be his girl, but I doubt you know him as well as I do—or what kind of risk he's taken by coming back here. Did you know there's already been one killing in town today? Judge Gwyther, a Justice of the Peace, was shot and killed in broad daylight, with a dozen witnesses looking on—all of whom claim they didn't see a thing." Margaret smirked, seemingly pleased to see the shock registered on Catherine's face.

"How horrible," Catherine replied, subduing her sudden fright at this news. "But I can't believe you're the kind of person who doesn't deplore such lawlessness. Not if you were once Rory's friend."

Margaret was silent, but the taut lines of her face softened somewhat.

Guessing that there were still tender feelings for Rory behind Margaret O'Reilly's stony exterior, Catherine boldly pressed on. "Margaret," she said, touching the woman's elbow. "I have a feeling you saw everything that happened the night Big Pat was killed. You may not have been in the bar, but I think you were watching from the back room, weren't you?"

Margaret's head came up, her eyes wide with surprise. "How do you . . . ?" she began, then clutched at her belly, apparently gripped by a sharp pain.

Catherine's arm went around the woman's shoulder until the spasm passed. When Margaret turned to face Catherine once again, there were tears in her eyes. Sensing a breakthrough, Catherine was determined not to let the moment pass.

"Margaret," she said gently but urgently, "for the sake of what Rory once meant to you, for justice's sake, please tell me exactly what happened the night Big Pat was killed. Surely you don't want to bring your unborn child into a world where wrongs are condoned, and violence simply leads to more violence?"

Margaret was weeping now and trembling. "It's true," she sobbed. "I did see it all. But I cannot speak of it . . ." Her voice broke.

Catherine embraced the distraught woman. "Margaret," she pleaded, "I know you're afraid. And I don't blame you. But it will do you good to unburden your conscience—if only to one other person."

Margaret's words came out in a rush then. "Rory came to the shebeen that night to see me," she began, and Catherine did not contradict her, allowing the women to hold on to her illusions. "I was in the back room, putting things in order before closing," Margaret continued, more coherent now. "And before Rory could seek me out, the men in the bar began to taunt him about his brother. Just two days before, Connor had blown the Trenton mine, putting a great many men out of work. The miners were drunk and angry, looking for a fight. When the commotion started, I opened the door a crack and looked out. They circled around Rory and began throwing punches at him."

"Was your brother Murphy among them?" Catherine asked.

"Yes," Margaret admitted, "much to my regret. But," she added, suddenly belligerent, "my husband, John, was not involved. He's not mixed up with the Mollies, no matter what you may have heard. He's a good man, John is."

Catherine knew very well that O'Reilly was involved, but she let it pass. What mattered was that Margaret had witnessed the entire incident.

She urged her to continue. "What happened then?"

"They all jumped Rory," Margaret said, beginning to weep again. "He had no choice but to take them on . . . and—and he killed Big Pat, in self-defense."

Catherine took the plunge. Murphy might not be willing to speak up for Rory, but perhaps Margaret could be persuaded to.

"Would you be willing to testify in Rory's defense?" she asked softly. "You were there, and you know he didn't intend killing anyone. He's facing a murder charge. If he's caught and convicted, he could go to prison!"

Margaret stiffened, and her eyes widened in alarm. "I

told you I cannot speak out publicly," she said, her tone icy once again. "It could endanger my husband. He might get involved, and" — she looked down at her belly — "this child needs a father."

"Please," Catherine begged desperately. "You can't let an innocent man go to prison. Rory needs your help."

But Margaret had already turned away, quickening her pace down the dark road.

Chapter Twenty-nine

Once back at the house, Catherine tucked an exhausted Cally into bed, then sat down at the kitchen table to wait for Rory and his father. The conversation she'd had with Margaret kept running through her mind. If only Margaret did not live in such fear of John O'Reilly! Catherine knew the woman still had tender feelings for Rory, and she could only hope that after their emotional talk, Margaret would reconsider and be brave enough to come forth with the truth. She knew, however, that it was nothing they could count on.

As the hours passed, and the men had still not arrived home, Catherine grew increasingly anxious. At eleven thirty, unable to sit still any longer, she decided to rinse out Cally's soiled dress and hang it outside to dry. The August night had turned cooler and the fresh air felt good on her face. In the distance she could hear peepers chirping their songs, but all else was still. The silence made her even more nervous about what was happening at Heckscher's Grove.

Irish Fire, hitched temporarily to a tree stump at the back of the house, stood near. After hanging the dress on the line, Catherine moved toward him, talking softly. The horse bobbed his head upon hearing her voice.

"I've been neglecting you lately, haven't I, boy?" she whispered as she stroked his sleek neck. "I had such wonderful dreams for you, and now, since I haven't any way to repay James Hambleton the money he loaned me, it appears as though I'll soon have to give you up." Just saying the words aloud saddened Catherine—and frightened her. What would Rory's reaction be when he learned she'd signed over the colt as collateral, for money that was stolen from her? He would be livid, she knew. And he had every right to be.

Catherine knew now that Rory had been telling her the truth when he'd claimed to be Irish Fire's owner. Having come to know Rory's true worth—the real man beneath the hard exterior he presented to the world—she wondered how she could have ever doubted him. Beside her, stood the foal of Bess's Dream, a true racer, bred in a Baltimore stable. The horse had been Rory's dream too, and Catherine's— but now all of their bright hopes for Fire seemed irretrievably lost.

"Oh, Fire," she whispered, pressing her face against the horse's smooth muzzle. "I'm so sorry."

The sound of thundering hooves suddenly shattered the still night, and Catherine's head snapped up as she soothed the started animal beside her.

Rory reined Bess into the yard, stopping only a foot from Catherine. Before him, draped across the saddle was the bulky form of Patrick O'Shay.

"Rory! What happened?" she cried. She watched in horror as Rory swung down from his mount, steadying the heavy weight of his father with one hand.

"He's been shot," he said. "It's bad. Help me get him in the house, will you?"

Oh, dear Lord, no! she thought, moving immediately to help Rory with his heavy burden.

Using all his strength, Rory eased his father's huge bulk

off Bess's sweating back, catching him in both arms and carrying him like a child through the front door which Catherine ran to open. The front of Patrick's trousers was blood soaked.

"Find something to make bandages," Rory instructed as he laid his father down on his narrow bed. Patrick let out a groan of pain. "Easy now," Rory whispered to his father. "You're going to be all right. We'll get you patched up and you'll be good as new."

"No," Patrick gasped. "Never mind me, Rory. Go give it to them bastards." He winced in pain, pressing his eyes shut.

"He needs a physician," Catherine said, even as she ripped apart a threadbare sheet. "Where can I find one? I'll go if you can handle things here."

"No," Rory replied in a low voice, taking the strips of cloth from her. "The doctor's at Heckscher's Grove. Gomer James was shot. Three times. I doubt he's still alive. Total chaos broke out as Gomer went down behind the bar where he was pouring drinks. My father and I were standing near the bar, and while Gomer was being pumped full of bullets, someone else took that moment to wing a shot in our direction."

"And he got me, too, the son of a bitch," Patrick wheezed. Immediately, he was overcome by a spasm of pain. He doubled up, clutching at his bloody groin. "Whiskey," he gasped. "Get me some whiskey!"

Rory nodded to Catherine, who ran to the kitchen where she'd seen a bottle of spirits. With trembling fingers, she fumbled the top off, then hurried back to Patrick's side. Rory took the bottle from her and tipped it carefully to the old man's lips. As the burning liquid trickled down his throat, Patrick gasped and choked, then opened his mouth for more.

"Leave it," he ordered Rory in a fast whisper as the whiskey dribbled down his chin. "I want you to get 'em, son. I don't need you here. I'm a dying man anyway, and it's just as well I go quick with a bullet than slow with miner's lung."

"I'm not going anywhere."

"Dammit, boy! When will you ever listen to your old man? I'm telling you to leave me. Doc told me I didn't have long to live, said he was surprised I was still walking the streets. Go on, get. Before you go, bring Cally in here. I want to see my baby one last time."

"Don't talk like that. You're going to live," Rory insisted. He was trying to stanch the steady flow of blood from the old man's groin, but Patrick pushed his hands away.

"No!" Patrick gasped. "Leave me."

Rory shook his head. "No, Pa. Never again will I leave you."

Catherine's heart constricted as she heard the naked emotion in Rory's deep voice. She felt as if she shouldn't be watching this scene between the two men who had been alienated for so long.

"I left you once and have lived to regret it," Rory continued. "Let me take care of you now. You're losing too much blood."

But Patrick O'Shay would not have it. He shook his head stubbornly, then was seized by violent, uncontrollable tremors. When they passed, he took a deep breath and asked for more whiskey. Tenderly, Rory cradled his father's head and held the bottle to his lips. This time, Patrick did not wince, but drank a long draught.

Settling back then against his straw filled pillow, Patrick whispered, "I did not mean what I said to you the other night at O'Reilly's shebeen. I don't hate you son . . . I've never hated you." The words were difficult to form and took most of the old man's ebbing strength, but he was determined to speak them. "Maybe for a time, after your mother passed away, I did hate you . . . but only because I thought you'd gotten more of her love than I did. I was envious of the love she lavished on you. But you were her first-born, the product of the passion she and I had shared before leaving the ould sod. Once in America, we never again had the time or peace of mind to be together in that special way. Day and night, there were endless chores for both of us, hungry mouths to feed—"

"It's all right, Pa," Rory said. "Please don't exhaust yourself trying to explain."

"No, it isn't all right. I treated you unfairly. I know I was the reason you ran away from home."

An odd sound came from Rory's throat. Catherine looked at his stricken face and knew he was reliving the day he'd walked away from his family. "You weren't the reason," he told his father in a choked voice. "This town and the colliery, the darkness of the mines, the miserable, hopeless conditions all of us worked and lived under, those are the reasons I left."

"Even so, I've wronged you, son. Can you forgive me?"

Rory replied in strangled, barely audible tones, "There is nothing to forgive. It is I who should be repentant."

Patrick O'Shay, lost in his own train of thought, seemed not to have heard his son. "How I've missed you over the years . . . but I'm glad you're here with me now, at the end. I'm proud of the man you've become, son." He gave a long, quavering sigh. "You've a good woman by your side; take care of her, Rory . . . and of Cally. She'll need you now. You're the apple of your little sister's eye, you know. She adores you. Dear Cally, just like her mama."

Rory was silent, his head bowed, his shoulders sagging.

Slowly, Patrick O'Shay moved his right hand along the worn coverlet, covering both of Rory's hands. "I love you son," he whispered hoarsely. There were tears in his eyes.

Rory's own eyes filled. He took a deep breath, then said softly, "I love you, too, Pa."

Patrick closed his eyes, smiling wearily. "Bring Cally to me. I want to say good-bye to her."

Rory nodded, then silently went to do his father's bidding.

Catherine stood near the door, trembling and afraid.

"Catherine McGuillicuddy," Patrick whispered. "Come. Sit down beside me."

Catherine moved the only chair in the room to the side of the bed. Blood was still seeping from Patrick's wound, and an occasional violent tremor shook his broken body. But Patrick O'Shay was not yet ready to die. He had words left to say.

"I want you to tell your father that there's never been a truer friend than he was to me and my Kathleen. You tell him I admired him for taking his little girl out of this goodforsaken place."

"Yes," she whispered, "I'll tell him."

"And you hold tight to Rory, you hear? He's stubborn and bullheaded, just like his old man. But he's a good fellow . . . damned good. I know he's no murderer. I've always known, but I let the brothers condemn him anyway. I regret that now . . ." He stopped speaking, wincing as his body convulsed, then relaxed. "I—I want you to make sure he gets out of Shenandoah as soon as I'm gone. Will you promise me that?"

Catherine nodded, reaching out to grasp his shaking hand. "Yes, I promise. Rest now."

"And Cally," he persisted, his face a mask of pain. "She needs a mother . . ."

"We'll take care of her," she said firmly. "Don't you worry."

"I won't . . . not anymore," he whispered. Catherine had to strain to hear him. "I'm going to my Kathleen now. It's been too long, Kathleen. Too long . . ."

His hand tightened in Catherine's grasp. Then suddenly, it went slack.

Patrick O'Shay was dead.

Catherine bowed her head, weeping quietly. Then she heard Cally whimpering. Looking up, she saw the young girl break from Rory's grasp and rush toward the bed where she flung herself on her father's chest.

"No," she wailed over and over. "No, Pa, don't leave me. Not you, Pa!"

Finally, Rory took her arms from around Patrick's neck, and cradled her in his own arms, crooning words of comfort as he rocked her back and forth. When at last her sobbing quieted, he carried her back to her own bed where she lay motionless, staring at the ceiling. Catherine followed Rory as he walked into the kitchen, watching in horror as he pulled his revolver from its holster, spun the loaded six-shot cylinder, then snapped it shut. The anguish in his eyes had been replaced by a look of dark menace.

"What are you going to do?" she asked.

"What I've got to do."

"No. I won't let you. Put the gun away, Rory. You're in no condition to leave this house."

"I'm going after the man who murdered my father."

"To do what? Kill him too?!" She stepped into his path, barring the door, her eyes wild with fear. "I won't let you," she said again. "Where will it end? Another murder will lead to another and another. If you kill one of the Mollies, then the others will be after you."

"They're already after me, dammit! Don't you see, Catherine? The bullet that plugged my father was meant for me! He stepped in front of me to save my life. No one wanted my father dead; he was just a town drunk, someone for them to laugh at. It's me they want. And by God, this night they're gonna have me, but not the way they intended. Now, get out of my way."

Terrified but determined, she stood her ground. "You're not leaving this house."

"Don't make me hurt you, Catherine."

"You won't hurt me," she said, lifting her chin and looking fearlessly into his angry eyes. "And you won't hurt Cally either by walking out of this house to your death. She needs you, now more than ever. Will you turn your back on her again? Will you?" she demanded.

Her blunt words hit their mark. For a moment, his face contorted in pain. Then, it hardened once again into a stony mask of terrible rage.

"I wish you hadn't said that."

"It's true! This night you have a choice. You've already killed a man, but you had no alternative. Tonight you *have* choices. If you walk out this door to deliberately commit murder, I—I will not be here when—and if—you return. Neither will Cally."

"Then I guess," he said tensely, "this is good-bye." He pushed her aside and walked out the door.

Chapter Thirty

Utterly stricken and defeated by Rory's words, Catherine stood motionless at the open door, unmindful of the cool night air which chilled her body.

He was gone. And if he killed a man tonight, there would be no doubt in anyone's mind that the deed was intentional. He would go to prison — or worse, hang for this crime.

"Damn you, Rory O'Shay," she whispered. "I won't let you do this."

Quickly, she ran to Cally's room. The little girl was lying curled up on her side.

"Rory's gone, isn't he?" Cally asked in a tear choked voice.

"Yes," Catherine replied simply.

"I heard you two arguing. You're not going to let Rory kill anyone, are you?"

"I'm going to do my best to stop him."

"Go on," Cally whispered through her tears. "Go after Rory. Don't worry about me. I — I'll stay here with . . . I'll be all right. I'm not afraid."

"I can't leave you here alone. Come, I'll take you to the Franklins."

"No," Cally said, shaking her head. "I don't want to leave.

I've been alone before. Besides, I—I keep thinking Pa's just sleeping. I promise to stay in bed. Hurry now, or Rory will get too far ahead."

"You're a brave little girl, Cally O'Shay. Yes, I'll hurry." And with that, Catherine ran from the silent house, making straight for Irish Fire, who was straining at his rope. "Easy boy," she crooned to the horse. "You've got to help me now. Rory's about to do a very foolish thing, and it's up to you and me to stop him." She untied the rope, stroking the animal with one hand as she did so. Sensing her nervousness, Fire snorted, prancing in place, his head jerking back. "Easy . . . easy." She tried to calm the horse, knowing he smelled Patrick's blood which had dried on the ground. She could see the fright in his eyes. "Come," she whispered, leading him away from the back of the house, away from the trail of blood.

In the dark night, she could hear shouts from some distance away. Voices, angry voices, filled the air. Trouble was boiling up out there.

Quickly, before she could lose her nerve, Catherine swung herself up and onto Fire's bare back. The horse stepped back, startled by the unaccustomed weight. "Whoa!" she called, as he reared up and tried to toss her to the ground. She hung tightly to his flowing name, yanking hard to get him under control. But Fire, who had never been ridden, kicked up his hindquarters, bucking wildly. Catherine was abruptly flung forward, but she clung to the horse with both hands, her legs pressed tightly into his flanks. Snorting, rearing, galloping madly in circles, Irish Fire did his best to toss Catherine from his back.

Knowing the horse was her only hope of catching Rory, Catherine held on for dear life. Trying to remember how Rory had handled the animal in training, she spoke now to Irish Fire in stern, steady tones while she forced her own nerves under control. Little by little, the unruly horse quieted, halted his mad dashing about and slowed to a walk.

"I knew you were good trainer, O'Shay," she said aloud. No matter that Rory had said his last good-bye to her; she had not said good-bye to him! "Let's go, boy," Catherine whispered to the horse who was now calm but eager to race. Brushing his sides with her boots, Catherine urged him on.

As they sped into the now deserted streets of the town, she could hear the angry shouts again, closer now, somewhere beyond the town limits. She dug her heels into the horse's flanks, pressing him to go even faster. He responded instantly, all grace and speed, his hooves kicking up dust as he fairly flew through the air. As though he could sense Rory's trouble, Irish Fire was unstoppable, racing through the dark, swiftly leaving the sleepy streets of Shenandoah behind him. Horse and rider, bodies perfectly attuned now, moved as one. Hair streaming, heart pounding, Catherine was fearful but oddly exhilarated. Beauty and the beast flew through the night.

Soon, Catherine could make out a noisy mob milling about in the roadway twenty or thirty yards ahead.

Oh, Lord, she thought. Rory has found the man who killed Patrick. She slowed the horse to a trot, straining to see what was happening.

"String him high!" she heard someone shout. "Anyone who harms a Molly must answer to his brothers!"

Catherine's heart stopped as she drew closer and finally saw Rory. Face bloodied and bruised, he sat atop his horse, hands bound behind him, a length of coarse rope tied about his neck. They were going to hang him!

"No!" she shouted to the mob, kicking Fire into a hard gallop. "No! Cut him down!"

But only a few heard, and those who did rushed forward to halt her headlong dash into the middle of the crowd. Holding tight to the plunging horse's mane, she kept her eyes fixed on Rory's face, knowing only that she must reach him before it was too late.

The last thing Catherine saw was Rory's wide-eyed stare, and — John O'Reilly's, who touched a lighted cigar to Bess' rump. Then, someone yanked her savagely to the ground where she fell face down. She heard Bess whinny then, and the mob's excited cries as the frightened animal charged out from under Rory.

Catherine whipped the hair from her eyes, lifted her head and turned toward the tree. She screamed. Again and again and again.

There, dangling grotesquely from the taut rope was Rory, his body swinging helplessly in the air.

Chapter Thirty-one

Only seconds before the noose burned into his neck, Rory had seen Catherine and Irish Fire charging into the lynching party. His heart constricted at the sight of her, hair flying, eyes burning fiercely. Jesus! What the hell was she doing? These savages would tear her apart! And there was nothing he could do to save her. . . .

He had run into the bloodthirsty Mollies only a short time before. They had come at him swiftly, yanking him off his mount and onto the ground where the whole mob fell on him at once, punching his stomach, his ribs, his face. When he'd first seen the Mollies, Rory's hand had gone to his holster. And then—he hesitated, remembering Catherine's plea. For her sake, he thought, there would be no more killing.

Not drawing had been a fatal mistake. Within moments they had his hands tied behind his back and the noose around his neck.

O'Reilly had just touched the glowing cigar to Bess' rump when Rory saw Catherine yanked off Irish Fire. One last hope surged through Rory then, and just before Bess charged away from under him, he gave one long, low whistle.

The rope went taut then—but Rory's neck did not snap.

O'Reilly had bungled the knot, and this would be a slow, agonizing death. The noose dug into his neck, burning and choking him. He felt his weight dragging him down, the rope pressing against his windpipe. Twisting and swaying, he gasped for air. *Come on, Fire,* Rory prayed, even as everything began to turn dark. *Come on, boy* . . .

And then he felt it, a gentle nudge to the toes of his boots. Vaguely, he was aware of some disturbance in the distance that seemed to have drawn the attention of the mob away from him. His oxygen-starved brain balked as he tried to will himself to be still, to not sway like a pendulum. Slowly, Fire eased himself beneath Rory's body, moving back and forth as Rory moved. *That's it, boy . . . steady now . . . steady. . . .*

The yearling came to a halt as he felt Rory's booted feet touch his sleek back. He held his stance even as gunshots shattered the air and the men around him shouted and ran about. Synchronized perfectly to the movements of his master, Irish Fire held firm and steady as Rory finally stood upon his back, easing the strain of the noose. Now, Rory struggled with the rope that bound his hands together. If he didn't get the rope from his neck, he would suffocate.

Catherine, screaming wildly at the sight of Rory hanging from the tree, scrambled to her feet and lurched forward. On the road behind her, four shots were fired into the air, and the mob rushed away from the tree to see who was coming. It was help, she knew.

But it was too late. Rory was dead.

Oh, Lord, she cried, tripping and stumbling through the distracted crowd, making her way toward Rory. It was then that she saw Irish Fire move to the hanging tree. She watched, mesmerized, as the yearling carefully manuevered to give Rory a footing. She saw Rory move then, struggle with his bonds. He wasn't dead! She plunged forward as the lynch mob scattered and fled.

"Mary Catherine!" The familiar voice cried out behind her. Only one person in the world called her by that name. It was her father, finally come to Shenandoah to track down his wayward daughter. But she couldn't stop, not now.

Finally reaching Fire's sweating side, she reached up and tried to help Rory undo his bonds. Too tight. They needed to be cut away, but she had no knife.

"Hold on, Rory! Hold on. I—I have to get a knife." Tears blurred her vision as she stared up at him, poised so precariously atop Fire's back. If the horse moved, Rory would be dead. Even now, his air supply was blocked and he was close to blacking out.

"Here, move away, Mary Catherine. Slowly." Ned was beside her, moving carefully, trying not to upset Fire who stood solidly in place, eyes unblinking. Pulling a knife from his trouser pocket, Ned reached up and deftly sliced the bonds that held Rory's wrists. Then, he slipped the knife into Rory's hands.

Shaky, but still in control, Rory raised his arms to cut away at the dangling rope. As it gave way, he swayed, then fell sideways to the ground, landing hard. The knife flew from his grasp. Only then did Fire step away, whickering softly. Swiftly, Ned knelt, scooped up the knife and sliced away the noose around Rory's neck. Bright beads of blood welled up from where the knife had nicked his skin, and there was an ugly rope burn, like a necklace, circling his neck.

Rory coughed and gasped, breathing raggedly as pain and relief swept over him. He lay motionless for a moment, gathering his senses.

Catherine moved to cradle his head in her lap. "Oh,

Rory," she breathed, tears streaming down her face. "I thought you were—"

"I know," he said hoarsely. "So did I." He took her hand in his and their fingers entwined. "You little fool," he whispered, looking up at her. "You saved my life."

Fire snorted loudly then, moving near to nuzzle Rory's leg. "And you, too, Fire."

The horse blinked, and Catherine had to laugh, despite the seriousness of their situation.

After Bess was located, meandering in a nearby field, Ned and Catherine helped Rory to his feet and into the saddle. Catherine climbed up on Irish Fire once again, and with Ned following on his own horse, the three of them made their way slowly back to Shenandoah. When they arrived at the O'Shay house, Connor was seated in the kitchen with Cally on his knee. His face was grave. Seeing Rory, Cally bounded up and threw her arms around him.

"You're safe," she cried happily. "I knew Katie would bring you home to me again."

As he held Cally in a tight hug, Rory's eyes went to his brother's grim face. "Yes, I'm home, Cally. Home to stay." To Connor, he said in a low voice, "Father is . . . is gone. One of the Mollies shot him tonight."

Connor nodded briefly, his face filled with hatred. "A bullet no doubt meant for you. What else are you going to do to hurt this family, *brother?*" he asked viciously.

"Connor," Catherine admonished.

"No, let him continue," Rory said. "He has a right to voice his opinion."

"That's right, I do. And my opinion is that you don't belong in this family. You never did. You killed our mother when you left, and now you've killed our father. Who will be next? Cally?"

Rory itched to smack Connor, but he held himself back.

He knew his brother was distraught over their father's death. "I'm sorry you feel this way, Connor," he replied calmly. "I never meant to hurt any of you."

"Never meant to hurt us, eh?" Connor shot back. "That's why you murdered Big Pat and then ran for the hills? What the hell did you think would happen to the rest of us with the Mollies looking for revenge? Did you know that the night you left Big Pat lying dead in O'Reilly's shebeen, five Mollies paid me a visit? They were looking for you, big brother. I took a beating on your account. A beating that left me with a broken nose and a few lost teeth."

"Connor . . . I'm sorry. I didn't know. Had I known, I would have—"

"Would've what?" Connor spat. "Returned home? I doubt it."

"Well, you're wrong," Rory said forcefully. "Don't you know I went into the shebeen that night looking for you? I'd come home to move you all out of this town, but Pa wouldn't listen to me. He was in a rage. So I went looking for you. I'd heard rumors you were running with a wild bunch of young bucks." He laughed harshly. "I guess I wanted to try and save my little brother from making the same mistakes I'd made. A few days later, I heard you were the one who blew the Trenton mine. I also heard you went underground, seeking Ned's help out west. *I* wanted to be the one to help you. For the next year and a half, I went looking for you. I met up with Jack Reese in Utah. I knew he was following you too, and I wanted to know why. Things didn't work out as I had planned, though. When I came to, Reese was gone, and so was Bess' new foal. That's when I headed for San Francisco."

Connor had had a moment to get a grip on his temper. Listening closely to Rory's words, he'd become visibly calmer. "You mean you were following me for that long?"

"Yeah. That's quite a system Ned had worked out. One day I'd think I had you, and the next you'd be gone, leaving no scent for me to pick up."

"And Reese?" Connor asked. "What did he tell you in Utah? Did he tell you why he was after me? Did he tell you who'd hired him?"

Rory shook his head. "I didn't even get a chance to talk to him. He must have seen me coming, for when I reached his camp, he came up behind me and whacked me on the head." Rory gave a wry smile. "Guess I never did learn to keep an eye out for my backside."

Connor averted his gaze. "Yeah," he mumbled, remembering the day he'd hit Rory with his revolver. "I guess not. Look," he said quietly, turning back toward his brother. "I'm—I'm sorry for the things I just said. I—I had no idea you were following me because you wanted to help me."

"Why else would I follow you clear across the country?"

Connor shook his head. "I don't know," he mumbled. "I—I guess I thought you were going to drag me back here to face charges."

Rory placed one large hand on his brother's shoulder. "I wouldn't have done that to you, brother." He squeezed his shoulder once, affectionately, and then released him.

Connor looked up, a sorrowful light in his eyes. "But I did it to you," he said softly.

"Yeah, well, I was planning to come back here anyhow," Rory said, shrugging off the matter. "Sometimes, a man can't go on with his life until he goes back to the beginning. I've got some unfinished business in Shenandoah. It's time I got it settled."

At that moment, there was a knock at the door. When Catherine opened it, she found a tall man dressed in policeman's gray standing before her.

"Yes?" she asked hesitantly. Perhaps he had come to

inquire into Patrick's death, or perhaps he'd already heard about the attempted lynching. Whatever the reason, she was glad to see him, for there was no telling what the Mollies would do now that they'd bungled the lynching.

"Evening, ma'am," the officer replied. "My name's Yost. I'm a member of the Coal and Iron Police. I'm here for Rory O'Shay."

Icy fear gripped Catherine. She started to shake her head. No! She wouldn't let them take Rory away!

Rory approached the door then, moving to stand behind Catherine. Placing his hands on her shoulders, he addressed the officer. "I'm O'Shay," he said in calm tones.

"Sir, I've a warrant for your arrest—"

"What?" Catherine exclaimed, feeling giddy and sick. "What do you mean a warrant for his arrest? What are you arresting him for?"

"The murder of Pat Daugherty."

"No! No, you cannot!" Catherine cried. She whirled around, staring up at Rory with wide eyes. "Tell him, Rory! Tell him you're innocent. Tell the man you didn't murder anyone!"

Rory shook his head. "I can't do that, *macushla,* you know that. Please . . . just don't say anything more." He looked over her head at the policeman. "I'll come with you," he said quietly. "I'd just like a few minutes to say good-bye to my family."

The officer nodded. "Very well. I'll give you ten minutes."

Catherine watched, horrified, as the policeman drew a pair of handcuffs from his pocket. As he moved past her, into the house, she caught his sleeve and stopped him. "Now see here!" she cried. "This is madness! Rory O'Shay is no murderer! I demand to know who issued this—this warrant!"

The tall officer lifted an eyebrow, astonished at her

outburst. "The district attorney, ma'am. I was given the warrant this evening. If you have any questions, I suggest you direct them to District Attorney Kaercher in the morning. My duty is to take Mr. O'Shay into custody."

"I see. And where were you, Officer, when Mr. O'Shay was nearly lynched by a gang of Mollies not an hour ago? Where were you then? Look! Look at his neck. He still has the rope burns! If not for my intervention, Rory would be dead right now! And what about his father? Patrick O'Shay was shot and killed this night! Tell me, Officer, are you going to serve a warrant on any one of the twenty men who tried to hang Rory, or on the man who murdered Patrick O'Shay?"

A look of complete bewilderment fell over the policeman's face. He turned to Rory. "Mr. O'Shay, is there something you'd like to tell me? Is what this woman tells me true? Were you accosted by a group of men? Was your father murdered this night?"

"Tell him, Rory," Catherine pressed. "Tell him about O'Reilly and the others! Tell him—or I will."

Rory was silent for a long moment, his face impassive. Finally, he said, "No, officer. I have no statement to make."

"Damn you, Rory!" Catherine hissed. "Don't do this!" She took hold of his hand and pulled him to the far side of the room, away from the others. In a hurried whisper, she said, "What is the matter with you? Don't you want to see justice done? Surely, you don't intend to let O'Reilly and his men get away with what they've done?"

"I don't see as I have any choice," he replied.

"You do! Tell the police. Tell them *everything*. Then they can help you."

"And you think, with just my testimony, they will round up that group of cutthroats and cart them off to prison? Think, Catherine. Every one of those men will have an alibi for tonight. They'll each have at least ten witnesses who will testify they were nowhere near that tree when I was supposedly hanged."

"But you've at least got to try," she pressed.

"To what end? I'm going to prison myself. I will no longer be here to protect Cally and Connor should they need me. If I open my mouth now, I'll be placing both my brother and sister in danger. And you, too, Katie. Never would I do that to them . . . to you." He reached up and gently brushed one hand across her cheek. "Please, Catherine, don't make this more difficult than it already is. I killed Pat Daugherty. I will pay the price, whatever it is. Once and for all, I will face my past." He trailed his hand down to the nape of her neck and pulled her face to his. He kissed her hard. It was neither a passionate kiss nor a tender one. It was a kiss that said good-bye.

He released her slowly, his blue eyes boring into hers. "Good-bye, Katie," he whispered. "I—I'll think of you always. You've made the past weeks bearable." He gave a small laugh, shaking his head. "No," he said. "Not bearable. You've made them the best of my life. Good-bye, *macushla*."

He turned away then, and moved across the room toward his brother. Pulling paper money from his trouser pocket, he said to Connor, "This is for Pa's funeral. The rest is for you and Cally. Take care of her, brother . . . and yourself." For a moment, his blue eyes glinted dangerously as he looked at the waiting policeman. "I'm ready now," was all he said.

The officer clapped the shackles to his wrists. The two of them started for the door.

Catherine stood rooted to the spot, her heart breaking with every step Rory took. "Rory," she called out, her voice cracking.

He turned to look at her, his eyes filled with pain. He

hadn't wanted her last view of him to be like this—not with his hands bound as an officer led him from the house. He had wanted nothing but happiness for Catherine Diamond. He had never intended for her to be hurt as she was being hurt by this wretched night.

"Be brave, Katie," he said. "Take Fire and go back to San Francisco with your father. Make your dreams come true, Katie; you can."

"But not—not without you, I can't. Never without you."

Then Rory was gone.

"Come, Catherine," Ned Diamond was saying. "Come on, let's go now. There's nothing more to be done here."

Chapter Thirty-two

The day of Patrick's funeral was hot and muggy. By ten in the morning, just as the funeral mass began, the humidity had become nearly unbearable. Catherine stood staunchly behind Cally, holding tightly to the girl's shaking shoulders. The smell of musty morning garb, kept in trunks until needed, filled the air as the few mourners gathered near the gravesite. Connor and Ned stood beside Catherine. The only others present were the priest and a few of the O'Shays' closest friends. Margaret O'Reilly was among the mourners, and Catherine intended to speak with her before the day was out.

Rory had not been allowed to attend. The morning after his arrest, Catherine had boarded the Reading Railroad and traveled to the Pottsville jail. She was not allowed to see Rory. No visitors, the official said. Nor could she post bail for him. Murder was a non-bailable offense. Rory would remain incarcerated until the date of his trial. Despite Catherine's daylong, repeated pleas to the authorities, they stood firm in their resolve to keep him secluded. Catherine had returned to Shenandoah feeling angry and depressed.

It was too much to bear! Pat Daugherty had been a wanted man, with a price on his head! How could Rory be kept in prison for killing him?

Before anything further could be done on Rory's behalf, there was the matter of Patrick's funeral. Connor saw to the details, going numbly through all the painful procedures.

The mass was lengthy, much too long for all those who stood beneath the hot August sun. Poor Cally, Catherine thought, listening to the priest who droned on and on, his words punctuated by the little girl's sniffles. Catherine was reminded of her own mother's funeral years before, and the tears that welled up in her eyes were for the woman who had been taken from her at such a tender age. Thinking of how hard it was to be raised without a mother's gentle touch, Catherine vowed to do everything she could for Cally.

Rory should be here, she thought angrily. Cally needed him, and after all he had been through with Patrick, he should have at least been allowed to honor his father by attending the funeral. He was hardly a hardened criminal! And why were the authorities so adamant about not allowing anyone to see him? It just didn't make sense.

Looking up, she realized the mass had ended and the small crowd was beginning to disperse. Taking Cally's hand in her own, she hurried to intercept Margaret O'Reilly before she left the cemetery.

"Margaret," she called. "Margaret, wait! Please, I—I need to speak with you."

Margaret O'Reilly slowed her pace, but only a bit. "We have nothing to talk about," she said as Cally and Catherine came up beside her.

"I think we do," Catherine said. "I'm sure you've heard Rory was taken into custody last night for the murder of Pat Daugherty."

"So what if he was? There's nothing I can do for him."

"Oh, yes, there is. And we both know it. You were at the

shebeen that night. You saw what happened. I'm asking you to go to the police and tell them what you saw."

Margaret O'Reilly shook her head, casting a quick glance around them. "You're wrong," she said in a hushed voice. "I saw nothing."

"But that's not what you told me the night of the picnic. You told me you know Rory is not guilty of first-degree murder! Please, Margaret! You've got to help him."

Margaret resumed her quick pace, skirts swishing. "Like I said, Miss Diamond, I saw nothing." With that, she took a long stride forward, trying to get away from Catherine.

But Catherine would not be so easily deterred. Urging Cally along, she caught up to Margaret and moved in front of the woman, blocking her way. Catherine's gray eyes were stormy as she spoke in a low, level voice. "Your husband tried to hang Rory the other night. He was the ringleader of at least twenty other men. If you don't come to Rory's aid now, I'll go to the authorities and tell them all about John O'Reilly's part in the near-lynching. Before this day is out, your husband will also be in the Schuylkill County prison."

A horrified expression settled over Margaret O'Reilly's features. Suddenly, she clutched at her protruding abdomen, breathing heavily. After a long moment, she straightened, fixing Catherine with a look of disbelief. "You wouldn't," she gasped.

Although Catherine feared at first that Margaret was having labor pains, she dismissed that worry when the woman made no complaint. Margaret could help Rory get out of prison, and Catherine would do anything toward that end. "I would," she said. "And I will."

Margaret O'Reilly shook her head, an ugly smile spreading across her face. "You don't know what you're up against, Catherine Diamond. You don't realize what type of people you're dealing with here. You say my husband tried to hang Rory O'Shay, but there will be at least a dozen other men who will tell the authorities John was at Heckscher's Grove with them. It will be just your word against theirs, just as it would be my word against many others if I were to testify that Rory killed Big Pat in self-defense. Don't you see? There's nothing either one of us can do." She winced slightly, her right hand going again to her belly.

"We can tell the truth," Catherine offered, watching Margaret closely.

"No. Not even the truth will help Rory now. Even if he did get out of prison, the Brotherhood would find him. I suggest you take yourself far away from Shenandoah, Miss Diamond. Go back to where you came from before the Mollies make you their next target." With those words, Margaret stepped around both Catherine and Cally, and hurried toward home. Her gait was awkward and she tripped twice, but she plunged forward.

Catherine watched her go, feeling defeated.

"What are we going to do?" Cally asked, tugging at Catherine's hand. "How can we help Rory now?"

Catherine looked down at the small girl who so resembled her oldest brother. "I don't know," she answered truthfully. "I just don't know."

Together, they stepped up their own pace, hurrying to catch up with Ned and Connor, who had gone on ahead. They had gotten no more than a few feet when a smart-looking carriage pulled up near the cemetery. A woman dressed fashionably in a black mourning outfit stepped down from the conveyance. Her face was covered with black veiling, but Catherine would have known that tiny frame and graceful bearing anywhere.

"Jenny!" she called out. "Jenny Latham!"

The woman looked up, shading her eyes with one gloved hand. "Catherine?"

Jenny Trenton Latham hurried across the dusty road, her arms outstretched. "Oh, Catherine, I didn't think I'd ever see you again! What are you doing here, in Pennsylvania?"

Catherine pulled Cally along as she ran to meet her friend. "I could say the same to you," she said as they met at the side of the road. "What are *you* doing here?"

"Well, I—I returned to Shenandoah to visit my father. When I saw the notice of Patrick's death, I hurried here as fast as I could. How—how are his children?" She looked to the little girl who stood silently beside Catherine. "This couldn't be Cally, could it?" At Catherine's nod, Jenny exclaimed, "Oh, my! How she's grown. You don't remember me, do you?" she asked Cally. "I'm Jenny. Your oldest brother and I used to be very good friends."

Cally looked up skeptically at Jenny. "Margaret was once Rory's friend," she said. "But she's not any longer. Rory's in jail and not even Margaret will help him get out."

"Jail?" Jenny echoed. "Catherine, what's happened? Is Rory truly in jail?"

"Yes," Catherine said. "He is. He's being held for the murder of Pat Daugherty."

Jenny appeared shocked. "Oh, my . . . Have—have you been able to see him?

"No," Catherine interrupted. "They're allowing no visitors. As things stand, Rory will be fortunate to have a fair trial." Looking down at Rory's little sister, Catherine said, "Cally, you run and catch up with Connor and my father, all right? I'll come along shortly. Jenny and I have to talk."

"You promise you won't be long?" Cally asked, her red-rimmed eyes wide. "I don't want to be alone at the house."

"You won't be alone, honey. Connor will be there."

"I—I know," Cally replied, looking down at her shoes. "But he's not talking much today."

Catherine gave Cally's hand a squeeze. "Yes, I'll hurry," she promised. "Now run along."

As Cally reluctantly walked off, Catherine turned her gaze back to Jenny. In a leaden voice, she came right to the point. "So tell me, Jenny, what happened back in San Francisco? Did you go to the police? Did you tell them it wasn't Rory who pushed your husband down the stairs?"

Jenny lowered her lashes, fumbling with the drawstring on her handbag. "I—ah—I don't want to talk about it, Catherine."

"Well, I do."

"Please," Jenny whispered, looking up at Catherine with wide brown eyes. "My life is finally getting straightened out. J.D. and I have worked through our differences, and Jasper finally has both his parents with him. I—I can't jeopardize my future by bringing up that horrible episode."

"And what about Rory's future?"

"San Francisco is three thousand miles away. Rory will be fine. I—I'll hire a lawyer for him here in Pennsylvania, the best, Catherine, I promise. Rory will be cleared of this murder charge, and then the two of you can build a new life together."

"And how do you expect us to do that with another murder charge hanging over him in California? It's just a matter of time before the San Francisco authorities contact Shenandoah."

"But you can leave Shenandoah. You can find a place where no one knows who you are—"

"And do you think—even if we managed to get away—that we'd be happy? I'd be living in fear, wondering with every knock at the door if it was the police coming to take Rory away from me! How you can even suggest such a thing is beyond me. I—I thought you were Rory's friend."

"I am!"

"No, you aren't. If you were, you would have gone directly to the San Francisco police and admitted you were the one who pushed Albert down the stairs."

Jenny squeezed her eyes shut and turned away. "I—I'm sorry, Catherine. I truly am. But I—I have a son to protect, and J.D. wants to marry me. . . . " She paused, sighing heavily. "I am sorry," she said once again. And then she moved away, toward Patrick O'Shay's freshly dug grave.

Catherine stood still for a moment, anger at Jenny Latham engulfing her. Certainly Jenny could hire a competent lawyer to represent Rory here in Pennsylvania, but after that what could be done to establish his innocence in the death of Albert Latham? She knew Rory himself would never implicate Jenny. He would hold Jenny's terrible secret until his dying day—just as he had held the secret of her childhood love affair.

With leaden feet, Catherine walked toward the dirt roadway that led back to Shenandoah. As she approached the carriage Jenny had just left she saw a man open the door and alight. He stepped into the road, his lean frame blocking her way.

Catherine looked up into the frightening countenance of James David Hambleton.

"Miss Diamond," he drawled. "It's been too long."

Catherine came to a halt, and straightened up. She didn't reply but returned his gaze unflinchingly.

"We've unfinished business, you and I," he said.

"We do," she acknowledged. "But at the moment, I've nothing to say to you. This is a day of mourning, Mr. Hambleton. I'd appreciate it if you'd let our business wait until another day."

J.D. Hambleton laughed. "I'm certain you would," he said, smiling. "But I'm no saint, Miss Diamond. I conduct my business when it pleases me."

"Even so," she said, trembling inwardly. "There's a little girl who needs me right now. She's just lost her father, and I will not keep her waiting."

"Fine. Just pay me my two thousand dollars and you can go to Cally. I won't stand in your way."

Damn him! she thought angrily. And damn myself for ever dealing with him in the first place! What was it Jack Reese had said about this man? She still couldn't remember

. . . and yet, she knew it was something that had great bearing on Rory's future. Her mind took flight, careening in all directions. She forced herself to concentrate, and as she was thinking, she said, "I—I haven't got two thousand dollars."

"Then I guess your Thoroughbred belongs to me, Miss Diamond. I'll come to the O'Shay house to collect him and save you the trouble of arranging for transport."

Even as the man spoke, Catherine could hear Jack Reese's ugly voice. What *had* he said? Slowly, his words came back to her.

I don't want Hambleton's money . . . the man paid me a fortune to see the Trenton mine blown sky-high. All I had to do was get the youngest O'Shay boy to light the match. . . .

J.D. Hambleton had been the one to hire Jack Reese! J.D. was the man who wanted to see Jenny's father ruined!

"It was you!" Catherine breathed. "You're the one who hired Jack Reese . . . it was you who wanted to sabotage the Trenton mine and put Samuel Trenton out of business. Of course!"

"What are you talking about?" J.D. demanded.

"Samuel Trenton had taken Jenny and your unborn son away from you. And you wanted revenge. What better way than to sabotage the Trenton's mine?"

J.D. reached out and pulled her roughly away from the side of the carriage. "You don't know what you're saying," he hissed.

"I think I do," she replied. "With all the mayhem the Molly Maguires were creating, you must have figured it wouldn't be a surprise to anyone if one more mine was blown. So you hired Jack Reese, a member of the Brotherhood, and paid him a huge sum to plant dynamite at the Trenton colliery. You thought everyone would assume the Mollies were responsible."

"You're insane," he hissed.

"No, I'm not. And we both know it. What you didn't

count on was that Reese would trick Connor O'Shay into blowing the mine. When you learned Connor had set off the dynamite—and survived the blast—you paid Reese to follow him across the country and kill him. And when you learned Rory had shown up in Shenandoah and was looking for his brother, you ordered Reese to take care of him, too, didn't you? You wanted to repay Rory for what you thought was his betrayal of you and Jenny."

"No," he said in a low voice. "You're wrong. It's not what you think, not at all." His eyes were looking beyond her, toward the cemetery where Jenny was kneeling at Patrick's grave.

"Are you saying you didn't hire Jack Reese?" Catherine pressed.

J.D. appeared flustered. "No! I—I mean, yes. Yes, I did hire Reese. But only to cause trouble at the Trenton mine. I didn't think the man would go so far as to have the colliery blown up. I'd told him I wanted no bloodshed. It was Reese who decided to involve Connor. I had no knowledge of his plans."

"So you paid Reese only to cause trouble at the Trenton mine? Nothing more?"

James Hambleton nodded, suddenly looking very weary. "Yes. That's correct. When I'd heard the mine was blown up and so many men left without jobs, I was furious. I once was a coal miner too, Miss Diamond. I don't think I'll ever forget the hardships I endured in this town. It wasn't until my mother was widowed that we left here and went to Philadelphia. There, through a stroke of good fortune, she met and married a very wealthy man. After that, I never again went to bed hungry. When my stepfather died a few years later, he left everything to us. It was then that I decided to get even with Samuel Trenton."

"And yet your plan for vengeance nearly cost Connor O'Shay his life," Catherine said.

"Yes," J.D. admitted. "But once I'd learned what Reese

had done, I came directly to Shenandoah and met with Trenton. I told him everything—I even admitted to being the cause of his recent troubles. The old man was bent on pressing charges against Connor, but after our little talk, he changed his mind." J.D. laughed mirthlessly. "Trenton changed his mind about a lot of things that day. Suddenly, it seemed, I was good enough for his little girl. I told him outright that I aimed to get Jenny and my son back. He wished me luck, and even told me where I could find Jenny. That's when I headed west. I was hoping I'd see Connor before I left, so I could tell him that Trenton wouldn't be pressing charges. But . . ."

"You mean Connor isn't going to have to face criminal charges? There never were any charges?"

"That's right."

"But I thought—I mean, Connor thought Jack Reese had supplied evidence that Connor had murdered a mine super."

"The only person after Connor was Jack Reese. No one else."

Catherine felt weak with relief. All this time they had been worried about Connor's safety—and all this time his name had been cleared.

"And Rory?" she asked. "What about him? Wh—what about the charges against him for the murder of Albert Latham?"

Instantly, J.D.'s open, sincere expression vanished. A dangerous gleam came into his eyes. "I can't help you there, Miss Diamond. Never would I implicate Jenny in anything so messy."

"Implicate her!" Catherine nearly shouted. "The woman was there! She was the one who watched Albert fall to his death! How can the two of you let Rory be blamed for such a thing! Listen to me, surely you have the means to mount a strong defense for Jenny. We both know she didn't intend to push Albert down those stairs. I—I'm certain she wouldn't go to prison for Albert's death."

"And you think Rory will?"

"Of course he will! Albert's neck was snapped, just like—"

"Just like Big Pat Daugherty," J.D. finished. .

"Yes," Catherine whispered, terrified for Rory. "Please," she said, ready to beg on Rory's behalf. "You've got to help Rory. He won't help himself. He'd go to prison with Jenny's secret on his lips. We both know that. He's a damn good man . . . too good." She wiped viciously at her moist eyes. She wouldn't cry! she told herself. She wouldn't.

"I won't involve Jenny's name in any of this," J.D. said harshly. "She's been through too much in her young life. She deserves some happiness. And I will never allow my son to hear his mother branded a murderess."

"But Rory is innocent!" she pressed.

To her surprise, J.D. said, "Of course he is. And you needn't worry. No one is going to arrest Rory for Latham's death."

Startled, she gave him her full attention. "What? What do you mean? I—I thought you said you would never let this scandal touch Jenny."

"I won't," J.D. said simply. "But neither will Rory face charges in San Francisco."

"I—I don't understand."

"Before I left San Francisco with Jenny and Jasper, I had a long meeting with Senator Sharon and the police commissioner. It's amazing how mountains can be moved for the right price. Trust me, Miss Diamond. Rory O'Shay will never be taken in for the killing of Albert Latham. Even before I left the city, Latham's murder was no longer listed as such. It seems the coroner's initial findings were in error, and Albert actually died by accidental means. Jenny will inherit the man's fortune, and Rory's name has been stricken from all records. I do believe both the police commissioner and the senator have already forgotten the name of O'Shay."

Again, Catherine felt a wave of relief wash over her. She took a deep breath to calm herself. "So they believe Rory is innocent."

"No," J.D. corrected. "They still believe he murdered Latham. But it doesn't matter. Because of my intervention, Rory is a free man in the state of California." J.D. looked beyond Catherine's shoulder, toward the cemetery. Jenny was moving toward them now. J.D. returned his gaze to Catherine. "What I've just told you—about the Trenton mine explosion, and about the Latham killing—is strictly between you and me. I don't want Jenny to ever know."

"But—"

"Not ever," he said forcefully. Then, on a softer note, he said, "I—I know Rory is being held now in the county prison. I'll arrange for his defense, if you'll accept the offer. No matter what the cost, I'll see he has the best defense lawyer in the state."

Jenny reached them then. Quietly, she tucked her gloved hand into the crook of J.D.'s arm, giving him a sad smile. J.D. patted her hand with his own.

"Catherine," Jenny said. "Would you like a ride back to the house?"

Catherine looked at the couple Rory had sacrificed so much for. "No," she said flatly. "I'll walk."

She turned and started down the road, not caring if she ever saw Jenny Latham or James David Hambleton again.

"Miss Diamond," she heard J.D. call after her.

Against her better judgment, she paused without turning around.

"About the Thoroughbred," he said. "He's yours. As for any other debts, if indeed they ever existed, consider them paid."

Catherine closed her eyes for a brief moment, then continued walking without replying to J.D. *Fire was never mine to sign away in the first place,* she thought bitterly. *And as for your money, you contemptible fraud, you'll get it, I swear!*

If it took her until the day of her death, she would pay J.D. Hambleton every cent she'd taken from him.

Chin held high and her back straight, she headed down the dusty road toward Shenandoah.

Chapter Thirty-three

The first week of September came and went. Rory was being held at the county prison, and Catherine still had not been allowed to visit him.

"I don't understand," Catherine said to Connor as they sat in a railway car, returning to Shenandoah. "Why won't they allow anyone to speak with Rory? It's barbaric!"

"I know," Connor agreed. "But I've a feeling John O'Reilly is behind this. He's got connections, he does. It's no secret the 'Old Man' owes his incumbency to the Mollies. I wouldn't be surprised if O'Reilly has put in a special request that Rory be tried and condemned swiftly."

Catherine knew that the "Old Man" Connor referred to was none other than John Hartranft, the governor of Pennsylvania. Governor Hartranft held the power to reprieve and pardon, and had, in the past, done just that for more than a few known members of the Molly Maguires.

Catherine mulled over Connor's words. It appeared then, there was nothing left for her to do but have a private conversation with John O'Reilly.

As the train pulled into the station at Shenandoah,

Catherine told Connor she would see him back at the house. Then, she headed directly for the O'Reilly shebeen.

It was still early in the day and there were only a few men in the saloon. Margaret, her face pale, stood behind the bar. Her heavy body moved slowly as she carried a seidel of beer to one of the customers. Seeing Catherine, she dropped her wet rag on the bar and motioned for her to step into the back room, which served as a kitchen.

Catherine followed her, ignoring the curious stares of the few patrons.

"What are you doing here?" Margaret demanded when they were alone.

"I think you know. I came here to ask you one more time to get up on the witness stand and tell the jury what you saw."

Margaret turned her back to Catherine. "I saw nothing," she whispered in barely audible tones. "I wasn't here that night, Miss Diamond. How could I know what truly happened."

"Stop it! Stop lying!" Catherine nearly shouted, pulling the young woman around to face her. "You know Rory killed Pat Daugherty in self-defense. You know it! Please, you've got to testify!"

Margaret O'Reilly looked away, a pained expression in her eyes. "I—I can't," she said hoarsely. "My husband, he—he wouldn't allow it."

"But can you stand idly by and let Rory be indicted for first-degree murder?"

Margaret shook her head, tears forming in her eyes. "Please," she whispered. "Don't say any more. I—I'm sorry, truly I am . . ."

"You've got to help Rory. He needs you now."

"But I can't—"

"Please," Catherine repeated.

Margaret clutched nervously at the worn apron tied

about her distended waist. Her work roughened hands were moist with perspiration. "If—if I were to testify," she began slowly, "you do realize it would only be my word against eleven other men—one of them my husband."

Catherine felt a tiny flicker of hope stir in her breast. "Then you'll testify?" she asked in a whisper.

Margaret nodded. "Yes," she said resignedly. "I'll do it."

Just then, the door leading to the bar was thrust open and the huge bulk of John O'Reilly filled the small room. "Do what?" he demanded in a harsh voice. "What will you do, Margaret?"

Margaret O'Reilly shrank away from her husband. Shaking violently, she held up one hand in front of her face, as though she expected him to strike her. "Nothing!" she cried in a quavering voice. "I—I didn't say I would do anything, John. Honestly. I—I was just—"

John O'Reilly moved menacingly toward his young wife. "Just what?" he demanded. Before either woman could stop him, he delivered a vicious, backhand blow to the side of Margaret's face. The impact forced her to her knees. A small yelp of pain came from her lips as she lurched heavily forward, breaking the fall with her hands. "No, John," she whimpered. "Please don't beat me . . . don't hurt the baby."

John O'Reilly gave an indifferent grunt as he sneered down at his wife. "I should give you a real shellackin' for talking to this woman!" he roared. "I told you to stay away from her! Didn't I tell you to stay away from her, Margaret?"

Margaret, clutching her stomach now, nodded quickly. "Yes," she sniveled. "Yes, you did. I—I'm sorry, John. I'm sorry. P—please don't beat me."

Catherine, horrified by what she'd just witnessed, knelt beside the pregnant woman. "Are you all right?" she asked, taking her by the shoulders. "Margaret?"

" 'Course she's all right!" John O'Reilly boomed. "Now

you get up and get out of my saloon, miss. I don't want you around."

Catherine glared up at him. "I will not," she said defiantly. "How dare you strike a woman — especially one in her condition? She's very near her time. Why, she shouldn't be in this saloon at all! She should be in bed, resting."

John O'Reilly gave Catherine a deadly look. "This is none of your business," he warned. "Now, get out of here before I do something I might regret."

Catherine, although inwardly trembling, didn't move. She stayed beside Margaret, holding onto her tightly as quick, sharp spasms rocked the woman's tense body. "Margaret?" she asked anxiously. "Are you all right? Shall I get a physician?"

Margaret shook her head, unable to speak. Holding her belly with both hands, she shuddered once more, then quieted. "I — I'm fine," she gasped, taking slow, deep breaths.

"No," Catherine insisted. "I don't think you are. Come. I'll help you to bed."

John O'Reilly slapped a beefy hand atop Catherine's shoulder. "You'll be helping my wife to go nowhere," he hissed. "Now, take your hands off her and get out of my saloon."

Catherine looked up at the huge man towering above her. He was strong as an ox, and his feral eyes held a deadly threat. She was mad to confront him, she knew, mad to involve herself in a family dispute, but she couldn't leave Margaret alone with this man. And, impossible as it seemed at this moment, she hoped to persuade Margaret to corroborate Rory's story.

With a calm she did not feel, she said, "I will not leave. I came here because both you and your wife know Rory O'Shay did not walk into this saloon with murder on his mind. He killed Pat Daugherty in self-defense." She paused, and then—knowing she was being absurd and unrealistic—she said, "I—I came here hoping one of you would testify in Rory's behalf."

John O'Reilly looked stunned, and then he laughed in Catherine's face.

"You little fool," he muttered. "If I had my way, O'Shay would have died the night I helped string him to that tree." His laughter echoed in Catherine's ears as he reached forward and grabbed Margaret roughly by the hand. "Get up," he said to his wife. "Go upstairs and wait for me. We'll talk later."

Margaret nodded, and struggled to get to her feet. Suddenly, she doubled over in pain. "Oh—John," she said weakly. "I—I think it's time. Quick, c—call my mother, please."

All anger drained from the big man's face as he knelt beside his wife. "But Meg," he said, his voice soft now and soothing. "Are you certain? The babe isn't due for at least another month!"

"I—I'm certain!" Margaret cried, her eyes wide with fear. "Oh, it's—it's early, John. Go fetch my mother—and the doctor. Please!"

John O'Reilly got to his feet with surprising agility, pulled the barroom door open, and yelled to someone in the saloon. It was Murphy, Margaret's brother, and in an instant he was off and running to get help.

O'Reilly moved back to Margaret, who was panting and sweating now. Picking up her awkward bulk in one fluid movement, he tried to reassure her. "I'll carry you to bed, Meg," he said. "You'll be fine. Lots of babes are born this early. There's nothing to worry about."

Catherine, who had stepped aside when O'Reilly reached for his wife, asked, "Is there anything I can do?"

John O'Reilly glared at her. "I'd say you've done enough, Miss Diamond. Your coming here today has upset my wife, and I warn you, if anything happens to our unborn babe, I'll hold you responsible." With that threat, he left Catherine alone in the small room.

Catherine stood there for several minutes, feeling utterly defeated. It was unlikely that Margaret would consider defying her husband now—and even if she did—her physical condition would prevent her going to court.

She stepped toward the door then, and was just about to open it when she heard someone race into the saloon.

"Condy!" a man's voice yelled. "Where's O'Reilly?"

"He's gone upstairs," another voice answered. "You can't bother him now. Margaret's started her pains. What's the matter, boy? Is there trouble?"

"Yeah, I'd say so. A telegram just came in from Lansford. You know the job O'Reilly ordered for tonight? It was bungled. They killed Jones all right, but the three brothers sent to do the job were spotted, and a posse's being formed right now to go after them."

"You sure about this, boy?"

"Sure I am! The townspeople are taking up arms and screaming for justice. They're red hot to kill the Mollies!"

"Gawddamn!" the other man exploded. "Let's go, boy. We've got to round up the brothers for a meetin'. We've got some alibis to set up."

Catherine stepped into the barroom just in time to see the two men head out the door. Another murder had been committed, and, as she herself had heard, it had been ordered by O'Reilly. She left the saloon, praying the killers would be caught—and that they would tell all they knew about John O'Reilly.

By sundown, Catherine was in the kitchen of the O'Shay house preparing dinner, Cally at her side. Absently, Catherine peeled the many potatoes she intended to boil as

Cally laid four plates and cutlery on the battered table.

Connor stepped into the room, Ned behind him. Both men wore frowns.

"What is it?" Catherine asked, dropping the paring knife. "What's happened now?"

"It's not good," Connor said. "Not good at all."

"What? Tell me. Has it to do with Rory?"

Connor nodded. "Ned just returned from Pottsville. Rory was arraigned today before the district attorney."

"And?" Catherine pressed. "Have they set a trial date?"

Connor ran a hand along the back of his neck, shaking his head. For a moment he was speechless. Taking a deep breath, he tried to calm himself. "It's not good," he said again, a catch in his voice.

"Tell me!" Catherine insisted, nearly hysterical. "He—he's not dead, is he? The Mollies didn't get him while he was in jail, did they? Connor, *please!*"

Ned stepped forward then, moving to stand beside his daughter. "I'm sorry, Katie," he said. "Rory pleaded guilty to the murder of Pat Daugherty. There won't be any trial. Sentence has already been passed."

Catherine gripped the back of a chair, her hands shaking uncontrollably. "What?" she said, incredulous. "You must have it wrong. Rory wouldn't have done such a thing." *Oh, but he would,* her mind screamed. *He would . . . and he had.* Like someone groping through a thick fog, she pulled the chair out from beneath the table and sat down, her body numb. "Wh—what was the sentence? What's going to happen to Rory?"

Both Ned and Connor averted their eyes. Connor, unable to stay a moment longer in the room, turned to walk out.

"Tell me," Catherine demanded of him before he could leave.

Connor did not turn around. "He's to be hanged by the neck until dead."

"Oh, God!" She began to tremble and could not stop.

Ned tried to soothe her. "Katie," he said, "You've got to be brave, girl. It's out of our hands now. There's nothing any of us can do. He's to hang for his crime. We've got to accept the fact."

Catherine whirled on her father. "And no doubt you're pleased with the sentence! Now, he'll be out of my life for good. That's what you've wanted all along, isn't it, Pa?" she cried.

"No, Katie, this is not what I've wished for." Ned Diamond appeared truly wounded. He attempted to place a placating hand to Catherine's shoulder, but she shied away from his touch. "I never meant to hurt you, Katie, only protect you. You must believe me. I—I only tried to keep you away from Rory in order to protect you from this very day. You knew from the beginning he was a wanted man, and yet—"

"And yet I fell in love with him. And I'd do it again and again and again! Rory is no cold-blooded murderer! We all know that! This is madness! There's got to be something someone can do."

Ned shook his head. "There's nothing save a stay of execution from the governor himself."

"Well, I'll not stand idly by and do nothing! I—I'm going to see Rory."

"They won't let you in, lass. They still won't allow visitors."

She wasn't listening. Rising suddenly, her eyes stormy and hard, she declared, "They'll let me in, or else." With that, she raced out of the house toward Irish Fire. Within minutes, she had him saddled and ready to go. In a clatter of hooves, she set off toward Pottsville and the only man she would ever love.

Pottsville, though also an anthracite mining center, was not as drab as Shenandoah. Here, amid the lush, rolling Pennsylvania hills, many prosperous mine owners had built impressive mansions, imparting some elegance to this city which also served as the county seat.

Today, the peaceful, picturesque town was buzzing with excitement. Three members of the Molly Maguires, suspects in the murder at Lansford, had been apprehended in Tamaqua, atop Cemetery Hill. The news had spread like wildfire, and telegrams had been sent to Lansford and to Raven Run, asking that any witnesses to the murder come forward to identify the killers. Responses were already coming in.

Catherine drew Irish Fire to a halt before the red sandstone Gothic jail. A small flame of hope had been ignited in her breast. Perhaps, with the capture of the three Mollies, Rory might not hang for killing one of their henchmen. Hurrying toward the main entrance, she clung to that hope. If only Rory hadn't pleaded guilty! she thought. If only his case could have been brought to trail . . .

Once again, Catherine's request to see Rory was denied. The warden, though extremely civil and mild mannered, was firm in his refusal.

This time, Catherine stood equally firm in her determination not to yield to the unusual ruling.

"I'm not going anywhere," she told the warden, "until I see Rory O'Shay. I will stand here for as many hours or days as it takes to make you change your mind."

The warden shifted slightly in his seat, his round, impassive face giving no indication of what he was thinking. Catherine couldn't tell if he was exasperated with her demands, admired her firm stance, or, indeed, thought anything at all of her. He simply continued to gaze at her levelly, then repeated, "I've strict orders to allow no one at all, under any circumstances, to visit with the prisoner."

"That is outrageous!" she declared, her voice rising. "Who issued such orders?"

For the first time, the warden seemed to lose his composure. "I am not at liberty to say," he responded.

"Was it Governor Hartranft?" she demanded. When he didn't answer, only widened his eyes, she pressed, "It was, wasn't it? And why did he issue such an order?" Before the warden could answer, Catherine continued, in a rush, "I'll tell you why! It is because the governor of this state is being manipulated like a puppet by the Mollies. He owes his incumbency to that wretched group, and he knows very well that if he doesn't flex his political muscle once in a while on their behalf, he'll soon be out of office! I'm right, aren't I? Yes, I know I am. Just as I know that John O'Reilly, head of the Shenandoah division of Mollies, is the man responsible for Rory being held in your jail."

"Ma'am,' the warden interrupted. "You are jumping to conclusions. You'd best take care what you say about anyone involved with the Molly Maguires."

"I will not!" she replied, angered that even a lawman had been cowed by a band of criminals. "In fact, after I leave this jail house, I intend to pay John O'Reilly a visit. If no one else will confront that blackguard, I will!" Seeing she was getting nowhere with the warden, she swung around, intent on leaving Pottsville for the O'Reilly shebeen. If it was true that Governor Hartranft was being manipulated by the Mollies, then there was only one man who could change the situation . . . and that was John O'Reilly. Already she was at the door, her hand on the latch.

"Wait," the warden called after her. "You aren't really going to confront O'Reilly, are you?"

She whirled around, her gray gaze clear. "I am," she said. "For Rory O'Shay, I would face the devil himself."

A flicker of admiration suddenly showed in the warden's

eyes. "I don't think that will be necessary," he said. "If you'll wait here, I'll go tell Mr. O'Shay he has a visitor."

Five minutes later, Catherine was escorted, not to one of the cells, but to a small, locked office at the rear of the building. She was surprised, and somewhat disconcerted, to discover it was the sheriff's office. She was even more surprised to find Rory there, clean-shaven and well fed.

The door shut noiselessly behind the warden as he left them alone.

"Rory . . ." Catherine breathed, unable to believe she was actually with him at last. As he rose from the couch on which he'd been seated, she drank in the sight of his handsome face, his clear blue eyes, his dark, unruly hair. She noticed that his clothes, the same he'd worn the night he'd been arrested, were clean and pressed. He looked comfortable and at ease, not at all like a man on his way to the gallows.

A queer expression settled over his features when he saw her. "Katie, what are you doing here? Christ, when the warden told me I had a visitor, I didn't think he meant you!"

"Are — aren't you glad to see me?" she whispered, shocked by his cold manner. Yearning to run into his arms, she forced herself to remain near the door. There was something in his gaze, some indefinable light, that told her he would not welcome her embrace. Wrapping her arms about her waist, she suppressed a sudden feeling of dread. Something was wrong. For some reason she did not understand, Rory was not happy to see her.

"You shouldn't have come," he said, remaining near the couch.

"Did you think I could stay away? Why did you do it, Rory? Why did you plead guilty to a first-degree murder charge?" Her voice was low, despairing. "We could have built a strong defense, Rory. We still can!"

His voice heavy, he said, "You don't understand. You shouldn't be here . . . not here, and certainly not alone. You did come alone, didn't you?"

"Of course I came alone! Connor and Cally are beside themselves with grief by what's happened to you. And my father—I'm sure he's gloating over your sentence."

"You're being unfair to your father. Ned was here most of the day."

She looked up, startled. Then, immediately dismissing the idea that her father might want to see Rory freed, she said harshly, "No doubt he came only to be sure the sentence was carried out posthaste.

"No," Rory said. "He came to try and obtain a stay of execution."

She shuddered at the word, hugging her waist as she pressed her eyes shut. She heard him move across the room, and when she opened her eyes, he stood before her, his own eyes filled with pain. Gently, his hands clasped her arms.

"I want you to leave this place, Catherine. I want you to leave Pennsylvania entirely. Your father is taking the morning passenger train. He's going to San Francisco. I want you to be on that train."

She couldn't believe he was saying such words to her. Did he actually believe she'd leave him now? Now, when he was sentenced to be hanged?

"No!" she said fiercely. "I won't leave."

"You must. Every minute you linger in Shenandoah, your life is in danger."

"My life? You are the one who—who is going to be . . ." She stopped herself, unable to utter the dread words. "Oh, God," she cried. "Why did you have to plead guilty? Why?"

"Because I am," he said heavily. "I killed Pat Daugherty."

"But you had no choice!" she cried. The tears she'd fought so hard to suppress finally burst forth and streamed down her grief-stricken face.

Rory pulled her tightly to him, pressing her slim body against his own. "Hush," he soothed, his voice tight. "Please, don't cry, *macushla*. Everything will be all right, you'll see." He stroked her back, trying to soothe away her pain. And she clung to him, her face pressed against his chest as her hot tears soaked his shirt front. "Catherine," he said, "tell me you'll get on that train tomorrow morning; promise me."

"I—I can't," she said in ragged gasps. "I won't leave you now, not like this." She hadn't meant to break down, to give into the despair that engulfed her. Taking a deep breath, she wiped at her tear-stained face, then looked up at him. Very slowly and very clearly, she said, "I love you, Rory O'Shay. I'm not going anywhere without you."

Her words, spoken directly from the heart, shook Rory to the core. He shuddered, as though he'd been struck physically. Then, he stepped back and held her at arm's length.

"Don't, *macushla*," he whispered. "Do not say such words—not now."

This was not the reaction Catherine had expected. This wasn't at all the moment she'd envisioned. He was supposed to echo her words, tell her he loved her as she loved him! But he didn't. He just stood there, an odd light in his eyes.

"But I do love you!" she insisted. "I do. And you love me, too . . . don't you, Rory?"

He didn't answer her. The moments ticked by, endless moments made longer by his silence. Catherine felt as though she were dreaming. Surely, this couldn't actually be happening. They weren't truly standing in a jail house with Rory awaiting a hangman's noose. Had she really admitted her love? And had he really refused to say that he loved her too?

Oh, Lord, her mind screamed. *Let me be dreaming!* She

hated the cold light she now saw in Rory's gaze . . . hated the harsh pressure of his fingers on her arm. Why didn't he say something? Why couldn't he tell her that he loved her?!

"Rory?"

"Don't do this, Catherine. Don't make this any harder for me than it already is . . ."

"But I love you," she said again, desperation overcoming her pride. "Please, Rory — don't look at me like that. If you won't do anything to save yourself, then at least let me be with you one last time. Let me hold you close and burn the feel of your body into my memory."

He stiffened, his gaze impenetrable. "Don't do this," he said again.

She looked at him searchingly, unbelievingly. "You can't really want me to go away now."

"I do," he replied woodenly. "I want you to leave. Go back to San Francisco."

"But I thought—" she persisted in a small, choked voice.

"Thought what? I told you more than once there could never be any future for us. I was a wanted man the day you met me, and now my past has caught up with me. There is nothing more to be said." He turned away from her and walked back to the couch.

Catherine could feel her heart breaking. She had bared her soul to him, had laid her heart at his feet — and he had spurned her!

What a naive little fool I've been, she thought bitterly. She had truly believed that he loved her. But now, when he had only days to live, he would not say the words. He didn't love her, never had.

And yet . . . she couldn't let go.

"Oh, Rory," she said in anguished tones. "Tell me our times together meant something to you. Tell me you—"

He swung toward her then, his eyes wild and agonized. "It's over," he said cruelly. "Can't you understand? It's over!

Go back to San Francisco with your father. Perhaps, someday soon, the man of your dreams will come to you. Perhaps then, all of your fantasies will be fulfilled."

She flinched at the words, shattered by their finality. There was nothing more she could say now.

Turning slowly away from him, she called out for the warden, waiting silently until he came and unlocked the door. Numb with pain, she walked out of the sheriff's office, away from the only man she would ever love.

Chapter Thirty-four

Later, Catherine would not remember how she had gotten back to Shenandoah. The long ride from the Pottsville jail was only a blur. She could think of nothing except that Rory did not love her, had never loved her.

Back at the O'Shay house she found that Cally had gone to bed early and Connor had disappeared somewhere. Only her father was present, sitting at the kitchen table, obviously awaiting her return.

"It's late," he'd said to her. "I was getting concerned."

She looked up, startled. "I—I'm sorry, Pa," she said, her voice barely a whisper. She was tired, so very tired. "I didn't mean to cause you any worry."

"Did you see him?" Ned asked. "Did they allow you to see Rory?"

"Yes, I saw him. And you were right, Pa. I never should have gotten involved with Rory O'Shay." She moved as if to go to bed, but Ned caught her arm.

"What do you mean?" he asked. "What happened, Katie? What did O'Shay do to you to make you say such a thing? When you left here you were—"

401

"I was a fool," she interrupted. "I thought he returned my love, but I was wrong. I—" She broke off, shaking her head sadly. "I don't want to talk about it, Pa. I'm weary of talking."

"I understand, lass," he said sympathetically. "You go on to bed now and get some rest. In the morning we'll head back to San Francisco. We'll put all of this behind us."

Catherine nodded. "Yes," she said. "We'll go back home . . . and maybe then I'll be able to forget."

But come morning, Catherine could not force herself to board the train. She could not leave Shenandoah. Rory may have turned his back on her, but her love for him remained undimmed. If he would not accept her help or comfort in this darkest hour, she could at least look after those she knew he loved—Cally and Irish Fire. She would stay in Shenandoah until she knew Cally was going to be all right. As for the yearling, she wouldn't even consider taking him away now, back to San Francisco. Irish Fire was Rory's horse; he always had been. Fire had brought them together, had, in a way, been Catherine's good luck charm. She would stay and care for the horse. Perhaps staying close to Irish Fire would somehow bring Rory back to her. The notion was absurd, she knew, but she was past rational thinking.

Deaf to her father's pleas, Catherine stepped off the train just before it steamed into motion. She waved good-bye to Ned, sure in her heart she'd made the right decision.

She spent the rest of the day at the O'Shays, occupying herself with small, domestic chores. Cally, quiet and at times tearful, moved listlessly from room to room. Catherine hadn't the energy to try and cheer the small girl. Indeed, there was little to be cheerful about. It was only a matter of days before Rory would be led to the gallows, although Cally didn't know that.

That night, after fixing a light meal for Connor, Cally and herself, Catherine tucked the little girl into bed.

"Connor says I'm not to worry about Rory," Cally said, as she reached up to kiss Catherine's cheek. "He says Rory will soon be home with us. He's certain of it."

Catherine gave the child a trembling smile. "I hope he's right, Cally. I hope Connor is right."

Alone in her own narrow bed, Catherine tossed and turned restlessly, unable to sleep. The hot, late summer night was sultry and airless, and she couldn't stop her mind from churning with an unrelenting flow of painful memories. Her mind and body screamed for release. She ached to be held in a warm, comforting embrace — Rory's embrace.

Finally, she flung the sweat-soaked sheet from her fevered body, climbed out of her lonely bed, and went outdoors, seeking relief under the stars. Pausing near the horses, who stood quietly at the back of the house, she brushed her hand across Irish Fire's sleek back. The yearling nickered softly in response. "Because of you," she said to the horse, "Rory is alive today — but he won't be for long. I only wish we could ride off together and rescue him from prison . . ." Her voice trailed off as she moved sadly away from the animals and headed down the silent road. The air was still; not even a breeze rustled the leaves. All was hushed, trees and ground bathed in the silvery iridescence of a harvest moon. Some called it a lovers' moon. Knowing that, only underscored Catherine's sorrow.

Padding silently on bare feet, she left the well-worn path and traveled down the hummock, unconcerned about her own safety. What was life without Rory beside her? Nothing mattered anymore. Oh, dear Lord, why was life so cruel? Why hadn't she the power to penetrate the thick wall of Rory's self-imposed guilt?

Absently, she crossed the rickety foot bridge that led to the peaceful covert where she and Rory had spent their last blissful night in each other's arms.

Perhaps, if they hadn't returned to Shenandoah, they might have been able to build a life together. But no, she realized, Rory would have always felt the guilt of his past — until he confronted it. And that confrontation had ended in tragedy. Whether they'd stayed in San Francisco, or come back here — her relationship with Rory had been doomed from the beginning.

Even the hope of brief golden moments — moments snatched from reality's hard grasp — was gone now.

Burdened by intolerable grief, she sank to the ground beneath an umbrella of late-blooming rhododendron, stark white and shimmering in the moonlight. The soft, fragrant petals brushed her face, catching the tears that streamed from her eyes. But not even sobbing could ease the ache in her heart. There was no release.

A short distance off, a songbird chirped, startled by an unexpected rustling in the woods. Catherine listened to the flap of the bird's wings as it took flight. Once again, all was still, but Catherine's senses had been alerted. Face curtained by her long, unbound hair, she leaned forward, listening intently. . . . Her body grew rigid as she suddenly realized she was no longer alone. Swiftly, she whirled about, hair flying, eyes wide, as she saw a man and a horse standing before her. Her heart began to pound wildly, uncontrollably.

It was Rory and Irish Fire! The blood drained from her face as she looked at Rory's dark, haunted eyes. Was this just some vision, conjured up by her anguished mind? Fearful that the sound of her voice might make him vanish,

Catherine just stared up at him in wonder.

Finally, as he took a step toward her, she forced herself to speak. "Rory! Is it really you? What are you doing here? How did you get out of jail?"

"It's a long story," he said, wearily. "Long and painful."

"But I—I don't understand. I thought—"

"That I was going to hang for Big Pat's murder? I thought so, too, when the officer showed up at the house that night. I thought they were pulling me in for Daugherty's murder. But they weren't. It seems that my snapping Big Pat's neck had saved them from paying the hangman to do it. As I think you know, there was a price on Daughtery's head; he was wanted for murder in Buffalo, and for two murders committed right here in Schuylkill County. What the police really wanted from me was information about the Heckscher's Grove killings."

"You mean the night your—your father was . . ."

"Yes," he said, nodding grimly. "That night. John O'Reilly was the one who shot and killed my father. And I had the evidence to prove it."

"Evidence?"

"O'Reilly bungled the job, as he did when he tried to lynch me. Hurrying into the crowd after firing, he dropped his pistol—and I picked it up. From what the sheriff tells me, that same gun was used in a number of clan jobs. The Mollies keep their weapons rotating among the boys. More than a few people have seen John O'Reilly slap that pistol down on the bar in his shebeen."

Catherine was confused. "But I don't understand," she said. "Why did the police hold you in jail? And why were we told you had pleaded guilty to a murder charge and would be hanged soon?"

"I'm sorry you had to go through this, Catherine. Believe me, I didn't want to stay at the jail, and I sure as hell didn't want word getting out that I'd pleaded guilty, but the sheriff thought it was the safest route. We both knew John O'Reilly was after me. He knew I had his gun, and he knew I would testify that he was my father's murderer."

"Then if all of this is true, why are you here, now? Aren't you in danger still?"

"Not with John O'Reilly, I'm not. As we speak, he's locked up tight in the county jail. I'm sure you've heard about the murder in Lansford by now, haven't you?" he asked. At her nod, he continued, "Well, one of the boys involved in the murder decided to turn traitor to save his own neck. There's enough evidence from his statement alone to put John O'Reilly behind bars for quite a while."

He fell silent then, fixing her with a penetrating gaze. "I thought," he said softly, "that you were planning to return to San Francisco with Ned."

"And why would I do that after I'd made a promise to you? I told you I would stand by you through all of this."

"Yes," he said, "you did. But you made that promise before—before the scene in the sheriff's office."

She lowered her lashes, not wanting to think about what had been said between them at the Pottsville jail. "A promise is a promise," she whispered.

"Even so, I—I thought you might go. You had every right to. I—I'm sorry for the way I acted at the sheriff's office, but at the time, O'Reilly was still on the loose. I couldn't let you stay in Shenandoah, and I knew, if I told you the truth, you wouldn't leave. I thought, if I played the heartless blackguard, you would walk away."

She looked up at him, her heart aching at the pain in his voice. "Did you truly believe that, Rory? Did you truly think I would ever leave you?"

Rory gazed at her for a long time, his eyes half closed, as though considering, reflecting. Then, he looked away, off into the night, shrugging his shoulders. "I didn't know," he said very softly. "In the past, the ones I've loved the most have always left me, or me them. . . . I just thought—"

"You thought I could leave you, now, after all that has happened? I don't believe you, Rory. You never really thought that."

"No?"

"No. If you had, you wouldn't be here at the covert. Why did you come?"

"Why did *you* come?"

This time, she looked away, plucking a white blossom from a nearby bush. "I think you know . . ." She tore off one petal, letting it flutter gently to her skirt. Another followed, and then another, and another. In her mind, she chanted, *He loves me, he loves me not. He loves me, he loves me not* . . . The last petal was gone, leaving only a bare green stem. A vagrant breeze brushed by her then, lifting a few of the silky white petals from her skirts, carrying them away to the ground beside her.

And then he spoke. "He loves you," he said, so softly she barely heard. "He loves you . . ."

The tears that coursed down her cheeks glistened in the moonlight.

Rory smiled, dropping to his knees beside her. He reached out to her—just as he had done that night atop the windswept knoll overlooking San Francisco Bay—his hands tenderly touching her wet cheeks, caressing away the teardrops, his own eyes moist with unshed tears. "I love you, Mary Catherine. I do. Never have I said those words to another woman. I'm saying them now and I mean them with every fiber of my being." His touch suffused her with a comforting warmth. "Forget my behavior at the jail house. I was playing a role I thought I needed to play. I—I didn't want you to stay in Shenandoah and be a target for

O'Reilly. Christ, Katie, when you told me in the sheriff's office that you loved me, I—I felt like jumping on the man's desk and dancing a jig! I wanted to shout for joy, but I couldn't."

"Oh, Rory—" she whispered, her voice catching.

"I love you, Katie. You are the treasure of my heart, the bright beacon that guides me when I've lost my way in the dark. I want you beside me forever and always. Marry me, Katie. Let us create a new generation of O'Shays and shower them with all the love we have for each other."

Oh, what wonderful, beautiful words. Her heart swelled, expanded, and spilled over with happiness. She nodded, unable to speak. And then she was laughing and crying all at once as he put his strong arms around her and drew her gently down on the thick carpet of fern that covered the ground.

Twining his fingers in her long hair, he rained kisses across her face, murmuring endearments as he nuzzled her nose, her cheeks, her ear lobe. Stretching out beneath her, he fitted her slim body to his long frame, breast to breast, thigh to thigh. Then, his hands traveled down her rounded curves to the twisted hem of her nightdress, tugging at the thin fabric till it tore. He cast it away, just as he'd cast off his past, putting it forever behind him.

Much later, they lay quiet and content on their bed of ferns, listening to the woodland night sounds and the gentle swish of Fire's tail. Moonbeams slanted down through the treetops, and a fine gray mist had moved in, veiling the rhododendron and saplings, enclosing Catherine and Rory in a magical, private world. Shivering slightly, Catherine snuggled closer to Rory's warm chest.

"Chilly?" he asked, drawing his coat over her.

Catherine shook her head, not wanting to stir from their private nest. "Did you know that J.D. and Jenny are in

Pennsylvania?" she asked drowsily.

Rory nodded. "Yes," he said. "Jimmy came to see me the other day before Pa's funeral."

"And the warden let him in?" Catherine asked, sitting up with a rush of anger.

He gave her a slow smile. "Calm down now, Katie. You know Jimmy. He always sets the right price."

"I can imagine," Catherine replied, relaxing once again. Laying her head back against Rory's shoulder, she asked, "So J.D. told you what he did before leaving San Francisco?"

"About Latham's accident? Yes, he told me. I'm glad all that's behind us, and I'm glad Jenny has J.D. with her now. She'll be happy at last."

"Yes," Catherine agreed, not wanting to think about James Hambleton or Jenny Latham. "My father left for San Francisco this morning. He—he plans to rebuild the Diamond. I think he's hoping to finance it by playing the stock market again."

Rory gave a small laugh. "Knowing Mad Ned, he'll do just that. But I wonder how he'll take the news that we're getting married? That's not going to set too well with him."

"No, probably not at first. But give him time. I'm certain he'll change his views once he comes to know you as I do."

Rory laughed, kissing the top of her head. "My dear, Katie, your father will never come to know me as you have. Even though I've been cleared of all charges, he still sees me in an unfavorable light, and probably always will."

"Oh, I don't know," she said, giving his ear a playful nip. "I think his opinion of you has changed quite a bit since we arrived in Shenandoah. I know Connor's opinion has, and I'm glad. Do you think Connor will stay in Pennsylvania now?"

"I don't know. Probably not. There are too many painful

memories here for him. Actually, I think he's restless to return to San Francisco and Sallie."

Catherine smiled. She was certain that Sallie would be more than pleased to see Connor again—and if anyone would tame the beautiful, madcap girl it was Connor.

"And you?" Rory asked. "Do you want to stay in Pennsylvania?"

She closed her eyes. "I'm not sure," she replied slowly. She would be content to make her home anywhere with Rory. "I—do you want to stay here?"

He was quick to answer. "No. Even now, I can hear our home calling to us . . . listen, can you hear?"

She lifted her head, gazing up at him with questioning eyes.

"There. Did you hear that? There's a plot of land high in the California hills beckoning us . . ."

She smiled at him. Yes, she thought, she could hear. And there was a snug little cabin just waiting for their return. Rory had made her his woman in that small retreat, and it was there that they had shared their innermost secrets, there where Catherine had found the true meaning of her life. She glanced over at Fire who stood close by. In the moonlight, she imagined she could see a satisfied gleam in the yearling's dark eyes. Irish Fire had linked them together in the beginning, and now he was here with the two of them as they planned their future. Fire would be a part of that future. Someday, Catherine knew, she and Rory would have the stables Rory had talked about—and Fire would be the pride of those stables.

She settled back against Rory's chest, contentment washing over her. "Do you think Cally will like living in California with us?" she asked, trailing a finger across his heart, down across the taut muscles of his stomach, and beyond.

There was a low rumble in his chest. "You witch," he murmured. "Cally will adore San Francisco."

"A witch, am I?" she cried, stroking him. "I am a lady through and through!"

Unable to endure her provocative caresses any longer, Rory rolled to his side, pressing her down to the ground beneath him. "Yes, you are indeed a lady, Katie dear. *My* lady." And then his mouth swooped down to capture hers in a searing kiss that left no room for more words.

Catherine did not mind. They had a lifetime ahead of them. Talk could come later.

TIME-TRAVEL ROMANCE
BY CONSTANCE O'DAY-FLANNERY
*Discover the sensuous magic of passions
that know no boundaries, with
Constance O'Day-Flannery's captivating
time-travel romances!*

TIME-KISSED DESTINY (2223, $3.95)
Brought together by the allure of sunken treasure and the mysteries of time travel, neither 1980s beauty Kate Walker nor 1860s shipping magnate Michael Sheridan dared believe the other was real. But with one enchanting kiss, the destiny that had joined them across the barriers of time could no longer be denied!

TIME-SWEPT LOVERS (2057, $3.95)
Somewhere during the course of her cross-country train ride, beautiful corporate executive Jenna Weldon had fallen backward through time! Now, in the arms of Morgan Trahern—the original Marlboro man—the astonished Jenna would experience a night of passion she would never forget!

TIMELESS PASSION (1837, $3.95)
Brianne Quinlin awoke after the accident to find everything gone: her car, the highway—even the tall buildings that had lined the road. And when she gazed into the eyes of plantation owner Ryan Barrington, the most handsome man Brianne had ever seen, the enraptured lovely was certain she had died and gone to heaven!

Available wherever paperbacks are sold, or order direct from the Publisher. Send cover price plus 50¢ per copy for mailing and handling to Zebra Books, Dept. 2320, 475 Park Avenue South, New York, N.Y. 10016. Residents of New York, New Jersey and Pennsylvania must include sales tax. DO NOT SEND CASH.

GIVE YOUR HEART
TO ZEBRA'S HEARTFIRE!

COMANCHE CARESS (2268, $3.75)
by Cheryl Black

With her father missing, her train held up by bandits and her money stolen, Ciara Davenport wondered what else could possibly go wrong. Until a powerful savage rescued her from a band of ruffians in the Rocky Mountains and Ciara realized the very worst had come to pass: she had fallen desperately in love with a wild, handsome half-breed she could never hope to tame!

IVORY ROSE (2269, $3.75)
by Kathleen McCall

Standing in for her long-lost twin sister, innocent Sabrina Buchanan was tricked into marrying the virile estate owner Garrison McBride. Furious with her sibling, Sabrina was even angrier with herself—for she could not deny her intense yearning to become a woman at the masterful hands of the handsome stranger!

STARLIT SURRENDER (2270, $3.75)
by Judy Cuevas

From the moment she first set eyes on the handsome swashbuckler Adrien Hunt, lovely Christina Bower was determined to fend off the practiced advances of the rich, hot-blooded womanizer. But even as her sweet lips protested each caress, her womanly curves eagerly welcomed his arousing embrace!

RECKLESS DESIRE (2271, $3.75)
by Thea Devine

Kalida Ryland had always despised her neighbor Deuce Cavender, so she was shocked by his brazen proposal of marriage. The arrogant lady's man would never get his hands on her ranch! And even if Kalida had occasionally wondered how those same rough, powerful hands would feel caressing her skin, she'd die before she let him know it!

Available wherever paperbacks are sold, or order direct from the Publisher. Send cover price plus 50¢ per copy for mailing and handling to Zebra Books, Dept. 2320, 475 Park Avenue South, New York, N.Y. 10016. Residents of New York, New Jersey and Pennsylvania must include sales tax. DO NOT SEND CASH.

Now you can get more of HEARTFIRE right at home and $ave.

Preview Four Brand New ZEBRA *Heartfire* Romance Novels...

FREE for 10 days.

No Obligation and No Strings Attached!

♥

Enjoy all of the passion and fiery romance as you soar back through history, right in the comfort of your own home.

Now that you have read a Zebra HEARTFIRE Romance novel, we're sure you'll agree that HEARTFIRE sets new standards of excellence for historical romantic fiction. Each Zebra HEARTFIRE novel is the ultimate blend of intimate romance and grand adventure and each takes place in the kinds of historical settings you want most...the American Revolution, the Old West, Civil War and more.

<u>FREE</u> Preview Each Month and $ave

Zebra has made arrangements for you to preview 4 brand new HEARTFIRE novels each month...FREE for 10 days. You'll get them as soon as they are published. If you are not delighted with any of them, just return them with no questions asked. But if you decide these are everything we said they are, you'll pay just $3.25 each—a total of $13.00 (a $15.00 value). **That's a $2.00 saving each month off the regular price.** Plus there is NO shipping or handling charge. These are delivered right to your door absolutely free! There is no obligation and there is no minimum number of books to buy.

TO GET YOUR FIRST MONTH'S PREVIEW... Mail the Coupon Below!

Mail to:

HEARTFIRE Home Subscription Service, Inc.
120 Brighton Road
P.O. Box 5214
Clifton, NJ 07015-5214

YES! I want to subscribe to Zebra's HEARTFIRE Home Subscription Service. Please send me my first month's books to preview free for ten days. I understand that if I am not pleased I may return them and owe nothing, but if I keep them I will pay just $3.25 each; a total of $13.00. That is a savings of $2.00 each month off the cover price. There are no shipping, handling or other hidden charges and there is no minimum number of books I must buy. I can cancel this subscription at any time with no questions asked.

NAME

ADDRESS   APT. NO.

CITY   STATE   ZIP

SIGNATURE   (if under 18, parent or guardian must sign)   2320
Terms and prices are subject to change.

ZEBRA HAS THE SUPERSTARS OF PASSIONATE ROMANCE!

CRIMSON OBSESSION (2272, $3.95)
by Deana James

Cassandra MacDaermond was determined to make the handsome gambling hall owner Edward Sandron pay for the fortune he had stolen from her father. But she never counted on being struck speechless by his seductive gaze. And soon Cassandra was sneaking into Sandron's room, more intent on sharing his rapture than causing his ruin!

TEXAS CAPTIVE (2251, $3.95)
by Wanda Owen

Ever since two outlaws had killed her ma, Talleha had been suspicious of all men. But one glimpse of virile Victor Maurier standing by the lake in the Texas Blacklands and the half-Indian princess was helpless before the sensual tide that swept her in its wake!

TEXAS STAR (2088, $3.95)
by Deana James

Star Garner was a wanted woman—and Chris Gillard was determined to collect the generous bounty being offered for her capture. But when the beautiful outlaw made love to him as if her life depended on it, Gillard's firm resolve melted away, replaced with a raging obsession for his fiery TEXAS STAR.

MOONLIT SPLENDOR (2008, $3.95)
by Wanda Owen

When the handsome stranger emerged from the shadows and pulled Charmaine Lamoureux into his strong embrace, she sighed with pleasure at his seductive caresses. Tomorrow she would be wed against her will—so tonight she would take whatever exhilarating happiness she could!

TEXAS TEMPEST (1906, $3.95)
by Deana James

Sensuous Eugenia Leahy had an iron will that intimidated even the most powerful of men. But after rescuing her from a bad fall, the virile stranger MacPherson resolved to take the steel-hearted beauty whether she consented or not!

Available wherever paperbacks are sold, or order direct from the Publisher. Send cover price plus 50¢ per copy for mailing and handling to Zebra Books, Dept. 2320, 475 Park Avenue South, New York, N.Y. 10016. Residents of New York, New Jersey and Pennsylvania must include sales tax. DO NOT SEND CASH.